imPERFECT
BLOOD

C.N. ROWAN

VINCI

BOOKS

By C.N. Rowan

Vinci Books

vinci-books.com

Published by Vinci Books Ltd in 2026

1

A CIP catalogue record for this book is available from the British Library.

Paperback ISBN: 9781036710804

The EU GPSR authorised representative is Logos Europe, 9 rue Nicolas Poussion, 17000 La Rochelle, France contact@logoseurope.eu

The Story So Far

Once upon a time, there was a religious group in the South of France who called themselves the Good Christians. The rest of Christendom wasn't very happy about that and decided to prove that the Cathars, as they became later known, were wrong, and it was they who were actually the good ones. They proved this by killing every last one of the Good Christians, as well as anyone who'd ever provided them shelter along the way. Their priests were called Perfects, and they died. All of them.

All except one. In a misadventure involving the destruction of the Holy Grail, one Perfect called Paul woke up in the nearest dead body. And continued to do so each time he died. For hundreds of years. Learning other magic – or *talent* – under the mentoring of Isaac the Blind, founder of Kabbalah and angel-bearer, Paul staked out his territory in Toulouse. He also died. A lot. Mainly because he couldn't keep his mouth shut. But also because he couldn't bear to see others suffer. A kindred sister spirit he rescued, Aicha Kandicha – Moroccan warrior princess and destructive force of nature - helped ease some of the suffering he'd accrued himself over those hundreds of years of living.

And then? Then it all went to shit. Spectacularly.

After recovering Isaac's brother and fellow-angel-bearer, Jakob, from centuries of imprisonment inside a magical skull, a series of events unfolded that wasn't so much unfortunate as downright catastrophic, culminating in a battle with the possible creator of the world, the Evil God that the dualistic Cathars believed in as a counterpoint to the Good God. Aicha, Jakob and his angel, Nanael, sacrificed themselves to close a portal that was trying to suck them all into some hellish parallel world. And Paul? Paul did what he did best.

He died. But this time? He died with aplomb.

Because he let the Good God take control of him, made a vessel of himself to allow the world to continue existing. And because the Good God was, well, good − and because she appreciated making him spit his godly whisky everywhere when she told a dirty joke − she decided to give him two things.

One, the information that his friends were not dead, that they could still be found and brought back.

And two − a do-over. One more at least.

So Paul came back, waking up on the top of Bugarach with his *talent*, but unsure if his next death would be his last. And then, once he and Isaac downed a well deserved bottle of the oldest malt of Balvenie whisky anyone could ever imagine in a manner that would have made most whisky connoisseurs weep at such ambrosia in the hands of Philistines, Paul set out with one single mission in mind. To find his friends. To obtain the information needed to bring them back home. Because the Good God told him it was possible, so someone must know the answer...

Chapter One

There's a saying - home is where the heart is. I guess my
home is in some long-abandoned sink estate, lying as empty
as my heart.

They say patience is a virtue. I am not a virtuous man. Just
ask Patience. Lovely girl. Terrible at time-keeping though.

I know it's only been a month of looking for my lost
family, Aicha and Jakob. Know that realistically, it's but a
drop in the ocean of time, a mere splash of seconds and
minutes and hours collected together into a glass' worth of
days and weeks. Absolutely nothing at all.

That's not stopping me, though, from being about ready
to lose my shit.

Because I'm getting nowhere. And fast. Which is the
speed I like to get to places generally, but Nowhere is a
fucking dump – no beauty spots, nowhere decent to get a
beer, not even an all-night kebab shop when you really need

it, so what I'd like to do is keep the speed but actually get *somewhere*.

That, sadly, is not happening.

And so it is with fingers jabbing just short of hard enough to put stress fractures in the car's touch screen that I dial the number I know better than my own. Primarily because mine changes so often. Normally. Phones last about as long as my bodies do usually. Mere time splashes as a rule of thumb. Now I've been wearing the same one for over a month, and it *itches*. It's like it's getting too tight around the collar. Except it's the skin beneath the collar that's too tight, too strange and restrictive when I'm used to gadding about, flitting from body to body, never caring about the consequences for the meat-suit I'm currently zipped into.

No longer the case. At least, possibly no longer the case. And I'm not enough of a gambling man to take the risk that the Good God's enigmatic non-answer meant I do get to reincarnate again next time I die.

Nope. This time – this one, sole time – I'll play it safe and preserve my flesh for as long as I possibly can.

I've managed a month so far. This is considerably longer than most people who know me would have laid odds on.

The phone-line connects, and my heart sinks, which is a truly spectacularly horrible feeling when I'm linking up with the one person I love left alive in this entire world, a man who's my father in all but that already demonstrably unimportant flesh I've been shucking off for centuries.

But the truth is, speaking to Isaac makes me feel guilty. And I'm carrying around enough of that as is.

'Any news, lad?' His tone is bright, that forced sort of chipper voice – what positivity would sound like if it was fed through a wood chipper and then recycled afterwards into some inferior, cheap, brittle form of upbeat attitude. And it sounds appalling coming from a man who always remained genuinely positive, no matter the horrors the world unfurled and then presented with accompanying slides and diagrams in great detail.

Losing his long-lost brother again, after so little time reunited, must have been that final straw. The stone thrown by life that finally chipped the chipper.

'Not...not yet, 'Zac.' I have to force myself to breathe out, to calm down. 'But there will be. It's early days yet.'

'Oh.' Just that. Oh. Not even a word really, just a letter. And yet what a missive it is, how many scribblings of miserable disappointment is contained within that single sound.

And, being Isaac, being the best human being I've ever encountered, he paints on that veneer, and in the next breath, those same cheerful notes are back. 'Where are you now?'

Which is, of course, the question I didn't want him to ask me. Mainly because I don't want the follow-up question that's sure to come. I don't lie though. I tell him the truth, though I'd have kept silent, lied by omission if I could have. 'On my way back home.'

'Are you coming over?' And there it is. That's the question I really didn't want.

Because I can't. Not yet. Not now. It's all too fresh. The pain. Both in his eyes and in my heart. The loss is too recent, and the drive is too real and so is my pride because I know myself and recognise that for what it is too. There's a part of me that can't bear to go there in anything but an exultant mood, with the special secret that'll let us bring them all back, so I can put a smile on his face and make him proud. And I know he's proud of me anyway, the Good God love him, but I want to give him this reason. This particular, specific reason that'll make him smile again.

'I...I can't 'Zac. There's a real lead. A proper possibility,' I lie. There're no leads. Nothing warm anyhow. The Mother of the Sistren of Bordeaux, coven priestess and unlikely recent ally? She knows nada. Gwendolyne, my mother-in-law and shepherdess of the half-fae Cagot outcasts? Doesn't have a clue, though she's trying her best to find me some more information. The White Lady, mysterious guardian of the Portals and exactly the being I'd most like to speak to right now, who rocked up to help us score a win at Bugarach against the Evil God? Completely untraceable despite my very best efforts.

It's only been a month. But I'm getting nowhere. In fact, it feels like I'm going backwards.

So I fob him off. Make an excuse about how I'm close, really close. And kill the call. Because I can't face him. Can't see his suffering and pain. Don't need any more of it.

Aicha's out there. Lost. My sister, for all I care for such limited labels.

And I'll not rest. Not until I bring her home.

Chapter Two

Gollum warned you about sneakin'. And I'm even more
likely to throttle you if you do than he is.

'Dude!' I don't melt Gil into a glistening puddle of bloody
organs on the pavement outside my house. But it's a near
thing.

My heartbeat is going faster than the backbeat at a
Gabba Techno rave right now. Not because I really felt
threatened, walking out of my own house, even with my
back turned to lock the door. This is still my city. Inside the
house might be my sanctuary, my Fortress of Solitude, but
even out here, I'm plugged into the magical equivalent of
the mains.

No, I'm more in adrenaline overdrive because of how
close I came to killing the young man who did me a seriously good turn by saving me from the magical fae-dragon
Melusine a mere three months ago. Despite him having zero
magic. A favour I then repaid by chopping the head off his

patron and possible lover Franc, slimy telepathic river monster and previous co-habitant of Toulouse. Well, Aicha did. She always got the dirtiest deeds done. Another reason I need her back, albeit not even close to the most pressing.

'Sorry, Paul.' He's a strange one, is Gil. His expression is sheepish, like a kid caught taking three sweets when they've been told they could grab a couple. There's something integrally innocent about him, almost childlike. And that makes zero sense when you think about the misery he's lived through. Running away from –as far as I can gather from Isaac's updates on his backstory– a bunch of religious arseholes who wanted to go a step up from praying the gay away to torturing it out instead. Ending up living on the streets. Then finishing up as one of Franc's "lovely lads" – his eyes and ears on the streets, his banquet of tortured emotions behind closed doors where he fed on their misery. Gil should have had all the innocence knocked out of him, should just be a hideous mass of emotional scar tissue and impenetrable barriers built of mistrust and hurt.

But he's not. Somehow, he's held on to who he is throughout it all. Sure, he's quiet as a rule. But he's charming too. And the little grin as he flicks a strand of hair behind his ear – the one that acknowledges, yes, creeping up behind a super powerful Talented and making them jump when you've not got any *talent* of your own thanks to letting Franc eat it, isn't a particularly smart idea? It's charming with zero pretence or posturing.

I shake my head. Whether I like him or not, I'm a man on a mission. And I can't believe he's just chanced across me on one of the rare moments I'm passing through town by happenstance.

Still, I'm not a complete arsehole. Just mostly one. 'You hungry? Let's go grab something to eat.' The kid's still ridiculously skinny, ranging on gaunt. The past few months free of Franc and off the streets haven't added much meat to his bones.

He obviously has something to say. I can feed him while I hear him out. I owe him that much at least.

We sit down at one of the cheap plastic tables on the restaurant's terrace I've brought him to. It's just an elevated bit of wooden decking constructed onto the enlarged pavement. Cars do their best to go whistling by. But the weight of traffic, slowed by approximately half a million traffic lights down the Boulevard D'Arcole, make that whistle more a frustrated growl — like it's been pitch-shifted down to match the vehicular speed.

We've a few minutes before the food arrives. Not many. This is on the border between fast food and a sit-down meal. But their falafel and taboule are fantastic, and Gil can get something meaty at the same time. Maybe some of it might stick to his bones.

Not that he's unattractive. Now that he's wearing proper clothing unstained by life on the streets — simple but functional jeans and a plain black T-shirt, he looks more heroin chic than simply heroin fucked. Not that he did drugs when he was homeless, as I understand it. But he didn't look well when we first met. Washed out and beaten down. Life on the streets might not have taken his innocence, but it sucked some of the vitality from him.

Although that might just have been Franc. He fed on misery, but he didn't eat all of it at once from his "lovely lads and lasses", else he'd have had no handy standby snacks. He just reduced it so it didn't kill them.

Now Gil's looking well. No dark circles under those bright blue eyes, half-curtained by the hair strands that keep falling in front of them. He's grown it out over the past few months. Suits him.

Point is, he's looking well. And, were I not time-pressured, I'd make that clear to him with all the prerequisite small talk. But I am. So I won't.

'What can I do for you, Gil?' To the point. Aich would be proud of me.

'I need your help.' Ah. Those infamous words. 'I – I've found something.'

Oh fuck. 'What? Hold on, let me guess. A cursed amulet? A gateway to Hell disguised as a child's puzzle? The original Necronomicon in handy pocket size?' Although that would, of course, involve the supposed *Book Of The Dead* existing outside of HP Lovecraft's mind. Which was far more unpleasant than any supposed book of evil spells could ever be.

'The whereabouts of my brother.'

That one stops me short. 'I didn't realise you had a brother.' Actually, I suddenly clock I don't know anything about his family except that most – if not all of them – are unpleasant religious extremists.

'Yeah. One. Older than me by a few years. Ran away sometime just before I did.'

'Did he get the TLC – Torture! Let's Convert! – treatment too?'

Gil shakes his head and puffs at the falling hair strands, directing air up to push them aside from the corner of his mouth. 'No. He wasn't gay. Always seemed like the apple of their eye, actually. Then one day he just went. Took a backpack and a roll of bank notes and he was gone.'

I can feel my lips tightening. Can't help thinking that

what he didn't do was take his younger brother – the one being tortured – with him. 'Okay. What does this have to do with me? And, no offence, what does it have to do with you?'

The kid blinks at me, and this time it's his lips that thin. I can see the muscles in his jaw tense up, but he takes a second. Picks his words. Deliberate as ever. 'He's my brother. He got out. No one else did.'

Okay. Interesting. Seems Gil still sees a family tie, wants to reconnect. Guess I can understand him feeling a little lost, what with everything that's been going on. 'Fair enough, kid. But I still don't see what this has to do with me.'

'Well, I've been tracking him down, right?' Gil's expression smooths, switches back to an exuberant joy, and I can see he's excited to share what he's found while playing detective. 'Turns out, he followed a similar route to me. Ended up on the streets.'

'Right…' So far, so unsurprising. Naïve kid, mentally and physically abused and completely unworldly wise, stumbles out into the bright lights of metropolitan France with a wodge of cash. The chances of it ending well are pretty damn slim.

'So I got a lead. Found out where he was staying.' Gil's struggling to keep his voice calm now. It's funny to see this normally taciturn kid so animated. Makes me feel all the worse for having to piss all over his parade.

'Again, right… I get it, Gil. You think you've found your long-lost brother.' I scrub my hand across my face, trying to wipe away some of the accumulated mileage and stress I've picked up in the last few weeks that a rapid piping hot shower failed to wash off. 'What I don't get is – in the nicest of all possible ways – why the fuck you're telling me about it?'

Oh. Ouch. That one stung, and the expression he gives me back – that brief flash of hurt that burns across his eyes before he locks them back down – makes me feel every inch of the callous eight-hundred-year-old monster I make myself out to be.

'I thought you might help.' The tone borders on sullen. I've not so much punctured his image of me as slashed it wide open with a bowie knife. And then pulled its guts out with my bare hands until there was a pile of intestines and viscera on the metaphorical floor in front of it.

'Look, normally kid, I'd be all over it. But I'm kind of on my own main mission at the moment, and I haven't got time for side quests. Plus, I don't see what help I can really be. It's not anything to do with the Talented world –'

'But it is!' A gleam springs back to his face. One of triumph. He thinks he's caught me out, bless him. 'Sebastien vanished in broad daylight! One moment, he was with his mates in the centre of Lille, sharing a bottle. The next, gone!'

Lille. Sounds like his brother hadn't hiked away as far as Gil did from his origins. An uncharitable part of me wonders if it was because he was hoping he might be able to go back and scrounge a few quid from his parents if worst came to worst.

'Listen.' I keep my voice as gentle as possible. I've already pissed all over his illusions about me; there's no need to be brutal in disillusioning him about everything else. 'A bunch of homeless drinking? Hardly the most reliable witnesses in the world. He probably just wandered off for a quick leak, and none of them noticed.'

'Except they all said the same thing!' He's strident now,

demanding. By the Good God, I think I've actually managed to anger him. 'They said the shadows swallowed him whole.'

Hmm. I rub my chin. Shadow magic. Unusual but not impossible. I shake my head. 'Any other time, Gil? I'd have happily traipsed off up north with you, gone to see what we can see. But my schedule's somewhat hectic post saving the world. Aicha —you remember her? She took you off for a merry jaunt into your master's cold store larder?— is missing. And I need to find a way to get her back. The Mother's just given me a heads up about a possible location of the Nain Rouge, and I'm heading south, not north.' Considering the Nain Rouge found the White Lady for Aicha during that particular shitshow of an adventure, I'm hoping he might do the same for me.

'You owe me!' Oh, yep. He's definitely pissed off. I've never heard him raise his voice, not even when killing a demi-goddess. And now he's on the edge of shouting at me, his face reddening as he half rises out of his seat. A second later, he slumps back, but his stare is anything but defeated. 'You owe me for saving your life.'

'Hey, I didn't send you there!' If I sound overly defensive, there's a good reason for that. Because I am. 'It was Franc who put you in that room, and you saved your own skin at the same time!'

Now I feel truly rotten. Because, technically, what I've just said is true. But it doesn't change the fact that this strange little homeless kid – able to see the Talented world but with no *talent* left of his own – saved all of our bacon by siding with us over Melusine. And we repaid that by chopping off his possible lover's head.

But that's how it works in our world. I didn't make him any promises. Didn't sign a contract. He's not some fae I thanked and am now forever in hock to. Nope. I like Gil. He definitely did us a solid, and, if I'm honest, in my heart of hearts, I do owe him one. Normally, I'd take the time to help him out.

Normally, Aicha wouldn't be missing. Jakob neither. Times are anything but normal and haven't been for far too long.

'Sorry, Gil. Doesn't work like that.' I keep my own tone calm but let him hear the steel in it too. He won't change my mind. 'Let me get what I'm doing done, then we can see. Once I find Aicha, I'm happy to lend a hand, but that comes first.'

'And how long will that take?' The kid's shrunk in on himself now, hunched over like he was the first time Aicha and I saw him at La Chapelle, a formerly squatted church that's now a charity helping the local community that Franc took over as his fiefdom when he got hit by a curse from the Sistren of Bordeaux. And I feel like shit about it. Won't change my mind though.

I shrug. 'How long's a piece of string? As long as it takes.' I'm not going to fob him off with some make-believe timeframe. He deserves that much honesty.

'But I've got a lead now!' He's pleading, and it's hard for him, I can tell.

'Sorry.' Final word. Let it be clear.

'Fine.' He stands up, pushing his chair back. The waiter's just arrived with the food, and Gil takes his from the tray. Too many missed meals means he's not going to lose out on this one just to make a dramatic exit. 'I'll do it on my own.' He turns, starts to leave.

'Gil…' He swings back, hope in his eyes. It fades at my expression. 'Take care, okay?'

'Whatever.' He's completely closed again.

I sigh and get up, pulling a card from my etheric storage as I do. 'Look. Here's my number. This should go through to whatever phone I'm carrying on me. It's probably just the booze talking, but if it really is magic? If you find yourself in trouble? Give me a call.'

It's a worthless gesture, probably. The chances of it really being anything magical are miniscule. And if it is, he's unlikely to have time to make a quick call. But it's as much as I can give him right now. As much as I have to spare.

And still he takes it. Grabs the card. Bobs his head in acknowledgement. 'Thanks, Paul.' Grateful words. They sound genuine.

I'm not sure why, therefore, as he walks off, his head bobbing in rhythm to the traffic's grinding motion before he dashes through the rush to the other side of the road, I feel like such a terrible fraud.

Chapter Three

The fact Ella Fitzgerald sang about loving Paris in the summer shows she's definitely American. No one French loves Paris in August. Not even the Parisians.

Paris in the summer is even more oppressive than usual. It's like the buildings suck the oxygen from the air and replace it with concentrated fumes emanating from the cars and half-contained disdainful fury emanating from the Parisians themselves. Although most of the locals have already headed for the proverbial hills. France in August shuts down. Any business that isn't considered an essential service – the hospitals, the police, the tourist industry – here in the most visited city in the world closes its doors for most, if not all, of the month.

Luckily, the National Library is considered an essential service. Unluckily, it seems that the Urluthes, the strange spirits of story and imagination who reside there, might be integrally French. Or distinctly not interested in me anymore. Because despite getting dispensation to consult with them concerning portals to other realms from Leandre, the Lutin Prince, ruler of Paris and all its surrounding banlieues, they're nowhere to be found.

I've searched the building from top to bottom. Spoke to more than one statue on the grounds that it might be an Urluthe in disguise, seeing as how they clothe themselves in images from stories, at least in my one encounter with them. Hassled a couple of tourists with brightly coloured hair in case they happened to be characters from books I haven't read yet. Searched every reading room for Pierrot, the moon-touched clown who acts as the intermediary for them as they don't normally ever talk to humans directly. Nothing. No sign of any impossible magical creatures who inspire our love of stories.

I even try running out and back in again, screaming, 'Sanctuary!' and falling over. It gets me nothing but a few curious looks and a smatter of applause from some bemused Norwegians who've obviously decided it is some form of impromptu street theatre. They even try to tip me a few euros, but I have my pride still. I direct them to drop it in the donations box. Then I stuff a few fifty euro bills in there on the off chance that the Urluthes will take it like an offering made at their shrine. The slaughtering of the fatted calf. Or the fatted wallet, in this case.

Zip. Zilch. Bupkis. Nada. Rien. Again.

Because no matter where I turn on my quest to find a way to bring Aicha and Jak back, I run smack bang into the equivalent of a brick wall. Nobody knows anything, and those who might know – the Urluthes, the White Lady, the Nain Rouge – are all conspicuous by their absence from where they're supposed to be, the lead the Mother had earlier about the Rouge having turned into yet another dead end. If I wasn't actually assured of the possibility of success by something that comes as close to a deity as I'm prepared to admit might exist, I'd give up hope and head straight for the bottom of a bottle.

But Aicha is still out there. And she's never given up on me. Even when I gave up on myself. So I'll be fucking dead forever, my flesh as worm food, all my multitudinous enemies dancing a collective hornpipe on my grave, before I quit on this one.

However fucking long it takes.

I reckon my frustration must be running at Parisian levels right now. Everything is irritating. The oppressive heat, the bustle of bodies and endless noise. Normally I'd have revelled in all the different voices and different languages sharing this space. But right now it's more like another barrier. Something boxing me in. Breaking my concentration. Keeping me from doing what I need to do.

So when my phone rings, the squawking screech of the standardised ring tone, it's an effort of will not to hurl it at the nearest tourist. Despite the temptation – and, boy, is it tempting – I don't. You may applaud my self-control now.

'Hello?' My exasperation is entirely clear in how I snap off each part of the syllables like pistol shots.

'Paul?' The voice on the other end is so low, so quiet, I can hardly hear him. 'It's Gil. I've found him, Paul.'

'Found who?' Then I remember. His missing brother. The conversation in Toulouse the month before. I've not thought about it since I held my guilt over not helping him face-down in a glass of whisky till it stopped struggling. 'Scrub that, I remember. Where are you?'

'It's The Family.' I can hear the capitalisation. That I wish he was talking about some Italian mobsters speaks to how much I dislike religious extremists. Sadly, I know enough of Gil's story to know he means both his family and The Family. A group of cultish Christian evangelists who have a strong distaste for things like freedom of thought or sexual liberation. They probably frown at the idea of women in trousers as a terribly modern and sinful fad. Not the sort of people I want to mix with. Unless it's in the sense of popping them all in a super-sized blender and hitting the on button.

'Where?' Keep to the main point. Because I might have been prepared to let Gil head off on his own, but I can hear it now – the slight hitch in his voice, the tiny note of panic. This is a waltz back into Past Trauma World for Gil, and I'm feeling like the universe's worst shithead for having let him head off into it on his own. Aicha would've clapped me round the back of the head for it. Possibly with a baseball bat. And with reason.

'I've sent you a location pin.' The rustling of leaves is louder than his voice. He's pressing his way through bushes or undergrowth of some kind if I'm any judge. 'They've got Sebastien. I've seen him through the window. And Paul… he's hooked up to *something*.'

Way too vague. 'Something what?' It could be anything from The Machine from the Pit Of Despair to the sucker pad of some Lovecraftian Elder God with a description that vague.

'Some sort of machine.' Pit of Despair it is. 'But there's *talent* involved, Paul.'

Of course. Gil can still see magic even though he had his abilities eaten up as part of his deal with Franc. What he can't do is protect himself from it in any way.

Which is why when I hear a crackling noise like an ancient electrical device well past its sell by date fritzing off a dodgy plug and then a half-scream that cuts off in a way no human could choose, mid-instinctive shriek, I know what's happened. Fuck.

He's been spotted. And grabbed. And there's *talent* involved.

And I sent him off on his own. Double fuck.

I hang up on the call. There's no point doing that whole film thing of screaming, "Hello? Hello?" down the line. All that's going to do is draw the bad guys' attention to his phone if, as I assume, he dropped it. Better there's a chance they don't realise he's called for help. That he sent his location. More chance they won't move him before I get there.

Instead, I dial a number which might, actually, allow me to be of some help.

'Paul, lad? What news?' Isaac's greeting is warm, if, perhaps, just the tiniest bit hollow. He sounds tired, stretched thin. I wonder how hard he's been working himself, trying to find an answer for us as to how to get our friends home. That's something to feel guilty about later on though. First things first.

'A pin. Location pin.' I'm garbling my words, panicking slightly. Panicked Paul is no use to anyone except his enemies. Certainly no use to Gil. I force my breathing to calm, force myself to slow down. 'On the main phone. Gil's sent me a location pin. Can you forward it on?'

The main number on any card I give – the number people can always reach me on – is back at Isaac's, with call forwarding set to my current burner phone. I go through more handsets than Avon Barksdale, so there's no point giving out whatever my current number is. The location pin won't come through though.

Luckily, Isaac's on the case. The tone when I first started was enough to get it through to him. 'It's coming to you now. What's going on? Do you need backup?'

The Good God bless him. He's always ready to do that, to back my plays even though most of the time they're likely to be utterly ridiculous, bordering on suicidal. A quick look at the pin tells me the answer to that though. 'No time, 'Zac. Gil's been grabbed by his old family. And they're not that far away from me right now. Up towards Lille.'

'Fine.' I hear the hesitation. He doesn't want to ask. Knows it isn't the priority. Can't help himself though. 'Anything?'

The poor bastard. He's just as stressed out as I am about Jakob and Aicha being gone. We know they were alive a few months back. There's no guarantee of that the longer time goes on.

So it breaks my heart each time I have to tell him the same thing. 'Nothing. Not a single Good God damned thing. Tell you about it after I rescue Gil, though, okay?'

'Got it, lad. Take care, all right?'

'Sure, 'Zac. Speak soon.'

Click. I have to hope that was enough to reassure him. Because taking care of myself isn't the priority right now.

It's finding an orphan left in our care. And saving him from his fucked-up, so-called family.

I'm not ready to lose another one of our friends. Now I just have to make sure I've not done precisely that. Again.

Chapter Four

"...And they all went Marchiennes , all to get out of the rain." Although I doubt I'm going to find anyone Noah would have accepted onto his ark in this particular town.

The trees might offer shade, a momentary break from the sun's oppressive attempt to bake us back into the clay dust we supposedly came from. But it's what else might lurk in their depths, what might hide out of sight, out of the collective mind of the population that concerns me more deeply.

Of course, it's far cooler here than back home in Toulouse, cooler even than Paris was. That city sucks in heat like it draws in tourists, channelling it back down onto them in the streets, venting it up at them from the subway down below. Even in the urban spaces, the temperature's a fraction of what it is only a couple of hours to the south. Here, under the leafy boughs, it's almost bearable.

What isn't are the results of my actions.

I can almost see the glare of a certain Moroccan

princess, can almost hear Aicha's cutting remarks about what a selfish fucking dickhead I am. Gil isn't harmless – go hold a séance and interrogate Melusine if you think so – but he's almost defenceless in the face of the Talented world. And I left him on his own. Let him walk straight into the lion's den and stick his head in their mouth to inspect their rear incisors for dental cavities. Spoiler alert – they're in perfect, flesh-rending condition.

It doesn't surprise me, the location of the pin Gil sent. The forest of Marchiennes makes sense as a location for The Family. Close enough to Lille for it to allow them access to all the mod cons they might need even as they rail against the sins of the modern world. Far enough away from most prying eyes to let them obscure all the horrible, terrible things they do to those in their power. A secured gate on a closed community, combined with a pious air when walking out among the locals, deflects a whole lot of questions.

It's amazing how, after centuries of evidence to the contrary, we forget that acting holy doesn't mean your soul isn't pure trash.

We're deep in the post-industrial north here. Thanks to interventionism by the French government, there's still enterprise left; Renault and Citroen are forces to be reckoned with. But much has closed down. A bit more than a century ago, Emile Zola came to the nearby mines and left shocked. Confronted by the horrifying realities, he turned the pit ponies, those forced underground as foals, blinded by never seeing the sun, and worked until they collapsed and died, into a metaphor for the workers them-selves in his novel *Germinal*.

I wonder who's wearing blinkers in the area these days.

There's no need to find out. No requirement to go inter-rogate the locals, to try to judge who's likely to point out their location from pride or spite. Because the pin that Gil sent?

Leads straight to their back door. Or, at least, the back door into their enclave.

I park a couple of miles back, at a branching footpath off the road. Hike like a regular day-trip walker as close as the public right of way can take me. Then pick my way through the trees, wrapped up tight in a *don't look here* spell until I get to the brick wall of Gil's pin.

As a rule of thumb, religious groups who construct three-metre-high walls topped with barbed wire aren't to be trusted. This place only needs a sentry point complete with spotlights and a machine gun nest to make the prison vibe complete. It's not the kind of spot where people come to clap their hands and praise the Lord around a campfire to the twang of a slightly off-tune guitar. More where they come to plot a cheeky bit of ethnic cleansing on the weekend.

The whole place gives me a chill that runs down my spine and back up to sit ice cold at the base of my brain. The horrors we can inflict on ourselves, on our fellow humans without ever the need for magic. There's an odour of guilt and trauma, grief and torture.

Nothing good has ever happened here. How anyone could be fooled into believing they are involved in anything holy when this is the backdrop is beyond me. But then, religion has always been a handy tool for washing a brain effectively, even at a hot thirty degrees.

Plus, this place *isn't* without magic – or at least someone inside it isn't. Because there's a slight shimmer to the air, an oil-slick of deepest midnight blue that coats the place. A working. One that reminds me of the shit the Ahnenerbe had in place in La Rochelle when I rescued Aicha at the end of WWII. It's a *don't look here* of sorts. More of a *don't get interested in here.* I wonder if I'd have managed to get directions from the locals if Gil hadn't sent us . People will know it exists, sure. Will be aware that it's a religious facility of some sort. But their *manipulated* instinct will be to leave it alone. To not ask questions. To just plain not want to know wha's going on behind the expansive walls and slammed closed entrance.

It may not surprise you to hear that my instinctive desire is to blow the bloody doors off. Storm in there like Get Carter. Show them that they might have a little *talent,* but they're out of shape, and for me, this is a full-time job.

What probably will surprise you is that I don't. Because I have no idea who or what's waiting in there. And I still don't know if I've any extra credits left in the arcade machine of Life if I happen to die. Which is highly likely even without me going off quite so cock a hoop.

So instead, I keep the *don't look here* swaddled around me. Then I harden the air into blocks, invisible compressed bricks, that I proceed to hop up, like some sort of weird cross between *Mario* and *Assassin's Creed*. It's a-me. Murderio.

The other side, initially, looks much like what I've left behind. Thick dense foliage obscures everything from wall height. Solid oaks grow closely enough to block the view even from three metres up in the air.

Good. It means they won't see me coming.

I use the same method to bring myself down, hopping catlike from point to point, landing silently, alert. Aicha would be proud of me. Good God, I wish she was here with me to bring the ruckus. We'd have this cleared up in no time. And she's never been a fan of zealots. Or those who try to hurt our friends.

But she isn't. It's just me. So I better get the job done. And properly too.

I slide around bough and bark. There are no leaves on the ground despite the heat. Guess there's either been enough rain to keep the trees healthy or some well distributed watering system running off an underground well. Either way, it helps me keep silent as I get close enough to see what, I assume, is my final destination.

The Family obviously isn't doing badly for themselves. It's an ancient farmhouse, complete with barns and stables, and the farm in question must once have belonged to some seriously wealthy landowners based on the main building. Probably profiting off the backs of the same beaten-down locals Zola in *Germinal*.

It's more manor house than farm. The building bends around in an L-shape, but even the shorter part is larger than Isaac's countryside folly. White-washed walls are run through with timber beams, and the roofs are that distinctive elongated slate form that's been the rage around here for a couple of centuries at least. Long grass lawns, manicured finer than a Parisian society lady's nails, stretch from the back door to where the forest has been neatly culled and contained, kept from intruding any farther into this genteel scene.

It'd stink of money if it didn't stink even more strongly of misery.

There really is an almost palpable odour that springs from it. Maybe it's my imagination with the heat, but I can almost smell that particular sweat. When it comes from fear instead of exertion or heat, it carries a distinctive scent. Maybe it's the hormones swirling about in the mix, the fight-or-flight mechanism gearing up to make the necessary choices. But when you've been in that place – been terrified for your life or the lives of others or stood in judgement over those facing their certain doom at your hands as often as I have, then you can smell the difference. An extra tang. Like the last lingering trace of burnt lemon juice, and it speaks of suffering to come.

The grass underfoot, baking and browning under the mid-afternoon sun waiting for its next watering session, seems to carry that same smell.

I keep the *don't look here* pulled tight around me. There may be magic involved, but it doesn't mean everyone on site is magical. I've no idea how many people are even likely to be here. Never asked Gil too much about his past.

Never made the time.

Once I'm sure he's safe. Once I've made sure whoever has laid their hands on him knows they can't do that to my people, there'll be time to berate myself for what a shitty friend I've been.

And if he isn't safe? Then I'll make sure they never do any laying on of hands – religious or otherwise – ever again. By severing them at the wrists. Then force-feeding them the bloody stumps.

There're a few possible places where they might be keeping him. Either one of the outbuildings – away from the main congregation, allowing them to wallow in happy ignorance. Or else a wine cellar or storage room in the central building that's been repurposed as a prison cell.

I doubt this will be the first time they've held someone against their will, the first time they've inflicted their own upon those who are unwilling.

My money's on the barn or the stables. Probably the former, but it depends. Seems unlikely they still keep horses, so they could have repurposed the other building. I doubt they go in much for fun-time activities like horse riding here.

I creep across the verdant lawn, pulling my sword from my etheric storage as I go. Religious nutters living in isolated enclaves have a worrying tendency to be both well-armed and equally well-trained. It's funny how often people think God wants them to be ready for war considering how every single major religious text suggests the exact opposite. It makes me wonder why the Good God even bothered helping us out on Bugarach if she really did make this world. I'd have let the Evil God just burn the whole place to the ground after all the fucked-up shit humans had done in my name. Raze it, start all over again.

It's probably a good thing I'm not a deity. I'd do a terrible job at the whole thing.

It's a couple of hundred metres across the grassy space, and I can smell my own worry coming through in *my* sweat. Because cults —and let's be clear, this is a cult— can be very efficient in their viciousness. If there's a member with any form of sniper rifle and *talent* on watch or one comes around the corner who can *see*, with whatever the black market can offer in terms of assault rifles, then I'm liable to get my brains splattered across the waving sward beneath my feet before I even realise it. A quick death. I've lived it often enough. Now, though, I really don't want to die. It's a pressure that's dug its claws into the animal part of my brain and is riding it like a bucking bronco, refusing to let go. Finding Aicha and Jakob, wherever they are in the myriad realities that touch our own. Getting them back. Before I die. It's a constant weight, a driving terror. I die so damn easily that the odds are I'm going to pop my clogs before I find them. And I might not come back.

I'd say it's a failure I can't live with. It's more important that it's a failure I don't die with.

I make it to the barn without getting my head painted across several metres of grass behind me. Which is a nice thing, all in all. The building itself mirrors the main house. There's the huge slate roof, the same size near as damn it as the main wall itself. Plus skylight windows looking out from along the top, suggesting a second level inside. The windows along the side of the building are four panes inside each of the frames, held together by what looks like wrought iron fixtures. It'd be pretty if I couldn't see the solid metal bars behind. That and the crackling wards covering it.

'Fuck.' It's a small half-breath of a word. I really hoped I wouldn't have to deal with wards. That it was perhaps some sort of instinctive *talent* usage that Gil saw. That the *don't look here* of sorts over the whole enclave was just a manifestation of some latent abilities.

Wards mean it's deliberate. That someone knows how to sling magic around. It takes the danger levels up another notch.

There's one small bit of good news though. If this building is warded, it means I've probably hit the jackpot in terms of which building he's in. I sneak along the wall, being very careful not to touch it in any way. That's a guaranteed way to set all of the Big Bad's alarm bells ringing and bringing the owners out to rain screaming death down on me with extreme prejudice. Let's not do that. Getting closer, I peer through the small, smeared panes.

Yep. I hit the bullseye. Now I just need to find whoever did this to Gil and hit them in their eye too. Preferably with a railroad spike. Driven home with a sledgehammer.

The glass is so dirty it verges on opaque, but I can see enough. Gil's naked, hung like a slab of meat from one of the oak braces that stand in the large interior space. I was wrong about it having a second level. The skylights allow the sun to come streaming in, lighting him up. Ropes loop up and under his arms, keeping them stretched out. The resemblance to the traditional image of Christ doesn't pass me by.

He's been beaten. That much is clear. It's only been a couple of hours, three maybe since he called me. Already the marks across his torso and around his face are exploding over his skin, fireworks of mottled greens and blues. They'll darken to midnight purples by tomorrow. If he lives that long. He looks half-dead already.

It's hard to be sure how much damage has been wrought to his visage. There's some sort of device strapped up over his nose and mouth, obscuring the view. It's a bit like a cross between one of those masks they use in hospitals to put you to sleep before an operation and one of the ones fighter pilots use to fly ridiculous speeds at even more ridiculous heights. It's a brown rubber that sits, triangular, across his breathing holes, attached to some sort of translucent piping, running away towards something I can't see. The angle of the window obscures it no matter how I try to crane my neck to look.

A noise – a half-squealed groan carries from inside but not from Gil. He's not alone. Another figure is across to his right, equally tied. He's rake thin, his ribs pushing the skin to breaking point each time he pulls on a breath. His face is similarly patterned to Gil's. But the bruises on his arms are older. Self-inflicted. Puncture-mark kisses from the needle's embrace, by my reckoning.

That must be Gil's brother. Considering he's been here longer than Gil – and the poor state of his health before he was taken, if I'm any judge – I can't imagine how he's survived. Guess the Brothers Gil are both made of stern stuff. Even when suffering from the ravages of addiction.

The same sort of breathing apparatus covering Gil's face is strapped across his, making it hard to make out his features. Lank black hair drooping across his left eye obscures most of the rest. No way of telling whether there's any real family resemblance. Of course, it's probably hard to tell anyhow when he's been beaten black and blue.

What most interests me at the moment is the machine they're strapped up to. Because it's not pumping gas into them − or at least not only that. I can't see gases − though, considering air is a gas, that'd probably just mean I'd be blind all the time, so small victories, I guess. But I can see *talent*. And there's plenty of that swirling through those tubes.

It's fascinating. Mixing magic and machines isn't exactly frowned upon, but it's a rarity. The Nazis were into it in a big way. And the horrific experiments they performed to try to intermingle the two is part of the reason why anyone sane in the Talented community has steered well clear of it since. But on top of that, it's not an easy thing to pull off. They just don't tend to play nicely together. Imagination says injecting magic into modern technology should super-power it, leading to incredible flying cars or guns that fire piranha-teethed demons at your enemies. Reality says it tends to make things go boom. Particularly when you're holding them. It's a large part of why the Nazis didn't win the war despite their best attempts at being utter cunt-bungles.

So I'm totally intrigued as to what this is, that seems to be functioning perfectly. And, talking of functions, what precisely it's doing to my friend and his brother so as I can stop it with extreme prejudice. I'm performing that peculiar little dance when you duck and weave like a punch-drunk boxer, trying to see round obscured views despite it being a physical impossibility.

With the result that I don't hear the person stepping out of the shadows behind me.

Not until I feel the shadows wrap themselves around me. Around my brain. Around my eyes.

Darkness takes me, and the world is gone.

Chapter Five

MARCHIENNES, 26 AUGUST, PRESENT DAY

Time to wake up. I'd say, 'I'll sleep when I'm dead,' if the lack of slumber I achieved when kicking the bucket each time didn't prove me categorically wrong.

My eyes crack open with great resistance. It feels like someone's mixed up a bunch of the sleep gunk that forms in your eyes when you're super tired or ill, mixed it with cement, and then poured it back into my corneas. It takes a barrel-load of conscious effort to force them open.

Once I do, I almost wish I hadn't bothered.

Everyone is allowed to have their own fetishes, and I support the right to indulge in your own desires. You'll never catch me kink shaming. But I, personally, don't ever want to wake up spread-eagled and tied up to a wooden frame with freaky medical equipment strapped over my face. If you do, then knock yourself out. Hell, that's probably part of the game. But for me, it's never going to be good news. Especially when said equipment is aglow with *talent* and the woman who has pulled the aforementioned knocking me out might, in reality, be young enough to be my fifty-times-great-granddaughter but looks old enough to be my grandmother.

And evil enough to make Satan decide to clean up all his toys. And lay the table for good measure. Not a woman to mess with.

She's definitely old, but that doesn't mean she's let herself go. Her hair is dyed black and has been combed to within an inch of its life, then pulled back into a single, austere ponytail. Facially, she resembles a Studio Ghibli grandmother witch but without the twinkly eyes and smile. In fact, the corners of her mouth are probably the least wrinkly part of her face. It suggests she has rarely, if ever, smiled. Probably considers it a wasteful expenditure of energy or the like. And her eyes have definitely never twinkled. Burned with righteous fury, like they are now, sure. I imagine they're as cold as an Artic drill hole any other time. Freezing or burning. She'd never bother with anything less than that.

Her clothes are puritan, cloth cut, reminiscent of a Victorian school mistress. Hell, she looks almost old enough to have been one. Although I imagine she'd have been happier running a workhouse than a schoolhouse. In all, she carries the vibe of an unpleasant elderly relation who one has to invite out of some sense of familial debt to birthdays or Christmases but who you know perfectly well will spend the whole time telling your niece that she needs to stop dressing like a boy and find a husband. In front of her girlfriend. Tolerance is not her middle name, which is ironic because she looks like it could be her first one. That or Patience or Virtue or something equally ridiculously unsuitable.

So far, so remarkably unremarkable considering our setting. But there's one thing that does catch my eye. On her face is a large red stain extending from her hairline, down across one eye. A patch that looks as though an iron might have fallen onto her forehead when she was young. Except it isn't puckered or damaged. The ruin to her skin is wrought by age, not by scarring. I'd say it was a birthmark. Except it glows with *talent*.

She's watching me, of course, sitting in what looks like an old high-backed winged chair, the thin cushioning covered in green velour. Absolutely ramrod straight. She doesn't strike me as a character who ever allows slacking in her presence. And that goes for herself too.

'So. Awake, are you?' There's a disdainful sneer to her voice. Apparently she doesn't think very highly of me. Just wait until she hears me talk. 'Are you Gil's *friend*?'

The emphasis on the word "friend" doesn't leave me in any doubt that she doesn't mean in a best buddies, drinking beers, and shooting the shit kind of way. And the distaste with which she says it makes it very clear exactly what sort of a nasty old bigot she is – though it was already pretty clear from the whole "tying us up and strapping us to some sort of weird magical device" schtick.

Speaking of which, said device is the reason why I haven't started cracking wise and insulting her in equal measure. Because it seems to be effectively nullifying my *talent*. Which is both deeply worrying and also just putting a cramp in my generally insolent style.

And still that stain on her face keeps pulling my eyes towards it, like when you're walking down the street and double take at someone's scars or over-sized birthmark even as you realise you've been incredibly obvious in doing so and start to die from the deep shame of such a tactless action. Because something about it is shouting at me, demanding my attention. And not just because it's *talent* imbued. There's something about the shape or the pattern that's tugging away at my memory. Sadly, I can't dive into my mind palace, the handy mental construct I built in my brain to allow me to hold on to all the information I'd lose otherwise, to find out what. Not because it'd be rude, but because I suspect if I glaze over, this woman – who I assume is the Matriarch of The Family considering her *talent* and general aura of horrible, authoritarian fuckwittery – will start torturing me to get my attention back.

'Noticed, eh?' The words are seal barks, harsh and surprisingly deep for a woman. I wonder if a packet or two of Gauloises cigarettes might be her guilty indulgence. 'The Family's always believed. Always soldiered. God's sword. Hunted fae. Hunted wizards. Cleansed them. Sanctified the land.'

Oh, I was wrong. I thought she never smiled, but her lip corners quirk up at the thought of murdering magical beings. Her eyes crinkle with delight at the thought of bloodshed and holy fire. She's a Crusader born and bred. Me and Crusaders have never got on, not since the originals decided to wipe out my entire creed for daring to think differently. Tends to leave you indisposed towards their like afterwards.

'A curse. Supposedly.' Now her eyes narrow. The words, already staccato, short cut, are practically spat. 'Fae *bitch*. It was. A curse, that is. At first. We died. Even children. Typical faery evil.'

Now, far be it for me to defend the fae. Getting stuck in Faerie, their home plane, was frankly terrifying, and I was more than happy to unalive a whole bunch of them to get home if necessary. In the end, Aicha slaughtered the queen of the Winter Court in one-on-one combat, but I did also threaten King Oberon over in the Summer Court with a homemade suicide bomb packed full of iron, and I was fully ready to pull the trigger. So, yeah. I'm not exactly squeamish about killing fae.

But at the same time, they aren't fundamentally evil. That's missing the point. They're amoral, in the sense that they're outside of our sense of morals and social codes. They aren't human. Aren't tied to our morality. So of course they're fucking amoral.

And frankly, if you were some kind of mad, cryptid-killing religious nutcase who'd just stabbed me with a very pointy piece of iron? Then I'd be trying to curse you with my dying breath too. I mean, it'd only be a word combination like, 'You're a cuntknuckle,' in my case, but if I could bring a bit of death to you and yours instead, I'd definitely go for that.

While I've been marshalling my thoughts concerning the ins and outs of fae versus human morals, she just carries on regardless. 'Next day. On returning. After the hunt. The heir... bled out. Horrible mess. And the mark? The mark came. The curse. With one aim. Against us. Our family. To kill us all'

Now she's back in her element. And that particular element is hellfire, by my reckoning, looking at what burns in her regard. Ironic when you think she considers herself on the side of the angels. Mind you, considering all the murdering they got up to back in the day, according to the Old Testament, perhaps they'd be backing her play after all. I feel momentarily guilty at the thought. I can't imagine Nithael or Nanael getting down with any indiscriminate slaughter and certainly not with a wrinkled old pussbag like the one in front of me.

'But it couldn't. Couldn't kill us. Nor our faith. Our belief. It became our strength. A blessing. Powered by God.' She's on her feet now, practically leaping up, which considering how ancient she is, must be relatively difficult. But there's nothing like extremism to push us beyond our limits, I guess. She pulls a crucifix out from under her stiff white collar and dangles it by the chain in front of her as she advances on me like she thinks I'm Christopher Lee and she's Van Helsing's long detested maiden aunt or something.

'Tasteless bit of jewellery.' The face mask obscures my words but doesn't stop them entirely. Oops. Probably doesn't fit with the whole "keeping my mouth shut" manoeuvre I was trying for. It's enough to stop her in her tracks though.

'You dare? Blasphemer!' Oh, that seems to have pushed her buttons anyhow.

'Well, I mean, you've got me apparently strapped up to The Machine in the Pit of Despair, ready to start sucking my life away one year at a time.' A blank look greets me. If there was any further evidence required that she needs to die, I just got it. Who hasn't seen the *Princess Bride*? Movie's a classic. 'So I might as well dare, right? And if there's ever anything tackier than a cross as a decoration, I don't know what it is. How about having something a bit more cool, like the loaves and fishes? Maybe a healed leper or him throwing over the stalls in the temple? That was metal as fuck. Even the rolled back stone would be awesome. But the cross? Hardly going to be Jesus' favourite moment, is it? I never got the idea of focusing on his death rather than his life.'

'Burnt! You should be!' She's practically spitting with rage now, almost frothing at the mouth.

'Thanks, Angry Yoda. That was their reaction last time around when we suggested it wasn't a good look. Not that it stuck then either. But just goes to show how you're just as much of a shithead as the ancient establishment for all of the loner Crusader vibe you're after.'

'Enough!' She's calmed herself, grabbed back hold with that iron will. 'Very clever. Filthy heathen. But you will. Help us, that is. Despite yourself. That sorcery. Wicked villainy. It will serve. Serve us. Once it's burnt.'

Damn. That doesn't sound good. I'm just about to suggest we get into the nitty gritty of our differences of creed, perhaps over a nice cup of tea in the main house instead of strapped up to a wooden frame, when she grabs hold of what looks like a sceptre made of glass.

Looks like she doesn't need a giant wooden lever to set The Machine to maximum. At least, I assume that's what she does when every nerve in my body explodes into a symphony of riotous pain at the same time as everything goes black.

As Franc would have put it, buggerations.

Chapter Six

*Let it be noted here and now that I'm not a big fan of
people whose response to a difference in theological opinion
is to render you unconscious. Although I suppose it makes a
change from burning us at the stake.*

The thing about pain is you never really get used to it. Not
the immediate shock of it anyhow. It doesn't matter how
many times it happens. When you get plunged under that
wave of real, pure agony out of the blue, you're going to
gasp it in and drown. For a moment at least. No two ways
about it.

But what you can do is learn to survive it. Get past that
initial, agonising overload. Break it down. Compartmen-
talise it. Separate yourself from it, at least a hand's width.
Recognise that the sensation is one thing, and you are the
other.

The pain might not leave. But you can at least think
again. Exist once more instead of just being nothing but

animalistic suffering, shutting down all your higher functions. *Cogito ergo sum.* I think, therefore I am. If you aren't thinking, you aren't real. But if you can string two thoughts together?

You're still alive. At least to some extent.

As I get back control of my brain, master the suffering enough to take stock of my situation, I realise I have no idea where I am. I'm hanging, suspended in an inky blackness. It's a bit like that moment when you first wake after a heavy sleep. When the eyes are still sealed shut and you're still a long way from being back in the body's driving seat. My mind is moving sluggishly, but it is moving, and I know that somehow I've been separated from my body.

And I also know that I'm not alone.

I can feel it now that I'm more aware again. A link, that same murky deep-ocean-blue colour as the magic I saw before, running off into the prevailing darkness. A main vein. And I can see what it's pumping.

Talent.

It's pulling on mine, trying to draw it from me. So far it's only a trickle. The little bit it's managed to grab hold of is moving like treacle, bunging up the pipes. Looks like my *talent* doesn't want to leave me, the Good God bless it. I gave it up before. Sacrificed it on the pinnacle of Bugarach. It was the least I could do, considering the sacrifice Aicha and Jak had made. But the Good God, bless her, gave it back. And now that someone's apparently trying to sacrifice it for me, it's clinging to me for all it's worth, sticking to me like glue.

But there's more than just me hooked up to this arterial piping.

Other offshoots run from it, and I can see what they're linked to. Amorphous glowing shapes. Ones I've seen when

I've looked deep inside people for reasons, good or ill, over the years. The anima that makes them who they are. The part of the whole that we define as us.

The soul, if you will.

Two other beings are linked on, and it doesn't take a genius to work out who they are. Even thinking that, I realise I can feel them. Not just their presence – although that is a radiance that carries through this non-existence we find ourselves suspended in. No. I can feel their thoughts, their hopes, their dreams. Their nightmares.

Those two are deeply intermingled. Trauma ties so many things together that should never be connected.

The one on the right is Gil's brother. He's lost in his suffering. Not only the burning of this accursed machine the Matriarch has us in, but the other burning too. They call smoking heroin chasing the dragon. Right now, the dragon's chasing him. Breathing fire through every inch of his body, wracking his soul with misery just as surely as whatever is being done to us.

Interestingly, I can see there's magic being drained from him. And also, interestingly, I can feel he knows he isn't going to die. However much he wishes he would.

The other soul is Gil. And he's fighting the pain, of course. A tougher young man I've rarely met over the years. To hold on to a faith in anything after all the suffering he's lived through is a tribute to his will. One which is the equal of the woman outside but channelled in a totally different direction. Gil's chosen to hold on to his innocence in the face of a world that corrupts all it touches. Of course he's refusing to be submerged by simple physical pain.

He'll win that battle. But that's not what's worrying me. What's worrying me is that it isn't magic being sucked from Gil. He sacrificed that to Franc when he became his minion or ward or lover, whatever the strange deal was between them. He has nothing left to give in that department.

No. It's not magic. It's life.

Looks like my *Princess Bride* reference wasn't far wrong after all. Because the machine is sucking at his life, stealing away the years in front of him. Draining him to a husk. Eventually.

I can sense this isn't a quick process. Gil's coming round more, becoming more conscious. He feels my realisation, and cold dread floods back off him. We're outside of words right now, but we're connected. My realisations are his. And his terrors are mine to see.

Gil – the boy who stabbed a dragon fae in the chest, who walked into Franc's cold storage full of hanging human joints and walked out still sane – is drowning in fear. He's mortally afraid of the woman outside of wherever it is we are.

I catch glimpses riding on the emotions. When they found him as a kid, reading a teen magazine. Found the images of young men he'd torn out and stashed under his bed frame. The "healing" they performed on him. Correcting him back to the life they expected of him. After all, he was the second heir. The spare, as they used to call it in the days of nobility. The one waiting in the wings in case the anointed successor kicked the bucket or went completely off the rails.

Considering said heir is currently deep in the grip of heroin withdrawal, I'd say it would be safe to assume that's precisely what happened.

So beatings. Burnings. Eyes wedged open with matches. Forced to watch gay porn while they pumped him with horrible chemicals intravenously, making him vomit until he felt like his stomach would follow, crawling up a throat that felt liable to dissolve from the burning stomach acid. Barbaric actions. I can't help wondering once again how Gil hasn't ended up utterly broken by all he's lived.

Although maybe I shouldn't be surprised. It's why Aicha saw his worth from the get go. Recognised another one who survived that which should have broken them, splintering them into nothing but cracked shards. Those who can remain whole when they pass through such a crucible know each other the moment they meet.

Gil pulls back. Breaks some of the contact. Guess that's more than he wanted me to see. I'm not here to take from him what he doesn't want to share.

Instead I head back to his brother. Touch with his soul. Because the machine is sucking Gil's life, so I want to know why Sebastien is so sure he's not going to die when that's precisely what I envision the future has in store for Gil and I.

There. The difference to Gil. Sebastien was the golden boy. Always doing right. Following all the rules and guidance to the letter. Taking on the mantle. Living up to endless expectations.

Drowning under the pressure.

And then, one day, he's in Lille. Sent there to…oh.

Sent there to dispose of a body.

I can see it now. A dried-up husk. Sebastien jumps out of a car, hammers his way into an abandoned building. Dumps what was once a living man into the bathtub. And now I can feel it. The first doubts. Worry. Hurt.

Shame.

And so he doesn't head straight back. Before he left, heading off to dump a body, he pocketed some things he shouldn't have. A big roll of bank notes for one. He drives around in the car. Looking for salvation. Or a way to forget what's just happened.

A dingy bar. A first taste of alcohol. Tears on the bathroom floor, among the puddles of stale urine and the smell of cigarette smoke that years of an indoor smoking ban have never managed to remove.

And a new "friend". Who offers up a taste. A straw brought to the lips, and a flame stuck to the brown sticky substance on the crinkled foil in his hand.

Bliss. Total and utter relief through complete release. Letting go. Giving in and handing over control to a higher power. Just not a religious one this time, no matter how much it feels like a divine experience. Sebastien finds his new god in the pipe and then the needle. And never goes home again.

Not until now.

Now he knows what's coming, and I can see it too. The Family views his trespasses as mortal sins that can be cleansed and purged if they torment him hard enough. They'll make him suffer, traumatise him once he's clean from the drugs until the very idea of a needle makes him physically sick. They're going to corrupt the only thing he's ever found peace in, and he knows they're going to win. Because Sebastien isn't Gil. Isn't a force to be reckoned with, who hung on to his own sexuality in the face of their corrective efforts and found a way to escape without drugs, to remain the person he chose to be. Sebastien knows perfectly well he'll crumble before the Matriarch's will. Shape up once more. Become their willing little puppet.

And he hates himself for it. He'd rather die, but he knows he's too afraid. Knows instead he'll carry our desiccated corpses out to dump where we can be found, a strange mystery that'll excite the media circus' attention briefly but will never tie back to The Family.

That rings a bell with me. The dried up corpse he dumped. "The Mummy of Old-Lille" they'd called it. An old man, a Spanish painter who'd fled Spain's fascist repressions under Franco. They found his body lying in the bath he was presumed to have died in some fifteen years previously, based on his last written letters and the condition of his mummified corpse. I poke at the memory a bit more. He was supposed to have been fabulously wealthy and miserable with his wealth. A loner with no real connections.

Isolated. Unhappy. Rich. Sounds like a perfect target for a group like The Family to drain him dry. Literally. I wonder if he, too, held some latent talent. Or maybe he just started asking too many questions about why he wasn't allowed to leave, what had happened to all the money he'd given them.

So that's what Sebastien thinks the future holds for Gil and me. Better see what I can do about that.

Because there're three of us here, together. But there's still one more presence. One I can feel and who I drew a little bit of info about from the mind of Sebastien.

The force that The Family uses to hunt down magic users. To drain them dry. To power the Matriarch's shadow magic.

Something trapped in the crystal staff she grabbed to send us to this pain-filled purgatory while she extracts our essences, magical and otherwise.

I can feel it now. Whatever's at the other end of this cordon linking us and disappearing into the darkness. Not enough to know what it is. Perhaps who it is. Someone or something extremely powerful, that much is sure. But they clearly ran into something or someone even more powerful, who imprisoned them in the staff.

And I can tell what the Matriarch can't. That the thing, this spirit or sprite, has been leeching off parts of the magic it's been fed.

It hasn't only been serving the Matriach's will. It's been subverting a part of the magic to weaken its prison.

Now I don't know about you, but I've seen enough films over the years to know that freeing ancient, immeasurably powerful beings from the magical items imprisoning them is always bad news – unless they're voiced by Robin Williams.

This thing definitely isn't about to start doing funny impressions or speaking a million words a minute to have everyone in hysterics. It feels far more likely to try and shred everyone it can get its hands on into a million pieces the minute it gets free. Malevolence flows like backwash, up the connecting tether. Hatred and fury and disgust and *disdain*. I can get the anger. I've been locked up against my will. Trapped in a cave in Faerie, filled to the brim with bodies, no way of escaping. Two weeks there was enough to drive me to the limits of my sanity. Perhaps past them if I'm honest. But not to . Although that may be because Aicha came, saved me from that hellhole despite me having driven her away, furious at her for doing what needed to be done and killing Franc even at the cost of a few of his nearby lads and lasses. Did the right thing each and every step of the way, never letting the unimaginable horrors she suffered at the hands of the Nazis for five years break her faith in the value of humanity. Only one being ever carried such disdain for the human race. The Evil God. And I revoked his visiting rights to this domain thanks to the help of the Good God. Thanks to all the help and hope Aicha placed in my heart.

Brilliant. The religious, magic-hating zealot has a staff powered by a human-hating magical being. That probably qualifies as ironic. I'll verify it with anyone other than Alanis Morissette if I ever get out of here.

The only good news is the entity isn't close to breaking out. Much as I'd enjoy seeing it tearing the Matriarch's face off, there's a large swathe of humanity in the vicinity it'd do the same to as well, and that's not a fair trade.

The whole situation's a bit of an emotional rollercoaster. On the one hand –oh no!– something is trying to eat our magic and life force. On the other –meh– it's not a patch on Melusine, who did the same thing, and me and Gil sorted her out. Except –uh oh– of course, we had Aicha then. And she did the heavy lifting while Gil applied the finishing flourish. I just sat and watched with a few broken ribs mainly.

And, of course, the setup is restraining my magic. Keeping me from pulling on my *talent*. And while that's happening, Gil's life force is being eaten away.

Sadly, that's not the biggest problem. Because the biggest problem is I can see a way out of here straight away. But no one is going to be happy to hear it. Which should tell you just what a shitty way out it is.

Chapter Seven

Not since Baldrick said, 'I've got a cunning plan,' will any suggestion for a course of action be less well received.

I'm not happy in any way about my plan. But the sand timer that is Gil's very essence is ticking, so I lean into the connection with the two brothers. Let them sense my intentions. My potential actions.

Gil recoils. Tries to pull away, strains against this horrible tether tying us all together. His rejection, outright horror at the idea, comes hammering up the line. We're left in no two doubts about how he feels.

Sebastien understands. He's still not really conscious, but there's enough of him there. And I need him to understand, so I take my time, push the shape of my thoughts, possible intentions at him so he can be in no doubt.

He gets it. And he's fully on board. His agreement, acceptance, *permission* flow along the cords that bind us.

And Gil's anguish is a silent scream, a vibration like a

47

child's howl of denial in vibratory form, carried down the string of a tin-can telephone.

We feel it. Of course we do. But there's something else I feel, as well.

A tipping point. There's not long left before too much of Gil will be swallowed down. If I break the links soon, his soul will regenerate. He won't be all dead, not even mostly dead.

If we don't stop it soon? Not even Miracle Max will be able to save him.

So there's a choice. A simple case of mathematics. Because I can't save all of us. And if I don't make a choice, it'll be made for us. Sebastien will live, and Gil and I will be gone.

But he wants to die. While neither of us do.

Gil's still screaming without words. Not just at me, though some of it is. At the injustice of it all, and my heart breaks a little, long-shattered thing that it is. He hoped for a reunion, a redemption for his brother. A connection between two who escaped from The Family's evil clutches.

But his brother doesn't want to just escape from them. He wants to escape from existence. From all he did before. He doesn't want to heal. He doesn't want to exist anymore.

But he wants to save Gil. That much carries through, one pure note communicated from that writhing tormented soul, suffering in so many ways. I can feel it. I hope Gil can too because either way?

It's enough of a permission for me. So I start to *pull*.

It's simple, really. This staff's been used to feed mainly on the weak. Those who have *talent* but don't really know how to use it. But I've had mine for hundreds of years. Lost it twice. Once, I gained it back, of sorts, in a fairy queen's dead body I wore. A second time, returned by the Good

God. I've wielded magics beyond humanity's understanding and stared into the eyes of a mad, imprisoned god as it sucked down my reincarnation power and stood ready to swallow me whole.

This thing we're tied to now? Isn't even close to being in the same league as that god.

So while I can't access my *talent* to use it properly, it's not difficult to figure out how *talent* flows through this connection. And we're feeling each other, emotions passing back and forth through the link. Ideas. Images. Understanding.

Diverting the flow of the magic being swallowed up so that it flows in my direction instead of to the creature inside the staff is child's play for me. Except this isn't play. This is deadly serious.

Gil and I got added onto this little tangled skein after the creature started to feed off Sebastien. As such, we're almost on a separate branch. We're linked but further back in this magical circuit – Sebastien closest in, then Gil, then me.

And using the magic in this way – dragging it along a reversed polarity directly to myself does two things. It blocks off the flow of this branch, of Gil and I, stopping whatever is inside the crystal staff from feasting on us. The magic is locked into flowing in one single direction, and the *talent* that comes hurtling away from the staff starts to fill me to the brim. Based on the battering roar of fury and spoilt resentment flooding back along the connection, I guess it's not happy about that.

The second thing it does? It starts to kill Sebastien.

Not because I'm eating his life essence. No, not at all. I'm no energy vampire, powering my workings with another's spark.

But the creature is pulling with all his might. It can't get the magic, I'm taking that away from him, but Sebastien's life force? That's free to move still. I can't draw on it, can't save it. But the creature can.

And the creature is pulling hard.

It swallows greedily on what it can get from Sebastien. And I feel another thought strike it, as what I'm doing sinks in. What it means I'm capable of doing once I'm topped up magically. The creature heaves with all its might on Sebastien's soul, sucking him down, the tether a straw sunk right to the bottom. Drink Sebastien right up, drain him dry, use that energy, and maybe it can stop me from doing what I'm about to do.

It can't. But it kills Sebastien in the process.

Gil's emotions are howling gusts, tearing around this empty ether we're in. The magic may be blocking his life force getting out, but it's doing little to mute his emotional response as he feels his brother's soul ebb, flowing away into the magical darkness.

Sebastien's being gutters, weakens. It feels dry, feeble, like ancient parchment crumbling under an over-enthusiastic touch. I try not to think about how his body is doubtless mirroring that. Concentrate on what needs to be done.

Because all of this has happened at the speed of thought, in a microscopic sliver of a moment. And in that next fraction of an instant?

I cut the cord.

I snap my eyes open, hard, fast. Quick as I can. Relying on how often I've come to unexpectedly. Usually in a brand new place, in a brand new body. Disorientation can bite my arse. I need to move.

The mask hangs limp off my face, and my *talent* is mine again. It takes but a desire formed for the rope around my wrists to split, fraying in a second, allowing me to rip my hands free.

I ignore the croaky gasp from in front of me. Dash to the hanging figures. Ignore the one I recognise, the one who's travelled by my side. The one I sent off on his own because my mission was more important than his. Straight to the other one, dangling, limp.

Tear the mask off the face. Try not to gasp when half his face comes with it, cracking and flaking off in lumps, more ash than flesh. Not burnt. Desiccated. Sucked dry.

I knew it would happen. Doesn't mean I didn't want to be wrong though. Doesn't mean I feel in anyway right for what I did.

A groan from next to me. Time's limited. Now I'm scanning the room desperately. I feel another surge of magic behind me, but I recognise the flavour now, am ready for it. Fool me once, shame on me. Try to fool me twice, and I'm going to wrap those shadows around you like the old horse blanket I've set my eyes on, tie it up with bands of *talent*, and fling you back into your chair without even half a thought.

I'm not convinced that's exactly how the saying goes. It's exactly what I do though.

She's borrowed her power. Mine is fresh and full of fire at the unnecessary death required to get us free. Bending her own thrown-out *talent* against her is a moment's thought, a waved hand's requirement. The shadows skitter back at the touch of my magic, pool in close to their mistress, and I tie them off around her like the world's shittiest Christmas present. A murdering matriarch religious nutter. The perfect gift for someone you really, really despise.

With the Matriarch suitably restrained, I swing the horse blanket up off the floor, whirl it like a matador's cloak out to its full spread, and let it billow down to settle over Sebastien. Covering his body. Allowing him one last shred of dignity.

'Sebastien?' Gil sounds croakier than the Matriarch. Not that I think he's much concerned about his parched throat. '*Sebastien?*' The tone's rising now. The word more insistent, the question more urgent. Panic's setting in.

Nothing I can tell him is going to help with that. Nothing but a lie. And I'm not about to add to the wrongs I've done to the lad by doing that.

'He's gone, Gil.' I keep the words as soft as I can. As neutral. It's my fault he's dead. I can't offer any sympathy. It'd only be insult to grievous, unforgivable injury. Better not to add to his already mounting grief.

The young man, hanging, dangling from his rope-bound hands, throws back his head and howls. It's guttural, glottal noise, like the pain is crawling up his throat and grabbing hold of his tongue even as he tries to scream it out into the world.

That it's a noise I know well, recognise both from my own mouth and many others? Says no good thing about the many lives I've led.

It calms after a while. It always does. Pain can only be that pure for a short time, so sharp it breaks reality and traps a part of you forever in that instance. It feels like it'll never end, like this new reality you find yourself in must remain forever the same, grief's unshaken snow globe. But, of course, time does move on, does shake up things anew. And so the pain can't remain pure. It becomes diluted by the onwards rushing movement of life streaming forward. We're all just pebbles in the middle as it roars past us. It never even notices as it wears us down until we're rubbed clean away.

He looks at me now, and we're onto that next stage of the whole process. Where the anger is starting to filter that pain, distilling it into something that can burn in a heart until it consumes it.

'Why?' Gil's always been a young man of few words. Always been able to make his meaning clear with them. I wonder if that's why Aicha liked him so much. *Likes*. Likes him so much. There're no past tenses here. And I have to face the present too, where Gil is asking me why I let his brother die to save our lives.

Let's be honest. Why I killed his brother.

'It was the only way.' It's the truth. Of sorts. And Gil knows it too. Because it wasn't the only way. We could have sat there, fat, dumb, and happy until whatever it is that's in residence in the crystal staff I'm about to confiscate with extreme prejudice ate us all up. 'Just him or all three of us. It was what he wanted.'

And just like that, I've fucked up. And this isn't like when I get it wrong with Aicha, when she goes stock-still, serpentine, ready to strike for my fundamental idiocy. Gil strains against his bonds, and for a moment I'm glad I've forgotten to untie them because he looks like he'll go for my throat with his teeth, launch himself to tear any other such foolish words from them and swallow them down before I can utter them out into the world.

'Wanted to die?' He's raging, practically roaring his anger as he twists and writhes against the restraints. 'Of course he wanted to die! Didn't you, Paul? Didn't you?'

Oh, damn. Of course. The connection. The feelings and information flowed both ways. I'm better trained to protect my thoughts and emotions in a situation like that – my mind palace operates like a locked up safehouse in that regard – but seeing the state of Sebastien, I must have let some leak out.

He felt my suffering, my escape into the pipe. The itching, scratching need. My craven behaviour under its vicious insistence. Addiction rides you hard. Digs in its spurs. And does its best to never let go.

I don't drop my eyes during this revelation. Never let go of his maddened, red-rimmed gaze. Not because I'm not ashamed. But because he deserves to see. See that shame, the weight of what I've done. Not just now. By the Good God, not for a moment. All those times I was weak or stupid or pigheaded. Where I made the wrong choice and people died.

Where I made the right one, and they died too.

And the times when I didn't care. When I was lost in my own suffering, in all that grief that consumes us and drowns out any light. A bottomless abyss that sucks us down into the murky dark – submerged, swallowed whole.

'Do you know, Gil? What happened while I was in Paris, lips stuck to that pipe, sucking down the opium as fast as the reprobate running the den could give it to me?'

He looks at me, so fierce, so right; he shakes his head, his eyes never leaving mine.

'Neither do I.' I chuckle but there's no humour. And even he, even in the depths of his own anger and pain, can see I'm laughing at no one but myself. 'I've no idea. Do you know, even now, I can't bring myself to find out? Life carried on without me, but who died? Who suffered because I wasn't there? What about Franc, Gil?'

The boy flinches, and I raise a hand to show him it's not a dig, not at him at least. 'How long was Franc there, squatting in the Garonne before I came back, before he had to strike an accord with me? What did he do before then?

How many made their way to that cold store larder under the Pyrenees that you found with Aicha?' I sigh. 'And that's just the tip of the iceberg.'

'So what does that even mean?' I can hear his frustration, and what's worse, I can hear the want. Because even in his anger, in his utter fury and despair at what's happened, at my actions, he wants me to make it right. He wants to believe in me still. The poor bastard.

'It means I fucked up then and I couldn't face it. Just like I couldn't face what happened to Susane. Turned my back on it. On the world.' There's a dampness now, the first drops catching in the creases under my eyes, wetting underneath. 'And I didn't learn. Not then. Not really. Because once again, I've been suffering, and I turned my back on you to chase after the source of my pain.'

Gil looks at me, uncomprehending, and I have to get it through, make him understand. He wants to believe. I can't give him that.

'I got it wrong, Gil. If I was with you – from the start, came when you needed me, your brother wouldn't be dead. This is on me. Gil, I'm sorry, this is on me.'

And I hurt. Really deeply, inside. But what's terrible is what I hurt for. I hurt for Gil, sure. For his loss. But it hurts me to shatter his illusions about me. That I am some sort of saviour. That I'll make the right choices. I'm not the person for that. Aicha is. She's the one who'll make the hard calls in the right sense, the one who separated Franc's head from his shoulders for his terrible cold storage packed full of body parts, trimmed from the "lovely lads and lasses" he judged to have reneged on their deal. I was ready to strike a new agreement with him, to let him go to save a few lives there and then. An easier choice for me in that moment. A cop out, like so very often.

But still I force myself to keep Gil's gaze, to never let it drop, even at the sight of the new hurt blooming in his expression. And I try to snapshot that, to photograph it, to imprint it on my brain without the need to dive off into my mind palace. That. That's what it looks like when I make the wrong choices. When I put myself first. When I let others down. That's what I need to carry forward with me. And now I need to make it right.

'I...I'm going to do better, Gil.' Seems such easy words to say. Perhaps a little ridiculous to some, considering I saved the species, the world perhaps, a few weeks ago. But I didn't save his brother when I could have. That carries a weight all of its own. 'I'll be better. Make the right call. Be there when you need me, okay? I've let you down, but this is the last time. And I'm sorry for the price you paid. You're right. Just because he wanted to die, doesn't mean he should have. I wish we could have helped him find another choice instead. That got taken away. By my letting you down. I'm sorry.'

It's so hard. Not to flinch. Not to drop my eyes, to show my shame in the myriad of ways we've developed as a species to express all those complex emotions that are often too much for our simple language to really explain, all so redundant compared to what we can demonstrate with our posture, our positioning. I'll not do that. Not right now. Instead, I hold the gaze of the fierce, silent young man. Wait for him to... well, to do whatever he chooses. Chastise me. Curse me out. Claim an owed blood debt that he can call in any time. I'll take any of those right now.

Instead he just stares. Silently. A lack of noise as weighted as his gaze is, tears half-denied still squeezing out from the corner of his eyes, their load so heavy even his ferocious self-control can't hold them back. He blinks them away, then shakes his head, slightly, as one does when trying to clean out the brain's cobwebs or the lingering traces of a boozy night, to clear the head. Or perhaps to deny my apology. Or the reality we find ourselves in. I can't say, because he doesn't. I can only guess.

Eventually he speaks. 'Later, Paul.' Then he turns that raptor gaze to the side. 'Her first. Then we'll talk.'

I turn back towards our captor. The shadows have evaporated by now, of course, and all that's left is a thin-lipped ancient crone. She's still ramrod straight in the chair, quivering with her eyes bulging. I've not silenced her. Perhaps she doesn't think we're worth her bilious words, and she's biting them back. Perhaps she knows if she does start to speak, she'll beg for mercy, plead for her miserable existence, and her pride and mania won't allow that.

I don't give a rat's arse flying on little furry angelic wings and strumming a harp with the still-attached tail. She's done.

Chapter Eight

I wonder if the Matriarch considers modern technology a curse as well. Or does she browse the internet on Google Crone?

'Shall I kill her?' It's almost a casual question that drops from my lips and scoots across to Gil's ears. She's done enough, and I've killed enough. One more won't hurt. I'm happy to add her to the tally.

Gil doesn't answer. I flick my eyes back and see that his own are fixed on her, and that smouldering anger is starting to burn hotter again. Also, I've not untied him *still*, which is bordering on rude. Especially now his anger's not so focused on me but on a target who right royally deserves it.

I undo the knots with a thought. He almost collapses, his feet flattening, his knees buckling. But he catches himself, half-crouched. Posed like some sort of dancer, all poise and determination. His arms, which must be aching like hell, muscles drenched in lactic acid, are outstretched. It makes

58

me think of Jet Li about to pull off some amazing crane kick, and I wonder if he's about to snap a foot to her jaw, finish her off himself.

I don't want him to do that. My soul can handle the weight of it. I'm not sure his can.

'What's with the mark?' Throw something out from left-field. Knock that determined presence off balance. Get him thinking, talking again. If he still wants to kill her afterwards, fine. That's his choice. But I'll make sure he's in a fit state to actually choose, at least.

'What?' The word sounds rusty, like he's forgotten how to speak. Mind you, I'm surprised that howl didn't snap his voice box in half. That he can form any sound at all is a miracle.

'The one across her face.' He can see it. He's staring so hard at her, she's lucky his *talent* got munched down moons ago by Franc; else she'd be bursting into flames right now.

'A blessing.' Huh. I wasn't expecting the Matriarch to reply. Looking round, I see she's also matching his furious stare. But she's not letting him see her shame. She's showing him she doesn't have any. Only a fervent, righteous pride. Fucking hell. I'm astounded he hasn't slapped it off her face.

'A curse.' Grated hate. That's what each syllable holds. But Gil isn't done. 'The origins of our family. The Family. She' —he inclines his chin towards the ancient woman, his eyes never leaving her— 'would have you believe it was cleansed, that it came from a holy source, from a religious mission. But I've done reading since. Spoken with Isaac about it. Dug a bit deeper. It wasn't ordained, a divine quest. Wasn't revenge for killing some fae who deserved to die for being different.'

He laughs once, a bitter humour that drops from his lips

as he shakes his head. 'No. It was none of that, was it, grandma? It was all from a woman scorned.'

She sits, still back like a stiff board, never needing to touch the back of the chair. And now there's her own anger building in her eyes. But her lips are pursed, buttoned shut once more. Looks like she has nothing to say to the likes of us.

'Did you ever hear the legend of the Count Ralph of Carrouges?' he asks.

I'm about to shake my head when I stop. It does ring the vaguest of bells. 'Maybe?' I could dive off into my mind palace, of course. Find out what has set that particular bell ringing. But I reckon Gil's going to tell me. And that the telling in and of itself might do him some good. At the very least, it stops him from killing the woman who is, apparently, his grandmother in hot blood. Once he's calmed down fully, cooled entirely, if he wants to kill her in cold blood, then I won't stop him. But not when he's still het up. Not when he might regret it for the rest of his life.

'Grandma always told us,' he says slowly, dragging up the words from deep inside himself, 'that it was a sign of our devotion. For generations, the senior member of the family has worn that mark. When one dies – never soon enough, always in a prolonged, dragged out old age, then it appears again on the face of the next. A miracle, she told us. The mark of our faith. A fairy curse reforged. The sign that showed The Family to be the guardians of the true faith, the righteous ways.'

He shakes his head again, disbelievingly. 'I swallowed it all, you know. As a child. Hook, line, and sinker. After all, how could it not be the truth? She was more terrifying than any Old Testament prophet. Always seemed to see your every thought. Read you like an open book. And Grandma always burnt books that didn't agree with exactly what she had to say, didn't you? Bonfires of boy wizards or Gauls powered by magic potions or anything else you considered blasphemous.' He points at the crystal staff. 'But this isn't?'

Now she speaks. I can see her jaw unlock like a snake, ready to distend, to swallow up our sins with her words. 'It is not. It is *strength*. Our greatest blessing. Not for all though. Not for you, *boy*. Not for the unclean.'

I can hear the disdain. If she's a serpent, it's what drips from her fangs. Words have been her main weapon, a poison spread through the community, keeping them obedient. Afraid. Traumatising them all into being true believers. Or running like Gil.

Or breaking like Sebastien.

'No, grandma. Not for me.' Gil's anger is up again. I tense, readying myself to step between them, to offer to finish the deed for him again. But he doesn't move. Just gestures at the covered, dried-up corpse still suspended under the blanket I threw up to offer the barest smidgen of dignity. 'It was all for him, wasn't it? Look where that got him, Grandma.'

Now, for the first time, she looks less sure. 'Shouldn't have happened.' She's trembling slightly now. Perhaps the first touch of doubt is creeping in. Or perhaps she's just a wizened old woman sitting in a draughty barn, chills creeping in even during the summer's heat. Or perhaps it's looking her death in the face. That's always been enough to make even the bravest shake.

'Shouldn't have happened. Shouldn't have…taken him. Just the curses. The evil. The magic. The stain he carried. Perhaps too rooted. Too much rotted. If I acted sooner. Taken it earlier.' Her voice is rising now, strident, any doubt gone. 'That was why. Why he sinned. The poison he took.

The devil's stain. The one inside. It corrupted him. Drove him…to filthy acts. He didn't choose. Didn't want to sin. Didn't embrace the devil. Not *like you.*'

Good God. To stand there and hear such despicable hatred railed on you by your own grandmother. The utter contempt that carries in her words. But stand there, lets it wash over him, a reed unbowed by the river's passing.

'It was never a choice, grandma.' He sounds sad now, a child shaking their head at the confusing, jumbled up mess the adult world is. 'I am who I am. I wish I realised that a lot earlier. Wish I was able to help Sebastien realise it too. Maybe we'd both still have our *talent.*'

He looks over at the blanket rocking slightly in the barn's hole-poked breeze. 'Maybe he'd still be alive.'

'No!' The Matriarch's denial is so sudden, a shriek so loud, it's almost more shocking than anything that's come before. The change is dramatic, unbalancing. She's not leapt to her feet, but she stamps one so hard, I'm surprised her shin bone doesn't shoot out of her kneecap. 'It was your choice! You! You were the taint! The poison! The rot in the barrel! Apple spoiler! Snake! Vermin! Unholy, you are. Always have been. I knew, of course. Knew you were marked! Both carried it! The devil's workings! In your souls! I left it there. Left it too long. This *talent.*'

She spits at the word, but hardly pauses, doesn't break stride in her rant. 'I should have acted. Purged you both. I waited too long. Hoping. Praying for purification. For you. For him. Both made righteous. Soldiers in our cause!'

She shakes her head, spittle flying from her lips as she does. 'Never for you. You were lost. A lost cause. A hopeless sinner! And once I knew? I was too kind. Too kind.'

I have to fight not to scoff at the idea of the Matriarch

ever being kind. Apparently, based on the dirty look she shoots me, it's a fight I lose.

'I wanted. To be sure. To only take…the evil. The curse. The *talent*.' She gestures at the machine behind us. 'Not the rest. Not your life. To let you live.'

'But why?' I don't want to intrude, but that's the bit I don't get. 'What's with all this feeding magic to an evil spirit to help it escape its prison? Doesn't seem very Christian-like to me.'

The realisation of the silence hits me. You could hear a pin drop. In fact, I actually do hear the matron's head turning, the grind of fluid-depleted joint-on-joint action.

'What?' Flat incomprehension. 'What was that? What did you say?'

'The magic? Oh, and the life force from Gil as well. Plus, I guess, the dude whose body you dumped in Lille.' And of course, Poor Sebastien. A lost boy, broken by her expectations, sacrificed to stop anyone else suffering at her hands again. My voice wavers, but I set that thought aside, strengthen my resolve. 'Feeding your congregation into a magic-sucking device to power your fucked up theology. By the way, who sold you the patent for that?'

I squint suspiciously at the staff. 'Melusine, is that you?' I'm pretty sure Gil stabbing her with her bladed sceptre through the heart did her in. This definitely isn't that particular ossuary-based item. The staff here looks like it's made of crystal, not bones. Plus, De Montfort dismantled the other one for his *Evil God Punch N Judy* show. Which mainly involved me getting punched.

Still, stranger things happen at sea. Ask Odysseus. So I continue squinting at the staff for a minute, fully ready for Melusine or one of her family to pop out in a surprise reveal like some sort of magical version of *Candid Camera*. It doesn't happen though, thankfully. I could do without battling a demi-fae dragon on top.

'What?'

Looks like I've managed to completely jam up the Matriarch. She seems to be glitching, stuck on the word "what". I decide to do the human equivalent of switching her off and then back on again by telling her what she, apparently, didn't actually know.

'Oh, your fancy glowing stick?' I nod towards the object I just subjected to my most suspicious of stares. 'Definitely not in any way a religious relic. It's actually a prison for some demonic and malevolent force who's been using all the power you've conveniently been channelling towards it like a metal file smuggled inside a prison birthday cake. Only without the pretty cheerful decorations. The icing on this cake is your apparent complete ignorance and mortal stupidity, along with planet-sized pride that came close to releasing it on the world at large.'

'How close?' Gil asks.

I wave my hand back and forth. 'Nyeh. Hard to say. Ten years? Maybe twenty?' Based on the relieved sagging of Gil, that seems like an inordinately long time to him. To me? After eight hundred years and after seeing the long game strategy of plotting that someone like De Montfort can put in place, it seems like the blink of a gnat's eye.

Now that the immediate pressure's off, Gil can get back to his reckoning with the Matriarch. Who doesn't look convinced by what I've told her. Bigots are rarely so easily swayed from their convictions, though. 'You lie. A test. A test! That's what you are. A test from God. My faith? Will not falter. Will not fail. I used it wisely. I used it to hunt. To find them. Those like *him*.' Still the distaste in her mouth when she mentions Gil, the absolute arsegrape of a human being. 'Those with this *talent*. It meant I could help. Bring them in. Cleanse them. And grow the flock.'

Interesting. But believable too. Swoop in with strange abilities. Take away those that have probably caused the owner, who was unaware of their latent power but perhaps catching occasional glimpses of the hidden world below their own, serious concern for their mental health. Heal. Impress. *Terrify*. Good ways to gather yourself a fervent congregation.

Another thought starts scratching away at the back of my head. 'Hey, Gil, didn't you say something about a Sir Giles or something? Where does that all fit in?'

'Sir Ralph.' Gil's still staring at the old woman. He's shifted to a more comfortable position over time. Standing normally once more. But the intensity of his gaze has never left her. 'She's right in one sense, of course. That is where all this started. But it was never holy.'

He looks over at me, and I see the slightest trace of that innocent grin flick across his face. It relieves a little bit of the pressure in my chest. Something's going to be all right. I'm not sure if it's him or us. I try to force myself to think it'll be the former, try to ignore that quiet little selfish part that wants to hope it'll be the latter.

To hope that he'll forgive me.

Chapter Nine

Sounds like it's story time. I get the feeling the Matriarch
isn't going to like what he tells me. Good. Fuck her.

'Sir Ralph likes to hunt.' Gil's eyes go back to the
Matriarch, scanning her. 'So when his wife Louise falls pregnant, he organises a big one. Off they head, trumpets blowing. And while on the hunt, they see a huge stag, white as
snow, with gleaming antlers.'

Uh oh. 'That's either someone under a curse or a fae.'

Gil nods. 'Pretty obviously. Everyone gives up except Sir
Ralph, who goes plunging deeper into Motte Forest. He gets
lost, totally turned around, and ends up at a castle that
shouldn't exist. This is his land, and yet here is a magnificent chateau, banners draped down the sides, all gleaming
spires and white stone walls.'

I nod grimly. I don't know whether it's the knowledge of
this particular tale slowly coming back to the forefront or if
it's simply having run into enough like it over the years, but

I can see where this is going. 'Let me guess. He finds a fae inside and gets seduced by her.'

'Quite.' Gil nods. 'Some legends say it was an enchantress or sorceress but most say a fae. Of course he falls madly in love. Or at least lust. So after he goes home and sells his wife a sob story about spending the night in a poor woodcutter's hut, he declares he's moving into a spare room to give her space to be comfortable with her pregnancy. Except as soon as night falls, he creeps out and heads to the fae's castle once more.

'This goes on for a while.' Gil's shaking his head gently again. I'm not even sure he knows he's doing it. I think he's genuinely disappointed in old Sir Ralph even though magic's involved. It's that touch of naivete I have no idea how he's still held on to and hope he never loses. 'Eventually, though, she gets woken up by terrible pregnancy pains and sends the servants to fetch Sir Ralph to reassure her during the night. Only they find him gone. So the next night, she follows him.'

'It's lashing with rain, but she's determined, her stomach round and skin soaked.' Goodness me. Gil doesn't speak much, but when he gets going, he's quite the storyteller. 'She follows him to the castle that shouldn't exist and sees him go in. Waits outside all night and sees him leave before dawn breaks the next day. Once he's gone, she sneaks inside and somehow manages to catch the fae by surprise. Filled with furious jealousy, she seizes up a nearby blade and drives it into the fae's heart, killing her.'

'Him.' The word is so unexpected, so shocking to my rapt state as I hang on every word of Gil's story, I turn, fish-faced, physically gawping at the Matriarch. 'Not a her. Not a woman. His paramour? Another man. Another sin of our ancestor.'

Gil snorts. 'No wonder you really hated me. Whatever.' He turns in my direction. '*He*, apparently, still managed to gasp off a curse to fall onto her and her descendants, yea, verily, unto the end of the earth. The fairy died, and nothing seemed to happen immediately. So Louise turned and headed home, no doubt to give her errant knight of a husband, in the modern sense of the word, a piece of her mind. Only, when she got back, she found Ralph dead. A sword wound in his chest. The exact place she drove the blade into his fairy lover.'

Oops. Those were different times. However pissed off she was with her husband, she probably didn't wish him dead while being pregnant and with lands to run. The story isn't quite done though.

'She was consumed by a fever, haunted throughout by visions of a red spot. Then when her son was born, his face was marked. A red spot marring his handsome features. The mark of the fae's curse. Legend said it was supposed to have been broken on the generation when only daughters were born – the curse being solely passed down to the men, but" –he nods at his grandma– 'apparently not.'

'What does the curse do?' Because although the mark is prominent, "making people slightly less conventionally attractive," isn't the usual way a fairy curse runs.

'It kills us.' The words of the Matriarch are flat. As if the curse has already sucked the life from them. Or the staff she used has instead. 'Slowly. We suffer fever. Madness. Then a wound. A bleeding chest. Then death.'

Now that sounds more like a fairy curse. 'So where does the staff come in?'

'I – don't know.' Oh, that has to hurt. I bet the Matriarch hasn't admitted not knowing something in decades, if ever before. 'Don't know how it came. Came to be ours. Not precisely. But it was a gift. A gift from God. To stem our pain. To manage our curse. To cleanse the land.'

Interesting. A mysterious item containing a terrible malevolent force inside, to be freed by feeding it *talent*, was handed to this family in their hour of need. A staff that proceeded to then set them on a path of religious extremism, hunting the Talented-in-waiting. I wonder if this was De Montfort's doing. Whether this was one of his doubtless myriad backup plans he had in place in case his other nefarious plotting failed.

An intriguing thought but unprovable and merely academic now he's truly dead, of course. Gil looks over at me. 'What will you do with it now?'

Good. I wondered if he might claim it. It's his in many ways. His birthright, the only inheritance he could ever get from this fucked up place. Hell, he could even use it to perform magic, to replicate his sacrificed *talent*. But he recognises the danger inside it. Knows that I'm the safer pair of hands, the best option. Which is terrifying but still, nonetheless, true.

'Get it to Isaac.' Now there's a properly safe pair of hands. As long as he doesn't dismantle it out of academic curiosity, of course. 'He'll be able to shore it up. Make sure whatever's inside stays sealed in there. At least until they work through their anger issues and all that.'

He nods, and the deal's done. Simple as that.

Which just leaves one question. 'What about her?'

He looks over at me warily. 'What about her?' Same words, different inflections.

'What do you want me to do with her?' The subtext is clear. Shall I kill her for you? Keep your hands clean.

'I don't want *you* to do anything.' And just like that, my heart stops. Freezes. Time does too as my mind goes into overdrive, racing. Because I'm so desperate to find the words to persuade Gil. To get him to let me do it. I know he's killed before, but that was in a moment of desperation and to save us all. I know I said I'd let him kill her in cold blood, but I still don't want him to. There's no innocence left in me. It's a tragedy to see him throw away the rest of his, which he's kept safe through so much misery, for someone as worthless as her.

'I don't want you to do anything. Nor will I. She's got no magic now, right?'

I nod. It's easy to see she's mostly Talentless again. When I broke the link holding us to the staff, I weakened any other links too. It takes only a sweep of my hand, a blast of pure *talent* to slice through the last connecting strands.

She cries out. Clutches her chest. Her eyes widen as her hands come away bloody.

'Then we don't need to do anything.' Gil sounds satisfied. Grim and satisfied. Strange tones to hear from that young man. 'Leave her be. Let the congregation see her as she is. Let them see her taken by the fever, wracked by the madness. Weakened and bloodied. Powerless. Let the hold she has over them snap. The fear dissipate. I doubt her successor will be able to keep them subdued without that image of Grandma to keep them in line.'

He laughs bitterly once more. 'Mother was always cruel but always weak too. Always just Grandma's shadow.'

And he turns, walks out of the barn. After swooping over and plucking up the crystal staff, I follow. As we go, the first wracking coughs, wet and phlegmy, start up from the frail old woman we've left slumped in a chair behind us.

It's a quiet drive back to Toulouse. Mind you, it's not as if it's a raucous party on a long journey with any of my friends. Somehow I've ended up being the outgoing, extroverted one. But I'm quiet too. On tenterhooks. Terrified I've ruined our friendship by doing what had to be done because I turned up too late.

But as the drive goes on, I get a feel for the atmosphere, and it feels…normal somehow. Gil's not being quiet due to nursing a grudge, full of anger and resentment. Gil's just quiet because that's who he is. A quiet young man.

And as we hit the grinding drag of the gridlocked Peripherique, the ring road around Paris, a thought hits me. 'Hold on, Gil. You said she was your grandmother?'

He nods. 'That's right.'

'So your mother is next in line?'

He gets what I mean. Not just next in line to take over The Family. Next in line for the curse. He's silent for a moment, then nods again. 'Yep.'

'So what happens? When it hits her?' *And when she dies?*

He shrugs. 'Not sure. The curse will settle on her. Way I look at it, each generation survived for decades once they had the curse, enough years to have and raise kids, so I can't imagine it'll kill her straight away. Doubt it'll be much fun though.'

I try to keep my gaze fixed on the road ahead as he drums his fingers on the plastic armrest. Eventually, he speaks again. 'Once it settles on me? Well, I'm banking on a couple of things.'

He stops tapping. 'Firstly, I'm never planning to have children. I can't imagine the curse wants to fizzle out, so I'm hoping it'll just hold off for a long time, keep hoping I'll change my mind.'

Clever lad. He's probably right. Fairy curses are almost semi-sentient half the time. From what I've seen in the old stories, it might just work.

'Plus, if she was right, and it was a male tryst? Well. Perhaps it will be kinder to me, who's rejected all their ancient hatred.' It's not a bad thought, albeit a slightly hopeful one.

'And anyway,' he says, turning to look at me, 'if that doesn't work. Well, you and Isaac will figure it out, won't you?'

And the Good God be damned if that isn't almost a physical blow, a strike straight to the stomach. And it's only the desperation not to disappoint this kid any further that keeps me from careening off the side of the road and crashing into a ditch. Because somehow, despite me turning him away, despite me killing his brother to keep us alive, Gil still believes in me. And I have absolutely no idea why he does, but I'm determined I won't let him down.

'We absolutely will, kid,' I say once I'm confident I can manage it without choking up. 'We absolutely will.'

The Good God damn me if I'm not absolutely determined to make sure that's the truth, whatever the future might throw at us. There's no way I'm letting this brave, unbreakable, determinedly innocent kid down. Not ever.

Not ever again.

It's hard to be alone once more.

I drop Gil back at his place in Auch, the small town to the west of Toulouse where he's living. Close inside our wards, where we can keep him safe…in theory, and far enough away from the memories of the city where we killed the creature he swore fealty to.

I wonder how often he curses the day he met me.

The car feels empty, too quiet, that compact interior

suddenly feeling several sizes too large. I turn on the music, filling it with thumping basslines that seem to echo, the sound waves bouncing off the walls, off the space left by my side.

But I don't have time to dwell on that. Because, whatever's happened, however badly I've messed up, it doesn't change what I need to do. I need to find Aicha. Need her input, her advice, her cutting assessment of whatever pig's ear I've made out of a situation this time. Now more than ever.

Because I'm worried it's not just her who's lost.

The promises I made Gil are still there, still ringing in my ears. The promise to do better, to be better. Because the Good God knows how much I've relied on Aich for that, to keep me strong, pointed in the right direction. And without her here, with so much falling on me, with me already failing? I need to find her *now*.

Rubbing my hands over the steering wheel, I run my grip around it. Then set off, back towards the Pyrenees, to the last known location of the Nain Rouge before he vanished again, according to the Mother of the Sistren. Aware I've not been to see Isaac still, but that's okay. I'll catch him next time. It won't be long. And maybe I'll drive back with Aicha and Jakob in the back seats, the conquering hero, bringing our people home.

It won't be long. I'm sure of it.

Chapter Ten

I'm missing my drive. On this drive. Heading for Isaac's drive. Drive, drive, drive, drive. Funny how words lose all meaning. Just the same way meaning can.

Two months. Two fucking months. And nothing.

I want to cry, except I don't really. What I want to do is turn this car, which has been my home for a large part of it, into a molten slag heap. And possibly a large section of the Haute-Garonne region too. Definitely the Pyrenees after yet another non-starter of a search.

And now I'm heading back. To face the music, which will be all the worse because it won't be played, not a marching band blast of recrimination in my face, the one I deserve for failing to get any closer to locating the missing members of our team. No, it'll be all kind words and pats on the back. *Never mind. You've done your best. Have a whisky. Take a break.* But I'll see it. The way his smile will waver, his chin will droop. How his eyes lose a little of that sparkle.

My failure is a full blown symphony that's playing constantly in my head, discordant fingernail screeches to show I'm letting everyone down. Isaac. Aicha. Jakob.

Myself.

Because I remember. No matter how much he'll tell me it doesn't matter, that I'm trying and that's what counts. I remember watching him tear through the world, searching for the tiniest sniff of a hint as to what happened to Jakob two hundred years ago when he vanished. Watched it eat him alive, not knowing the truth of what could have occurred.

Watched him diminish at the loss.

So now I can't allow it. Can't let it happen again. And so I've done what anyone would do in the situation. I've thrown myself into the search.

And avoided Isaac at all costs.

Of course, there's a name for . And that name is cowardice. Which doesn't seem to be the right way to honour Aicha in her absence. Were she here, she'd slap me round the back of the head till I could feel my brains poking out of my tear ducts and then drag me by my twisted ear round to see Isaac. So that's what I'm going to do. After several weeks away and several months since I called round, it's time to stop being a cowardy, cowardy custard.

Driving back up the motorway from the south of Toulouse towards the ring road is a silent affair. I've not been able to bring myself to listen to music on any of my drives. Tunes aren't bringing me any solace at this time. It's something Aicha and I did together, driving towards unimaginable danger, blaring out some banging beats, taking the piss out of each other. Plus, it makes me remember her insistence on us getting our own theme music. Until we make that happen, I'm not in the mood for getting my groove on.

As I get closer and closer, an uneasy feeling starts to grow. It's one of those ones where you know you've forgotten something, where you keep looking at the clock, part of your brain pointing out the position of the hands, insisting it means something, but you can't remember. Not until it's too late.

So it is with me now. It's only when I get onto the ring road itself, only as I'm driving round towards the motorway that heads in the direction of Auch, that the realisation of what's been missing sinks in because suddenly, finally, I feel it.

The wards. The wards I gave to Isaac. The wards Nithael supercharged so they extended all the way down to the south of Auterive. The wards that should have been thrumming on my skin like static electricity for the past seventy kilometres or so. The wards that are only evident in their absence.

The wards. The wards are down.

The only thing that keeps me from breaking the land speed record is that, at that precise moment, I feel the wards' touch. Either they've just come back online, or I've reached their current limit. A limit which is a damn sight closer in to Toulouse than it used to be. My foot stays firmly pressed to the floor though because the wards dropping temporarily or shrinking dramatically definitely isn't good news. I don't know what's happened, but I know one thing without a doubt.

Something is wrong.

By the time I tear up the scree driveway and burst through the weathered oak door leading into Isaac's farmhouse kitchen, I'm so aglow with *talent*, you could probably take a photo of me from space. Assuming you could make technology and magic play nicely together, which is about as likely as summertime snow in Hell. During a heatwave.

Movement. I sense it out of the corner of my eye, that change in the bulb-cast shadows, that momentary flickering as a shape launches at me from above, growing as it does.

I duck, my hands up and glowing, *talent* pooling in them as I stumble over the threshold. There's no way I can keep upright, so I twist, scraping my back along the cold tiles as I raise them to intercept...

Hubert. The short-toed snake eagle who roosts some-times in Isaac's rafters. He normally limits his bombing runs to Isaac, hammering into the space above his head where Nithael might be said to be present, as though challenging the angel for aerial dominance. That he's attacking me instead, has reached that point of boredom, makes me wonder how little Isaac must have been leaving the house. And that nobody comments on my spectacular prat fall – or hurries to try to help me up – only causes me to worry further still.

The warm glow of the lights illuminate a place that's a mixture of rural and scholarly, with the worn wooden table scattered with occult scrolls and scriptures worth more than my house in the centre of Toulouse. Two glasses of amber perfection sit upon it too, a single ice cube bobbing about on the tops like Kate Winslet after having let Leo DiCaprio drown for no apparent reason. And sitting there is the closest thing to a father for me in the past eight hundred years. Inventor of Kabbalah magic, body host to a Bene Elohim – an angel from another dimension – and the best man I've ever met. Isaac.

He still looks every inch the university professor, although in the same way as Harrison Ford in the first part of *Raiders* did. He is the embodiment of the charming older man who melts hearts and panties without even realising it. Despite having been as close as family for centuries, I still have no idea if he's ever been in a relationship. Mind you, he's always been married to his research. And his angel – the Bene Elohim Nithael, pulled down from the higher dimensions hundreds of years ago and bound up into his body and soul by Kabbalist workings tattooed directly onto his body.

The tweed jacket complete with elbow patches he's wearing looks rumpled, but that in and of itself isn't that concerning. Ironing is hardly a priority for either of us, and honestly, I'm worried enough that Isaac will forget to eat when I'm not around. Making sure his outfits are neatly pressed? Never going to happen, even when Nith deals with most of the housework. It's an advantage having a super-dimensional being who can make the plates clean with a thought. And I'd guess living with Isaac would give a being of pure thought and order serious OCD. Getting Isaac's clothes to stay neat approximately a second after he's put them on though? There are limits even to angelic powers.

But Isaac looks pale, pasty, washed-out. That change to the flesh where it gains an unnatural sheen – dough-like, as if every muscle were kneading it into the required form, then holding it in place to stop it sagging down into a shapeless mass. Isaac looks *ill*. That's not supposed to be possible.

'What's goi...' I start to say, but Isaac waves me to sit down, pointing a finger at the tumbler of whisky. Right. First things first. Picking up the glass, I tap it against his in salute and then take a draught. Good God, that hits the spot. It's nowhere near enough to distract me from the sorry state my mentor appears to be in, but he was right. Best to start off with this, like an alcoholic version of the Japanese tea ceremony. A moment of quiet communion before we get to the nitty gritty of what has befallen my friend.

There are limits though. By the time I've taken a third drink from the glass, reducing it from gulps to sips now I've settled my nerves, and he's still not started explaining exactly what the fuck is going on, I've started to get a bit antsy. Moments of quiet reflection before diving into the crux of the matter are fine. The key word, though, is "moments". Brevity is paramount. This particular moment is starting to overstay its welcome.

Just as I'm about to crack and start pounding my fists on the table, demanding answers like some intense interrogation on a TV cop show, he sighs. It's a sound loaded with wear and weariness, that speaks of a soul weighed down with grief and strife, and I cannot tell you how it splinters my heart into a thousand shards to hear such a sound come from the mouth of the man sitting in front of me. Nobody deserves to carry such suffering but least of all him. I know as well as the next man that Life isn't fair. She doesn't have to be quite such a blatant bitch though.

Isaac rolls up his sleeve, and the questions I had die on my tongue, my brain overloading with a whole new fresh batch, clamouring in a panic so loud, I can hardly think. I know Aicha, my best friend, would say "hardly able to think" was my normal modus operandi, but this is even harder than usual.

You know, in a supernatural action film or a Marvel flick, when the bad guy gets injected with some super serum or whatever? His veins bulge, filling with black sludge till his muscles start popping out and he transforms into the new Big Bad. This looks like that only without the instant gym bod to accompany it. All the blood vessels up Isaac's arm are raised, bulging outwards with what looks like rancid squid ink or as though all the blood cells have died and are rotting inside the veins, swelling as they decompose. What it doesn't look like is a healthy arm.

The riotous bickering of shrieking questions in my normally empty head is tying my tongue into a bow line knot, but eventually the biggest, most pressing of them all beats the rest into submission and makes its escape, riding my vocal cords. 'What the absolute living fuck, 'Zac?'

Pithy and to the point, I feel. I mean, it's either that, or I start gibbering and weeping in incomprehension and terror. Isaac can't get ill! He can't. It shouldn't be possible with Nith along, riding shotgun, the angel burning away any mortal fallibilities in the physical vessel they share. And he certainly shouldn't be doing an impression of an arm in a manga film just before it explodes into a thousand tentacles. Isaac's supposed to be all right. Always. He has to be.

He just has to be.

Except, of course, life doesn't work that way. Nope, as said before, Life tends to like to hit you where it hurts. Repeatedly. With a nine-iron. An electrified nine-iron.

'You remember all the demon essence De Montfort got his hands on?' Isaac picks up and cradles his glass in both hands, his eyes fixed on the refracting light that shimmers across the liquid's depths.

Now I can feel my emotions arriving, steamrollering all the confusion out of the way. I might not have a clue what's going on, but I can understand one thing from what he's just said. De Montfort was an absolute conniving smeghead who manufactured most of the misery that befell me over the centuries, and all of our recent woes. And being a cunning stunt of a man —also true when you reverse the starts of the words— he came up with a way to nullify the angels for the final battle. Demon essence. It was all over the creatures we battled when he put the end game in place, and it was implanted into the wards on Bugarach, locking Nithael and Nanael out until he was ready for them. Isaac spent most of his time trying to break said wards. Time in close proximity to the essence itself.

'This is from *then*? All those months ago? You've had this going on since then, *and you didn't tell me*?'

My tone might have risen a bit on the last few words. The volume too, judging from the indignant squawks from above my head.

'It wasn't always this bad.' Isaac doesn't lift his eyes up. There's a pleading tone to his voice though, a prayer for understanding. 'I thought we had it under control. You've been busy, consumed by the search...'

The words die away, and with them my anger does too. A numb shock spreads through me, pushing out the fury, leaving me stunned. When I speak, my voice sounds tiny, ridiculous, like a hurt child. 'You thought I was too busy for you, 'Zac? Too busy for this?'

Now he looks up at me, and I can see the pain there. The pain and the guilt, which seems ridiculous because if anyone should be feeling guilty here, it's me. I'm the one who didn't even know he was suffering. Who deliberately kept away from Toulouse these past few months. 'I thought we had it, lad. Really, I did. And if it meant you'd find them, that seemed more important.'

Guilt floods through my body like a swollen river, bursting through the banks, sweeping away the anger. No, I'm not angry anymore. I feel the guilt. Guilt and shame. Guilt because Isaac thinks I've been searching for *them*, when, if I'm honest, I've been searching for *her*. And shame because I've failed. I'm no closer to an answer than I was when I set out, and in the meantime, I've left Isaac to *this*, whatever this is.

Grabbing hold of myself, I try to stem the flow of crippling emotions. There'll be time for self-flagellating later on – or else crawling into the bottom of a bottle long enough that I stop feeling for a while. Right now, I need to get to grips with what the hell is going on and start working out how we can solve this. As much as it pains me to say, Aicha will have to wait. Though saying that doesn't hurt half as much as seeing the sorry state Isaac is in.

I finish up my whisky and push myself to my feet, plucking Isaac's empty tumbler from his hands. Heading past him into the cosy, if somewhat outdated florally-tiled kitchen area, I beeline for the cupboard packed with the good stuff. In the back is the bottle of Balvenie Thirty I picked up to keep him company while I went scouring for a way to find our friends. A couple of grand's worth laid down in barrels for three decades prior to bottling. If there were ever a moment that merited cracking it open, it's right now. I grab it, along with the petite crystal serving jugs I bought to go with it.

Back at the table, I pour us each a healthy measure into our tumblers. Then I pull out the serving jugs and drop a couple of ice cubes in each. This calls for a subtle drop of ice-water to release the flavour, not the raucous barbarity of an ice cube in the glass itself. I plonk a serving jug down in front of Isaac, along with his drink, retake my seat, and look him in the eye, never letting my gaze waver.

'Demon essence. Demon Fart. Start talking. The whole story.'

So he does. It turns out that when, as we battled at the top of Bugarach to keep the Evil God from breaking through and De Montfort was slinging demon essence left, right, and centre to disrupt the Bene Elohim brothers from going all heavenly horde on him, it didn't just keep them from bringing all their angelic force into play. That in and of itself had been a revelation earlier on, during the assault on the cottage itself. We still have no idea how they got hold of any demonic energy and didn't know previously about the disruptive effect it had on angel *talent*. No, on top of that, when we got back down from the mountain, cheering our victory, even if it were a cheer muted by our heavy losses, he found a small spot of black, like a super condensed beauty spot on his purlicue, the piece of skin between his thumb and first finger.

'At first, Nith didn't seem too concerned, lad.' Isaac taps absent-mindedly on the crystal. A clear, light ring echoes out. He takes a sip, then coughs, the burn of the whisky hitting the back of his throat. Except he doesn't stop coughing. Instead, he fumbles out a cotton handkerchief, holds it to his mouth as they wrack his body. I'm up on my feet, on my way over, but he waves me back to sit down as they ease up. But I don't miss the stains on the handkerchief as he folds it away, the rusted splodges that cover it, both old and new.

'When the wards came down that first time, it splashed over me. Just a few drops, but I felt it. A strange sizzling, but it was pandemonium, lad, as you well know. I couldn't worry about it there and then. And once it all calmed down, I didn't notice it. Not at first. Not until after we got home. And by the time I did – once I saw it in the shower, realised it was still there, well, you were already planning on how to find them and get them back for us. So I thought it best to let you concentrate on that, especially as Nith didn't seem worried about it either. So I let it be. And it didn't seem to be a problem, not at first.

'Although Nith couldn't get rid of it, he seemed to have it under control. It wasn't spreading, so we thought we had plenty of time. Better to leave you to get on with the search, and I could do some digging here, see what I could find out.' Isaac gazes over my shoulder at the waning light outside.

I can imagine the research. No doubt he prioritised anything he thought might help me in finding a way to bring back our lost family rather than his own worrisome state.

Isaac takes another sip, and that, at least, drags his attention back. 'Well, I did some digging, but I couldn't find anything. There's no documentation of this interaction between angelic and demonic energy.'

I can hear the frustration dominating his tone. Admitting his research failed him is probably Isaac's least favourite thing to do. It's hardly his fault. As far as we know, Nith and Nan are the only beings from the higher dimensions who've strayed down here and stuck about. Similarly, real demons – as opposed to just monsters or fae creatures who think it's amusing to jump through a suddenly available weak point in reality to scare the shit out of some would-be conjurers – don't come up here, ever. They're too busy having a right old time down in their own dimension. It's not Hell, not like we imagine it, and they're not bad guys despite what all the scriptures would have you believe. Higher and lower just means further up or down the vibrational ladder. Angels are beings of pure thought. Demons are beings of pure physicality. Honestly? Further down the dimensions sounds a lot more fun. No wonder none of them actually want to come up here. None of them that is, except…

I shoot to my feet, nearly knocking over the bottle of Balvenie in the process, though I manage to grab and right it before any of the precious cargo is spilled. Some horrors are just too terrible to contemplate.

'Did you reach out to Mephy?' I'm not shouting. I'm not. I'm just talking forcefully at a very loud volume, loud enough to rattle the windowpanes in their fittings as I ask him if he's reached out to not only the only bloody demon we know but also the only bloody demon ever to be physically manifest in our reality ever. At least the only one to ever stick around.

Isaac shakes his head. 'I've no way of getting hold of him.'

'*Which is why you should have contacted me, you daft old bastard!*' Okay. I might be shouting now.

'*I didn't want you to see me like this so you wouldn't worry, you bloody ingrate!*' Isaac's tone matches my own as he shoots to his feet, glaring at me.

We stay here for a moment, both frowning furiously, our chests heaving from all the pent-up emotion, the glisten in our eyes tears that aren't sure whether they're reporting for duty to Camp Anger or Team Sorrow. Both at the same time is the answer, of course.

'Feel better now, lad?' Isaac's voice is back to its normal softness, and just like that, the tension's gone from the room, taking with it a lot of those ugly emotions I've been drowning in since I walked in.

'I do actually.' It's amazing, but it's true. Maybe we both needed to get that off our chests, clear the air. I top up our glasses and tip mine in his direction. Santé.

Now I just have to worry about his health. And about that blood-soaked hankie he tucked away, and how much of it looked fresh, while he looks quite the opposite.

So I drink my whisky. And try not to imagine a world in which Isaac dies.

Chapter Eleven

TOULOUSE, 26 OCTOBER, PRESENT DAY

'Is there a doctor in the house? Not a fucking medical
one. A doctor of demonology. No? Useless, the lot of
you.'

I think a lot of unTalented people, were they to somehow
stumble onto the hidden world bubbling away like a witch's
cauldron just below the surface of their own, would assume
that us Talented use magic to communicate across vast
distances. Me? I use a phone.

Don't get me wrong, all that magic stuff was super
handy when landlines were rare and magicians' lairs were
hidden in the middle of swamps or atop lonely inaccessible
mountains that weren't top priority for cable installation.
Nowadays, why reach for the best sigil-drawing chalk or the
finest crystal scrying bowl when you can just pluck the latest
tech wonder out of your inside pocket? Plus, it has Angry
Birds. Hey, I said I'm good with the movement of technology, not that I'm bang up-to-date with everything. For

someone over eight hundred years old, I'm doing pretty well. Give me a break.

Of course, if Johannes Faust, the wizard who opened up the portal for Mephy to come through to our plane, binding them together in the process, doesn't answer, I'm fully ready to go old school and polish up the old Palantir. He likes to party and isn't always as conscientious about keeping a working, charged up phone on him as I'd like. Plus, my tendency to lose my own constantly means it's an unknown number – for him and me. I let it ring three times, hang up, ring back for four, then two, then let it ring. The pattern's really useful for identifying that it's me calling but only if he's properly compos mentis. Otherwise, it's just a load of missed calls from a number he doesn't know.

I get lucky. After the ninth or tenth ring, he picks up. 'Hello? Who is this?' Glad we bothered working out the identifying pattern of rings then. There's a trace tone of irritation that suggests I've interrupted him. It's early evening, but that means little with Faust. It could be I've bothered him while he's getting ready to go out. It could be he's just got back in and wants to go to bed.

'Faust, it's me. Paul.' I always feel a tad ridiculous stating my name. Instinctively, with the people we're close to, we feel they should recognise us the instant they hear us, that our bonds are so tight that a single syllable should be enough to clue them in. That instinct doesn't account for poor network signal though. So I'd rather clarify now than go through that awkward song and dance where someone knows they should know who they're talking to but hasn't a clue and has to try to dig the information out, never giving away their own ignorance. There's no time for that right now.

'Paul! How are you?' The irritation disappears, and I

can feel the warmth radiating through the speaker. Let me tell you, it does good to the soul, even one as old as mine, to hear that sort of reaction. There are times when I imagine I must just be an irritant for all around me, a Stormcrow as Grima labelled Gandalf, bringing nothing but tempests and trouble wherever I go. That despite my propensity for landing myself and all around me knee-deep at best but often more like neck-deep in the shit, I still have friends? That is both miraculous and reaffirming. When it's hard to see your own value, sometimes it's best to seek out its reflection in the eyes – or, in this case, the voices – of others.

'I've been better, Jo.' There's no point beating around the bush. This might surprise you, but I have a propensity for getting side-tracked. I can't allow that to happen right now. 'Jo, can Mephy hear this? Can you put me on speaker?'

'Sure, hold on.' I hear that muffled crunch of a hand wrapping around the phone's mic, meaning he's probably moving location, no doubt looking for the demon-dog himself. Mephistopheles – the fairground funhouse mirror image of Nith and Nan.

Forget what you've seen in every horror movie ever. Demons aren't constantly trying to tear their way through to our dimensions. And angels? Angels aren't coming to save us. There've been ways to talk to each over the ages – the equivalent of smoke signals wafting up or down the vibrational ladder – but neither seems interested in coming to hang out for a game of Goldeneye and hammering down a cold six-pack. None except for Nith and Nan from the Bene Elohim, and Mephistopheles, the demonic King of the Crossroads.

Of course, just as Isaac's partnership with Nithael speaks to his magical prowess, so Mephy being called forth to our plane of existence is a measure of Faust's. My time studying hard with him – and partying even harder – was a revelation. Just not in the 'Book Of' sense that most people associate with demons. Mephy isn't evil, not at all. The lower planes don't mean worse. Just more connected to the physical, the intensity of sensation as opposed to the joy of pure thought and contemplative ethereal bliss that defines the higher ones. Personally, I'd prefer to go party down below every single time.

I can hear the fabric-scratch rustling of someone making their way to another room without muting the phone. Then Faust pipes up. 'Mephy, can you stop licking your balls for a moment? Paul Bonhomme's on the phone.'

Me, personally? I reckon that right there is the reason he's not fucked off back to the rave-up down below. A growling voice, sounding like Patty and Velma from the *Simpsons* after a particularly hard night on the cigarettes and whisky, carries over the line. 'I can multi-task, Faust. I can lick and listen at the same time.'

'That involves me having to see it though.'

'I'm not going to charge you, don't worry.' A sound not dissimilar to a balloon getting slapped with sandpaper starts up again, and Johannes sighs.

'I think that's as close as you're going to get to his undivided attention, Paul.'

Normally, I'd have enjoyed the banter. My time living with the pair of them was a blast, and when times have been tough and I've needed to remember what it is to live again, they've always been my first port of call. Right now, though, issues aren't just pressing; they're doing a full dry clean service first.

'Guys, listen.' I feel a bit stupid saying it, but I know the two of them are almost as easily distracted as I am. They need to be focused on what I'm telling them. 'Isaac's infected.'

'Don't worry about that.' Mephy's tone is indolent, bored, and I want to tear my hair out and scream. He hasn't got it. 'We know remedies for every STI under the sun. Been there, done that, got the T-shirt and burning sensation when I piss.'

Faust's voice is quieter, cautious. Concerned. 'Infected how exactly, Paul?'

Of course Johannes got it. He knows of Isaac. Knows not only his lifestyle choices but also who he's bonded with. This isn't a result of having headed off to Spring Break without a rubber johnny in the wallet. He knows this is something more serious.

'Infected with demon essence.'

Silence reigns like an absolute monarch. I'm just about to go all Robespierre and start fomenting revolution against it, guillotines and all, when Mephy speaks.

'Are you sure, mano?'

There's no humour in the gruff tones now. He doesn't sound bored anymore either. The voice has dropped, low but insistent.

'Absolutely certain, Meph. Look, you know how I called you, told you about the demon essence on those Nazi soldiers who rocked up to the house?'

'Of course, mano. And called us in to help before giving us a ring a few hours later as we were about to board, telling us not to bother, that the world's been saved and you're off a-questing.'

'Well, I saved you having to fly. I know how much you hate it.' *Almost as much as Aicha does*, is the thought that goes through my head, but that just hurts, and the situation right now is painful enough, stressful enough. I push that away, concentrate on what's going on.

'Fair enough. I don't fly, no one gets bitten. Plus I can see all those legs just squished in, curled up all inviting, and I'm not supposed to indulge? Just teasing, that is.'

I don't have time to get into the weirdness of Mephy's leg kink right now. I need to pull the subject back on course.

'Well, there was more of it. On the creatures we fought. Woven into the ward that De Montfort had in place on the top of Bugarach. And somehow it got from the wards onto Isaac. Maybe even onto Jakob and Nan. And since then, they've been…infected. It's growing, consuming their arm. And it's almost at their neck.'

'Nan? Jakob is ba—' Faust starts, but is cut off by a rumbling snarl. It's not a threat, not to him at least. It's animalistic hackles raising, Mephistopheles expressing himself primally. He's not happy.

'Get here. Now.' There's no space for argument, no room for further discussion. Isaac and I exchange glances. His says, *Can we trust him?* Mine says, *Yes?* There has to be a question in it. Normally, I'd trust Mephy with my life. Problem is, it isn't my life on the line.

'Faust?' What a terrible way to have to say someone's name. To use it to ask if their bosom companion for centuries can be trusted. Just emphasising it in that way feels like a betrayal. I can only imagine how the answer feels. But this doesn't feel like the creature I got smashed out my skull in the bars of Berlin with and then set up with a pretty poodle or two.

'Come, Paul. Both of you.' That's enough for me. I know Johannes, know his voice. There's no doubt in it. Mephy might be worked up, but it's not against us. Faust is vouching for him. That'll do.

We say our goodbyes, then get off the line and onto the net. Normally, I'd prefer to drive, but Isaac's looking shaky just standing up. The idea of letting him have a turn at doing part of the fourteen hours plus of driving doesn't exactly fill me with joy. Driving's considerably harder than standing, and that already looks almost beyond him. It'd be a different matter if Aicha were here...

That thought's too difficult, too painful to deal with, so I push it away. As much as I want to be out there, searching for a way to get her back, right now I need to be here, helping 'Zac. Aicha's a big girl. She's far more capable than me. Far more capable than anyone. Isaac's dying. Everything else has to take a backseat.

Looking online, we can get to Salzburg in a couple of plane hops, switching aircraft in Frankfurt. The other option'd be to fly to Munich and then drive down, but the Frankfurt flight's in three hours, while the Munich one isn't till the morning.

'You ready to go?' It's so hard not to let my worry show, not to fuss at the man trembling like all of his near-on thousand years just landed on his shoulders in one fell swoop. Instead, I busy myself, grabbing a few supplies for the journey and tossing them into my etheric storage, my handy little pocket-dimension lockbox.

'Of course I'm ready, lad. Born bloody ready.' Isaac's attempt at a brave face is even worse than mine. I wonder which of us is more worried. We're both living up to my last name at the moment, plastering on the bonhomie to try not to acknowledge exactly how worried we are. Sometimes those are the things you have to do to survive.

Before we leave, I stash the malevolent staff I took from the Matriarch when I rescued Gil, and spectacularly failed to rescue his brother. Even with Isaac weakened, there's nowhere safer for me to leave it, and frankly it's been giving me the creeps each time I reach into my etheric storage. Far better to have it stashed out the way here, until such time as Isaac's well enough to work out a way to dispose of it permanently.

After buying a couple of seat tickets, we jump into the Tesla. I take the driving seat, and Isaac doesn't even muster a show of complaint. If there's a clearer symptom of how unwell he is, I can't imagine it. Although, considering the car was a present for Jakob, to let him get a taste of the thrills on offer in the twenty-first century after having been enslaved for hundreds of years inside a skull, perhaps driving it doesn't bring him the pleasure it once did.

Either way, he lets me take the wheel, and we pull off down the gravel track, towards Blagnac Airport. Me trying to concentrate on the road and stop my gaze from drifting down to the black-stained mess of an arm that Isaac's cradling unconsciously to his chest. Eyes on the prize, Paul.

There's a demon who can tell us what's going on, who can help us. Isaac's going to be fine. We just have to get there, and Isaac's going to be fine.

Eyes on the prize.

Chapter Twelve

Time to climb into a small metal tube and get hurled
through the sky thanks to impossible physics again. Can't we
just go battle a world-threatening deity instead?

My faith is long gone. I don't believe in heavenly hosts, in
angelic choirs, in the blowing of trumpets and the gates of
paradise swinging wide open. So I don't believe in the other
place with the thermostat stuck on full blast either. But if
there was one thing that might make me believe Hell existed
and that someone got a sneak peek at what was going on
down in the lake of fire, it's airports.

The soaring glass walls aim to speak of futuristic origi-
nality but are somehow identical to every other terminal
ever. The lost people stumble meanderingly, searching for
which of the horrendously oversubscribed and underserved
queues they need to stand in. The machines you're made to
pass through time and again beep at you for metal that
doesn't exist, can't possibly exist because you've stripped

yourself bare. And still they beep as you search for a last crumb of forgotten steel somehow secreted about your person. Forever.

And don't get me started on passport control.

The day cannibalism becomes necessary for humanity, the day Soylent Green becomes a reality, just set up the slaughterhouses in airports. A people processing plant. That's all an airport is.

As you might be able to tell, my patience with the building we now find ourselves in is limited at the best of times. This is not the best of times. My worries for Isaac, whose pallor seems to be growing chalkier by the moment, are gouging their way through my already practically non-existent patience. I just want to *go*. For a hub of transport, airports really aren't designed to make you move very quickly at all.

Luckily, we don't have any check-in baggage and I printed out the tickets at home. Waving my Talented version of psychic paper at various special access queues lets us shortcut the madding crowds. I don't even bother working out what I want them to see, just push the urgency of our passage out through the paper as a message. The security guards and border control probably think we're the new President of France and his second-in-command or something. I'm pretty sure one of the armed police gives us a small salute as we go past. I couldn't give a damn though. As long as we're getting where we need to go, without me losing my tenuous grip on my temper and melting the whole place into a slagheap of molten glass and steel, then we're winning in my book.

'Are you all right, lad? You seem a little tense?' Isaac is, as ever, the master of understatements.

'Never better, 'Zac,' I grind out from between my teeth,

which are almost certainly developing stress fractures. Maybe I should invest in some gold grills to protect my dentures, like the Dirty South US rappers. Although even thinking about going through airport scanners with a mouth blinged up like that is enough to cause heart palpitations.

Isaac's hand wraps round my arm gently but firmly. I've no choice but to stop. Not because he's strong enough to check me in mid-stride, but because if I don't, I'm terrified I'll pull him over, that he'll fall and break something. My heart, probably.

'Paul, my lad, listen. I'm fine.' I do listen. I listen to the quaver in his voice. When I look him in the eye, he has the decency to look abashed, but he doesn't look away. 'Okay, I'm not fine. But I will be. We'll solve this. Nith has it under control. Mephistopheles will have answers for us. Look at me!'

My eyes were sliding away, down towards the stains on his arms that are tearing me apart with worry. Now it's my turn to look abashed, and I snap back to him.

He carries on, 'We'll find a solution. Somehow, we'll solve this. You aren't going to lose me.'

There's this strange sensation in my chest. A bubbling mixture of laughter and tears. It seems to swell bigger and bigger, desperate to escape into the outside world. The daft old bastard. Even now, when he's sick beyond measure, he's more worried about the impact on me.

The tears come. Because he's right, of course. I can't lose him. Not now. Not ever but especially not now, having just lost Aicha. My sanity feels glass-pane brittle. One hard tap, and it'll shatter. Nothing left but Paul-shards. I'm not sure it'd be possible to rebuild myself again afterwards.

Never in my life have I been more grateful for my *don't look here* spell than I am now as it covers up my relentless sobbing in the airport. I seem to have cried more in the past few months than I did in the last two centuries. After Susane, my wife, died, I felt like I was using up all the tears I would ever own. Guess I've finally replenished my supplies.

Isaac magics up a hankie out of somewhere and passes it over, then waves it away once I try to give it back. That might have something to do with the elephant-trump of a blast I just blew into it to clear out my running nose.

'Feel better now, lad?' He pats me on the back, the ridiculous old sod. Worrying about my wellbeing above and beyond his own, as always.

But I do feel better. There's little in life more cathartic than sobbing your heart out, even if we seem to find it some sort of an inexcusable sin for a man to cry in a public place. Shame never did us service.

Thanks to my handy magic paper trick, we have a little time to spare, so we grab a couple of coffees at the small coffee bar by the boarding gates. I'm tempted to order an Irish one, seeing the bottles arrayed along the back. But Isaac notices where my eyes are going, and his brow knit together so tightly they become like some sort of Noel Gallagher monobrow. It's terrifying enough to persuade me to stick to the alcohol-free version. Good God, it's as if he thinks I have a tendency to descend into heavy drinking whenever things get difficult or depressing. It's a bugger sometimes when people know you so damn well.

When they call for boarding, we're among the first on. I sprang for the business class seats. They're a pale imitation of the sort you get when you fly serious distances, but they've a bit more leg room, a bit higher quality service, and right now, Isaac deserves every luxury I can make happen. It's so difficult not to treat him like an invalid, like he's made of glass and everything around him is a rocket propelled baseball aimed straight at him. Which, incidentally, would be the only way to make a game of baseball interesting.

The flight to Frankfurt, Germany, passes peacefully. We luxuriate in the approximately five centimetres of extra legroom we have, but the little snack we get is passably nice, albeit still lacking in flavour. I once heard that it's the altitude that affects our ability to taste things properly. Mind you, that might just be an urban legend the airlines have put out to excuse bland offerings.

Two hours later, give or take, we stumble out into the main terminal of Frankfurt airport. Which, let's be frank, just looks like an almost carbon copy version of the terminal we just left. Perhaps slightly larger. Maybe this one is from one of the more prominent circles of Hell. Though at least we don't have to go back out past the security and searches. We just need to find our gate, which should be a straightforward task. Big digital displays rattle off destinations and numbers. Placards point to gate groupings in each direction. There's efficient German organisation at work everywhere, but something about stepping inside an enclosed metal tube that then zooms about through the atmosphere at high levels reduces human cognitive behaviour back to that of a traumatised seven year old. If someone isn't leading you around by the hand, everything becomes markedly more difficult than logic says it should be.

Nonetheless, I manage to find our gate, which considering the airport is approximately half the size of Venezuela and we've little time to spare for the connection, is no small feat, and we stumble back up the attached steps and into an airplane nominally identical to the one we just got out of. The crew are the only real difference, albeit they look as equally exhausted as the last lot. The glory days of aviation are long gone, I suspect. As with most industries, they're more interested in extracting every last drop of juice from their employees than providing any form of healthy work-life balance. Makes me glad I just have to deal with getting murdered by horrendous monstrosities from other dimensions. Still beats a nine-to-five.

There's the usual fussing around, trying to get bags that contain more than my etheric storage into the letterbox overhead bins. The crew maintain the patience of all the saints combined as they deal with people who seem to be new to the existence of seatbelts. And rules. And manners. I briefly consider getting up and punching the smarmy suit who's mansplaining to the steward that he has to keep his bag because he's far more important than the safety and wellbeing of the rest of the aircraft, and, *"It's Mont Blanc, for chrissakes,"* in honour of Aicha. But while I'm sure it'd get me a round of applause, it won't get me closer to Salzburg and the answers hopefully awaiting us there.

We taxi-out –and by we, I mean the pilots while I munch crisps and jab at my phone, but I think that counts as a team effort– and saunter straight onto the runway and off into the wild blue yonder. Though the blue yonder is noticeably more grey yonder than it was in Toulouse. After a few minutes, we pierce through the clouds and out into the joyous sunshine. It still does my soul good after all this time. Sunshine for the win.

It's only a short hop over to Salzburg, less than an hour planned in the air, so just enough time for us to grab a couple of glasses of champagne and perhaps some sneaky pretzel snacks or something when the seatbelt sign goes off and the service starts. The cabin attendant on duty looks about twenty, with his hair cut in a styled quiff that Harry Styles would be proud of. He manages to deal with the pretentious bastard businessman and get him to calm down with his demands at least slightly. And without pouring burning coffee right onto his bald spot. Impressive. Young or not, he clearly knows how to handle the cabin.

When he passes back down the galley and stops next to me, I assume I'm in for some of that five star, business class service. Perhaps a top up on the peanuts or the like.

What I don't expect is for him to say, 'Your time has come,' as his eyes turn ink-black and in a voice that sounds like the creak of a gravestone cracking open from enormous sustained pressure underneath. Which, let's be honest, is never how you want a gravestone to open. Nothing good ever claws its way out of its own grave. Apart from *Community*.

Then my eyes focus past this imminent and menacing threat as I become aware that the passengers sitting opposite have swivelled round to stare at us with those same black-stained eyes. Not only that, but so have the passengers sitting in front of them, and through the gap in the seats in front of us, I can see the glint of similarly unnatural regards, looking like they've had their sclera, the whites of the eye, coloured in with a marker pen. Which, I'm fairly sure, isn't going to do your eyesight any wonders, so probably don't do that at home.

When, 'Your time has come,' echoes out again, I can't guarantee it's chorused by every voice on the plane apart from us, but it has to be pretty darn close if not.

Looks like we're dealing with actual, real-to-fucking-god mass demon possession.

In a sealed metal tube, tens of thousands of feet up in the air.

This is not good news.

Chapter Thirteen

I don't suppose there's a handy exorcist on the plane?
Perhaps sat by the emergency overwing doors? An exit-cist.

For a moment after the chorusing voices, I dare to hope this
is just a show of power – a threat against further involvement in whatever this fucking demon thinks we're involved
in other than saving Isaac and Nith. Either that or they
really want to create their own version of a Greek chorus,
and it's our turn to deliver our lines. That hope quickly
vanishes when the stylish young cabin steward attempts to
bite a hole in my cheek.

Good God damn, but it's hard not to make his head
explode. When you've been in as many magical showdowns
as I have, the moment someone with *talent* starts throwing
down, the second that power starts getting flung about, your
go-to reaction becomes to pull out the big guns and start
blowing things up. There are two reasons why I don't. The
first is that it isn't the kid who's *talented*. He's just a conduit

for the demon scuzzbucket who's seized control of everyone on board, by all appearances. As much as it'd be the easier option, I can't just start killing them all. They're innocent victims. Isaac would be less than impressed, and Nith'd probably give me the angelic equivalent of a clip round the back of the head.

The second reason is that I'm pretty sure that causing an explosion inside an aircraft wouldn't do wonders for any of our life expectancies.

So as the kid lunges forward, his meticulously capped and polished teeth coming about a millimetre from tearing my throat out as I rear back, I have to settle for cold-cocking him straight between the eyes. He slides down between the seats, wedging at an uncomfortable-looking angle. While I feel bad for the bruise he's going to have in the morning, at least he'll still have a head to wear said bruise on. Pretty self-restrained of me, really.

'We can't kill them all, lad! They're possessed!' Not the most useful time for Isaac to transform into Captain Obvious, but honestly, I've enough to deal with right now without even worrying about that. Like, how to subdue an entire plane full of possessed crew and passengers without ending up scattering airplane and body parts over a several mile radius.

Oh, fuck. The pilots. What if they're possessed too? Our odds of surviving a subsonic impact with the ground are slim enough, but everyone else on board wouldn't stand a chance. I'm about to share the thought that's hit me with Isaac when I feel my jaw slam off to the left while the rest of my face stays in the same place. Apparently, Business Bro sucker punched me when I wasn't looking.

He's already swinging again, but he's no brawler, and I suspect the only weightlifting he does is picking up his phone to check out his bank balance. Possessed or not, there's only so much the dude's body can actually *do*. It's easy enough to duck the swing, and there's a satisfying crunch as I pop him in the face with a left. It staggers him backwards, and I grab Isaac.

'We need a defensible position!' Even as weakened as he is, I'm confident Nithael will have him covered, but it doesn't stop the worry. This is something completely new we're dealing with, and I've seen the zombie films. What effect will it have if he gets bitten, with him already struggling to fight off the demon essence? All right, I'm making the schoolboy error of believing Hollywood has a fucking clue about what it's talking about, but we're operating blind here. I'm just taking the worst-case scenario and running with it. Demon-possessed Isaac with Nithael's powers? That's bad news in the same way an ocean is quite a bit of water.

The only thing going for us is that these passengers weren't trained fighters before getting possessed. The demon can push them to extremes, but there's still a limit to how hard they can hit, how fast they can move. Seeing as we're in business class, most of the threat is behind us, so I start pulling Isaac towards the cockpit door. As we go, I flip open the overhead lockers with my magic, raining bags down on the heads of our dead-eyed pursuers. I see Business Bro's laptop bag on his seat and grab it, wrapping the handle round my hand, wielding it like Captain America does his shield. An older woman, her hair coiffed into a tight bun and her body Louis Vittoned to within an inch of her life, lunges from the seats in front of ours. I get the laptop up in time, so she smashes face-first into it. There's enough different crunching sounds that I'm pretty sure she's broken the screen and her teeth.

I'm lucky we're only about five rows back, and there's not that many passengers in business class. I'm almost caught out at the last moment, when the cabin manager – a portly thirty year old, who obviously ducked behind the bulkhead to get a minute's peace from the incessant, inane demands during take-off, throws himself at my blind side as I start to turn left. It's more a case of feeling the movement, the rushing air, and hearing the rustle of the cheap polyester uniform than seeing him. I duck, bending my right knee, and pivot back round, catching him on my shoulder and lifting. The momentum sends him flying at chest height, straight towards an oblivious Isaac. He's looking over his shoulder, obviously distraught by the chaos and carnage behind him. Nithael comes in with the save though. I see the flare of white light, and for once I'm glad Nith is weakened because it neither blinds me nor makes me start babbling in tongues. The senior cabin crew member bounces off Nith's shield, ricocheting into the nearest seat and out of sight.

I push Isaac behind me into the alcove leading to the flight deck door. The potential threat of possessed pilots is still at the forefront of my brain, but if the door opens, I'll hear it before they can become a clear and present danger. I hope. With us in a defensive position, I can see the full-scale of the mayhem behind us.

Turns out my guess was right. As far back as I can see, there's nothing but squid-ink eyeballs fixed on us, teeth gnashing, hands crooked into make-shift claws to tear us apart. Men, women. Even a few children. A little girl in a flowery dress over a pair of combats –which is a hell of a style and one I want to see become more widespread– is climbing over the seats, using her smaller stature to bypass the crush of the crowd. If what's happening to Isaac wasn't already enough, the sight of her being exploited in such a way would make me vow to disassemble the demonic fuckknuckle into their component parts and feed them to their loved ones. Assuming we can survive this.

The only thing saving us so far is ratios. Who says maths isn't helpful? The number of bodies to the space available for free movement is impeding the majority from reaching us. It means I'm in mostly one-on-one scenarios, and the possessed I'm fighting are struggling to get enough room to attack efficiently. Plus, I've noticed that there's a synchronicity to the movements. They can all advance freely enough, but I'm guessing coordinating attacks from multiple different bodies at the same time is taxing the demon's multi-tasking capabilities. I can't imagine the sort of mental gymnastics that'd be required. Hell, I find talking while walking in a straight line without falling over my own feet hard enough sometimes.

Problem is, the demon has the numbers game on their side. Sure, organising an effective singular attack is taxing, but they don't need to. They can just throw enough bodies at us till we're overwhelmed. Nith's got the kid who vaulted over the seats restrained, but other bodies are now following suit, and the danger's mounting. Everything's a blur. I'm moving at top speed. Punch, kick, twist. Block. Snap my head forward to bust a nose. Swing my elbow sidewards as pain tells me teeth have connected with my midriff. The number of scratches and bite marks are multiplying rapidly, and I'm in a major quandary. There may be no other option than to start killing or start dying.

A hammer blow from the left hits the sweet spot on my temple just above the eyebrow and drives me to one knee. Can't even see who did it. There's too many of them. I have bodies looming over me on all sides. Only my back is clear. I can feel Isaac's desperation, but I don't have the time nor energy to reassure him.

I'm jabbing at kneecaps, throwing punches at groins, anything to clear enough space to regain my feet. Legs are raining in now, sharp kicks to my midriff, trying to force me to stay down, to fall prone where I can get stamped to death. The sound of my ribs cracking is like kids going mad with bubblewrap. My *talent's* healing me as fast as it can, but I'm still seeing stars. Auras of lights crackle in the corner of my vision, and I can see grey edges. We're very close to the decision point. Who's going to die? Me or them?

I still feel no closer to an acceptable answer.

Jesus, I don't want to kill these people. I really don't. On the flip side, I don't want to die either. There's no telling if I get a re-up or not, and I have to save Isaac and find Aicha. Have to get her back. Have to repay her just the tiniest bit for all the times she saved my worthless hide. But these people are innocent. And there're kids, for fuck's sake. If the killing starts, I'm not sure Paul Bonhomme will be left afterwards. Just a bloodstained shell.

If I don't make a call soon, though, that's going to be a call in its own right. My *talent* is starting to waver, and there's nowhere for me to draw more from. I'm suspended twenty-five thousand feet up in the air. And I don't think the demon mob is likely to let me call time-out and take a quick nap to replenish some energy. Already, my healing's having to concentrate on the debilitating or life-threatening injuries. Each blow to the head sends my vision tunnelling, and sooner or later there's going to be a hit hard enough to rattle even my thick skull enough to knock me out. Then that'll be all she wrote.

I'm struggling now, the press of legs too dense to do much except try to cover my head and extremities. Nothing but the roaring tide of noise. My brain narrows in on certain sounds – the bamboo-cane whip of arms against sleeves as they shoot forward. The muffled-drum kick of a foot against my shin as I wriggle in position to take the bruise without a breakage. But there are more feet stamping down, making my bones do their best impression of a breakfast cereal – snap, crackle, *and* pop. There're little defensive options left. Good God damn it, I don't want to make this decision. I can't. I just can't…

And then, suddenly, everything goes still.

It's like someone just pressed pause on life.

The silence that spreads is uncanny. It makes me think of when a grenade's gone off nearby, the concussive deafness it gives before the ringing in the ears starts. But what comes isn't a ring. It's like the toll of a chime bell in the wind but held, sustained, reverberating and building, and now it no longer sounds like a chime but like the sonorous clap of a church bell, perfectly tuned, cast out of flawless iron. And still it grows, and now it's as if I'm standing inside a choir, a hundred choirs, an entire reality of choral singers, each harmonising a single note, and by the Good God, it's beautiful, inexpressibly heart-wrenching. It's the sound love makes when you strike out against it and it remains undented, all the more staunch. There's no pain anymore. None. Not even an echo of an ache. All those deep-worn cares are gone, dissolved like nightmares under a mother's waking caress, and somewhere, some part of me knows I should be concerned by that. Trauma doesn't just disappear. Right now, though, I feel utterly at peace. No hurt of any kind. Just rest.

A hand wraps around my arm, holding me tight, which is weird because I was convinced nothing else existed anymore, just me and the sound. It brings me back to sense and senses, to what touch feels like, to what sight is. To a world outside of that moment of blissful communion. And now I know where that sound is coming from. It's emanating from the same form that's taken hold of me, that's pulled me back.

Nithael is singing.

All around me, the possessed passengers and crew are like petrified statues, unmoving. Their eyelids are all closed, meaning I don't have to stare at their freaky demon state, but they're still standing or crouching or paused mid-swing towards trying to snap another one of my ribs like a chicken wing's wishbone. And I know where they must be. I've just come back from there, after all. The song's transported them to that other state of bliss. And somehow that's taken them beyond the demon's reach.

And still the song doesn't lull or falter. Even now, grounded by Isaac, I can hear it augmenting, enriching, timbres and tones adding in, weaving through the whole. It's harmonious in a way that would make Beethoven weep. I wonder if I'll ever enjoy music again afterwards. Nothing can equal this.

Still it grows, louder and more pressing, and though I daren't look back —the thought of seeing Nithael at full power is frankly terrifying— my gaze darts down to the hand wrapped around my bicep. It's glowing, the illumination building alongside the note. It's a one angel heavenly chorus, and it looks like it comes with its own full scale light show too. The brilliance is blinding now, even just in my peripheral vision, and as much as I want to watch, want to see, I have to press my eyes shut. It's too much. Way, way too much. Despite how long I've lived, I'm only mortal. I want to stay that way. The combination of the light and sound feels like it could burn the human condition out of my soul. I'm not ready for that.

So I feel it rather than see it. The note reaches a point where it's more than my ears can hear, more than my body can take, an overload of stimulus – sound that's painting perfection across my nerve endings, sending it scuttling back to my brain, and I can't tell you if it's damaging it or making it whole. The inside of my eyelids are lit up like someone's pressed a torch straight to them, a golden aura streaked with faint pink blood vessels rather than the calming dark I seek.

Then we reach a crescendo, a point where even with Isaac holding me down, I must surely have left the simple constraints of the atmosphere, carried on the notes, transformed into stardust, subsumed back into the endless, perfect whole. Then it's gone. But not fading, not an ending like that. No, I feel it expand outwards from us, radiating like a shockwave. Maybe that's it. Perhaps reality itself is shocked by what Nith just did, by what it's possible for reality to be. Maybe what I feel is existence recoiling, grief-stricken that what we were just experiencing has been taken away. Except grief isn't the right emotion. Though there's a sense of loss, of lessening, it's peace that permeates my heart. We may not be there yet as a species, as a world, but it's possible. There's another path than us just annihilating ourselves in flaming world death. The light-carried note rockets outwards away from the aircraft, and perhaps, just perhaps, some people elsewhere in the world will find a calming lullaby that soothes away their rage before it can't be undone. Maybe there'll be a peal in an ear where the weight of living feels too smothering, too Sisyphean, and that grain of hope sees them through the dark another time.

I hope so. Really, I do.

Right now, though, much as I'd love to stay in this meditative state, blissed out, I can't. I feel the falter of Isaac's grip, feel him sit down hard, and my eyes snap open at the same time as all the bodies drop. They're all out cold, and we're in complete silence, only broken by the laboured breathing behind me.

I'm up on my feet in a second, half-scrambling in my turn to check on 'Zac. There's no holding back a sigh of relief when I see him still with his eyes open, but if I thought he looked ill before, now he looks atrocious. He's pouring sweat from every pore, and his hand is trembling, tremors that speak of deep-seated illness, of a progressive march towards a near end. This isn't good.

He's smiling weakly, and he has every right to. Maybe the credit should all go to Nithael, but they're a team, and I don't doubt he prodded the angel into action. Then his smile fades, his brow creases, and uncertainty takes hold of his eyes.

'The silence, lad,' he mutters, almost unintelligible despite the utter, complete quiet.

Ah.

That's the point.

We're on an aircraft. Complete quiet is a bad sign.

As if on cue, I feel this strange weightlessness in my stomach, like someone's just filled it with helium, then sealed me back up, letting it bob around among the rest of my internal organs. I'm no expert on flying, but I reckon that might be G-force. Pressure starts pushing me towards the door of the cockpit, which I'm going to have to breach ASAP.

Because if I haven't missed my guess, we've lost all power, and gravity's decided to start pulling us in.

Straight towards the waiting earth, down below.

Chapter Fourteen

I guess even if I had known Nithael was about to let off the magical equivalent of an electromagnetic pulse... I still wouldn't have been able to pre-EMPt it.

The good news is the blast of angelic power seems to have fried the magnetic locks keeping the cockpit door sealed.

The bad news is it seems to have fried everything else at the same time.

We bounce through the door, aided by the gravitational pull, the metal door snapping into a latch holding it open. Through the wide-screen panoramic windows, there's a whole lot more green and grey and a whole lot less blue than we should be seeing. Pointing at the floor isn't a good look in an airplane. I don't think the ground wants to be friends with us.

Both the pilots are out cold, slumped in their seats. Luckily, their shoulder harnesses seem to have arrested their forward movement, stopping them from collapsing onto their flight controls, which look like two joysticks nicked from the early 1990s. I count my lucky stars they didn't collapse on top of those. The Good God knows what would have happened if they had.

As we enter, the place is distinctly dim, six blank screens in front of the pilots. From what I remember from the movies, those should all be on, jam-packed with information, and the whole place should be lit up like a department store Christmas tree.

Turns out I'm right. A second later, there's the distinct *click* of a generator engaging, and the two screens in front of the captain –based on the number of stripes on her shoulder– spring to life. The co-pilot's side and the two middle screens, one stacked on top of the other, remain resolutely dark. Whether that's normal or not, I've no idea. Sadly, the aircraft stays determinedly quiet. Looks like the engines didn't just start themselves back up automatically, convenient as that would be.

I look over at Isaac, who shrugs weakly. 'Don't ask us, lad.'

'Don't ask you?' I manage to keep my voice calm. Ish. 'While I appreciate the save, 'Zac, I'd hoped for a proper one, not just a delay for a few minutes till we kiss the ground at Mach 1. What happened?'

'No idea, lad. Nithael sang. It's, well –' His eyes flick back towards the door behind us. 'You've seen exactly how powerful it is. Neither him nor Nan have ever done it in our existence. That was the only thing he could think of that might work other than you killing every one of the passengers.'

'Yes, thanks, Nith. Now I don't have to do it because gravity will. Fuck!'

I pull the captain, a lithe, dark-haired woman in her

112

early forties at my guess, back, trying to get a clearer look. There're some switches on the side of the bottom of her chair. Pressing them doesn't seem to do anything. I guess they got fried in the Heavenly-EMP. Trying those, though, means I spot some levers just below. With a bit of fiddling, I nearly scare myself to death when the seat drops heavily floorwards. Calming my breathing, I slide the chair back-wards. As I do so, her headset slips loose, and I can hear the sibilant whisper of radio chatter coming through.

'Sky God Four Eight Bravo, do you read?' The urgency, both in the voice and our situation, is enough to distract me from how fucking ridiculous the call sign is. Almost. I can't help wondering if any one of the deities associated with the firmament might strike us down just for being called such a stupid name.

I manage to slide the headset on, although the micro-phone ends up getting in between my teeth, leaving the horrible taste of foam on my tongue. Setting it correctly, I shout, 'Hello? Hello?' several times. There's no response. Just as I'm starting to worry it's like the time Aich and I had walkie-talkies, and she ignored me if I didn't finish each transmission with, 'Over,' Zac leans forward and pulls one of the earpieces away from my ear.

'I think you have to push the transmit button, lad,' he says, pointing at the big red trigger on the control stick.

Over the years, some people have said that I'm my own worst enemy for loudly letting everyone know just how stupid I can be. Yet, I refrain from admitting I was terrified of pulling that trigger in case it fired rockets or machine guns. Now that I think about it again, those would be pretty strange optional extras to include on a commercial passenger jet.

'Hello, hello?' I try again, and still there's silence. Panic is arriving even faster than the ground is, and that's pretty fucking quick.

'Release the button, lad,' Isaac murmurs in my ear, and I let it go in time for my ears to be filled with squawking.

'... you, Sky God Four Eight Bravo? I repeat, is that you, Sky God Four Eight Bravo?'

Umm. 'I have no idea? Can you tell me how we can check?'

Silence for a moment. 'Who is this? Say your identity and callsign.'

'Yes, hi, my name's...' *Quick, think of an alias. Don't tell them your name on the recorded radio.* 'Isaac.' *Good God damn it, I'm an idiot.* 'We're on a plane.' *No shit, Sherlock.* 'Everyone's unconscious, even the pilots. Oh, um, and the engines are dead.'

Honestly, I have no idea how the poor air traffic controller doesn't run off screaming at this point. Not only are they clearly dealing with an utter moron but in an impossible situation. Yet, instead, the same voice, still utterly calm – albeit that kind of calm that speaks of steely self-discipline rather than zen meditation or pharmaceuticals comes back on the radio.

'All right, we're going to do everything we can to help you. I've got a direct line to a pilot. I'm going to pass you over, and they're going to try to help you, okay?'

Wow. 'Sure, okay.' The voice is so reassuring, I can almost believe this might end well even though every single rational thought tells me we're going to end up in a screaming collision with the Earth's surface.

A different voice comes on the line. 'Okay, can you hear me?'

'Yep.' *Keep it simple, Paul. Don't start blathering.*

'Are you pulling the trigger on the sidestick to talk?'

'Yep.'

'Do me a favour. Look on the screen. Can you see the horizon at all? The bit at the top of the brown part?'

There's a lot of brown on the screen, but at the very top, I can still see some blue. 'Yeah, I can.'

'Is it straight, horizontally?'

I peer at it. 'Almost? Like, it's a bit wonky but not much.'

'Okay, good. So on the stick you're holding, can you pull it very gently back? Tell me if it does anything.'

I do so, and the whole aircraft lurches upwards, so I instinctively release it. The nose dips again but not as much, and I can see more sky. We don't seem to be plummeting quite as quickly towards the ground anymore; although, based on the numbers on the side of the screen, we're still going down.

'That seems to have slowed our descent down a little.'

'Okay, resist the urge to yank back on it, just hold a little bit of pressure on, okay? Don't try to stop it coming down altogether; it won't work. Right, so in the middle of the centre console, at the bottom, you can see two levers marked engine one and two, with a switch in the middle. See them?'

Damn, that ground's closing fast. Damn, damn, damn. 'Erm… yep, got 'em.'

'Okay, switch them off.'

I want to argue about wanting the engines on rather than off, but I have to assume the guy knows what the hell he's doing. I certainly don't, so I do as I'm told.

'Turn the selector knob in the middle to the right, where it's marked ignition.'

Click. 'Okay, done.'

'Great, now turn on the left engine switch for me again.'

At first, I think they've jammed; they don't seem to

move whatever I do. As ever, Isaac's far more cool in a crisis and leans forward, lifting the switch, allowing it to push forward.

'That's done.'

'Brilliant. Let's give it a few seconds. What's your name?'

Ah. The old "keep them talking, keep them calm" trick. It's one I've pulled a few times myself in the past. When someone's in a situation miles above their head, when they're so far outside their comfort zone, they've forgotten what comfortable feels like. Simple words that forge human connections can guide people to perform wonders.

Sadly, judging by the total lack of noise, I don't think it's going to be enough to get me to make this plane turn on and start flying. Why the fuck didn't they just put an on/off switch on it? All this flicking on levers and getting a big fat load of nothing is fraying nerves that are more worn than a pair of fifth generation hand-me-down jeans.

'I don't think it's working, dude!' Maybe I'm just stating the obvious, but the ground is closing rapidly, and I really don't think we're going to make it. After all the times I nearly got obliterated by magic, it looks like malfunctioning technology might finally do the job. There's probably something prosaic in that about the advancement of humanity, but I'm too worried about being transformed into a pancake, complete with my own complementary strawberry jam serving, to work it out.

'Okay, listen to me. Turn that engine off, turn on the other one. Let's see if we can get that one working. In the meantime, I'm going to talk you through how we're going to get this on the ground. Your landing gear is already out, so that's going to make life a whole lot easier. We can do this together, all right?'

Oh, he's trying. The Good God bless him, he's really trying. Even over the staticky broadcast, I can hear the pep and vim he's trying to inject into his speech to keep me bucked up, believing we're going to get out of this. Isaac and I exchange glances, and I know he knows too. We're not going to make it. There's no way I can learn enough in the minutes –best-case scenario– that we have before impact to land this plane with no engines and no assist. If Nith has his metaphorical breath back, he'll probably be able to save Isaac, but I'm not sure what I have up my sleeve to stop me from getting smooshed. And nothing I can think of is going to do anything to protect the rest of the poor souls on board.

I do as I'm told and try to ignore my heart plummeting.

Isaac closes his eyes tight. His lips are moving, though I can't hear a sound. I wonder if he's praying to his god, the same god he's never lost faith in despite hundreds of years of evidence that what we think of as gods are just other dimensional beings poking the ant hill with a stick to see what happens. I can't blame him for making peace with his maker though. If he does end up meeting him soon, best to already be on the right footing with him.

Then his eyes snap open, and it's like the reverse of what I saw out in the cabin. Where the possessed had eyes subsumed in pitch darkness, the gaze now fixed on me is like two pocket torchlights if you'd powered them off an infinity stone. I'm no longer staring into Isaac's eyes. I'm looking directly at Nithael, and it is almost as terrifying as the demon mob but for different reasons. I'm used to being the big cheese, the centre of the drama, the main character the action revolves around. Right now, I feel like a gnat buzzing around a phoenix, and spontaneously combusting any second seems entirely possible. I'm definitely too close to the angelic flames right now.

I freeze like a rabbit in the headlight. Except I feel like a rabbit would have a better chance of survival delivering a flying headbutt to an articulated lorry than I would clashing with the being in front of me. Then they smile and say one word.

'Fly.'

I'm about to reply, 'That's exactly what I want us to do, but we seem to be doing a better impression of crashing right now' – proving that even when I'm cowed by truly awesome extra-dimensional beings, I'm still a mouthy twat, but I don't get the chance.

Because Nithael, and by extension, Isaac, leap backwards, twisting in midair, and crash through the rear-side window.

Chapter Fifteen

THE SKY, 26 OCTOBER, PRESENT DAY

I'd say don't try this at home, but unless you live inside a fucking airplane, that's unlikely to be a problem for you. Lucky you.

Tere's a moment in every film ever involving an aircraft, where a window gets shot out, or something hits it and it fractures, pencil-thin cracks fractaling the surface before shattering into smithereens. Then utter chaos ensues. Deafening noise as the whole world gets sucked out through the tiny hole, usually till someone hits it who's big enough to plug the gap.

Here's the surprising part of it, which I've just found out is true. Hollywood actually didn't exaggerate for once.

A millisecond after Nith/'Zac smashes through the glass, I have the joy of feeling my eardrums pop so hard, I'm surprised I don't get a sonic boom shooting out of each orifice. Plus, I get the sensation of someone having jabbed red-hot knitting needles into each of my tear ducts. Next moment, I'm outside the aircraft, along with an assortment of items from the cockpit – glasses, iPads, pens, anything not strapped down, basically. I might be wrong, but I'm pretty sure finding yourself on the exterior of an aircraft before it has landed isn't a good place to be.

I've never gone skydiving. Only lunatics like authors and lawyers do such insane things. Personally, I'll stick to battling berserker ogres armed with insta-death magical weapons. Far less stressful.

However, I can imagine this is the bit that adrenaline junkies look forward to. The free fall, the sense of weightlessness. I assume that's what they're all constantly chasing, that incredible sensation of man surpassing his limitations and challenging the very gods themselves.

Personally speaking, I don't notice any of that. I'm too busy screaming in sheer utter terror. I'm back in "baby just after birth in the delivery room who's had their arse slapped for no apparent reason" mode, and I'm about as cognisant and compos mentis as a newborn too. This may be what they mean by blind panic, but honestly, my eyes are screwed too tightly shut to be able to see anything anyhow. The wind's tearing down my throat so hard, I've no idea if I'm still screaming myself hoarse, and the noise is being whipped away or whether the apparent hurricane I've found myself in the middle of, judging by the windspeed and noise, is just plucking on my vocal cords like an Appalachian banjo player. Either way, they feel liable to snap at any moment.

Then familiar hands wrap themselves under my arms, around my chest, and suddenly, I'm not falling anymore...

I'm soaring.

I crack an eye open and crane backwards to look over

my shoulder. Isaac's above me, holding on to me tightly, and above him…

Nithael has unfurled his wings into reality.

The electric plumes are cutting their way into the physical plane, seizing and dominating the air currents, pulling them into service. If I thought the angel was phoenix-like before, that was nothing in comparison to now. His feathers crackle like neon fire as they slice the air, and I can't look for long because the angel's like a miniature phosphorescent sun, and it'll blind me if I do. Even looking away, I can see sizzling lines in my vision, echoing exposures of the sight above me, tempting me to sacrifice my eyes for one more look.

We wheel and turn, soaring majestically. I've never felt jealous of Hubert before, but damn, being an eagle's a pretty sweet deal. Then I hear wings flapping harder, a sound like a sack-tied tempest being let out in bursts, like Aoelus' gift to Odysseus is being put to use. And we accelerate.

Not a little bit. I have no real relative idea of any of the speeds we've been doing – not when we were in the plane, not when I was plummeting towards the ground, not when Isaac grabbed me. What I do know is that we're suddenly going a damn sight quicker than any of those. The air is tearing at my cheeks, making me do a Jim Carrey impression against my will, and I finally think to loop some of my *talent* up around Isaac and me to keep me secured in place and the speed from killing us. If I'd been a bit more on the ball, I'd have done it earlier, taken some of the physical slack off 'Zac, but plunging towards certain death did a number on my reasoning faculties. It's only selfish deadly terror that gets me to tie myself in place.

The left wing drops, which I know because the horizon,

which I've always been very comfortable with having on the aptly-named horizontal, suddenly becomes a vertical line. My stomach doesn't seem to have got the same memo as the rest of my body, I'm fairly sure, by the way it feels like we've left it several metres behind. Then we drop, and rational thought becomes impossible.

Falling was one thing. Now we're diving, and my head's filled with static. My utter dread's working like a white noise generator. It's almost a safety function, like if I actually think about what's happening, I'll just have a heart attack instantly and drop dead even quicker than we're plummeting down, down, down towards the earth. If I could identify anything, I'd make some sort of comment about how I can spot cars moving around, make out the shapes of individual trees' greenery, tell the slate texture of certain roofs. Instead, a sole thought manages to pierce the terror, and that's to wonder why I haven't passed out, considering the G's we must be pulling. And whom I can issue a formal complaint to about that.

Then there's a noise and sensation reminiscent of reversing a car into a brick wall, only multiplied – an articulated lorry into a cliff face, perhaps, or what I can imagine it'd be like to hit a dock with one of those ridiculous super yachts of the rich and braindead. Our speed's dropped dramatically, enough so as to leave space for my thinking to start working again, and I risk a peek back up to see what's happening.

Oh. Wow. That's quite something.

The aircraft we just got sucked out of is resting on Nithael's impossible back, the engines nestled in among his wings that span from tip to tip of the plane's and beyond. Those magnificent downy appendages are making tiny motions, beating against the air, and it's enough. Enough to check the aircraft's downward velocity, to steady it and slow it down.

We're damn close to the ground now, but I can see a stretch of black ahead of us, like a road's dream of grandeur slicing through the surroundings. I'm aware of noise from Isaac, but I'll be damned if I can hear what he's saying.

'What?' I scream, battling the air trying to whip the words out of my mouth and steal them away, moving my head as near to him as I can.

'Don't…look…here.' I make out the words, just. I can hear the effort they cost Isaac as well, but I'll have to worry about that later, when we don't have a sixty-tonne vehicle full of people literally riding on us.

What he's asking for is going to be taxing. Every single person involved in monitoring and controlling the skies, all the authorities below where the plane might end up crashing into, every person who's caught the slightest whiff of what's going on? They're all going to have their eyes skywards, fixed on us, trying to see. I'm sure Nith's been dealing with it up until now, but if Isaac's asking…

He needs his strength. I need to do my part.

So I start to weave my *talent*. But not into my normal *don't look here*, where people's eyes simply slide off us. No, now it's more like the reverse, a *definitely do look here* that I wrap around the metal carapace above us. With a minor working added to make us invisible to cameras and electronic equipment in general. It's far easier to make everyone's attention be so entirely fixated on the aeroplane that they don't see us underneath. Though "easier" is definitely a relative term. It's still using all my *talented* muscle to make it happen. This is a huge-scale working, but the stakes are equally high. I don't doubt 'Zac would risk exposing the

Talented to the world to save the lives above us. Doesn't mean I want either of us to have to shoulder that responsibility. I'd say Nith shouldering the aircraft is impressive enough.

We're closing rapidly on the terrain, though in a controlled manner now. Much preferable to the whole "plummeting, screaming in abject terror" shtick I had to go through earlier. The black asphalt rises up to greet us like a long-lost lover, arms thrown wide for a clinching embrace. Our speed's dropped from impossibly fast to still far too quick for my liking, but I can feel the deceleration. As we get low enough that I feel an instinctive need to ball my knees to my chest in case of an overly tall tree or cable, Nithael *heaves*.

As he pulls back, my head comes up, and for a moment I get the view I reckon most pilots must see before landing. There's a whole host of illuminations arrayed in lines of differing widths that lead arrow-like towards the tarmac just in front of us, and the runway's black surface is picked out by a thousand lights. It makes the whole thing look like something out of a video game. Then Nithael launches the plane forward, and I'm looking down at the lead-in lights again, twisting my head to see what's happening while trying to keep the *don't look here* on us, and the *definitely do look here* on the plane.

The aircraft whooshes over our heads, although it's a very diminutive whoosh compared to most flyovers. I guess that's to be expected when it's operating as an over-sized glider. As the tail whips into my field of vision, I see a loop of angelic energy fastened around it. Suddenly, we pivot, so I'm now upright again. As the plane connects with the tarmac – 'lands' might be too strong a word for it – Nithael heaves backwards. It's like a cowpoke wrangling a bull, only with a lot more metal. And a lot more lives at stake.

The screeching noise that fills the air makes the first point clear, like an angle grinder scraping across a car door repeatedly. Nithael's rope of *talent* goes taut, and the aircraft bucks. For a moment I think it's going to flip or come tearing off the side of the runway, ploughing into one of the other aircrafts or the terminal itself, but somehow Nith steers it from that single tether. It seems impossible to me, but I guess simple spatial equations are a doddle when you're a Bene Elohim. Somehow, the angel judges it perfectly, keeping the aircraft on the runway, decelerating it without tearing it in half despite the terrible metallic noise we're hearing, chunks of metal flying off along with the shower of rubber as the tires pop one after another. I reckon the odds of that aircraft ever flying again are zero. But at least all the people on board will get a chance.

Below us, flashing sirens come whipping up alongside the vehicle as it slows to a manageable pace and stops. Fire engines and police cars gallop heroically up to the now stationary aircraft, no doubt readying for explosions or hijacker gunfire. Instead, there's silence. Another vehicle pulls up, one of the airport's own, and someone jumps out and slams chocks into place, the wedges to stop the aircraft from rolling. Then they leap back in and peel off, away from the mystery. Sensible. This one's way above their pay grade in terms of potential risk.

It's done though. Everybody on board is safe. If I hadn't seen it with my own eyes, I wouldn't have believed it possible. I'm so proud of 'Zac and Nith. Unbelievable heroics, saving a day I thought not just lost but utterly destroyed, fed through the shredder, and then set on fire. The two of them should be proud of themselves. I'm certainly proud of them both.

As that thought strikes me, so does Isaac's chin, glancing hard off my shoulder. I feel his body slump against mine, and it's only the *talent* I looped around us that keeps me from sliding out of his relaxing grip. Panic starts to grab hold of me, as well as that icy-cold kind of fear that freezes your stomach acid into a dead weight in your guts. Fear for Isaac. I look over my shoulder just in time to see Nithael disappear from the normal, visible realm.

And then we pick up where I left off when 'Zac grabbed me out of the plane, and we start plunging towards the ground – again.

Chapter Sixteen

THE SKY BUT FAR CLOSER TO THE GROUND, 26 OCTOBER, PRESENT DAY

Oh no, not again. So this is what it feels like to be a bowl of petunias.

Whistling wind is a noise I can do without hearing again for a very long time. Preferably ever.

Luckily, we don't have far to fall, and I'm so jacked up on adrenaline from the insane shit I've just been through – insane shit that Hollywood can only dream of coming up with, whimpering in its sleep at its own inadequacy – that I can throw up a cushion of *talent* on the ground, resistant enough to arrest our landing but soft enough not to shatter our spines in the process. Between the healing on the aircraft and the loops tying me to Isaac, my power levels are practically running on empty, and softening our impact pretty much wipes me out magically.

There's a moment of me just lying here wheezing and gasping, trying to remember how to breathe without screaming, what it feels like to not be either at risk of imminent demise or strapped under the belly of a manifesting fiery angel. Then I remember Isaac.

I roll onto my front and try to stand. My feet don't remember what solid ground feels like, and I just lurch forward to faceplant in the cracked paving slabs, so I turn it into a scrabble, clawing at the ground to launch myself over to Isaac's side.

He's only a couple of metres away, so it's quick enough, and my first sensation is palpable relief. He's breathing. Oh, thank fuck, thank all the gods and life and Lady Luck, that fickle little madam who's actually chosen not to show me the middle finger for once. He's alive. Then I see his neck.

The veins are bulging out, swollen, and I can see the discolouration. They aren't totally seized up yet, but they're sludgy and blackened. Maybe they aren't yet turned to tar completely, but there's no question that they're infected, polluted, whatever the right term is for this sort of fuckery. Isaac's condition has just gotten a lot worse.

And he's not waking up.

I'm still packing enough *talent* that we're enrobed in a *don't look here*, thankfully. Police and air crash investigators will be combing the area soon, looking for debris and bodies. There's going to be two passengers missing, but everyone else is alive and on board – hopefully. Either that or the demonic magic will kill them all now that their usefulness is exhausted, and all Isaac and Nith's efforts will have been for nothing.

That's a grim thought. I push it away and concentrate on getting myself up and hoisting Isaac onto my shoulders. He feels so light, weightless, and that's a concern in and of itself. He should be a cumbersome load. The demon essence is eating away at him.

We've landed without too much impact. My air cushion

has smashed a couple of lights from the lead-in guidance system. I hope they're not too important for the next landing traffic; although, looking at the debris scattered across the runway, I imagine it'll be some time before they get the airport open again. We're inside the airport terrain but not far from the fences, and there's a road just the other side. Stumbling towards the barrier, I fumble my phone out of my pocket. It's still intact, which is amazing because normally with modern phones, they break if you breathe on them too heavily. While I do miss the indestructible old Nokia bricks, I am also not always the smartest tool in the box – possibly not in the entire warehouse – and it's very damn handy having something capable of doing most of my thinking for me via Google in my pocket.

Faust picks up on the first ring. 'Paul? Chrissakes, man, what happened?' His own panic is evident. That must have been hellishly stressful to watch from the ground. Although, I can confirm it was even worse from the air.

'Tell you later. Isaac's hurt. Do you know the road just outside the airport, on final approach?'

'No idea, but I can work it out.'

'Get there. Now. Isaac's not good, and I'm about done in.'

Nearing the fence, I dig deep inside myself to run a narrow ramp of *talent* up and over, staggering as I mount it. Isaac might be light comparative to normal, but I am wiped out and close to nervous exhaustion. Total collapse is being held off only by willpower and adrenaline, and even those are starting to run low. Soon, nothing short of an intravenous hookup of caffeine straight to the vein is going to keep me moving.

Once on the other side, I keep my *don't look here* up and manage to stay awake at the same time. Frankly astounding, although the worry for Isaac is frenetic enough to help keep me from total collapse. Then it's just a waiting game.

A few minutes later, a battered old station wagon, dulled grey and with dents that might be due to age and bad parking or, knowing the owners, from them clambering on top if it after some tequila shots, pulls up next to me. After we bundle Isaac into the backseats, a good fifty kilograms of canine muscle springs over the rear cushions. You could almost imagine Mephistopheles is just a really large Dobermann most of the time. Right now, though, his eyes are glowing black, which is precisely as odd as it sounds and intimidating enough to send the Hound of the Baskervilles scampering away whimpering with his tail between his legs.

Tendrils of shadow and shade peel away from his pelt and entwine around Isaac. It's hard to watch. I want to jump in instinctively. This is well outside of my wheelhouse though. If I don't trust Mephistopheles, I should never have come in the first place. But I can't help 'Zac myself. There're no other options.

Faust leans over and pops open the front passenger door, though I have to catch it as it starts to swing shut again. 'Jump in, Paul.' I can hear the strain in his voice, but if he thinks he feels stressed, he should try hooking himself up to my nervous system for a few minutes. Guaranteed to make his heart explode.

I grip the rim of the doorway and sling myself in. Manhandling myself is the only way to get anything done now. 'What's going on, Mephy? Is it bad? Can you help?'

The huge dog's head swings my way, his teeth bared, foam speckling his lips. 'I can talk to you, Cathar, or I can keep him alive. Choose.' Then I'm dismissed, all the demon's concentration focused on Isaac – a limp form prostrate across the leather seats, wrapped in Mephy's darkness on the outside, burning with another demon's on the inside.

It's a bloody mess.

There's nothing more I can do. His care's out of my hands for the moment. The old turn of phrase about waves of exhaustion hitting is fair but insufficient. It's a whole goddamn tsunami, breaching the levees of my consciousness, washing away my wooden huts of reason, demolishing whole swathes of my city of rational thought and swallowing them away into oblivion.

A few seconds after I strap in the seatbelt, I follow them away into unconsciousness.

It's the stopping of the car, that definite gravel crunch under tyres that speaks of arriving at a place, a final destination rather than just the temporary pause of a stoplight, that wakes me. My brain comes back online, albeit operating in limited safe mode, only basic functions available, but my eyes don't get the message. In their defence, they seem to have been cemented shut. When I start applying proper effort, I'm delighted to find it's just that my body appears to have produced superglue from my tear ducts. With a little furious rubbing, I eventually unstick them enough to get them open and stagger out. The back door pops open, and Isaac floats through it, still wrapped in Mephy's *talent* like a funeral shroud. I try to shake that particular morbid image away as the front door of the house swings open and the demon-dog and my mentor disappear inside. Luckily, the house is fairly distracting.

Faust's taste has always run to the gothic. I'm almost certain he kicked off the whole New Romantic scene in the eighties just so he could feel hip and cool for a minute. I think about telling him of my adventures with the group of wannabe goth vampires in England a few months ago, but firstly, they were a bunch of wanky poseurs, and secondly, they're all dead. Me killing them tends to have that effect.

His house is the sort of thing that Morticia and Gomez from *The Addams Family* would have up on their vision board. Multiple wings and turrets designed with the level of finicky intricacy that ran rampant during the original Gothic period. There are even honest-to-Good-God gargoyles looming over the doorway with leers like cat-calling builders. Top marks for style, definitely. Bit too serious for my tastes. Plus, keeping the place clean must be a nightmare even if you cheat and use magic.

Inside is a different story. Warm oranges and pastel yellows paint the walls and ceilings, with hardwood floors leading down the hallway towards a living area straight out of Austin Powers' wet dreams. Space chairs like half-hollowed eggs hang from the ceiling, with random lengthened lights. A huge leopard-print sofa and matching chaise lounge sit huddled together around the open fireplace, as if hoping the hearth would protect them from the hideous décor, or else as though they'd realised they were part of it and were trying to throw themselves into it in despair and a desperate attempt to save my eyes from the visual onslaught. It's like the seventies partied even harder, and this was the hangover it woke up to the next day. Which, to be fair, would be better than having woken up to the eighties but only just. None of it should work, and honestly, none of it really does. I'd love to say they somehow overcame the clashing riot of colours and styles, pulling it together into a homogenous whole, but I'd rather my pants don't sponta-neously burst into flames if it's all the same with you.

There are more pressing matters, but my eyebrow can't help itself. It arches up, higher than the ceiling that's been painted with some sort of purple-and-green polka dots scheme.

Faust shrugs. 'It makes Mephy happy.' Damn, that's some top quality friending right there. Putting up with this every day just to make someone you care about happy? Beyond impressive. You wouldn't catch me doing that for anyone. I'd have anxiety attacks every time I tried to watch TV. It'd become a ghost room, never visited, never mentioned, the Lounge-Which-Must-Not-Be-Named. As it is, this isn't my house, and even I'm not that much of a rude bastard, so I try to ignore the muscle that's started twitching in my eye at the oversized fish tank with lava lamps on either side and a faux tiger-skin rug in front of it. All is forgiven when Faust pops out to the kitchen and brings me a bottle of dark German beer though.

'Where's 'Zac?' I want to drink. The Good God knows I want to drink but not as much as I want Isaac to be okay. 'Is there any news?'

Johannes looks grave, a strange expression on a face normally so jubilant and joyful. 'No news yet, man. Being here will help Mephy, of course, but I got the impression it's going to be some time before we know either way.'

Now I drink, and fuck me, do I need it. I'm in that horrible stage where part of me's furious with Isaac for not having told me beforehand, so we could have got here sooner, and the rest of me is flushed with guilt at even thinking a single negative thought towards him while I wait here to find out if he's going to die. And, of course, there's always that niggling little bitch of a voice that keeps pointing out, quietly but insistently, that I should have noticed, should have seen the change. That I'm a bad friend, and all of this is my fault. A better human being would have spotted the problem earlier on even without being told. Instead, I was off trying to assuage my guilt about what had happened to Aicha, and I let Isaac fall by the wayside.

So as bitter as the hops in my beer are, my own emotions are far more difficult to swallow. Booze helps, of course. It might be an illusion – hell, it definitely is; alcohol absolutely causes a whole lot more problems than it helps – but it gives me the feeling of calming me down. Right now, I'll take anything, anything at all, that aids me in maintaining a grip. If Isaac dies, if it's my fault…

Whether Faust can see where my thoughts are going or not, I can't say, but he comes in with a timely interruption of them. 'What on earth happened back there, Paul?'

His refined tones are almost musical. Some people say German is a guttural language, full of harsh sounds and barking syllables. There's some truth in that, perhaps, but there's also a pitch that runs through Faust's voice, high and fine, reminiscent of the first pull of a bow over a well-tuned violin. It matches with the man himself. So like Isaac in some ways – tall, thin, elegant, with his scholarly credentials evident in both his speech and his poise, the model of an academic – and so different in others. I can't imagine Isaac up on the table, pouring shots in his underwear and a pair of stripper shoes he'd borrowed from who knows where. That's a quiet night when you hit the town with Johannes. I've seen him in that sort of situation after we're deep in our cups more than once.

I try to work out what he's talking about. That in itself is a good indication of just how befuddled by tiredness I am now. For most people, fighting off demon-possessed hordes, getting sucked out of an airplane window, and then paragliding under an angel would be what Faust was obviously referring to. Of course, it might also be a commentary on just how convolutedly bizarre my life is that I still feel the need to clarify.

'Which bit of "back there" are you talking about, Jo? How far back?' Beer's the wrong choice, really. It's too heavy. Too much weight into a stomach already filled with rocks and acid reflux rapids by the feel of it. Still, I've started, so I'll finish.

He peers at me over a pair of half-crescent spectacles that I know are just for show. His eyesight is perfect 20/20 vision. Not my place to call out other people's pretensions though. 'The literal plane crash we just picked you up from?'

I sigh. The problem with telling this story is it all keeps leading back to something else. So when I tell him about the plane, he wants to know about the demon. That obviously leads to us discussing how Isaac got infected, which brings us round to the whole confrontation with the Evil God and —

'Hold that thought, man,' Johannes interrupts. 'Mephy'll only make you retell it once he joins us, and I don't think you want to be running through it more than once.'

He's right, I don't. In fact, once is one time too many. Of course, I know it has to be done. Somewhere in the twisted mangled wreck of the last few months might be the answer to saving Isaac. Maybe not, but there's no way I can risk it. Both of them need the entire backstory, warts and all.

As I finish my beer, Faust goes to get me another and Mephy lopes into the room. I've never kept a pet – not that I'm calling Mephistopheles a pet; I like having my brain attached to the stem and my organs on the inside – but I was pretty certain dogs can't sweat.

Mephy is definitely proving that to be false. He's soaking, wringing wet, and I can see trembles in the shaking sheen of his coat even though his gait screams casually relaxed. I can't mirror it. With all the worry and exhaustion, I'm vibrating fast enough, it's a wonder I don't blur at the edges.

'What news? How is he, Mephy?' The fact he's playing it cool reassures me slightly. Surely he wouldn't look like that if he'd failed? The expression on his face, though, is grave enough as to give me pause on that optimistic thought.

'It's not over, mano. They live, for now.' The crux of the news delivered, he sinks down onto his haunches. I flop back into my chair. Isaac's alive!

Faust hurries back in, dropping an open bottle into my trembling hand as he passes. 'Did you say he made it, Mephy?'

The demon-dog rolls his head back and forth like he's weighing the question or else how to give it a truthful answer. 'They aren't dead yet. And both of you would do better to remember there's not just a *mano* involved.'

Huh. I can feel the colour rising in my cheeks slightly at the comment. He's right, of course. It's not just Isaac; it's Nith as well. Considering the angel saved both our lives and those of everyone on the plane, I'd do better to show more consideration. Plus, I can only imagine how much of a second-class citizen it must make Mephistopheles feel. If we're only worried about the human here, would we do the same if there was a problem for Faust and him?

'Sorry, dude. You're quite right. With Nith being a silent partner most of the time – at least for the rest of us, I wasn't focused on him.' Suddenly, one word from his last answer comes back to me, and an icicle forms inside my chest. 'Hang on, what do you mean by "yet"?'

The creature gives a deep huff, shaking his head to pop one of his ears back the right way out. 'What is happening to your friend shouldn't be possible, mano. Should not happen. Especially considering his boon companion.'

Mephy raises his head, and deep inside his black hole stare, I can see something that might be anger, might be fear, or some concoction mixed up from bits of each of them. 'The essence in him is growing, consuming him. I've checked its advance for now, but all that's done is bought us a little time. The problem's a long way from solved.'

'Can you cure it?' I'm not really sure if that's the right term. Is being infected by energy really a disease? I suppose it's behaving much like a virus, spreading itself through the host.

The canine's eyes regard me carefully. 'No.'

Just like that, the world seems to pause, then shatter all around me.

Chapter Seventeen

It's like Fred Savage hearing about the death of Westley.
He's gotta be okay. He's just gotta.

My world, my whole existence since I came back to life after
the pyres of Lavaur eight hundred years ago has held one
single constant: Isaac. He's not just my rock; he's my
anchor, my tether point that keeps me from losing touch
with humanity, from sliding off into a penchant for shiny
PVC outfits and cackling monologues. If there's anything
that's kept me out of supervillain territory, it's him.

So when Meph says no, my reality falls to pieces.

I can't breathe, not properly. Oh, sure, there's air in my
lungs. But they feel tight, cramped, unresponsive to any
order to keep me alive. I can count the ribs pressing on
them, the ribs my heart's expanding against. All the
different elements of my body feel the wrong size, like my
skin's suddenly too tight, as if it's shrunk in the wash.

My panic must be obvious because Mephy barks a

short, sharp gunshot crack that grabs my attention and pulls my focus back to him.

'I'm not finished, mano. I can't save him *on my own*. What I need is simple. I need you to get your hands on the demon who did this.'

'Great, why didn't you say so? I've got him right here.' I mime opening my hand but stick my middle finger up instead. Is it childish? Yes, but I'm pissed off. That's of no bloody use to me right now.

Mephy growls at me, a deep reverberation in his considerably muscled chest, but I'm too terrified at the thought of Isaac dying to give a rat's ass about my own wellbeing. 'Stop being a smartarse for once in your life, mano. I can't cure the angel's mano, but I can stabilise them, beat the essence back. Or at least there's someone – or something rather, who might be able to. If you're quick.'

The next second, I'm on my feet as if he were a teacher and I the eager school kid trying to prove himself, to show just how speedy he can be. 'Who? What? What can I do, Meph?'

'Do you know the alp?'

'Erm. The singular of the nearby mountains? One alp, many alps?'

I'm not an expert in dog expressions, but Mephy doesn't look amused. Mind you, neither am I. It's just, flippancy is my go-to response when I don't know an answer. Especially when I'm panicking.

Faust takes over before Mephistopheles loses his patience, and I lose a limb. 'Alp is the origin of the English word used commonly for most forms of fae, thanks to a certain JRR. It's the etymological origin of "elf", *bettgenosse*.'

Oh, fuck.

Faust obviously picks up on my expression. 'What's wrong?'

Ah, yeah. I didn't get that far back in the story. Doesn't look like I've the time to either now. 'Let's just say I'm persona non grata in Faerie right now.'

I can see Johannes' inquisitive mind firing up at that. 'Which court? Summer or Winter?'

I shrug. 'Both? Tell you about it later. Which court are they denizens of?'

He shakes his head. 'Neither. The alp may be the origin of the word "elf", but they're either native to Earth, or else they've been gone so long from Faerie that they owe no allegiance anymore. I'm not even sure if it is "they" or "he". I've only ever come across one, and that was a chance crossing.'

Now it's my turn to be getting fascinated, but again, this can wait. 'Okay, fae being or beings without allegiance to Summer or Winter. Lovely, friendly fellows who like to help all and sundry wherever they can, right?'

My voice inflects upwards on the last word, my desperate hope injected into it. Of course, Johannes is there to piss on my hopes from a great height.

'No, they're terrible, evil beings who delight in the misery and suffering of all who cross their paths.'

Right, so standard fae fucknozzles then, basically.

Half an hour later, I'm driving through the foothills of the Alps, which may also belong to the alp if Faust is right. This is where he crossed paths with the creature the one time he came across it. Apparently, it tried to stalk him through the forest, no doubt planning to do him mischief. It hadn't factored in Mephy, who stealthily tracked it through the undergrowth and apparently got within inches of fastening his teeth around the creature's neck. Sadly for them but luckily for me now, it changed into a dove and whizzed off at top speed into the canopy.

Which is the main problem ahead of me. Well, the main problem not including the whole having to deal with a malicious shithead of a trickster fae, something I've had enough of for at least one lifetime, probably several.

No, the main problem is that the little knobhead is a shapeshifter, which makes trapping him a tricky prospect. There's only one advantage I have regarding that. He's shit at it.

I don't mean he gets halfway and then stuck or something. No, just that he can't use it for disguise because every time he changes, he's always wearing his *tomkappe*, a jaunty little William Tell number of a hat that must look ridiculous on the monstrous creature at the best of times but even more so when he's doing a Cock Robin impression, emphasis on the cock.

Which would be great, until you get round to translating *tomkappe* and realise it means 'cap of concealment', only adding to me feeling like I've somehow ended up inside a solo Dungeons & Dragons campaign. Apparently, the little fucker can turn invisible as well as shapeshift, which might make this all a lot more difficult. Johannes' answer to the issue was a shrug, as he'd no idea how to combat it. Mephy's was to chuff, which resulted in me telling him to chuff off. I know, I know, not the smartest idea to the creature keeping your father figure alive, but I'm not feeling particularly charitable towards demons in general right now.

I asked Mephy to give me a timeframe for how quickly I

needed to capture the creature, but he didn't have one. Just 'fast as'. Then he mentioned I actually needed to steal the *tomkappe* because, apparently, it's a wondrous device capable of nullifying all essence. Of course, being fae or fae-like, there's a twist. The reason it nullifies it is because it slowly but surely turns you into an alp.

When I then asked if that's what's going to happen to Isaac if I get the hat, Mephy's answer was that he was fairly sure it's not. Either way, with Nith's angelic magic combatting the change, it'll be slow enough that it'll give us a lot more time to track down the demon-spawn who infected him than we would've had otherwise. Just another reason why I'd like to have a long, protractedly painful conversation with the arsehole.

The mountains aren't just capped by snow but coated in them, their white flanks blinding in their gleams and glistens as the sun comes up. I've hardly slept outside of passing out in the car on the way to Faust's house, but he whipped me up something to get me back up and on my feet for the time being. Then he sent me out with the perfect trap to catch an alp – a bag of coffee.

No, I don't know why. Neither did Faust nor Mephistopheles, just that all of the folktales say so. If it was anyone else, I'd have thought they were taking the piss and just trying to make me look like even more of a twat than I do normally, but no, apparently, it's a real thing. So, here I am, driving through the mountains with the plan to traipse through the Bavarian alpine forest, swinging a bag of coffee about and hollering my offer to lend it to all and sundry who might suddenly find themselves in need of a cuppa.

Good God, but I feel like a twat just thinking about what I'm about to do.

Pulling up at the last turnoff for the single lane road,

where the path simply ends in a small clearing before the wilds of nature take over, I head on into the mountains on foot. I've spent enough time in Faust's territory that I can access his resources, so I've topped my *talent* back up, at least. Birds sing chirpily from the nearby trees, which would be lovely if I didn't find myself squinting suspiciously at each of them, trying to spot if they have a rakish little bit of headgear on over their plumage.

Once I'm sure I'm far enough away from civilisation, I start swinging the coffee bag around. Then I put my legendary acting skills to use.

'Oh! A bag of... coffee! I'd – love – to lend... it to some...one.' Jesus, I sound like fucking William Shatner as I bellow the line out, waving the bag around. For a moment, I think I've struck gold. There's a rustling on the path ahead, and I'm hoping the alp's going to jump out. Instead, a very confused, slightly scared hiker appears, bedecked in waxed jacket and professional quality hiking boots. He accelerates, waving his walking poles at me as he goes past.

'No! No coffee for me, young man! No!' Then he's gone, practically running back down the path to get away from me. The fact that I wasn't looking at him but peering constantly at the top of his head, trying to make sure he didn't have a teeny tiny, hat on must only have added to how strange I looked to him. Meeting random madmen on the hiking trails is never the one you want to have happen. Then again, meeting anyone anywhere ever is always something I'd rather avoid as a rule of thumb.

Still, the presence of other humans suggests I'm not deep enough into the wilds yet. The alp's a horrible little bastard who preys on people, but he'll not want to be where there's too much of a population. Not in the daytime, anyhow, according to legend. At night he's more likely to roam, looking to slip into mountain chalets. He's a sleep paralysis creature, who then feeds on human blood. Neither of which are qualities likely to endear him to me.

But that's beside the point. What is relevant is that after about two hours of this particularly random way of exploring the German countryside, I hear a cough behind me. It's the sort of nervous noise an introvert makes when they think, perhaps, you might want to hear something they know, that it might help you and make your life better, but at the same time, they're terribly afraid that if they do get your attention, you might do something awful like talk to them.

I turn around, and there's what looks like, to most people, a little old man wizened by the ravages of age. His loss of height has clearly been balanced out by an acceleration of whatever hormone causes hair to grow because his beard is down to his knees, and his eyebrows are knitted together in a way that'd give members of the band Oasis serious monobrow envy.

I'm not so easily fooled though, so I *look* at him. It makes me wonder if Mr Tolkien might have met one of these, and his use of the word 'elf' afterwards was just to take the piss.

The thing in front of me is about as far from a daoine sidhe or any of the other high fae as you can imagine. It's like someone hit Fungus The Bogeyman with a baseball bat made from the ugly tree and then infected him with the bubonic plague. Buboes, raised off his mould-green skin, are so enlarged, you can see the pus sloshing about inside them when he moves. Warts looking like he might need to get them checked out by a dermatologist stat sprout even more hair than he has up his nose, which is to say, enough to make a wig for an adult fancy dress outfit...if you wanted your outfit to make you vomit until you passed out as soon as you put it on. His arms are stick thin, his belly's distended, and his hooked beak looks like it could be used for grubbing for worms or for disembowelling you and grubbing for internal organs.

And perched on top of his head is a jaunty little green felt number of a hat.

Call it a wild guess, but I reckon this is it. The foul fucking thing gives a tiny little bow with a nervous hop-skip from foot to foot.

'Borrowing? Lending?' The voice sounds like if you'd taught a crow to talk, then made it perform a ventriloquist act while gargling a pint glass of mud. As such, it takes me a minute to decipher what it's saying.

Now, doubtless some of you are wondering why, as soon as it appears, I don't just launch a magical attack on it. Perhaps lasso it with *talent*, fasten it to the ground so it can't move or the like. The reason's simple. I'm in its territory. We're in the daylight and out in the middle of nature as opposed to a warded house or den, but this is still an area marked by its presence and power. If I start flinging magic about while it's in the middle of following the rules of protocol that I've invoked by waving coffee grounds about – and who would've ever guessed that being a part of some peculiarly messed up set of faerie folk rules – then all sorts of bad things are likely to start happening. At best, the magic's likely to backfire and wrap me up instead. At worst? I might find myself powerless and at the mercy of a pestilent bloodsucker.

So for now at least, we need to play the game. Here goes. 'Yes, I do indeed have coffee to lend.' My words are full of careful intonation that make me sound like the kid in a school play who only got the part because the drama teacher fancies their mum. 'Do you have anything to lend me in exchange?'

The creature furrows its brow, which, thanks to its inordinate length, results in it bowing down in the middle low enough to get drenched by the snot-like substance oozing out of its nose. 'Wanting? Needing?'

'Oh, nothing much. If you happened to have a super magical hat, that would be marvellous. Don't suppose you do, perhaps?'

The alp looks at me quizzically, studying my face. When he sees I'm serious, he roars in laughter, slapping his thighs and hooting not unlike a baboon at the zoo when it sees my face. Theoretically, of course; not that that's ever actually happened. Curse you, Zoo African Safari baboon. When he calms down, he wipes his eyebrows, twirling them in the nasal excretion, which is like hair gel or wax, and shakes his head.

'Living? Returning,' he gurgles, holding out his hand for the bag.

Ah, damn it. Looks like he's not prepared to go for that. Instead, I think, he's asking me where I live ("living") and is offering to drop me a bag of black gold in bean form back at a later date instead ("returning"). Mind you, I didn't really expect him to just hand over the hat in exchange for my sack, even if it is full of magic beans. Worth a try though. In the meantime, we'll put plan B into operation. I tell him the address I'll be staying at and hand him over the coffee grains. As I do so, I look him in the eye.

'Now I'll be searching for you from hereon in, you understand?'

The little disease-ball nods solemnly. 'Knowing. Going!'

He snatches the bag and darts off into the undergrowth. I launch myself after him just in time to see him change into the world's nattiest squirrel, his hat jauntily positioned on top of his head, never moving as he races off, clutching a similarly shrunken coffee bag in his hands.

Damn it. That's my first hope dashed. He's glowing with *talent* but only as much as he was before, that strange deep-forest green that much of the fae have. The change didn't light him up in my magical field of vision. His shapeshifting is an integral part of him rather than some *talent*-based working. If he'd fired up his *talent*, he'd have shone like the sun for me, left a trail I could follow like a bloodhound even if he hid in the depths of the darkest treetops of the mountain forest. But he doesn't. There goes that option.

Luckily, I've more than one.

I throw a barrier up just in front of his face; he clatters into it at force, and for a moment I dare hope he's down, done for. But the next he's no longer earthbound. Now a bird, a swift, he shoots skywards. As he goes, the trees bend together, lowering their foliage, blocking my view of him. It's enough to stop me from pulling the same trick again. Fuck.

Instead, I use my *talent* to boost myself, pushing it down into my legs, giving myself enough power and speed to hopefully keep up with him. Launching myself upwards, I grasp the bough of one of the sneaky bastard trees that helped him out and swing myself up higher, *looking* for any sign of anything in the magical spectrum or else any creature looking surprisingly stylish for a woodland animal.

There's nothing to see. The alp – and my coffee – are gone.

Bollocks.

Chapter Eighteen

Plan A's a bust. Luckily I've a Plan B. Even without Aicha
here to kick my arse if I didn't. Look at me, all grown up
and everything.

It's been said before that I'm ill-prepared and make things
up as I go along, hoping for the best. The person who said it
found out I was well prepared to punch them in the throat,
but that's a different matter.

This time, however, I've not bet the house on my first
plan. I have been *sneaky*. Or, at least, my attempt at sneaky.
Which means anything other than just going in gung-ho
and making it up as I go along.

The bag of coffee I gave isn't just a bag of coffee. Oh,
no. Deep down, inside the granules is a tracker.

The great advantage of having done that is most creatures aren't prepared for gadgets. Magical beings tend to
look at technology with huge mistrust and generally try to

ignore it as far as they possibly can. So while the alp might well have some sort of clever little cantrip up his sleeve to destroy the spells I've woven into the coffee or the bag it's contained in, I'm willing to bet he didn't think about the possibility of me using an electronic tracker too.

Of course, I didn't consider the possibility of the bag shrinking when he did, so I'm freaking out a little, worrying that it might not have changed but instead got smashed to smithereens during the transition. I pull the receiver out and heave a sigh of relief when there's a nice strong signal, the readout telling me he's about three hundred metres away to the northwest.

Ah ha. Now, the game is afoot!

Of course, I don't just go crashing through the undergrowth, blundering after him. Even I can recognise that he's going to have plenty of time to hear me coming and do a runner if I do. No, instead I try to strategise. It's not easy, as my usual go-to strategy is "ask Aicha", but Isaac's life depends on it. I can do this whole thinking malarkey when those are the stakes.

I create bubbles around each of my shoes, working like a cone of silence. Perfect. Now even when I put my foot on something that loudly goes *crack* – otherwise known as "pretty much everything on the forest floor" – it'll be muted by my magic.

In terms of him seeing me, I can't think of what to do. Invisibility of any kind is hard work. It's why we go for *don't look heres* as a rule of thumb. Plus, pulling illusory magic good enough to fool innately magical creatures isn't just taxing; it's nigh on impossible.

In the end, I go for a bit of the old Predator trick. Rather than trying to make myself invisible, I invest my *talent* into persuading the light to bend around me a bit, like the air just off my skin is a slippery refractor. It doesn't make me invisible – not even close – but it blurs my outline and makes me camouflaged, blending in with the surrounding foliage.

Am I expecting it to fool a paranormal cryptid with connections to nature on his own turf? No, not if I'm honest. But I'm hoping it'll let me get close enough to pull something else that might catch him off guard and off balance. Like breaking one of his legs. Pretty sure that'll throw his balance off.

I feel like a regular ninja, moving through the brush and ivy, twigs left, right, and centre never making a single sound. Even Stephen Segal's opinion of himself isn't as good as mine right now. The tracker's screen is easy to see held out in front of me, leading me towards the weird little magical caffeine addict.

Part of me just can't get past that – of all the things that might work to get his attention. Coffee's been around for a while, don't get me wrong but not *that* long. If this guy split from Faerie long enough ago that he holds zero allegiance, doesn't even draw part of his power from the fae realms, is completely bonded to the human world? I don't think they'd have been sipping a cup of joe back when he first started harassing the local population. The only thing I can think of is the borrowing aspect. Neighbours have always needed a helping hand, and community used to be a much stronger commodity. Hell, it needed to be. If the bloke over the way died, you might lose something the whole village needed producing to survive. And no one had the spare time to be taking on more grunt work. The other thing, of course, is that the alp is a bloodsucker. If you're already addicted to getting the hit you crave from slurping down one liquid, perhaps you automatically start gravitating towards something like coffee when you discover it to get you through the time between neck bites.

The trees narrow, boughs intertwining more, stubby brushes and saplings occupying through-spaces, with nettles cloying at trouser legs and thorns hunting wickedly for flesh. I'm worried at first that it's a defence mechanism the alp's triggered, that the forest will come alive and seek to rend me limb from limb. Having been through the Wilds of Faerie recently, it's more than possible with a creature like this. Hell, I was throwing around that kind of *talent* myself only recently, before I died that last time, fighting the Evil God alongside Aicha, Isaac, Jakob, and the two Bene Elohim. So it's a great relief when the flora starts spacing itself out again, opening up, and I see the alp in a clearing ahead.

He's hunched up, one leg crossed over the knee of the other, on a fallen trunk stretched out from one end of the small open space to the other. The coffee bag's open in one hand, and he spreads some of the grains across the flat of his leg. Then he pulls out a small silver pipe, the size of the smaller part of a bendy straw, and snorts a line of coffee. Jesus. Looks like I was right about the addiction substitution behaviour. That has to sting, surely. He wipes furiously at his nose, spraying snot everywhere. No wonder his nose runs like a broken faucet. The Good God knows what that must be doing to the blood vessels up his nostrils.

He springs to his feet and does a weird little jig, like the hornpipe being danced by someone being electrocuted. So not only is he a deadly vampiric magical being, he's now hopped up on the equivalent of a pint of espresso delivered straight into the bloodstream. Excellent.

I creep a few steps closer, trying to close the gap. My idea is to throw a magical box around him, so I'm watching his feet. He's skipping so quickly, I'm hoping there might come a split second when he leaves the ground completely, and I can throw a working up to cage him. Simple but effective. If I can make it work.

Problem is he's so damn fast. He's like a hummingbird on crack, and I'm only going to get one shot at this. He looks like Snoopy from *Peanuts* doing his dance but at ten times the speed, and with all the cuteness stripped away. My confidence that I can time this right is low, and the pressure's on. Fuck this up, and the man I consider a father might die. That's some serious stakes to ride on a single throw of the dice. Not just betting the farm but the family as well.

There should be some way to even the odds. There has to be. But in the end, I've no choice. Because sooner or later, he'll get enough of that crazy caffeine out of his bloodstream, and hightail it back out of here. I just have to go for it.

His feet are still almost a blur, and considering it's a toss-up whether he's dancing or having a fit, he doesn't seem to be blessed with a natural sense of rhythm. But I keep watching, totally focused on his feet, and I think, *think*, I've learned his pattern. As with all movement, unless we're trying really hard, we fall into the comfort of repetition, and strange as the alp is, I think I have his. Every fourth time he hops from his right to his left, there comes a moment of air. It's not Michael Jordan sinking a hoop, but it's there. I hope.

The pattern loops back around, and I can't have much longer. At the precise moment where I think he'll clear the ground... I throw out my working, hardening my *talent* into a box around him, feet first and a microsecond later the rest, putting him inside a two-metre cube, an invisible cage.

For a moment, I think I've fucked it up. He stumbles, so my assumption is I hit his feet with the working rather than sliding it under them. If he gets in contact with the soil, the base won't be complete. A transformation into any digger – a fox, a mole, hell, even a worm – and he'll be gone, escaped. Then the stumble transitions into a shift, and he's a swift again, his wings flapping upwards for the freedom of the blue sky above.

Sadly, for him, the freedom's illusory, and he smashes straight into my magic at full pelt. If you've ever had a bird mistake one of your windows for a clear opening, you'll know how well that tends to work out for them. Sadly, the alp doesn't break his neck –that'd be too easy, damn it– but he does crash back onto the ground of the box, taking up his natural shape as he lands. He glowers at his surroundings, no doubt *looking* this time and seeing the *talent* that cages him. Then he looks at me.

'Trapping. Releasing?' His liquid-granite voice pitches hopefully at the end. Why he thinks I'd go to all the effort of taking him prisoner just to let him go because he asked nicely, I have no idea, but the Good God loves a trier.

'Sure. Soon as you give me the hat.'

The creature looks at me hard, like he's trying to strip the skin off with his regard, to free all the delicious blood running wild under the surface. It's eerie and only made more so when his mouth splits wide open to reveal two silver fangs that Jaws from *James Bond* would have given his right arm to have. As long as it could be replaced with a metal one, I guess.

'Giving? Removing.' Hmm. That smile doesn't say, "oh you've beaten me, you clever little human; here, please have my most prized possession". It says "I'm about to fuck you right up". I'm on my guard, but the problem is I can't imagine how he thinks he's going to pull it off from over there.

He reaches up with a scab-ridden hand and sweeps the hat off like he's about to bow low to an anticipating court. Except he doesn't bow. No, he looks at me. With all three eyes.

Because that's what he has underneath. A third eye. And I'm not talking in the "open your third eye, sheeple" kind of way. I mean a literal third eye embedded in his forehead. And it's not one you want to look at.

I once played poker with a cockatrice who was a very bad loser, and he took to staring at me by the end of it like this, convinced I had cards stashed up my sleeves. How it thought it was going to check once it had me and everything I was wearing petrified, I have no idea, but I learned my lesson. Never play cards with someone capable of turning you into stone. Medusa was seriously disappointed, absolutely gutted the following week on poker night, but we all have to live with disappointment sometimes. And at least she wasn't literally gutted like the fucking cockatrice ended up being.

There's something very similar to what that whining cockatrice bastard pulled on me in the alp's stare. The strength in my limbs fades, dribbling away, and I can feel my knees buckling. I try to look away, but it's no use. There's some sort of element to the *talent* that locks you in once you're caught. Fuck.

As my physical strength drains, so does my *talent*. I can feel the power wavering, and now the panic starts to bite. Pretty similar to how I imagine the alp will in a minute, when I can't hold him anymore. Looks like I'll be a snack for him. I can just imagine him doing lines of the finest Colombian black off my broken spine as he eats my arms. Not how I planned this to work out.

I'm weakening, wavering, and I'll not be able to hold him much longer. There's one last role of the dice I can make. Throwing out a new working? Impossible. He's draining my magic quickly. So instead, I pull the spell I've already cast, condensing it into one single location, drawing it together, and throwing all my will and workings at it to do one thing.

In the air between us, a small square turns opaque, then solid black. Right in the middle of the space separating me from the alp, breaking our eye contact, blocking my view. It's enough. I flick my eyes downwards instantly, and the magic starts surging back into my veins, filling me once more. He didn't take my power, just blocked my connection to it. Now I'm back, baby. My hand shoots into my etheric storage and grabs a mirror I keep for just such occasions. Then I go back for my sword and get ready to throw down with the power-draining arsewipe.

Except, he's gone. The clearing is completely empty, with no sign or sound of life, no hint of any creature in the vicinity, magical or otherwise. Remembering the properties of his hat, I start *looking* around wildly, expecting him to be creeping up on me from behind, ready to tear my throat out.

Nothing. Looks like the alp's not looking to go toe-to-toe with a magic user in anything resembling a fair fight. Which means he's not stupid. Damn it. Smart villains are a pain in the arse. Why can't I get an idiot to go up against for once?

'I make a mean cappuccino!' It's not a lie, but it is a sign of my desperation. Maybe something fancy'll draw him back to the area. 'I've got a hook-up for java beans straight from South America!' Okay, that one isn't true, but if offering him the highest-grade product for his addiction gets him to show his ugly mug, it's worth a try.

Nothing. No response but the wind whistling through the branches, stealing the last few leaves.

The alp is gone. I'm alone on the mountainside.

Chapter Nineteen

Okay, let's see if Plan C is any less of a spectacular fuck-up
debacle. A fuckbacle. Now there's a word to describe my
life.

That didn't go as planned, it'd be fair to say. Then again, it
was my plan, so I never expected it to.

Doesn't stop me freaking out, of course. I'm still franti-
cally shouting out offers of lattes and mochaccinos to the
empty sky. But, after a small period of time wandering
around, making ever more convoluted offers of caffeine-
based delicacies, I accept that he's done a runner and isn't
coming back. There's nothing for it but to head back to the
car. On the way, I give Johannes a call.

'Did you get it?' I can hear the urgency in his voice, and
it brings my panic bubbling back to the surface so as I have
to stop and brace myself against a nearby young oak,
preparing for news that'll break me as much as Susane's
death did.

But there's no preparing for this. There's only been one certainty in my time as a Talented. Not that the sun will rise, certainly not that life will end. I'm proof against the latter, and there's been enough super powerful individuals over the centuries that would've been maniacal enough to blot out the sun if we hadn't exploded their brains all over the concrete first. No, the one thing I've known, always, is that Isaac's going to be there. Whatever hare-brained scheme I get myself involved in, however terrible times become, there'll be a warm fire and a welcome glass of whisky waiting, alongside a shoulder to cry on and a heart full of wise words and limitless love.

'No.' I don't have the energy to launch into the full reason. I need to know. Now. What's my failure cost me?

I hear that squeak of an in-breath that speaks of a lip being gnawed on. 'Okay. He's still stable, but it's a struggle. Mephy can't do anything else now except sit by his side, pumping his *talent* into him to hold back the other essence. You've got one night, maybe a day as well. No more.'

My breath simultaneously returns and hitches. Good God, he's still alive. Thank fuck. I have another chance. But only one.

'Is he well enough to move?'

The speech from the other end of the line becomes indistinct, muffled, then Faust comes back on the line. 'Yep, as long as Mephy comes along for the ride.'

'I'm going to give you an address. Take him there. Will Meph have to stay once you get there?' That'd ruin everything. Too many magical beings in one place to play my last gasp, my Hail Mary of a plan.

Again, the two of them discuss it inaudibly. 'He can stabilise him enough for tonight, but it means you've got to get it right. He'll be okay until morning, perhaps midday. After that?'

After that, my world falls to pieces if I don't get this right.

Guess I better get it right then.

There's one advantage to fucking things up on a regular basis; I never assume my plans are going to work. Especially when they're as tenuous as "hike through the forest shaking a bag of coffee".

Now it's time to put the backup plan into action. Unfortunately, this time it *has* to work. Has to. There's so much riding on this. More than I can bear to be gambling, but I've no choice.

Night's falling fast by the time I manage to shoo the owner of the cottage I've just rented away, having assured him that, no, I'm not intending to have a wild rave full of drugs and devil worship. I don't mention the fact that there's an actual devil en route. Mephy doesn't get worshipped – unless you count all the people who go gaga about him when Faust takes him out for a run in the park.

The cottage is only about a ten-minute drive from where I had my showdown with the alp, and it's the address I gave him for the borrowed coffee. Johannes was eminently confident that, if we lent him the grains and gave him the name and number of the house, the alp would come hunting for blood there tonight. All the rest of this plan is based on his knowledge of the creature, mainly based on folklore and superstition, considering the alp's not what you'd call sociable. Faust got it right about the coffee. Here's hoping he's on point for the rest of it.

It is perfect. Rustic in the extreme, with an old flintlock musket over the heavy oak mantle of the entrance. A trio of swords hang on the wall, although, having fought with a French cutlass for most of my life, these are clearly shop-bought props rather than heirlooms. Low-slung ceilings are picked out with black beams so thick you'd think they'd just shoved a whole tree in there to load-bear. The doorways between rooms are low enough that I have to remember to duck, and if we were staying here longer than a day, I can guarantee you I'd end up braining myself on one of them within a week. And the moment I see the two full suits of decorative armour – I mean, the guy who lives here genuinely seems to think he's the owner of the Chateau De Versailles rather than a country cottage – then I can't help but grin. I set to work, dragging them into position, one on either side of the door. I've just found my hiding place for the wait. Scooby Doo, eat your heart out.

There's only one bedroom, but that's fine. I've no intention of sleeping. When the others get here, we get Isaac settled into the four-poster bed, the blanket looking like a giant crocheted doily.

Seeing Isaac is beyond painful. He's pale, gaunt, a wisp of the man he is normally. I know there's still a spark there, even if it's guttering under the force of the demon essence, but I can't bear to *look* at him hard enough to find it. Not when I know I'll see only that last spark wavering. The pressure I'm putting on myself is already immense. I can't afford to make a mistake now. Once we're sure he's well – or, at least, as well as he can be while fighting for his existence against the infection – Faust and Mephistopheles help me into position, hauling me onto the standpost once I've pulled the armour on, which gives me something to rest against for the unknown period of time ahead, and then they're gone. There's no way an alp will come near the two of them. They reek of power and danger, far more so than even I do. He'd definitely go hunting an easier target if they hung around.

The next part is hard. Waiting. Never my favourite pastime. Right now, it's torture. Not only that, but my hiding place means I can't move, not a muscle, not if this is going to work. So, of course, approximately seventeen milliseconds after Faust and Mephy leave, itches start in the crook of my right knee. My left calf keeps threatening to cramp up, and sweat dribbles down my forehead, directly into that sweet spot on my eyeball that makes it burn like I just rubbed suncream straight onto it. With sandpaper.

Staying like this is never going to work. Luckily, there's an out of sorts. I dip off into my mind palace, a sort of virtual reality console for my own brain. It's a really sweet setup and, most importantly, a repository for all my memories. Here, I can separate myself away from the itches and demands of my physical body. What I can't do is keep an eye on the outside world. So I set a little simple tripwire of a ward on the other side of the door. Not enough to scare him but enough to cause a little buzz in my brain. Still, I'm nervous about something going wrong. Which means I'll probably pop out every few seconds, but I'm determined to try and last a few minutes at least. Distraction is key, so I head into my cinema room to watch *Beetlejuice*. After I got kidnapped by a Nain Rouge called Cyril who wanted to force me into letting him run havoc across Toulouse by a seemingly *Saw*-inspired Escape Game, I promised myself that I'd get a viewing in as soon as I could. So, amped up as I still am, I give it a go.

By the time it's finished, the night's creeping steadily towards the witching hour, and even Michael Keaton can't keep me distracted for much longer. If the alp's going to make his move, it'll be soon. Otherwise, we've misjudged this, and I'm about to pay the heftiest price I've ever had to pay for a bad call. And the Good God knows I've made enough of them and paid heavily enough each time.

Now it's getting really difficult. Every time I popped out of my mind palace, my bladder's been screaming. Locking myself away inside my brain has been the only way I've survived without ending up with a pool forming round my feet. Not that I care in the long run – wouldn't be the first time I've pissed myself, and at least it'd be for a better reason than "I downed half a bottle of absinthe for a dare" – but it'd give me away. That I can't allow.

So I have old Warner Bros cartoons running on the big screen, hoping the flashy colours and instant gratification of visual slapstick can pull my attention away from where it's really fixed, which is the world outside. Then the clock strikes midnight, and I see him.

He's no more attractive this time round. In fact, if anything, he's uglier, seeming to have hulked up and doubled down on his hideousness in the process. Where during the day he'd been reminiscent of a plague-ridden Quasimodo, now he's more like a Marvel Zombies version of Abomination, his muscles swollen and distended, all pustulant sores, his skin the colour of meat left to rot till even the most feral of street dogs won't touch it. The creature lopes into the corridor leading to the bedroom, entering my field of vision, and then, approaching the door to the bed chamber, he starts to shrink smaller and smaller with every step till I can hardly see him, only tracking his movement rather than really making him out. He can't be much bigger than a bee by the time he leaps up towards the door handle. Then the next second, he's gone through the keyhole, and into the room with Isaac inside.

I'd like to say I'm quick as a flash to respond, but there are limits to how fast it's possible to move when, like me, you're wearing a full suit of armour.

I move, just not at a full sprint. Don't get me wrong, armour's nowhere near as cumbersome as the films would have you believe. If someone knocked me over, I'd just get straight back up again and smash their face in with a metal gauntleted punch. None of that rolling about like an upside-down turtle nonsense. But it still slows me down a bit. So by the time I open the door and get inside, the alp's back to normal size, already crouching on the headrest of the bed, poised to leap.

Because that's the sort of nasty little bogeyman the fucker is. He's a night terror, a chest crusher. I'd call him a sleep paralysis demon, but frankly, that'd be insulting to Mephy. Once the alp gets on your chest, you can't move, frozen in place while he drinks his fill of your blood, revelling in your panic and terror. Utter shitweasel.

I jam up the key hole with a big wodge of Blu Tack I've been carrying for just this occasion, blocking it up. According to all those folk legends that have got us this far, an alp can only leave a room by the way he went in. Now he can't go anywhere. Not without going through me. And I reckon the suit of armour might even the score on that account.

The monster tilts his head, sending another globule of his nasal sputum flinging across to splat against the wall in the process. 'Trapping? Wanting?' The voice is grating, irritated. But not worried enough for my liking.

'The hat, alp. Give me the hat, and we're cool.' I'm not

a hundred percent convinced about that. He's still a blood-sucker, after all. On the other hand, he's just obeying his nature, following his instinct. And Faust couldn't find any evidence of him having killed anyone. Doesn't mean he hasn't, but it's not his normal modus operandi, at least. So if we can make a deal here and now, I'll let him live. The fact he'll be considerably weakened by losing his natty head-wear helps me feel better about it.

The alp swivels his head back and forth like a blood-hound searching for a scent. I can't help but wince as a great lump of nose secretion gets flung outwards, makes contact, and clings to my breastplate. It's only my imagina-tion, I know, but it's like I can feel it glooping down towards my groin. Grim. Utterly grim.

His head pricks back up in my direction, and for a moment I think this is it. We're going to rumble. Full on Hell in a Cell; two fighters enter, one fighter leaves. His muscles are bunched, coiled, and surely, surely, he's going to hurl himself in my direction in a shower of bodily fluids, the disgusting bastard.

Then he grins, and my heart sinks. 'Giving? Leaving!' The grating gargle to his voice carries a victorious, vicious tone, and I know I've lost. He has a way out. In a heartbeat, I spring forward, all the weight of the armour forgotten, determined to seize him. If I can get the steel wrapped around him, grapple him, I stand a damned good chance of nullifying his magic and ruining his plans. Fairy creatures don't get on with iron or any of its alloys. It's their version of Kryptonite.

But I'm not quick enough. Before I've taken two strides in his direction, he's changed into a hummingbird and is darting towards the window frame on the other side of the room. By the time I've taken another, he's already there and shrinking again, changing into some sort of flying insect, an ant or the like. Then, a second later, he's found some path of egress – a crack in the mortar or a gap formed by the frame shifting with time and subsidence, and then he's gone.

The alp's escaped. I've failed. Isaac's as good as dead already.

Chapter Twenty

Of all the prices I've paid for all the mistakes I've made?
This one outclasses them all.

There's a reason most knights had pages. Getting armour on and off on your own isn't an easy task. Luckily I give precisely zero fucks what condition it's in once it's removed.

I tear it from my body, grief and fury supercharging my strength like an old lady lifting a car off their beloved dog that's trapped under the wheels. Except it's not a dog. And there's nothing I can lift off, nothing I can do to save the man I may as well call Dad.

The helm's flung across the room, half-burying into the wall, sending up a plume of plaster dust. We'll not be getting the deposit back, but that's the last concern on my mind right now. Then I shuck off the gauntlets. Tearing at the rest, shredding steel as I go, I pull my phone out of my etheric storage with my right hand and call Faust.

'*It didn't work!*' I can't keep myself under control. The

words are screamed down the microphone, as though if, if I can just express all the agony of failure in this one sentence, time itself will take pity on me and rewind, giving me another shot at it.

'Didn't work how? What happened, Paul?' I hear the change of sound quality, a distance added to the microphone, and I know he's put it on speaker so Mephistopheles can hear.

'The alp escaped. He went out through a gap in the window frame. You told me he couldn't!' Good God, I know I'm being unfair. I do. I just can't help it right now. The guilt and anger are tearing me to pieces, bubbling over, and I have to lash out, or else I might just pull down this whole building on myself right now.

'Paul, I said I didn't think he could! The stories all say he has to leave by the way he got in. But that's all we had to work on. Stories. You knew that, well as I did.'

I do, of course. When dealing with rare magical creatures and the strange rules they're bound by, there's no detailed guidelines. Just rumours and fireside tales. Doesn't help in the slightest. I don't want to be assuaged. What I want is to have someone to blame, a way to offload some of this tsunami of guilt and despair that's threatening to drag me under and drown me. It's not Faust's fault. He did his best. Doesn't matter who's fault it is though. We've failed.

'*Fuck*!' The clattering smash of the phone as it instantaneously disassembles itself on contact with the wall is as momentarily satisfying as it is unnecessary and stupid. Right now I couldn't give a damn though. Nothing matters. Not compared to the enormity of the bill that's just come due for that whole messed-up escapade that kicked off with me hanging from the wall in the shit-wizard's basement seven months ago.

Though, I suppose you could say it all really started with the tussle of *talent* against Nicetas in Lavaur eight hundred years ago. If Nicetas had never concocted his fucked-up plan to bring the Evil God through, killing me and hundreds of other perfects in an attempt to drain our souls and fill the Holy Grail, would Isaac's life have been better? Without me in it, Jakob never would have been kidnapped and imprisoned in that skull. Ben only targeted him, only ever dreamed of capturing the power of an angel because of his vendetta against me. Others paying the price for my actions, all over again.

If it wasn't for our chance encounter outside Foix eight hundred years ago, they would've had the centuries together. I can't help feeling like I must have been a poor substitute, can't help wishing he'd had his brother instead of me. Still, if wishes were fishes... Well, if wishes were fishes, we'd have destroyed the entire world's ecosystem pulling every last one of them from the rivers and oceans, and we'd still be as miserable as sin as a collective species.

Heading over to the bedside, I can hardly see through the tears pouring down my face. In this case, it's no bad thing. It's unbearable to see this goliath of a man in all the ways that count – heart, mind, generosity of spirit and word – reduced to the pale knock-off imitation that's lying in the bed. There's no sign of Nith either, and that doesn't seem right. Again, deep down, I know the angel's in there, fighting to hold off this bizarre infection, to keep it from ravaging Isaac and destroying him completely, but I don't see Nith suffering. Only my oldest friend. Only the one who shouldn't have to suffer. Nobody deserves it less.

The next few hours pass like a blur. I alternate between furious denial and terrified pleading with any deity who'll be kind enough to actually exist just long enough to listen to my pleas. After, I'll happily go back to not believing in them, but for this moment now, I want there to be an all-powerful monotheistic god, and for them to pull their finger out of their arse and save my friend. Then I'm shouting and screaming at the force I met in that hut outside reality when I last died, fighting the Evil God, stuck between worlds, insistent they return the favour I did by stopping Nicetas. Fuck this extra shot at life they gave me. Take it back. Give it to Isaac instead.

Next moment, I'm crouched by his side, murmuring encouragement in his ear. He can beat this. He can fight whatever the fuck this demonic bullshit is that's got into his system. Good God damn it, he has a literal angel riding shotgun, and he's *Isaac The Blind*, creator of Kabbalah magic, one of the greatest Talented ever to live. Between the two of them, there's nothing they can't do. Beating back this poison can't be beyond him. It just can't.

Then I'm in the lounge, a whirling dervish of destructive energy. Part of me feels awful for the proprietor, but that little voice of calm reason has been pushed down deep under the weight of my unreasonable fury and pain. Furniture gets turned to kindling. Plaster crumbles under fist blows. The fake swords bend under the pressure when I use them to hack away at an Ikea coffee table that dares to stand in my way. If the living room was the demon essence, I'd have whittled it away to nothing. Of course, sadly, it's not.

By the time the first rays of dawn start peeking nervously through the half-drawn curtains, I'm spent. Sitting hunched down on the floor amidst the wreckage I've wrought of a once quite charming living room, everything is gone. I'm completely numb. No feelings left. Mentally, I'm calculating how much of a sum I'm going to need to throw at the owners to assuage their own quite-justified wrath, but it's just a distraction, a mental exercise to keep me from thinking. I don't really want to think anymore. I don't want anything anymore. Just for this night not to have happened, for me to still have a chance to save him.

My heart's shattered, and the last thing I want is to be sociable, to talk to anyone, so when there's a knock at the front door, it takes the last stagnant drops of my willpower to force myself over to it. I'm expecting to find Faust and Mephy on the other side, doing that ever-awkward dance of trying to commiserate and reassure simultaneously, searching for the words that might somehow work as a magic balm on my troubled and torn soul.

So it's fair to say I'm somewhat caught off guard when I throw the door open.

And there, on the raffia doormat straight out of the 1970s, waving a paper bag with a distinct aroma of a certain life-giving bean, bushy eyebrows acting as a visor against the glare of the sun, stands the alp.

'Lending. Returning,' he says and holds out the bag for me.

Okay, what the actual fuck?

Chapter Twenty-One

It would be entirely fair to say I didn't see that coming. But now I have a chance. Well, 'alp a chance at least.

I am momentarily stunned into silence, but my reactions kick back in a moment later. Fuck the niceties. My fist's flying forward almost before I can consciously think about it, power channelled into it like Goku on crack, and the alp's head snaps back at the crunching contact.

There's no letting up. No messing about trying to trap him with magic. No obeying the rules of interaction and hospitality that don't even fucking work when you really need them to. Nope. I just follow up the first jab with a left to the stomach and then bring a hammer blow down with the right to his temple, sending him to his knees.

But I can see him blinking. It's not enough. He's down but not out. Fuck. I swivel on my right leg to bring my left foot smashing into his jaw as hard as I can, and still, still, he doesn't get knocked out. Fucking creature's got the opposite of a glass jaw. A reinforced concrete jaw. The kick sends him rolling and skittering across the floor, but I can see his muscles are tense, not loose and limp. It hasn't worked, and now he has space from me. Enough space to transform. I start pulling my *talent*, aiming it at the surrounding air, trying to harden it, but that's a lot of area, and I'm exhausted. Deep down, I know I'm not going to be quick enough. In my heart, I know I'm going to fail again.

And I probably would have if a dark shape didn't spring from the shadows, hurtling forward like a lion towards an injured gazelle. A moment later, Mephistopheles' teeth are fixed round the alp's throat. Tight enough that, should he try to change, he'll be able to tear out whatever form of throat he comes up with or swallow him whole if he decides to shrink. Not even counting whatever sort of demon power Mephy might have in reserve should the need arise.

'I wouldn't try anything.' Faust's voice is still a little distant but close enough we can hear him without him needing to shout. 'We don't need you alive. Just the hat.'

'Needing? Needing!' The creature's board-stiff, terrified, but the inflection makes the meaning clear. Both parties involved feel they need the hat. Sadly for him, I don't give a flying fuck what he wants or needs right now. Especially after the night I've just been through.

In a second, I'm over next to him and tugging at the *tomkappe*. It's a tight fit, sitting snug on his brow, and I'm struggling to get it off. Makes sense, I suppose. If you're constantly changing shape and size – and species for that matter, with the prerequisite of maintaining a jaunty little number on your bonce whether you're an eagle or an earthworm – then it has to be able to survive the ride without falling off easily. After some dedicated pulling, a thought occurs to me.

Pulling a knife, I bend down level with the alp, his head poking out between Mephy's massive jaws. 'Look, you can let me take it off, or I can start sawing. Both work for me. I couldn't give a monkey's ass whether the hat's clean. We can transform it into a fucking redcap for all I care. Main thing is that you aren't wearing it and my mate is.'

The knife's blade wends its way towards the alp's cranium, and I can see his eyes tracking the movement. 'Giving! Taking!' he shrieks a second later. Good God, that was easy. I'm not used to people giving up quite that quickly. Not when I'm making the threats anyhow. It's normally Aicha who's much more effective at them. I guess the drive of the situation's severity was enough for me to bring Kandicha levels of intimidation. I hope wherever she is, she can somehow sense this moment happening, and she's proud of me right now.

When I tug on the hat this time, it's still snug, but it comes off in my hand. Of course the sneaky bastard was using magic to keep it in place. Probably an integral part of his *talent*. Either way, he's been de-hatted, and I have what I need. My interest in him is fading fast.

One of the great things about good friends is they understand when you're under enormous amounts of pressure and will excuse rudeness generated by it. Despite them having just saved the day, I don't spare Faust and Mephy a second glance. As soon as the hat's in my hand, I'm racing through the bomb site that was once a cute little living room, down the hall and smashing through the door to Isaac's side. A second later, the hat's on his head, and I'm praying. Praying to anything and anyone who'll listen to a desperate Talented whose heart and soul are resting on this actually working.

At first, I think it won't. There's no visible sign of improvement, no glowing halo as either the hat's power kicks in, or Nithael gains strength from it to kick the demonic essence's metaphorical ass. Seconds pass that feel like minutes. Perhaps they are. I can't tell, can't look away to pull out a spare phone and see. This is a vigil, and I'm pouring every single drop of hope I can wring from my ragged, disillusioned heart into this moment, willing Isaac to be all right, for the magic to work. And nothing happens.

My heart's beating harder and harder, faster and faster as disappointment and despair threaten to consume me. It feels like it could burst at any moment. Dying from grief always seemed like such an overdramatic turn of phrase even though I've done it before. My wife's death killed me over and over. But I knew I had bodies to burn, death after death to squander if I so chose. Now this might be it. And it really feels like it might be, like this could be the moment that a strange journey from Perfection to the imperfect person the years and my choices have shaped me into might finally conclude, and I'll die and not come back. Without Isaac, I don't know that I can carry on.

Then I see it. The plague-like stains around his throat fade slightly. The veins retreat back from their prominence, retracting back under the skin. The unnatural wraith-like pallor of his face fades back towards, if not normality, then a paleness that doesn't suggest he's already dead but that his body's not received the memo yet. His eyelids flutter, that weird return to awareness after a long time out of the phys-ical realm. Then they crack open.

'Paul, my lad? Is that you?' He places his hand on mine,

and I can feel the trembling weakness still there, but he's back. He's alive. I'll take that, no question.

'Nope, it's not me. I'm his evil doppelganger who just saved your ancient ass using uber-strange German fae magic just so I can kill you all over again, you daft, stupid bastard. Don't ever do that to me again...'

The words all just run together. I can't keep them separated, can't keep up the pretence of humour. But Isaac pats my hand, sees the glisten in my eyes. He understands.

'Bit of advice if you're going to dopplegang, lad. Try to make some improvements. Not to look so bloody hideous, hey?'

I laugh-snort, that mixture that comes uniquely when someone catches you off guard with humour when you're an inch away from collapsing into a flood of tears. It does the job though. Wiping my eyes with the back of my sleeve, I get myself back up from my position, kneeling by the bedside.

'Right, 'Zac, Nith. Lie there, rest for now. I need to go check in with Faust and Meph, see what's going on out there. Oh, also, don't take the hat you're wearing off. I've not dressed you up as Robin of Loxley for a laugh. If that was the case, you'd have woken up looking like Maid Marion. I'll answer the list of questions I'm sure you have when I get back, okay?'

Isaac's agreement shows he's still a long way from recovered. Normally, his inquisitive nature would have led to me being bombarded with questions no matter how much I insisted on the contrary. That he accepts the delay shows how badly he needs to rest.

I head back outside, wincing as I pick my way through the carnage of the sitting room. The apologies I owe to the owner are considerable and pricey. There's no way he's going to be able to rent the place out for at least a week, and that's assuming he can get builders on-site pretty much immediately. Whatever it costs though, I'll cover it. Least I can do considering I did more damage than a group of Marvel superheroes having a brawl with a Skrull. Shame I don't have my own clean-up crew that follows me around.

Back outside, Mephy's released the alp, who's sitting on the floor. *Looking* at him, which I only do for the minimal amount of time as he is spectacularly hideous and I really don't want to lose the appetite I've worked up by destroying harmless furniture for the past few hours, I can see he's wearing bonds made of the same tar-like goop running through Isaac's system. Mephy and the alp have clearly reached an understanding. The understanding being if he even thinks about moving, Mephy'll bite his face off. Right now? I have no problem with that, whatsoever.

I cock a thumb at the wretched little creature. 'What are we going to do with him?' As pathetic, if stomach-churning, as he looks now, I remember very well those silver-tipped teeth, him preparing to launch himself onto Isaac's chest. 'Does he live or die?'

'Choosing? Living!' The creature's voice sounds like a cement mixer in mourning. Guess he knows the odds aren't exactly stacked in his favour.

Faust looks pensive. 'What are you thinking, Paul? Don't you think we've got what we needed? What are you worried about?'

I love Johannes. He's a wonderful human being, with a heart as big as the sky, a razor-sharp academic mind, and he's a blast to get wrecked with, even if my head might not agree the next morning. But there's something about the naturally studious even if they like to party. Something he shares with Isaac. A certain naivety towards the world outside of text, from the nuances of reality. It can be charming. It can also be intensely frustrating. Sometimes, it's like they dig out a section of their own central cortex that deals with common sense and sacrifice it to the gods of book smarts.

'What am I worried about? With regards to the blood-sucking vampire wannabe fae whose hat we've nicked? The one who can change shape at will, access even the most tightly locked up room, and track like a fucking bloodhound? I've no idea why I'd be feeling concerned in the slightest!'

The alp looks up at me. It's going for a puppy dog look, but that's ruined somewhat by the mucus forming a sticky green Sancho Panza moustache down each side of his mouth. Somehow, the look has the desired effect on Johannes. He squats down, and his tone softens as he looks at the alp.

'Why do you need the hat? Do you need it to live?'

Good God damn it, Faust. That was the exact question I've been trying to make sure we avoided asking. Not that it'll make a huge difference. If the choice is between this weird creature's life and the man I consider a father in there, I won't even hesitate. What I will do is beat myself over the head with super-sized guilt repeatedly later.

The alp tilts its head, and I can see it contemplating, trying to decide whether to do that integrally fae thing of being utterly misleading while telling the truth. It's a skill they have down to a fine art. There's a moment, though, where he reaches a decision. If I've not missed my guess, he's decided that honesty's the best policy.

'Healing,' it says. 'Breeding.'

The horror of the latter statement is only underlined by it scratching one of its pustules, popping it so that a miniature torrent of ooze pours out of it, pooling on the floor. If that's what the hat considers healing, perhaps he's better off without it. Concerning the second statement? I've no idea what the mating habits of an alp are, but that's knowledge I can happily go to my grave – or any number of graves, for the rest of eternity – never knowing. There's already enough trauma in my noggin to last unlimited lifetimes, thank you very much.

There's a bit of a Bilbo moment though, seeing the foul creature dripping pus and snot left, right, and centre across the trim little pathway up to the cottage's front door. He's disgusting, sure, but I also can't help feeling a tiny bit bad even if losing the hat isn't going to kill him. There's another question that's been scratching away behind my eyes, demanding to be asked.

'Why did you come back this morning?' Of all the utterly mindfuckingly bizarre things about this particular misadventure, that's the one I just can't get my head around.

The alp looks up at me with its weird triple-orb stare, and it takes me a moment to read the expression. Affronted is the word for it. 'Borrowing. Returning!' There's a tone of disbelief in his voice, as if he can't understand why I even asked the question.

Faust looks over at me. 'That's right. There are stories about people who've interrupted alps as they were about to feed, distracting them with promises of lending them things, such as coffee, the following morning. They turn up to borrow what they've been promised, then the person tries to persuade them to leave both the victim and themselves alone. Of course, normally then anything given is in payment. It's what made me think of the whole taking the coffee out with you and trying to make a loan. He must have come to pay back what he borrowed!'

Oh, brilliant. So not only did I sucker punch the alp, but I did it while he was trying to repay me for the cup of joe he'd borrowed.

Faust looks up at me, serious, intent. 'We can't kill him, Paul. He's done nothing wrong.'

The Good God damn it, he really hasn't. Sure, he's a freaky little bloodsucker who scares the shit out of people with sleep paralysis. But he doesn't kill them, at least not as far as we know or can prove. Plus, if a lion's hungry enough, he'll tear a village of humans to pieces to feed himself. The offending animal might get put down – can't allow it to stick around once it has a taste for human flesh – but no one's suggesting eliminating all lions because of the potential risk they pose to humans. No one worth the time of day anyhow.

Basically, the alp's been doing nothing but obeying its crazy, magic-created nature. I have to say, *talent* is a far crueller mistress than evolution. Non-magical animals have developed in a way that best suits them to their environment. Magical ones? They seem to get a whole raft of fun abilities but with such strange and twisted constraints as to hobble them half the time if you know their secrets. I might not believe in an overarching god, an omniscient being who creates and controls everything. What I do believe is that some absolute dickweed definitely kicked off the whole magical beings popping into existence thing. There're too many built-in design faults for it to be any other way.

The alp was minding its own business, merrily pootling about the mountainside when I turned up, fed its addiction, chased it around its backyard, set a trap for it, and then kicked the shit out of it and stole its most prized possession.

I look at Mephy, who's watching me with a look of canine amusement.

'Are *we* the bad guys here?' It's hard to believe, but the evidence certainly seems to point that way. Based on the chuffing laugh Meph gives, looks like he agrees.

Fuck. Don't get me wrong, it doesn't really change anything. 'Look, you can't have the hat back. Not while my friend's ill, okay? It's not possible.' Plus, if I'm honest, sorry as I feel for the alp right now, I'm not sure I really want it breeding.

Faust's been watching the whole exchange, wrapped up in thought, and I see him reach a decision. 'Do you have to feed on human blood to live?'

It's a good question and one the alp gives due consideration to. He puts on his thinking pose, which seems to involve him ramming his finger as far down his ear canal as is possible and then excavating great rich seams of earwax to flick into the nearby bushes. I can't see it replacing The Thinker as the standard pose any time soon.

'Needing?' His answer is drawn out, deliberated. 'Preferring.'

'Okay.' Johannes' voice is gentle, compassionate. 'I think we can help.'

'What? No!' Now it's Mephistopheles' turn to sound panicked and mine to try not to smirk. 'You can't bring that thing into our house, Faust! I have a finely attuned nose, a sense created to allow me to pick up the most delicate of scents and to treat me to an orchestra of information within it. Even you, you poor, half-sensed mano, must be able to smell that creature. It's like having spikes driven directly into my brain, like a rotting squid got zombified and crawled halfway up my nasal cavities, and that's with us outside.'

Mephy's agitation is clear. He's spinning around in

circles as he speaks, his head low. 'Imagine being inside! Being in an enclosed space! It'd kill me. I'd be struck smell-dumb or whatever the right term is for that. Stripped of the whole reason I stay on this stupid bloody plane. You want me to go back to the down below, don't you? That's what this is! It's all a tactic to get rid of me!'

The demon-dog's voice descends into a half-growled whine as he finishes, and he lies down, his paws over his snout as though trying to protect his poor schnozzle from the horrors he's envisioning.

Faust chuckles and walks over, giving Mephy a rub on the top of his head. 'Calm down, my friend. I'm not suggesting he moves in with us.' He turns his attention towards the alp again. 'Could you live here, at least for the time being?' he asks, waving his hand at the cute little cottage.

'Living? Staying.' The alp nods his head furiously, sending great dollops of sputum flicking back and forth, slamming into a nearby rosebush and peppering the front door, narrowly avoiding Mephy's forehead, which elicits another growl from the already unsettled demon-dog.

'Good, so here's what I suggest. I'll get you some fresh animal blood from the local butchers; the one in the next village over is run by a werewolf, so he should be sympathetic to your requirements, and we'll keep that refrigerated and available. Then, when I do you the deliveries, I'll bring you a couple of pints of my own blood so you still get some of the human variety from time to time. You can't have the hat back, so that's the best offer we can make you.'

The alp scratches at his chin, popping several grape-sized buboes in the process, sending more globules of pus splashing down to his feet, like the most vomit-inducing version of Alice's pool of tears you could ever imagine.

'Dealing. Accepting.' He nods once, firmly, unleashing a last half-litre of snot to splash at his feet. The dude really needs to stop snorting coffee on the regular and take up something less dangerous to his health. Like injecting heroin straight into his eyeball.

So with that, we reach an agreement. The deal is made.

Now the question is – what state is Isaac in?

Chapter Twenty-Two

SALZBURG, 27 OCTOBER, PRESENT DAY

I hope the creature doesn't mourn his hat too much when in
the mountains. That'd be an alp-pine scene.

It takes a considerable shower of money being rained down
upon the cottage owner to get him to calm down enough
not to either have an aneurysm or call the police when he
arrives to see the state of his cottage. That's then followed
with a deluge, a veritable monsoon of money, to get him to
agree to part with the building altogether. We're all long-
lived to the point of immortality with wealth to match here.
Excepting, perhaps, the alp, but I've not exactly got into the
nitty gritty of his finances and investment portfolio with
him. Even so, the number required to be transferred is a
string of ones and zeros large enough to make a dent in
even my bank account. Still, it's worth it just to assuage the
mounting guilt.

By the time we've calmed down the initially enraged
landlord by making him significantly richer and me signifi-

cantly poorer, it's early evening. The stress and sleep-depri-
vation of the last couple of days is hitting me like a ton of
bricks stuffed in a giant's sock and then wielded by said
giant as a billy-club to batter me senseless. I crawl into the
back seat of Faust's car, wearily hoisting myself in and even
doing up my seatbelt –safety first, kids– before Extreme
Fatigue calls its big brother Complete Exhaustion in for an
assist, and I don't so much as fall asleep as get dragged
kicking and screaming into unconsciousness.

Next thing I know, the gentle rock of the car frame over
crunching gravel pulls me back to, if not full consciousness,
then sufficient awareness to know we're back at Faust's
house. With a bit of fumbling, I get the seatbelt undone and
even manage to swing myself out of the car without face-
planting. No small task. Then it's inside and upstairs,
clinging to the ornately intricate bannister, shielding my eyes
against the harsh artificial lighting and the loudness of the
clashing décor. Groping down the corridor, I find the door
to my room. I get in and kick off my shoes, then turn,
taking off my jacket, and do the world's least graceful
corkscrewing swan dive onto the bed. A fraction of a second
later, darkness takes me, and for the next ten hours, that's all
she wrote.

When I do come to, it's to the shocking harshness of
sunlight streaming in rows through the wooden slats of the
shutters, making a cartoon jail cell of shadows on the
bedspread. I'm not going to lie. I don't feel recovered. The
last number of hours –Forty-eight? Seventy-two? It's too
much like maths for my bed-befuddled head– have been
seriously tough, both physically and emotionally and
massively draining. What I really need is a week sitting by
the fire, drinking fine spirits and ignoring the existence of
the world outside my front door. What I get, instead, is to

find out how much crisis has been averted and how much it's simply been distracted by the gaudy flashing lights and temporarily slowed down.

Such cheerful thoughts get put aside for the time, though, when a smell, heavenly in its promise of both greasy sustenance and tasty delivery, wafts up the stairs and seizes me by the nostrils. The next few seconds are like one of those old Warner Bros cartoons, where I'm practically dragged bodily from the bed, floating on the odour, down the stairs, so taken by it I can even ignore the screaming pastel orange paintwork, and hauled into the kitchen. A kitchen that is comparative to the size of a small flat, and of course, in complete contrast to the rest of the house. Because why have one style when you can mash them all together into a hideous abomination that'd make an interior decorator poke their own eyes out with a paint roller? At least I can understand the choice for this room. Faust and Mephy have gone super modern, all sleek chrome surfaces and appliances. It's the Terminator of the kitchen world. I half-expect the fridge to start interrogating me as to the location of John Connor.

Sat round an industrial-style kitchen table – black steel struts supporting a polished wooden plank – are the other three, but I don't even see them, mainly because of what's on the table. Bless them all, I don't doubt they'd have loved to go full-ham – sausages, bacon, those weird things that are bits of organs shoved into other organs, all of it. Instead, there's some scrambled eggs fluffed to a consistency that is surely only possible with a kitchen of this quality – and presumably the aid of a Michelin-starred chef – and a pile of pancakes, apparently made from the milk of human kindness and the eggs of the hens of deserved self-indulgence. I can feel my eyes widening, trying to become the size of the fine white china laid out for me, to drink it all in, to devour this feast of perfection with my eyes. There may be words being said; a tiny part of my brain, the miniscule amount not entirely fixated on the food can hear murmurings, like the sound at a public swimming pool when your head's submerged; it all just washes over me. I sit down, load up my plate, and set to work clearing it of every morsel in the least amount of time my jaws and gullet can manage. The answer? Not very long. I reckon I can beat that time though, so I load up and have a second go at it.

By the time I've worked my way through plate two and am loading up my third attempt, I've enough spare capacity left to look at the other people in the room with me. Mephistopheles is opposite, sitting on his haunches, perched on a wide-seated kitchen stool. Johannes regards me with amused indulgence, like a parent seeing their kid tearing through wrapping paper in a haze of excitement and sugar-fuelled mania on Christmas morning. And Isaac?

Isaac's smiling, looking at me with a strange gleam in his eyes, like he's close to tears or else to laughing or perhaps even to both at the same time. I stop chewing halfway through a mouthful.

'What?' I manage to get the word out despite being mid-mastication, only spraying half the table with pancake crumbs. Style and panache are my key defining aspects.

'You look like someone took the Ravenous Bugblatter Beast of Traal, starved it for a month, and then released it on a poor, unsuspecting population of pancake people, lad.' All right, that was pretty good. I still think mine was better. Time for a witty riposte.

'I know you are, but what am I?' Perfect. Killer delivery. Absolute zinger. No coming back from that one.

Isaac's eyes crinkle further, and he cracks. The laugh

that rings out is a soothing balm to my soul. Not going to lie, I've been far from sure I'd ever hear it again. That sound makes everything – all the bullshit we've gone through the last few days – the demon zombies, the near plane crash, the parachuteless skydive, robbing the alp – all of it worth it.

'Thank you, Paul.' He's calmed back down, and those three words are delivered quietly but with conviction.

'You're welcome, you old git. Next time you end up in the shit, tell me instead of keeping schtum until it's almost too late, okay?' Damn it, these pancakes must still be really hot. The steam's getting in my eyes, stinging them. I've no choice but to wipe them on the back of my sleeve.

Isaac nods, the humour gone, a much more grave expression in its place. 'It almost was. You're quite right, lad. My apologies.'

I look at him, really look at him. Not magically –I'm sure Nith is okay, and I can do without the headache that comes from staring directly at a Bene Elohim– but just appraising his wellbeing. His skin's taken on some colour again; that terrible drained effect has dissipated, at least somewhat. But he looks tired still, his skin drawn, the bags under his eyes a bruised blue. As much as I want to be able to chalk this up as a victory and get on to the next problem, I don't think he's out of the woods. Not yet.

'How much has it helped?' I nod my head at the felt cap perched at a jaunty angle. 'Also, don't think for one moment this makes us your merry men. I'm still the leader of this particular band of outlaws.'

They think I don't see the look they all share, a look that speaks of communal indulgence, like humouring a temper tantrum. I see it. It'll all be remembered, mark my words.

'Whatever you say, lad.' Isaac's tone is even more annoying, verging on smug. Bloody hell, what does a fearless leader have to do to get some respect around here?

Isaac rolls up his sleeve and shows me his arm. The black poison's retreated; his veins are back to normal instead of looking like he's about to pull a full-on Akira any moment, but the essence isn't gone. Not totally. Around his wrist is a band of black like a shitty tattoo of a watchstrap, a neat delineation between hand and arm.

'Nith says he's got it under control.' Isaac's voice is calm, measured, and I don't know if he's talking like that to help keep himself from getting stressed out or to help me keep cool.

'For now.' Mephy's voice is as growly as ever, but I can hear the effort to soften the blow with that particular line. I appreciate the effort, but it doesn't help.

Isaac nods though. 'He's right. Nith says the healing magic of the alp is keeping the essence at bay, but it's also trying to…change me.'

Panic floods me. I already know, but I don't want to know. Maybe it isn't that. 'Change you how?'

'Change me into an alp, lad.'

Damn it.

Chapter Twenty-Three

I really don't get it. Someone needs to give me an 'alp-ing hand.

Jesus. I've no idea what effect that'll have on Isaac's brain, on his reasoning capacity. Will he become like the simple, strange creature we left behind in the mountains, speaking in two-word answers, interested in nothing but drinking blood and getting high on caffeine? I suspect if that's the answer, Isaac will prefer death, obliteration before such a fate. But there's still the unanswered question about what will happen to him if the essence consumed them both entirely. Would it create a super powerful puppet for the demon to control? Would it create a whole new evil being? Or would Isaac just be gone, dissolved away in the tar-like sludge, devoured, finished? None of those are good options or even options I can live with. I need a better choice.

Now the panic's coming back, a reminder that one day, when all this madness calms down, there's some serious trauma and damage I need to find a way to deal with. The last few months have left their mark, and I'm a whole sight more jittery than I used to be. I look wildly across at Faust, at Mephy, not even having to speak. The question's there, clear in my stare, demanded by my eyes. How do I save him? How do I properly, totally save Isaac?

Faust turns to look at Mephy, who meets my stare, sympathetic understanding in his ink-black eyes. 'There's only one way, mano. Only one. Get me the bastard who did this.'

Even if there's a level of unimaginable difficulty – capture a manifest demon - to the act required for saving Isaac, it still calms me down. It's doable. That's all that matters. Doesn't matter to me how impossible said act might be. There's a chance of saving him. That's what counts.

It does bring up a number of other questions though, questions we've been far too busy to talk about or address, what with going *Grand Theft Auto* on the alp to get his hat. Now seems like a good time to start asking them. I take a moment, trying to work out how to phrase the questions all clearly and concisely.

'What,' I say to Mephy, waving my hand up and down Isaac's arm, 'in the everloving fuck, dude?'

Isaac gives a cough that I think might be intended to cover a snort. 'I think what our learned friend is trying to ask is, how is this possible? Nithael has no idea. In fact, he's quite insistent that it's not!'

Okay, maybe that was a more succinct way to put it. Because that's it. As far as I understand it – or understood it anyhow – the whole supposed rivalry between angels and demons that we get from the Abrahamic holy texts is bupkis.

What I gathered from conversations with 'Zac and, by extension, Nith is that while the demons have a bee in their bonnet about the Bene Elohim, it's all seen as a bit of a non-event by the angels. They're not threatened by them in the slightest; plus, and here's the point where it all stops making sense, *the demons are supposed to be powerless against them.* So how in the name of all the dimensions did we end up with demonic essence that can not only disrupt Nith's and Nan's power, which somehow De Montfort got his hands on, but can actually infect and overpower both an angel-bearer and an angel working together?

Mephy shuffles uncomfortably on his chair. For a moment, I assume it's the answer that's making him get like that. Then he leaps down and lands on a rug and precedes to drag his bottom back and forth on it, a look not far off ecstatic plastered over his face. Then he jumps back up, looking both deeply sated and slightly guilty.

'Sorry, was driving me mad. Needed a good scratch. Only time I miss fingers and opposable thumbs. When I want to really get access, you know, to get at an itch. To be able to get right deep up inside…'

'Meph!' Faust's interruption is as timely as the anecdote was horrific.

The demon-dog looks at us all, baffled. 'What? Oh, right. The issue with Isaac.' Meph's never understood our hangups about discussing pleasure. His attitude is if it feels good, go for it and then discuss it in great detail. I'm not entirely sure how Johannes survives some of the barrage of over-sharing.

Mephistopheles looks at each of us, then slowly lowers his head, bringing it down, down, his tongue drooping out towards his…

'*Meph!*' Now all three of us shout at him. If ever there

was not a time to be publicly pleasuring yourself, even in dog form, surely now's that time.

He mutters something about prudish humans but doesn't fellate himself in front of us, which is a win. Instead, he drags his concentration back to the matter at hand.

'So you're wondering how *that* happened?' He nods at 'Zac's wrist. 'Well, so am I.'

I bite back a groan but only just. Fucksake, I thought we might actually get some useful information, but apparently Meph's just as in the dark as we are. That is, until he carries on.

'How much do you know about the history of the angels and demons?' The question's aimed at Isaac, but I know I can read the subtext to his tone. The real question isn't "how much do you know"; it's "how much has Nithael told you?"

Isaac frowns, that kind of deep engraving of the lines where the flesh folds up, like the thoughts are digging so deep into the brain as to pull the skin in with them. It takes him a moment to answer. 'Not...that much.' I can tell the admission hurts. I'm not sure whether it's because he hates not knowing or because he's upset, injured by Nithael withholding it. Probably a bit of both.

'What do you know?' Mephy's tone's still gentle despite the ever-present growl. Pretty considerate of him considering we've interrupted his fun twice.

'Well, I mean, only what I've asked.' Isaac's tone wavers, uncertain. 'Obviously, I wanted to know about the connection between you, but, well...' He breaks off, still deep in thought, still with hurt intermingling with the thinking process, judging by his expression. 'Nith's always been a bit evasive actually.' He sighs, pinching the bridge of his nose. 'I always read it as dismissive, but evasive is definitely a better word now I think about it, and he's being very quiet right now, I can tell you. All I know is that he assured me that demons are no threat to angels, that their power cannot harm them, and that the enmity we've been given as gospel, no pun intended, isn't actually true. And then he's always changed the subject.' His tone goes hard, with a frosty bite to it. I'm pretty sure there's going to be some strong words exchanged with Nithael when he gets a chance.

Mephy chuffs. 'Typical bloody angelicos. Always on that "holier than thou" pitch, pretending that they're better than everyone else. They aren't better, mano. Not at all. They just went a different way, that's all.'

A different way. Hang on. A thought occurs to me. 'Are you saying that angels and demons were once from the same family? The same species?'

The demon-dog's tongue lolls out, taking advantage of the opening made by his canine grin. 'Quite right, mano. Quite right.'

Well, I'll be blowed. This is quite the revelation. Judging by the shocked and hurt expressions on both Isaac and Faust, it's news to them too.

'So, hold up, what happened?' I'm really confused. How did they end up heading in two such massively different directions as to finish up at two extremes of the dimensional ladder?

'Well...' The grin goes, although the tongue doesn't. 'Therein lies a long and twisted story, but suffice to say our civilisation reached an *understanding* of sorts. How to live forever but without using up the limited resources of a material plane. Now, for various reasons, we were dividing into two main factions, anyhow, over enormous stretches of time, but then came a crunch point. A decision. Do you want to go all cerebral, locked up in the essence of pure thought, taking delight in contemplation and meditation?'

Meph's eyes flicked up as he said the last part. Now he looks in the opposite direction. 'Or do you want to go down and get your party on? Where everything is permitted but no one can get hurt, and "do as thou wilt" is the whole of the law? Also, guess which place has the best cocktails and musicians? Unless you're happy with an eternity of harp playing, that is.'

I've no idea how much of what Mephy's saying is imagery and how much is reality, but I don't doubt he's simplifying it. Both so that we can all comprehend and also to make the angels look like a bunch of dicks.

'So how come Nith was so convinced demons couldn't hurt us?' Isaac's words are as tight as his expression – cut, clipped.

'Well, that's the point. He should be right. We're at different ends of the vibrational spectrum. Even when we're here, tied into the physical with these inferior frames – well...' Meph looks at us, then at his paws, then down lower at something else we're all trying not to pay attention to. 'Your inferior frames, anyway. Whatever. We shouldn't be able to interact with each other. Different frequencies. Angelicos and demonicos shouldn't be able to mix, certainly shouldn't be able to *infect*. But it has. And the angelico's still stuck with the same problem. Can't touch the demonico essence inside Issac's body. No doubt the old bird-brain thinks he can find a way around that because there's no one more arrogant than bloody Elohim, but what he's been finding out in the last period of time...is that he can't.'

There's not just one genius in the room with a wounded pride over their significant spiritual other having held out on them. But Faust's more invested in finding a solution.

'So what changed? And why?' I can almost hear the cogs in his head turning as he searches for the answer, trying to get there before Meph can give it.

The demon-dog cocks his head at Isaac. 'They did, of course. They changed it all.'

A look spreads across Isaac's face, one of dawning realisation with a chaser of horror to follow it down. 'Are you saying this is our fault?'

'Yep. You two − or four with your brothers involved − changed the rules. The angels came here and stayed. And what difference did that make, eh?'

The demon's teeth are bared slightly as he looks at Isaac, the growl rumbling again, and I know he's not talking to 'Zac but to his silent partner, the one who knows all this and didn't think to share the info.

Isaac goes quiet for a minute. And it hurts to see him looking like this. I get the impression these revelations are hurting him more than his battle with the essence threatening his very existence. Nine centuries of partnership, only to start learning these sort of basics now? Nith might only be guilty of omissions rather than straight up lying, but there's not a huge difference between them. Certainly not as far as Isaac's concerned, and I don't doubt they're having a little internal chat while he has us all on mute. Then he pops back, and the shock's reduced. The horror hasn't. It's just quieted, but it's still there in his eyes. 'It anchored the realms to this reality.'

Meph grins again, panting, his tongue like a matador's red cape waving for a mouse-sized bull. 'Exactly, mano. Exactly.' Then he bounds down off the chair and heads over to a water bowl, proceeding to slurp at it noisily and with evident delight.

Which leaves the three of us sitting around the table,

shell-shocked. And still somewhat in the dark, at least in my case. 'I don't get it. Sorry. Can someone explain why the dimensions being anchored is an issue, taking into account my inferior brain? Words of single syllables or cartoon diagrams will be appreciated.'

Isaac stands and starts pacing back and forth, across a few tiles of the floor, covering the distance so quickly he seems to be almost doing an elongated pirouette. 'The higher dimensions aren't supposed to be anchored. The lower ones neither. Look, you understand that there's a multiverse out there, right?'

I scoff, insulted. 'Of course! I saw the animated *Spiderman* film.' I'm basically an expert in the multiverse now. Thanks, Marvel.

'Well, it's not quite that simple...' Isaac must see my expression closing because he adds hurriedly, 'but it'll do for now. Point is, yes there're lots of different realities, infinite numbers branching off, intersecting and separating and starting and ending, right?'

Okay, that makes sense. 'Right.'

Isaac's in full-on lecturer mode now. Good. It seems to make him forget to be pissed off at the same information he's thrashing out. 'Well, those branchings are reflections of the cycle of mortality. Some live. Some die. So many changes but always expansion, Yggdrasil's growth pushing outwards through eternity.'

A bit poetic, but it's an image I can get my head around. He's paying attention to the instructions I gave him at the start. Good man. 'Okay. Go on.'

'Well, part of the whole vibrational shift was the angels and demons taking themselves outside of those splitting, changing realities. They separated away, sealing themselves into a single, continuous plane. If there are no alternatives occurring, no branching off, no different versions…'

This might be the simplified version, but it's still making my head hurt. I think I have the gist though. 'Then there's no way for them to get hurt or to die?' I look at him suspiciously, resisting the urge to nurse my now-aching head with a stiff drink. Nine in the morning is too early to start on the booze. Best to wait till second breakfast at least.

'Eh, close enough.' I can tell that both my friends are itching, practically bursting at the seams to start breaking out chalkboards and drawing up theoretical equations that would probably either lead to them inventing a whole new subgenre of magical theory or the world going pop like an overfilled balloon. Neither are things I wish to get involved in. Another thought strikes me, and I narrow my eyes. 'Is this all *quantum*?'

Isaac sighs in relief. 'Yes, exactly.'

'Right.' I nod positively. I understand quantum. It means "impossible-to-understand science but which explains everything, so just smile and nod". Those are instructions I can follow to the letter. I smile at the two of them broadly for a moment. But then my smile vanishes.

'Hang on, that still doesn't explain how you've changed things!' I feel like I've just got hustled, conned in a street magic trick – watch the dancing ball; don't see the left hand whipping into your breast pocket and relieving you of your fob watch and bulging wallet.

Isaac resumes wearing a groove in the tiles. 'That's correct. Obviously Mephy's a bit busy right now.' He cricks his head at where Meph is still face down in the water bowl, now doing his damnedest to blow bubbles and inhale all the liquid at the same time. 'But I think I get it. Nith and Nan coming down. That's anchored the planes to this reality. Am I right?'

The question's aimed at Meph, who pops his head up and winks at 'Zac. 'Absolutely correct. At least that answers the question that's been niggling at me forever.'

I shouldn't ask. I know I shouldn't. But still I do. 'What question?'

'How the hell you've survived so long, mano, even with your ability to reincarnate. Somebody had to have smarts in the team. Certainly isn't you.'

Ouch. Savage burn. I think I'd rather take a ride around the fiery lake. Less chance of me getting toasted.

Meph pads over, sighing contentedly, and leaps back up onto the bar stool. 'So, yep. The angels coming *here* meant this became an anchor point for the other realities. That's why I'm here.'

Now it's Faust's turn to look shocked. 'What do you mean? I thought that was down to me!'

'Oh, it was.' Meph clocks the expression on his friend's face and hurriedly tries to make amends. 'Absolutely incredible magic, really top-notch. Quite unbelievable for a puny mano, actually. Without that, I'd never have been able to make it across, never been able to stay. But the same is also true about their presence. I needed both of them.'

Based on Faust's expression, I'm not convinced he's managed to pull off a save here. There's a look of silent anger on both the other men that speaks of their absolute fury over their supposed best friends, closer than a husband or wife could ever be, withholding the one thing they treasure above all else. Knowledge. Specifically, in both their cases, forbidden arcane knowledge. It's the air they breathe, the lost ark they hunt each and every day. Both Nith and Meph have messed with academics. They done fucked up.

'Mephistopheles.' Faust's voice is low, quiet. Dangerous. 'Did you know you needed the angels in order to be here? Are you, perchance, here because of the angels?'

'No!'

Johannes' brow unfurls slightly. For a moment.

'Well, yes, of sorts, but not only that, no.'

Okay, this is definitely giving me a headache, and it has to be evening time somewhere. Fuck it. I stand up and walk towards the cupboard where I know Faust keeps his hoard of spirits. Of the alcoholic kind. When dealing with the likes of Faust, probably best to clarify that.

'Right, this is all far too intense. Who wants a drink?' Honestly, if I'm going to survive the rest of this conversation, I need a glass of whisky in my hand to get me through it.

Judging by the two hands and a paw in the air, looks like I'm not the only one.

Chapter Twenty-Four

I'm not saying booze will help. But it'll definitely make a
spirited attempt.

Settled back at the table but this time with the soothing *clink*
of ice on glass to work like a meditation gong and the
whisky ready to give me a warm hug, I feel able to concentrate again.

'Okay, this is getting pretty convoluted. Let me try and
get this clear. Angels and demons used to be mates but got
pissed off at each other?'

'Same species, but yes, close enough, I guess.' Isaac
corrects me. Ooh, approximating in front of academics. I
do love to live riskily.

'They went their separate ways, and because of *quantum,*
they no longer can interact.'

'Well, it's not that they can't interact…' Isaac sees my
expression, and for once, reads it absolutely correctly.
'Right, fine, yes. Carry on, lad.'

'But now because of Nith and Nan popping down for an extended vacation, they're, what, vibrating differently?'

I see them all rolling this round their heads like the whisky round my glass. In the end, Johannes nods. 'Not far off actually. More like it adds in an additional harmonic. One that both of them now share.'

'Making them able to now do each other damage. Meph, you're what? A spy for the demons? A balancing agent? For the light, there must be dark, yin to their yang. What exactly?'

Mephistopheles is sitting, hunched down as low as he can, his front paws on either side of a saucer of whisky, his eyes peering down his long snout half hidden by the bowl. 'Pretty much, mano. Though I'm not in contact with the other dimension. No more than they are. Just, we knew they were here, so when opportunity arose for me to come, it was felt wise.'

Faust narrows his eyes at the beast again. 'Felt by who?'

Meph shakes his head, his muzzle firmly closed. Apparently that's above our collective pay grade. Very fucking irritating but not the most pressing matter at hand.

There're questions unanswered that we've still not even got to. 'But what about the energy that's infected 'Zac? Where's that come from? And why were they working with De Montfort and Nicetas?'

Now Mephy raises his head, and the concern's clear to read on his face. 'I don't know, mano. Really, I don't. What benefit would the destruction of this world bring to one of my own? I can't understand it. As for them infecting the angel-bearer?' His lip curls back, and he looks like he'd like to bark in frustration, though whether at what they've done or his own ignorance, I can't tell. 'It shouldn't be possible.'

There's one other question we haven't raised. I don't like

asking, but I have to. 'Mephy, do you have any idea who it might be?'

The Dobermann-demon's head pops up, outraged. 'Know who it is? Why? Because you think all demons know each other? I bet you reckon we all look the same too. Do you know what that is, mano? Do you? That's racism, that is. That's…'

'Calm down, Meph.' Faust's gone from looking irritated with his old friend to amused again. I guess with the well-spring of information we're gleaning this morning, he's prepared to forgive Mephistopheles for holding out on him. 'You aren't a race. You're a whole other set of beings on a different vibrational plane. We've no idea how many of you there are. There could be a hundred of you or a hundred billion. We're clueless. Don't blame Paul for plugging you for info, especially when we've already proven you've been holding out on us, hmm?'

He arches his eyebrow on the last point to emphasise it, and Mephy gives a small whine that tells me Faust hit the bullseye with that particular gesture. 'I'm not holding out on you by choice, Johannes! It's not down to me.'

A statement that just raises more questions than it answers, and the demon can tell. He casts a despairing look around the room. 'All right, fine. Look. There are and always have been definite factions who don't like the angels, all right? That much I can say.'

'But why?' I hold a hand up to get him to hold on before answering, then pound down a good hard swig of the whisky. I need a safety blanket before we get into more brain-stretching infernal politics.

'Well, as you can see by us being here, it's possible for us to travel up and down the dimensional ladder. It was the angels who imposed the terms of the agreement on us, stating we had to stay off the material plane. Personally, I couldn't care less. Don't get me wrong,' he adds, seeing the affronted look on Faust's face. 'I'm having a whale of a time. Top tier fun. Would one hundred percent definitely recommend. But when you do die eventually, mano...' There's a kindness to his words, the verbal equivalent of a pat on the head on a favourite pet you know you'll outlive many times over. 'When you die, I'll head straight back home, and I'll not be in any hurry to get back up here. There's an endlessly entertaining infinity down there. I love the giggles here, and I'll definitely be taking the blueprints for this body back with me, but still, it's so very *limited*.'

The wistfulness in the demon's voice on the last word is evident for all to hear, and Faust turns away quickly, trying to mask his expression. I don't quite catch what it is he doesn't want Meph to see. Hurt? Guilt? Either way, by the time he turns back, he has his features schooled.

I decide to pull us back to the matter at hand, both to help them and to get to the crux so as I can start seeing a path forward. 'Okay, so the angels shut off interdimensional travel, and there's a group of demons who're pissed off because it stops our plane from being their personal sandpit. Am I right?'

'Crude but fair.' Mephy nods, then takes a good slurp of his whisky. I don't know how Johannes ever manages to go out on the lash with Meph and not get arrested. I'd be horrified if I saw a dog drinking like that out at a bar, and this is the demon in restrained breakfast drinking mode. When he really lets loose, he puts the most serious drinker to shame. Mephistopheles is why they coined the term 'booze hound'.

'So do you know who it might be?' I'm trying not to sound impatient and failing miserably.

C.N. ROWAN

'There are some options.' Fuck me, it's like trying to get a straight answer out of the fae.

Meph feels the combined weight of our three glares burning into him and hunches inwards, whining. 'Okay, look. Straight answer, yes. I have some ideas, but I can't just go throwing their names about, all right? Who it is shouldn't make that much difference. Whichever demon they are, you'll need to do the same thing. Capture them and then either bring them to me or bring me to them. Doesn't matter which; both will work.'

With that, the gigantic Dobermann invests his concentration into his saucer of hard alcohol and studiously ignores us all as he laps at it. I look around at the other two. Equally consternated and troubled visages peer back at me.

'So I think that's all we're going to get out of him for the moment. Does anyone know how to restrain a demon?'

Nothing is immediately forthcoming, but I'll be honest, I wasn't expecting anything to be. As far as we know, Mephy's the only demon on Earth – or was till some douchebag jumped over to tag-team in with Nicetas. This is unknown territory. I wrack my brains, trying to think about legends, religious texts, anything that might help us out.

'What about the *Lesser Key of Solomon*? How much truth is there in all that?' I think that's a pretty pertinent question on my part. Also known as the *Ars Goetia*, it gathers together a list of seventy-two demons, stating their powers and their position in the hierarchy of hell, as well as methods for containing and commanding them. It's all deeply apocryphal information, and in normal times, I couldn't be less interested in trying to pull creatures up or down from the other dimensions. But under the circumstances, what's the point in having not one but two erudite scholars in your party if they're not able to give you the goods when it comes to rolling a D20 for a knowledge check?

Faust strokes his chin, thinking back. 'Well, I've chatted to Meph about it, and he confirms the demons listed are all correct. My general assumption about that was the author managed to summon them for limited periods of time. As with the angels, brief visitations are possible. It's more, erm, long-term accommodation that's unusual or outside of the rules.'

'Okay, anything in there to go on?'

The two scholars look at each other doubtfully. No doubt they're trying to separate the useful information from the dross in that particular esoteric text by telepathy. Isaac answers eventually. 'It's not impossible... There are certainly some glyphs and symbols for containing demons.'

'But,' Johannes butts in, concerned, 'those are glyphs for containing them in summoning circles, when they're not fully manifested here. I'm not convinced they'll work when the demons are actually physically in our world. It's the difference between hanging up on someone when they're rude on the phone and trying to do the same thing when someone turns up and starts screaming at you at work. One is much easier to deal with than the other.'

Isaac's nodding sagely, clearly impressed by his logic. I don't know why I never got the two of them together earlier. It's like they're destined to be bosom buddies. Perhaps it was just an instinctive reaction to the likelihood of their respective companions not seeing eye to eye.

'Okay.' I can feel myself getting restless, the need to move, to do something starting to kick back in. Don't get me wrong, I'd love to take a trip to the Bahamas and go lie on a beach for a couple of weeks and forget about anything stressful, but the problem with Isaac's not gone, just delayed.

Plus, knowing my luck, I'd end up getting assaulted by a pack of randy harpies and a lovesick kraken. Again.

'Okay, right. So we don't know of any definite way to restrain a demon, *but* we've got two of the finest esoteric researchers ever known to humanity on the case. I have faith that one of you will come up with the goods. Not that it's a competition, of course, to see who gets the answer to this incredibly obscure, almost impossible to crack enigma.'

Oh, reverse psychology, you weapon of winners. Now both of the clever bastards are still staring at each other. Oh yes. But now it's with grim countenances, weighing stares, each trying to take measure of the other's mettle and worth. For two genius-level intellects, they sure are easy to manipulate, getting their competitive natures fired up. Should I feel bad about using my cunning wiles to influence them into doing my bidding? Probably. Do I? Not in the slightest. If I had a brain the size of a planet, I'd try to at least devote a small portion of that brainpower into not getting suckered. They're many times smarter than me. If they can't pick up on a simple trick like that, I'm afraid that's on them. Plus, if it helps me save Isaac's life, I'll trick anybody and everybody, and Isaac's not excluded from that.

Mephy gives me a bawdy wink. It's his form of a round of applause, the original act of which is blasted difficult to do with dog paws. I know because I've seen him try to pull it off before. 'I've nothing to add to that, manos all.' He gives a sneeze halfway to a chuff, then shakes the last remnants of it from his head. 'I'll help Faust. There's no surefire way to contain us on this plane that I know of. Between the two of us though, I'm sure we'll crack it.'

'Hey, that's not fair!' Isaac's voice rises, indignant. 'Having a demon to experiment on gives him an unfair advantage in this competition!' He flushes slightly, realising what he said. 'Not that it is a competition, of course. But even so, in the totally-not-the-case scenario of this being a competition, I'd like it to be noted by the judges that he has a significant advantage.'

'Theoretically noted for the totally non-existent situation you've not mentioned, Isaac,' I say wryly. 'Okay, which leaves us with one last, extremely pressing question.'

The three of them look at me blank faced. I can see their mighty servos picking up speed, chuntering away, calculating, trying to work out what they've missed, what essential piece of information we've not considered, what set of facts we've not effectively dissected.

Eventually, though, they give up. 'No.' Isaac scratches the back of his head vigorously, clearly put out at having to admit it. 'I've no idea what it is.'

I look at them flabbergasted. It's as plain as the nose on their faces. 'How are we going to get home again?'

Because I am telling you right now, there's precisely fuck-all chance I'm getting back on board a plane with Isaac while this demon's hunting us. Not on your life.

Chapter Twenty-Five

The only way you're getting me onto another plane is with
a fucking portal through reality. Although considering
recent events, I probably shouldn't tempt fate.Isaac

At first, the others aren't convinced we should leave. After
all, the demon attacked us on the flight between Dortmund
and Salzburg. There's no question in my mind though.

'Look.' I try to make them understand. 'All the prepara-
tions that De Montfort made? All his carefully laid plans?
Were all made in either France or England, and all were
aimed to come to fruition in France. We don't know for sure
why the demon's targeting us – whether it's to kill 'Zac and
Nith or whether it's another reason, something to do with
whatever they were up to with Team EGW.'

Isaac's hand shoots up. 'Goodness, I know I'm going to
regret this, but who's Team EGW?'

'Team Evil God Wankbugles. De Montfort, Nicetas, and
the like.'

Isaac slumps back down. 'Right, I can confirm. I do regret it. Carry on, lad.'

'Okay. So not only are the chances higher of us picking up the demon's trail if we go rather than sitting around waiting patiently for him to come and ambush us, which let's face it, we were fucking lucky to walk away from last time –'

'Fly away from last time.'

I stare at Isaac, my jaw dropping in solid disbelief. 'I'm sorry, are you auditioning for the role of Aicha in this particular amateur dramatics performance? Knock it off, will you?'

The interruption is almost made worth it by the charming shade of red that Isaac turns. 'Right, sorry.'

'Apology noted and filed away for further later inspection, at which point a decision will be forthcoming as to whether it's been accepted or not. Anyhow, where the fuck was I again?'

'How we were lucky to fly away from the last ambush.'

'Right. Quite. Look, point is, if we're fumbling about in the dark, they can just keep coming in on the offensive. I know here we've got Faust and Mephy to back us up, but back there, we're on home turf. Plus we can start chasing down any leads as to how they partnered up with Demon Fart and the whole EGW Team. Yes, Mephy?'

The dog demon has his paw in the air, which would be adorable if I didn't know he could make me wear my internal organs on the outside for a change if he put the effort in. 'This question's for Isaac. Is he always this puerile?'

Isaac nods gravely, sadly. 'I'm afraid he is, my friend. Despite my best efforts. Incorrigibly immature, he is.'

Mephistopheles' expression matches Isaac's. 'I'm so

sorry. So terribly, terribly sorry for you. It must be almost unbearable.'

I snap my fingers. 'And now you're back in the room, and you can remember I'm here rather than being a pair of rude dickheads. Point is, 'Zac, once we get home, you can dig through all your own...' I pause, thinking. 'Texts? Treatises? Parchments? Fuck it, let's just go with research material. Then we can go and have a look at Demon Fart's base of operations over by Paris easily enough, as well as see if we can't sniff out where he was camping out when he came down to Bugarach before putting the whole "tear the veil asunder, start the apocalypse, bathe in rivers of blood" project in motion.'

I wait for dissent. Not just because I've put forward a good argument but because that's just what I expect from my friends. I put something up for consideration; they try to tear it down. If they can, I rethink, or else I argue harder. If they can't, then we might have a workable plan.

Silence reigns. Guess the plan's a goer.

Except then I remember this isn't the plan. This was just the eventual aim, getting everybody on board with it. Now we need a plan.

'So...' I sigh, feeling the weight of the burden of being the one having to do the thinking when surrounded by geniuses. 'At the risk of repeating myself, how the fuck do we get back home?'

Isaac looks at me, baffled. 'Plane?'

Fucksake. That gets a negative finger gun, the "shoot that shitty idea down in a hail of bullets" finger gun. 'No. Next.'

Meph chuffs. 'Drive then.'

It's possible. We could drive, but it's going to involve a lot of stops, and I'm not in the mood for a road trip. As much as this is all very jolly, and I'm a hell of a lot more relaxed now Isaac's not about two and a half inches away from dying, it's still some way from all the pressure being off. Isaac's still infected by demon essence, and Aicha's still missing. They both need to be resolved as quickly as possible. A three-day drive – two if we really push it – isn't getting us there the way we need to.

'How long will the train take?' Faust pulls on his bottom lip, playing with it like a stress toy.

I pull out my phone and fiddle about with the search results. 'If we're lucky? Fifteen hours. Unlucky? Twenty-five. Fuck!'

I know. I know I've just spent three days basically on a jolly, trying to trap the strangest little bloodsucking fuckknuckle imaginable, but the only thing that was pressing on me at that moment was the possibility of Isaac dying. Now that's receded, my urge is to get into the mix, to find an answer to what the hell is going on more long term, and catch the scumsucking pond-life who thought it acceptable to try to kill everybody on board a plane just to take us down.

So I want to get *home*. I want to get home, top up my energies. Fuck it, centre my chakras or realign my third eye, however you want to put it, and then get on the hunt. Thinking about third eyes reminds me of another reason to hurry. Nith said the hat's going to turn 'Zac into an alp eventually if he doesn't take it off, but if he does, the demonic energy'll start rampaging again. The clock's definitely still ticking, even if it feels like the pressure's eased off a touch. It can easily come roaring back on any second.

We may have no choice. 'Mephy?' *Please say yes, please say yes.* 'Do you have anything that could keep a plane safe while we're on it, keep it protected from a demonic attack?'

Mephy growls, a deep dark vibration rattling around his chest cavity that speaks of a desire to rend and tear. 'No, nothing short of me going with you. I'd be able to counter the effect.'

Okay. Well, actually, that's better than nothing. It means pulling both him and Faust away from their research for a day, but it gets us home quicker.

A thought occurs to me. 'Johannes, could you and Meph do the research you need to at ours?' Hell, if we all travel there together, the three of them can crack on, safe inside the angelic wards while I go hunting demonic wascally wabbits. I quite like that idea.

Faust sucks in a breath between his teeth, a sound like a T on the inhale that speaks of doubt. That or a pretty shit impression of a kettle. 'I suppose we could, but I'd be missing lots of resources. I spent a lifetime studying demonology before Meph arrived and several since. All my notes, texts —'

'Research materials as the Philistine put it.'

'The Philistine already told you to stop interrupting, Zac.'

'Right, yes. Sorry, lad.'

Faust watches the interruption ping-pong back and forth with a wry smile. 'Yes, thank you, Laurel and Hardy. As you've so kindly put it, Isaac, yes I wouldn't have all my research materials. It would hamper our work, I think.'

I look at the three of them. 'So day trip for you two to Toulouse, then turn around and come back again?'

They all nod. Brilliant. Just a couple of days after the plane I was on got absolutely pulverised, and I nearly got torn limb from limb by possessed passengers, we're going to get on board a commercial airliner again.

Fabulous.

To minimise the risk, we decide to drive over to Munich and fly from there. It reduces it to one single leg where we have to be alert for trouble, and we'd lose as much time in the air as we do on the road as it's only an hour and a half to get there.

We pull up in the closest parking. The car's only going to be here for a few hours. Plus, when you look at the amount we ended up spending to buy a cosy forever home for the alp, even airport parking starts looking cheap.

We get lucky for once, which fills me with absolute existential dread because if there's one thing I'm not supposed to be, it's lucky, and I'm just waiting for the other shoe to drop. Probably complete with running spikes. Right on my face. Anyhow, there was a plane going four hours after we decided to risk it and enough space on there for us to book four single tickets going there, and two back.

Everything runs smoothly, which only adds to my sense of impending doom. We sail through friendly, efficient security with casual waves of our psychic paper, Meph included as Faust's emotional-support guide dog to everyone but Johannes' intense amusement. We stroll onto the aircraft, having had time to grab some impossibly complex and even more impossibly expensive coffee concoction involving milk, syrup, and apparently a Master's Degree in Fine Arts to complete the patterning of chocolate powder on the top. There are no delays, no waiting for air traffic controller slots, no people having panic attacks and demanding to get off at the last moment. There aren't even any business bros being snooty towards the cabin crew. Everyone seems to be impossibly friendly and polite. We leave early. Early!

Surely something terrible is about to happen any second.

But no. We come down with a graceful bump onto the

tarmac in Toulouse a bit shy of a couple of hours later, with smooth flying and a comparatively gentle touchdown. There's even a smattering of polite applause from the passengers, although I've never quite understood that. Congratulations! You didn't kill us! If I did that every time I was in mortal danger, well, I'd have two very sore hands. Although, to be fair, it's fifty-fifty odds most of the time whether I end up dead or not. Or was before my last death, at least. Compared to our flight eastwards, it all just feels very normal and ordinary, and I'm inordinately grateful. I may not develop a phobia of flying yet. Considering the backpack of trauma I'm currently carting around with me, I'm very appreciative of not adding anything more into it.

We say our goodbyes to Mephy and Faust, with promises to keep in touch.

Then start the tedious trek through the airport. It's not the biggest in the world – nothing like some of the gargantuan monstrosities like Dubai or Paris Charles De Gaulle, but we still have the joy ahead of queuing to get through passport security. At least we don't have bags to collect. You can guarantee if we did, there'd be some sort of delivery failure, and we'd be hanging about for another hour at least.

When we join the back of the line to get our passports – or in our case, our teeny bits of magical paper checked – I'm feeling pretty good actually. Sure, Isaac's not cured, but we've a game plan. Get home, charge up, find the demon, kick its ass. That's the sort of simple strategy with a single digit number of steps I can get on board with. I'm tempted to slide into the left-hand side lane, which is reserved for flight crew and V.I.P.'s – and totally empty – but we're in a lot less of a rush thanks to managing to take the plane rather than having to fuck around with any of the alternative options for getting back here. So I luxuriate in a moment of just standing in line, waiting my turn.

Which turns out to be a good thing. It means that as we slowly advance on the plexiglass box the frontier police are sitting in, we have time to watch them. At first, it's just a case of observing how they treat the various people — their frustration when people don't have their passports ready, the subconscious or institutionalised biases that make them take longer on this person than the next, studying every detail of their face and document before finally waving them through. However, as we get closer, it's not just us studying them anymore. I become uncomfortably aware that they're taking a lot of interest in us too. Far more than I'd expect. An unhealthy amount, it'd be fair to say.

By the time we're about five passengers back, the two police officers in the booth aren't even trying to hide their attention. They're staring at us openly, and I don't think it's because they're overwhelmed by my good looks. The one on the right, his hair cropped tight to a head so square you'd think he accidentally got it trapped in a trash compactor, pulls up his walkie talkie and starts murmuring into it. I can't hear the words, but there's a sense of urgency to him, and his eyes never leave us.

This does not look good.

Chapter Twenty-Six

TOULOUSE, 28 OCTOBER, PRESENT DAY

Not drawing the attention of armed agents of the mortal
authorities? A good general police-y to live by.

Isaac's been fairly oblivious up until this point, but after
getting a few significant and sharp nudges to the ribs, he
clocks what's going on. I'm just considering cutting out of
the line entirely, perhaps heading over to the toilets when I
become aware of a looming presence in the empty left-hand
lane. Turning, I find a squad of police officers. I notice their
hands are all resting on their weapons, ranging from a
holstered pistol to a fully automatic HK-G36 that could cut
a man in half and not even notice any real depletion of
ammunition. I'm not entirely sure it's really what you want
to be toting around inside an incredibly crowded building
when the weapon's firing velocity could punch straight
through all those elegant glass windows and keep going
through the nearest aircraft wall without breaking a sweat,
but then automatic weaponry isn't really my area of special-

ity. Give me a nice sword and the ability to melt people's brains and make them dribble out of their ears. Far more civilised.

I can't help noticing that not only are hands on their weapons, but several of them are less resting, more gripping, and even pointing them, if not at us, then ready to whip up before we can draw breath if we say or do the wrong thing. This only further reinforces my earlier analytical assessment that this *does not look good*. I turn up my charm to the highest possible setting and flash a million-kilowatt smile.

'Hello, officers, is there something the matter?'

Good God, I' forgot how difficult it is to talk to people of authority without instantly acting like the dodgiest criminal ever to walk the planet. It doesn't matter how innocent you are, the minute there's a figure of law and order looking at you, the urge to fidget, to babble incoherently and inanely, to shift and shuffle becomes almost unbearable. Even in a perfectly air-conditioned environment like an airport, even if it's the middle of winter, it doesn't matter, sweat will start beading instantaneously on your forehead. I can feel it running down my cheeks and pooling around the neck of my T-shirt even though I know I've not done anything wrong. Sorry, let me rephrase. Even though I know I've not done anything wrong that should concern the mortal authorities. Actually, I'll add on to that – that should concern the mortal authorities that they could possibly know about.

None of these thoughts are helping me to look cool and collected, I can assure you. My brilliant smile's flickering. I can feel the filament is about to give up the ghost, and my facial expression is becoming less confident happiness and more of a pained grimace as every millisecond ticks by. Still they don't say anything, and now I'm starting to get seriously worried.

Then the man I assume is their leader steps forward, a stocky bulldog whose salt-and-pepper hair colour speaks to experience. Possibly experience tearing human beings in half as a party trick, looking at the size of his biceps. He leans over slightly, his eyes never leaving my face, his left hand still on his holster, and unclips the cord acting as a guide rope to separate the two lanes.

'If you'd both be so kind as to come with me, gentlemen,' he says, and I'm impressed. All of the words are impeccably polite, and yet he still manages to convey that he'll destroy us both without breaking a sweat should we dream of disobeying him. It's no mean feat.

Of course, we could take him. Even without using magic I'd fancy my chances, and with *talent* on my side he'd never stand a chance. He might have decades of gym training and dealing with roughneck criminals on his side, but I have centuries of warfare and slaughter in my back pocket. Plus magic. They don't have anything that can equal that in their armoury.

Except that means hurting them. At best it means unleashing chaos in a busy public transport terminal and disarming a group of highly trained soldiers. I don't know why we're being sought by the authorities, but I can't imagine that would de-escalate the threat. Plus, it only takes one trigger to get pulled at the wrong moment, and real innocents might get caught in the crossfire. I can't risk that. Isaac and I exchange glances and then fall in with them. The leader strolls ahead, never looking back, which considering the firepower they've brought to bear due to our suspected threat level, takes some balls. Then again, considering the squad of heavily armed men and women he has flanking us, ready for action, I suppose that probably helps to reassure him.

On the flip side, the further we go into the system, the more we're recorded, our presence noted, our details taken, and the harder it's going to be to completely disappear again afterwards. Not impossible, of course, but I don't want to have to perform the magical equivalent of the plot of *Face/Off* every time I leave the house. What I want to do is go home, have a nice cup of tea, followed by a nice cup of whisky, then put my feet up and for all of this to disappear. Sadly, we don't always get what we want.

This situation could rapidly get out of hand if I don't deal with it. No one's really sure if the authorities know about *talent* and the Talented, not really. Personally, I'm pretty much certain they must. Somewhere, in each government's shadiest, most forgotten about building, there's doubtless some bunch of patriotic lunatics trying to work out how to defend the nation against fae invasions or enraged dragons. Those are people I never, ever want to meet. Unless I'm gravely mistaken, they'll be zealots totally dedicated to a notion of the flag. Dangerous people. Always.

I'm torn. I want to extract more information about what on earth is happening, why we're being escorted under heavily armed guard. Hell, for all I know, this is it. The jig may be up and the Talented world exposed. Perhaps men wielding machine guns all over the world are about to find out at exactly what temperature their gun barrels melt. If that's the case, we're going to enter into a struggle that'll make World War II look like a bit of a tiff, a pub brawl. A scrap behind the bike sheds over a half-crushed packet of nicked cigarettes.

On the other hand, it might not be that at all. In which case, the longer we stick around, the more chance we have of accidentally giving the game away. Going down in history as the clumsy buffoon who blew the Talented world wide open isn't how I want to be remembered. So I'm not going to take the risk. This sort of peaceful resolution is more Isaac's normal wheelhouse, but I don't want him pulling on his *talent* at all. It might accelerate one of the current magics coursing through his body. Demon or alp. I don't want him changing into either.

So it looks like it's down to me. Luckily, illusion magic is a forte of mine.

We're still progressing down the hall, although there's an ominous looking door coming up, clearly marked as off limits to all normal personnel. I reckon that's our destination. Time to act. The walkie talkies of all the soldiers suddenly crackle into life in a burst of static and panic.

'... attack in the main hall. Suspect carrying a.... Several people hurt and...'

The radios fall silent, dead. Change, on the other hand, electrifies the hallway. All around me, the troops are gearing up. Wartime mode, that state of being they've had drilled into them is coming to the fore, triggered by what they've heard. Hyper awareness and readiness emanates from them all. Their eyes are fixed on their leader. Let's see what he does.

His qualities shine through. After an almost indiscernible moment of hesitation, he snaps into action. First he clicks on his radio, attempting to hail the team on the other end. Nothing but the crackle of dead air. Now he's in full swing, problem-solving mode, combat ready.

'Deneuve, Villiers, take the new recruits. Go straight there, remain in radio contact. If problems continue with handsets, you've got my mobile number. Go!'

I've not even bothered counting the surrounding

soldiers, but most of them peel off now. A good half a dozen. All we're left with is the leader himself and two other soldiers – a tall, lean woman who carries a scar from her left eye to the top of her temple that I'm fairly certain she didn't get opening a beer bottle and a younger guy but with eyes that speak of plenty of experience in his limited lifetime, who makes his captain look small. I thought it impossible to get into the police while jabbing yourself with anabolic steroids, but if he's not, then scientists need to consider studying him as some sort of new subspecies of humanity. Looking that hench naturally just isn't normal.

This is worrying. Seriously. I didn't exactly expect them to let us go; you don't bring this kind of firepower to bear on two people and then just allow them to wander off because another emergency's happening. This is hardly a "driving at fifty-five kilometres per hour in a fifty zone" sort of situation. But I expected him to leave us with one of the green recruits, maybe two while he went rushing off to deal with whatever mayhem has broken out. That he's stayed himself with two of his toughest looking SOBs suggests he considers us more of a threat *than people getting killed in the main hall in public*. Jesus Christ, what the fuck does this guy think he knows? Who does he think we are? Like, don't get me wrong, we definitely are the bigger threat, but I wouldn't expect *him* to know that.

Still, we've trimmed off the dead weight. There're a lot less guns being waved about, which means a lot less chance of someone getting shot by accident. Me included. Now to deal with these three...

I'm tempted – so very, very tempted – to just make them forget they ever saw us. Except that's mind magic. Dirty shit to be pulling. I'm no fan of doing it, especially not to the unTalented. That's the kind of thing that leaves psychic stains. On them and on me.

Similarly, I could just knock them all unconscious with a wave of my hand. That one's not off the table, not yet. I won't do it quite like that. I'll need to come up with a plausible reason why these three rock-hard military individuals just keeled over. The only thing holding me back is feeling bad for them. People like this build their entire identities around their work. It's their purpose for existing, their way of defining themselves in relation to the world, understanding their place in it. Something like this – letting two… whatever they think we are… get away – is going to be a black mark on their records. They'll have to carry that around for the rest of their careers, and it'll be a blemish that'll stain their existence. Maybe I'm being overly sensitive towards this trio of hard-cases, but I carry enough stains on my own soul, some my fault, some not, to be in a hurry to stick some on anyone else's. Especially when they've done nothing wrong. They're just doing their jobs, ma'am.

Whatever I'm going to do, I need to make a decision and do it. I've no idea how far we are from the 'main hall' – to be honest. I've no idea which part would even be considered the main hall – but sooner or later the other soldiers are going to find nothing more threatening than a luggage trolley with a rickety wheel waiting for them and come charging back. I look over at Isaac. He's watching me with patient faith, which is frankly unnerving. What I really need is Aicha here to yell at me, telling me how spectacularly stupid I am and to stop being a total clusterfuck of a human being and come up with a plan.

Hmm. Worth a try. 'Zac.'

'Yes, lad?'

'Call me a twat, will you?'

I'm not sure what he expected to come out of my mouth, but apparently it wasn't that. 'Sorry, say that again?'

'Call me a twat. Tell me I'm a total dickhead.'

I'm speaking in lowered tones so the armed police don't hear me. That combined with a little cone of silence means we can plan. While they're not taking their eyes off us completely – they'd be more than ready if we tried to jump one of them – you can tell their minds are off with their colleagues. As far as they're concerned, we're contained. They want to be where the action is, not babysitting prisoners, however dangerous they think we are.

Thank the Good God for the cone of silence. Isaac obviously hasn't picked up on the memo and just carries on talking at normal volume. 'You want me to insult you, lad? Really?'

Lord love him, but it's hard work getting Isaac to understand the insane way my brain works sometimes. 'Yes! Tell me I'm fucking useless. Tell me to come up with a bloody plan.'

'Oh. Oh!' I see the realisation reach his eyes. 'Right, well, yes. Paul, you're…you're frankly slacking. It's…it's not good enough. You need to pull up your socks and find a way out for goodness sake. Honestly, you should be ashamed of yourself.'

Fuck my life. 'Okay, I wasn't really going for "slightly miffed headmaster" as a vibe, 'Zac. Ideally, I'm looking for "deadly warrior demanding I step up my game". Do you think you can manage that? Call me a fuckhead, man. C'mon. Say it with me. Fuck…head.'

'Oh, my word, lad. Seriously? Fine, you are a fumckhd.'

The last bit comes out in an obscured mumble.

'Louder. Say it properly, dude.'

'Fuckhead. Okay? Happy?'

I actually am. A grin spreads across my face from ear to ear. Don't get me wrong, I still have no fucking idea what's going on, what sort of a shitstorm we've just found ourselves in the middle of, but hearing Isaac having to force himself to use bad language and then looking thoroughly embarrassed and wretched after using the F word? While we're surrounded by gun-toting government employees? Well, it brings a touch of much needed levity to proceedings. Sometimes, whether it's someone to laugh with or at or someone to clip you round the back of the head to get your brain working, that's all you need from one of your team...

That's it. Of course. The way to get us out of this without them losing face or us looking too damn dangerous.

Shift the blame to an outside party. An assist from a potential unknown teammate.

The problem is making it plausible. This isn't really my area of expertise – modern weaponry and general sneakiness. I'm much more of a "blow everything up with magefire, then stab them with the pointy end of a bladed weapon" kind of guy. Luckily, I don't have to be a genius. I just have to look like one.

The question is what's a believable vantage point? Looking through the windows at the outside, I can see the concrete barrier of the multi-storey car park. Perfect.

We can worry about setting up the evidence correctly afterwards. Right now, all I need to do is make it believable. Pushing my *talent* outwards, I let the tendrils link themselves onto the three soldiers guarding us. With the unTalented, the energy it takes to persuade them of anything is minor. I can basically go and have a chat with their subconscious and get it pretty much on board with any sort of crazy scheme I can think of. So getting them to take a nap? Not too tricky at all.

What's trickier is what I'm trying to pull with the head honcho. The message I send to him isn't 'sleep'. It's 'get very damn tired and also let's lock all of those muscles up from the neck down'. Which means he's swaying, his eyes going bleary, but he sees his two soldiers go down. What he also notices, thanks to a very easy to conjure up minor illusion, are darts sticking out of their necks, along with the tinkling of glass. What he feels due to my hotline direct to his central nervous system is a biting sting to a similar spot on his own muscle-bound neck. Thanks to the muscular paralysis, he can't raise his arm to feel there's nothing there. Even through the fatigue, I can see the horrified realisation hitting his expression. Now that I'm confident he's on board with the charade I'm aiming for, it's easy enough to send him off to slumber land too, and I let him keel over next to his colleagues. His little grunting muffled snores let me know it's mission accomplished.

Happy they're all out cold, I bend down by each of them, aim a hand towards the car park, and fire a tiny pellet of power out lightning fast, letting it smash through the glass from where I reckon their necks would've been before magic and gravity persuaded them to lie down. As it hits, I catch the fragments of glass that pop outwards, then pull them back through the new holes, letting them scatter across the floor on this side.

Perfect. Now we have a believable alibi for the trio as to what happened. An unknown assailant with a high-powered dart gun picked them off from the car park. The lack of evidence up there will only point towards a professional. We could have taken the darts with us. The lack of drugs in their bloodstream might be harder to explain on a tox scan, but they'll just assume it's some super cunning new knockout agent, probably of Russian design. Sure it'll makes us look even more guilty of whatever they think we're guilty of, but it'll do in a pinch.

All in all, I'm fairly proud of myself. No one's dead, no lives have been ruined, no careers ended, and we can go home.

'Good work, lad. Knew you'd handle it.' I try not to flinch, hearing the wearied tone of Isaac's voice. That's not supposed to be there; although we're in entirely uncharted territory, so how I dare have any suppositions at all, I've no idea. Maybe the hat's draining his energy; maybe the demon essence is making itself heard again. Anything is possible, and the lack of knowledge is stressing me out almost as much as how frail 'Zac looks.

'No worries. You know me, always the brains of the operation.' Isaac's snort at my suggestion alleviates a little of the worry. If he can still laugh at my clowning, then he's not too far gone. Although, then again, I am damnably funny.

We're about to head off, *don't look heres* in place, ready to be gone and done with the airport when the chief soldier's radio crackles to life. Not something I'd have normally paid attention to, except for the words that come over it.

'*Dead man…angel bearer…*'

Call me crazy, but I don't think those are this team's call signs. The odds are infinitesimally small. There's only one other person who might be calling us.

I don't even reflect. Perhaps I should. Perhaps grabbing up the walkie talkie and responding isn't the best idea. After all, it's definitely what this motherfucker wants me to do, the animated shitbag. But still, I've nothing else. Nothing to go on. And any chance to shed some light on what the hell is going on –no pun intended– is worth taking. At least, that's my defence. It could be argued I'm just acting without thinking. Again.

'Who are you?' Urgh, it's a horribly stereotypical way to open up a conversation with a mysterious bad guy, but let's be honest, there's a reason for that. I'm not really holding out hope they're going to slip up and reveal all their plans, but hey. I've seen it happen in movies. Maybe this is my Hollywood moment.

Sadly not. 'The question is not who but what?' There's a sound to the voice that carries even through the shitty quality of the plastic speaker. It's what primordial ooze might sound like if it got surgically given a voice box.

I blink. 'I'm not sure I agree with that.'

The oozy voice previously was dripping with malice. Now a bit of uncertainty works its way in. 'What?'

'Well, I mean, I guess you're going for the whole intimidating "you don't know the power of the dark side" evil emperor schtick. But we know you're a demon. And I don't really think you identify as an inanimate object, Darth Shittyus. So having established you're not human – and I can't really believe that you believed that was going to catch us off guard after everything we've been through – I'm not really after your particular genus of lower dimensional being. I was more asking what we can call you.'

'You can call me your doom!'

'Urdoom? Weird name. I'm going to stick with Darth Shittyus. Mind if I shorten it to Darth? Or do you prefer Shittyus?'

The transmission falls silent for a moment, and I think for a second they've given up on the whole attempt to intimidate us. Then it crackles back to life.

'A valiant attempt at distracting me. Not good enough. I've heard about your tendency to bluster and bluff, dead man. Looks like it's not unmerited. Right now, though, I wanted to talk to you about your current situation. How did you enjoy it, having the mortal authorities turn against you? To have them hunting you down? You and I are going to play a little game…'

I narrow my eyes. 'Cyril? Is that you?'

There's no mistaking the confusion this time. 'What? Who is Cyril?'

'Cyril. The Nain Rouge. Is that you, man? Are you fucking with me again?'

'No! This is…' The voice catches himself just in time. Damn it, that nearly worked. 'This is not he. Why would you think that?'

I shrug, which is wasted on the conversation but never mind. 'Well, because last time he tried to trap me, he kept doing the whole knockoff Jigsaw from the *Saw* movies – "let's play a little game" bullshit too. Didn't work out too well for him. I ended up burning down his living room.'

The voice chuckles, sounding like methane bubbles popping on the surface of an acid pool. 'You didn't, though, did you, dead man? That was your little Druze bitch. And she's gone. We saw to that.'

The light switches in my eyes. The filter comes down. I'm seeing red. 'Talk badly about her again, shit-for-brains. I'm already aiming for more than just a little arson in your case, you brainless cockgoblin. I'm going to fill your nasal cavities with lighter fluid and shoot fireballs up your arse till your face explodes.'

Look, I know it's the reaction he's looking for. You know it's the reaction he's looking for. Come and lecture me on keeping my cool when he insults your missing-presumed-dead best friend and gloats about their part in it.

None of that takes away, of course, from it being precisely the reaction he wants, and it settles him. I can hear it in the oozy chuckle, like tar pits pulling down an old junker. 'Now that's more like the dead man I was looking for. All big threats and showy magic and nothing underneath but fear and failure. So do you know what? I'm going to give you a chance. I'm going to let you go for now. No more normal humans hunting you. They've all forgotten about you – for now. Oh, no. They won't be hunting you. See you soon, dead man.'

The radio goes dead, and icy waves run up and down my spine. Despite what he said and despite how I might sometimes act, I'm not totally oblivious. The way he kept repeating, *you*, the way he kept stressing he wasn't going to keep coming after *us*, putting all the emphasis on those words?

I look up at Isaac and see the same worn concern on his face as I'm sure must be evident on mine. 'If they're not hunting us…'

He finishes my sentence, clearly on the same wavelength. 'Then who are they going to be hunting?'

Yep, he read it the same as I did. Who has the cumbubbler put in the police's target sights?

Chapter Twenty-Seven

No more mystery, please. Let's get Jerry Maguire. Show me demon-ey.

Our exit from the airport is uneventful. We keep ourselves veiled of course. I may come over as stupid sometimes, but even I'm not dumb enough to take the word of a demon who's positioned himself as our enemy. It appears he was telling the truth though. We pass by the group Team Leader Gunnery Sergeant Hartman sent to investigate my false disturbance in the main hall, and they're all just milling about, patrolling, looking entirely unfazed.

Isaac's Tesla is exactly where we left it, which was far from certain in my mind after what happened in the airport. 'Zac himself goes to just slide on in, but I pull him back. Then I get down on my hands and knees, have a good scout around on the chassis of the car, and pop the front bonnet and boot to make sure no surprises have been left there. I'm not entirely sure what I'm searching for; I think we've established I'm no expert on modern weaponry, but anything that looks like a bundle of dynamite with a ticking clock on it, basically.

Nothing looks out of place or unusual, and in the magical spectrum, the vehicle looks undisturbed. Doesn't mean it's completely clean; my knowledge of spy equipment begins and ends with *The Bourne Identity* and *James Bond*, so they could have placed some super modern miniature bug on it. That I can live with. I don't have anything I really want to say right at the moment, and Isaac looks too worn out, greyed around the edges, to get into the discussion either. If they want to listen to us blasting out the radio to help stay awake for the next twenty minutes getting home, that's up to them. As long as we don't get blown sky-high between here and there, I don't give two shits.

When we get home, I secure the doors, making sure they're locked and bolted. The wards are still up around Toulouse, but still, there was that period when they wavered, so even though he looks shattered, I get my old friend to check all the area and wards properly to make sure no one's meddled in our absence. Honestly, the odds are low, but right now I'm taking zero chances.

Next thing, having tended to the metaphysical, is dealing with the body's needs. Digging through Isaac's freezer produces a bag of frozen bolognaise, the defrosting and warming of which is about as far as my culinary capabilities can stretch tonight. More importantly than that, I go break out the bottle of Dalwhinnie and load us both with decent measures, complete with a single ice cube each. While the spaghetti's cooking, I give Faust and Meph a call. It's only just occurred to me that, considering what happened to us, they might have run into similar difficulties back in Germany, but I find out it was plain sailing for them. Filling them in, I hear Mephy growl when I describe the demon's voice on the walkie talkie.

'Do you know him?' I can't quite keep the hope muted in my voice when I ask. If we can find out who we're up against, it reduces the chances of them blindsiding us.

Mephy hacks, a wheezing bark, as if trying to dislodge a hair stuck in the back of his throat. 'Not certain, mano. There's a few that could fit that description. None of them are good news though. See if you can get me anything else to go on.'

'Brilliant. Not only useless but depressing and vaguely ominous at the same time. Thanks, Meph.' It's a bit harsh, but let's be honest, I'm not in the best of moods right now. The involvement of the unTalented makes me distinctly uneasy. Even De Montfort, hellbent on destroying the world as we know it, didn't get mortals involved, excluding the Grail hunters he'd kept on ice. I suppose had the Evil God managed to get through, that would probably have blown our whole secret wide open, but we had bigger fish to fry at that point. Kraken-sized ones.

'Calm it, mano. We're all on the same side.'

I want to snap at him, to tell him how I don't feel like anyone's on my side right now, but that's petulant bullshit. If I hadn't already known they have my back – which I do when I'm not feeling like an angsty, pissed-off teenager – then they more than proved it by saving Isaac. This is just me lashing out at friends. Once is forgivable. Repeating it is just being an arsehole. More of an arsehole.

Apart from that, we've little to report from either side, so I end the call, trying to ignore that sinking feeling. It feels like slim hope drowning in the pit of despair. A pit filled with a viscous black tar.

And we've still not addressed the other issue, the one that really has me panicking. 'Who's it going to be, 'Zac?'

Isaac startles, almost dropping his beaker. He must have half-dozed off. There's no way he'd have endangered the precious liquid in his hand otherwise. As much as I'm trying to ignore it, he looks wan, worn out. It's not doing him any favours to keep pushing him, but I'm far from convinced he's going to accept what I want. For him to stay here, to research what he can while I go and deal with the demon. Assuming I can fucking find him, of course.

He looks at me sheepishly, which hurts in my chest. There's no reason to feel embarrassed considering what he's going through. 'Sorry, lad. Off with the faeries there for a minute.'

'Really? I didn't hear agonised screams or see torrents of blood erupting from your general vicinity.'

Isaac tuts, but he can't quite stop the corners of his mouth turning up. 'Not literally, as you well know, you blasted fool of a lad.'

'I prefer "fool of a Took" if you're going to go with that sort of phrasing.'

'You're a bloody long way more rash and irritating than Pippin, my lad. You need to show a bit more brains and restraint if you want that title.'

Ouch, talk about a savage burn. 'Anyway, any ideas who the demon might go after? Because I don't know about you, but I'm not sure they could have been more obvious about their intentions if they'd just told us, "We're going to fuck up someone you love for the fun of it." There's one of our people about to catch it in the neck, but who?'

There's no answer. Isaac's eyes are closed; even under the shadow of his felt cap's tip, I can see it. Leaning forward gently, I pluck the tumbler from his relaxing hand. He's had enough shit of late without having to deal with waking up to glass shards all over the floor. And probably his crotch, looking at how he was holding it. Then I tip what's left of his glass into mine –because it's still thirty-year-old Dalwhinnie. I'm not wasting it. Are you mad?– and tiptoe outside.

Whether I was hoping the cooler evening air might get my brain into gear or whether I just wanted to take in the fresh scent of the forest, pine, and the last promises of crocuses carrying on the air, I can't say. Either way, no new ideas assail me as to what's coming next, and eventually I give up. I'm still running on empty from the last few days, and all the strain of the stress and deep-grained worry I've been porting around with me is still there. I might not be on the verge of nervous collapse anymore, but I'm a long way from fighting fit. In the end, I accept my limitations, and that no answers are going to come to me tonight, not in the state I'm in. Instead, I enjoy my whisky, listening to the susurrations of branch and bark, and stare at an open sky lit by unlimited stars. Then when I'm done, I creep past the dozing Isaac and make my way through to the spare room, closing the door on the day and the troubles I know are brewing but can do nothing about. Between the drink and the moment of communion with the calm of the world outside, by the time I'm undressed and the light's out, so am I.

The next morning, I'm still bleary, but the exhaustion's gone down a notch. I've had a long rest, and I've recharged my hit points, even if I'm not fully refreshed. This is as close to fighting fit as I've been for some time. I'll take it for now.

The kitchen's empty, meaning Isaac woke up at some point and moved himself to bed. I'm glad about that. Maybe I should have done it myself – got him up and into his own room before I went to mine, but he'd looked comfy enough, and he's never struggled to sleep. Even less so with his body effectively being a celestial battleground, warring between angel, demon, and fae. I thought letting him rest there and then was the best option for the time being.

Although, there's a part of me that wants to go charging into his room to check on him. It's almost that parental existential terror that causes a mum or dad to creep in during the night and lay their heads close enough to hear their breathing, to feel them moving just to reassure themselves that the inconceivable hasn't happened while they weren't there to save their loved one. There's a little niggling bit of my brain that's insisting he might not be there anymore, that he might not be Isaac. That in his exhaustion, the battle might have been lost, and either a monstrous demonic force or a strange and vicious alp might be lying in his place. Or perhaps nothing at all. Just a lifeless, cold sack of bones, the battle having beaten them all. Or not even that. Just an empty space where he once lay. Gone, lost. Totally destroyed.

I'm not going to go check though, no matter how much thrills of panic keep running through me, no matter how much those dark and terrible thoughts flit through my brain, grabbing at my attention. Instead, I force myself to pull out a frying pan and crack some eggs from the fridge, making my attempt at an omelette. By the time I'm finished, it's more like clumpy scrambled eggs pushed together in a block, but it's food and edible. That's all I'm looking for at the moment. At least as far as eating goes. Far more pressing is my need for coffee. After much stumbling about, I locate a French press and some ground beans. From there, getting the kettle on is child's play, even for someone as sleep-drunk as I am, and soon I've a mug slightly smaller than a kiddie paddling pool full of black gold and enough ketchup on the eggs that they almost taste good. I tuck in, and for a moment everything seems almost right with the world even though thinking about coffee grounds reminds me of one of the particular fates potentially awaiting Isaac.

Then I shatter any feeling of calm or zen I might have by turning on the TV, straight into a news bulletin.

'... believed to be planning wide-scale terrorist attacks. Authorities are currently unable to confirm whether he's a lone wolf or connected to other potential cells nor have they commented on his motives or likely targets. Born into the Father of Holiness group, based just outside Lille, a small sect known for their austere practises, they have distanced themselves from the young man, insisting he has not been a part of their community or in contact with them for several years. There's some evidence to suggest he may have been living rough until recently, but there're still no solid leads as to why this young man is so dangerous or what he's done – or plans to do – that has made him the centre of the largest manhunt in recent memory. If sighted, authorities are advising you to keep your distance and contact...'

Click. I don't need to watch anymore. Of course. Now that I think about it, who else would the demon target? Who else has worked with us closely in recent times and is, despite his many charms and qualities, entirely unable to fight back against anything that low-down, dirty, scum-sucking trident-fucker might throw against him?

Gil.

Chapter Twenty-Eight

From scrambled eggs to the ATF scrambled for Franc's ex.

Panic. Sheer gut-wrenching panic is the first thing that hits me. Then shame. And guilt. Always guilt. Because last time I turned my back on Gil, he nearly died. Now his whole life has just imploded for the terrible, unforgivable crime of ever having known me.

An innocent paying by association. By the Good God, I'm so tired of that being true.

There's no question of a lazy morning recuperating now, of course. The bastard demon's already got the drop on us. He's made good on his threat – not only targeting one of our people but bringing the combined might of the unTalented authorities to bear as well. It's a fucking mess, and I can't deal with it on my own. So as much as I'd love to just let him sleep, I have to wake up Isaac.

There's that moment as I enter like the one I described for a parent earlier, when I get in and I can see his chest moving up and down, the sheets lifting in time. When the hat's still clearly on his head, and there's no sign of black demon sludge wriggling up his neck to take him over. When I can breathe easily again because I know, at least for now, that he's still alive, still okay.

Once I've shaken him, rousing him to something resembling conscious – or at least as close as I can get him to it – I pass him the cup of coffee I made. After all, what I'm about to drop on him is heavy, and I'm going to need him as compos mentis as is possible. Plus, I'm not a total monster. If you're going to wake someone up, at least give them a cup of joe to curse at you over.

It tugs at my heartstrings, seeing the state he's in. Isaac's aging froze at a slightly later age than mine. They say you're supposed to get wiser as you get older. Isaac's just got more experimentative in terms of body modification, leading to him carrying a whole other entity around with him thanks to some radical tattooing. Thing is, externally anyhow, there's not normally that much difference between mid-thirties (where I froze) and early-forties (where he did). Normal unTalented I've met tell me there's a whole host of differences going on behind the scenes, as the equivalent of your cam-belt starts wearing out, and the spring in your step becomes more of a pained hobble, but on the outside, the age gap might be visible, but it's not extreme.

Today, that's not the case. Right now, Isaac looks *ancient* compared to his normal rejuvenated expression. If I'm his adopted son, I've definitely put him through the wringer over the years – stumbling in drunk at all hours, keeping him up all night with worry. Although, of course, his worries were more to do with the very possible threat of me dying horribly. I guess most parents have that fear, actually. It just happened to come true more often than not with me.

But even when I came in wearing a new body, marked by whatever eldritch evil I'd been battling with, he'd always looked fresh and relaxed. Didn't matter what time it was, what state I was in. How long he'd had to stress about whether he'd ever see me again. Each and every time, he always welcomed me home with a pat on the back and a glass of the good stuff, looking fresh as a daisy.

Not right now. No. Now he looks like he's been carrying the One Ring for too long, like it's left him stretched out. There're wrinkles everywhere, and the colourless greyscale that's become his standard skin colour palette only highlights each and every darkened entrenchment. There's no sparkle to his eyes, none of that usual visible emotion that permeates his expression, running the gamut from baffled amusement to forgiving disappointment. He just stares at me dully, as if he's struggling for a moment to know who I am. If there's anything that's scared me so far – and trust me, there's been plenty – this puts them all in the shade. I don't think there can be anything more disturbing, more unsettling than seeing your parental figure lose their vigour. Except perhaps to see them lose their memories of you.

Eventually he blinks and accepts the coffee mug handle, uncertainly, unconfidently but takes it nonetheless. I try to ignore the slight tremor that sets the surface rippling.

He takes a swig, the mug bottom obscuring his visage, and when he puts it back down, it feels like a weight lifts off my chest. There's more of Isaac back there now. If his eyes still aren't on fire with knowledge and curiosity, the spark's in there, even if it's sputtering.

'What is it, lad?' It's a strange tone to hear from Isaac. Querulous, on the edge of annoyed. He didn't sound like that even when I destroyed King Arthur's round table by accident. My bad. Should've known having sex with a fire elemental on it was never going to end well.

I shake the thoughts from my mind. Time to get focused. 'I know, 'Zac. What the bastard's got planned. Who he's targeted. It's all over the news.'

Now the spark flares back up. Good. He's still in there. We still have time to solve this. 'Who? Who is it?'

'Gil. They're saying he's a terrorist, and they've activated a nationwide manhunt for him.'

The difference between the man before me and the man I pulled resentfully from his slumber is night and day. He may be so tired, so worn down by the internal struggle that even *coffee* has no effect. But someone being in trouble? Specifically, someone who can't really protect himself, particularly not against the threats of Talented society? That's enough to replace all his blood with energy drinks. He leaps to his feet and starts scrambling for clothes.

'Damn it, they'll be coming for him, lad. And soon. What do you reckon? This as a feint to keep us off guard?'

'And then while we go tiptoeing in, looking out for the unTalented troops, they'll hit us with some sort of attack.' Which, of course, is something we've not really discussed. 'Why, 'Zac? Why is all this happening? I know Nith has been pretty tight-lipped about everything, but do we have any idea why the demons are doing this? Is it because of Nith?'

Isaac worries at his lip as he casts around for a clean shirt. 'He's of the opinion it's what Meph said. To do with them tethering everything to this reality. Whether it's to sever that tether or to take advantage of it.' He pauses, looks at me, and I can see the hurt there in his eyes. 'He either can't or won't say.'

Oof. Keeping secrets from the being you body-share

with makes keeping your partner in the shade look like a non-event. No wonder he's looking so wounded by it. 'Is Gil still safe?'

'Of course! He's stayed put. I spoke to him after you dropped him back in Auch, lad…'

He stops. Goes white. A moment later I realise what he was about to say and why he's looking so horrified.

He was about to say behind the wards. Except they're not anymore. When they dropped for that moment as I came back to Toulouse? When their power weakened, when I found out about the essence having spread up his arm…

The wards shrunk back to their old size.

Gil is completely defenceless.

Chapter Twenty-Nine

The dead river monster broke his heart. I'm terrified what a demon might do to Franc's Gil-ted lover.

I'm out of the room like a shot, scrabbling in my pockets for my phone. There's a little black book on the sideboard where I know Isaac keeps all his numbers, like the old-school OCD maniac he is. I've not called Gil since I killed his brother. Honestly, I've no idea how he feels about the whole thing. "No idea" seems to be my thing, when it comes to Gil. No idea how he is. No idea what to do with how I feel about having fucked up and let him down so badly, then left him alone in Auch to deal with the loss of his brother. And now, no idea what to do about the fact he's been declared Public Enemy Number One by the government, thanks to having the misfortune of knowing me. By the Good God, I can't even begin to list all the ways I've let the young man down in recent times, and now my worry is starting to peak, transforming into panic, that I might have left it all too late yet again, left him alone too long. Left him to pay the price for my fuck ups once more.

Gil's phone rings and rings. No answer. Maybe he's forgotten it somewhere. Left it in the kitchen while he's watching telly. Or knocked it onto silent mode without realising. It's possible. Except, if he was watching TV, he'd have seen his own mugshot and surely picked up the phone to call Isaac.

My feet are itching now. If I could do a Road Runner impression, get them whirling round in a blur to power me off towards Auch, I would. Visions of Gil banged up behind bulletproof glass while the high-ups in the various services interrogate him for acts he would never do flash through my head. They're chased out by images of the sort of Talented who might throw their lot in with a demon working against humans, what they might do to him if they get their hands or claws or talons on him. We need to *go*. Now.

Luckily, Isaac feels exactly the same and comes speeding round the corner, half falling over his own feet, struggling with a canvas-coloured trench coat, trying to dress and get out the door simultaneously. It's only because I point out his patent brown leather shoes are missing that he doesn't run out in his socks. A second later, we're in the Tesla, wheels spinning up a cloud of shingle and dust as we tear off. There's no time for careful driving now. We're heading for Auch at top speed.

I pull together a *don't look here* and try to trust Isaac's driving. It's hard, at the best of times. This isn't the best of times. However, for once, he's really motoring. He's moving like a bat out of hell. Luckily it's only a few turns and then we're on the motorway heading straight there. Forty minutes, and we'll be in the city itself.

Which means we need to make plans now. I can see how

hyper-focused Isaac is, and I can understand. Me too. I want to get to Gil, to find him safe, to pull him out of this danger we seem to have inadvertently put him in. But that doesn't mean we have to be stupid about it. For once, it's my job to do the thinking, to stop us just charging in headfirst.

'You have remembered it's a trap, 'Zac, haven't you?'

'Hmm?' Isaac's eyes are fixed on the road ahead. We're doing at least a hundred and fifty kilometres an hour, weaving around cars and trucks that can't even see us. Normally, I'd just let him concentrate, but I need to get this through to him, need him to divide at least some of his attention onto what I'm saying.

'It's a trap. Remember?'

'Oh. Oh, yes.' Nope, he completely forgot. Thought so. He eases off the accelerator. Just a touch. Not enough that it'll make any real difference to how long it takes us to reach Auch but enough he can listen to me, can think about what I'm saying without running a serious risk of ploughing straight into the back of an articulated lorry.

'So what does that mean?' I ask. This is not my usual role. Normally, I'm the one running in gung-ho, and the others are making me do some actual thinking, not even caring that it makes my brain hurt. This role reversal's not playing to my strengths, but I don't have any other choice.

'Mean?' Isaac's distracted. I can understand it. Doesn't mean I don't find it frustrating still.

'Yes. What does it mean? Does it mean we should still just charge in there? Should we sneak our way in? Be on the lookout for the cops and the army? The demon himself? Possessed people? What?'

Isaac contemplates this for a moment, rolling it around his vast intellect while he careens around a small rusted Fiat doing half the speed limit for no obvious reason other than it might fall to pieces if it goes any faster. Italian car design at its finest.

'Yes?' That's the answer his gigantic brain comes back with. Fuck my life.

'Okay.' I just start talking, conscious stream style. 'We know the demon's set this up to get to us. They've already seen we're loath to hurt any unTalented. They know we're not going to be cold-hearted and ruthless when it comes to the deaths of average Joes caught in the crossfire.'

'Right.' Isaac nods firmly, appreciatively. It's not helpful, but it is validating. I'll take that for now.

'So the unTalented forces might get used as a protective barrier or a deterrent. Put them between us and Gil, make us work twice as hard and burn twice as much power for half the results.'

Isaac's still nodding sagely. Honestly, I'd rather he started speaking sagely because it'd stop me from having to do it, so I throw in a question again. 'But do you think the demon will want the human authorities to take him away?'

'No...' Isaac says it slowly, stretching it out, thinking it through. 'No, they'll want him where they can get their sticky mitts on him, to get us to come to them.'

Good man. He's come to the same conclusion as me, but I really wanted to double-check I didn't miss something in my calculations. 'Right, that's how I see it too. So the demon will have Gil guarded. He might make us go through soldiers and cops to get to him just to fuck with us, but once we get there, it'll be a strictly Talented affair.'

'Unless they've a load more possessed.'

Oh, fucksticks. I didn't think of that at all. That's even more plausible. 'Shit. So then it could be soldiers, cops, civilians, all of them up in the mix, all of them full of demon energy...'

'All of them trying to kill us. Right. Let's slow this down a bit.'

Isaac lifts his foot off, and we come down to normal speed. Good call. We're going to be there soon enough. Rushing in more than we already are is just going to get us killed. That's not going to do Gil any favours.

'So we're going to be facing an unknown threat. We know the demon wants us dead –'

Isaac interrupts. 'But they're not willing to do it themselves.'

Good God damn, that's a good point. That's very true. 'You're right. Even in the big showdown with De Montfort and Nicetas, they didn't show their face. If they did, it might have changed the tide. So why didn't they?'

Isaac's fingers drum the steering wheel, drubbing it between thumb and forefinger. 'Nith. Nan. The pair of them together. They're scared of the angels.'

Nice. 'That makes sense. Sure, they've managed to weaponise their energy to reduce the effectiveness of the Bene Elohim, but that doesn't mean they're in a hurry for a head-to-head showdown. And right now, you might not be at full strength, you or Nith, but I bet it's the same again.'

Isaac nods, grim faced. 'They'll use patsies. Proxies. People or creatures they can use to do their dirty work, that avoids them having to show their blasted face.'

Which prompts a thought. 'Do they even have a face? Are they manifesting, tied to a body like Nith and Mephy? Just because that's how it works in the only cases we know about doesn't mean it always works like that.'

'*Damn it!*' Isaac's roar nearly makes me jump out of my skin. 'Damn it, damn it, damn it!' He pounds on the steering wheel, alternating hands so that at least we don't go careening off into a ditch to emphasise how upset he is. And he is mightily upset. I've never seen him lose his temper to this degree, ever.

After a couple of minutes of what is his equivalent of swearing like a trooper and working out some of that frustration on the poor, defenceless wheel, he calms down enough to express what he's venting about.

'We know so bloody little, Paul.' I can hear the frustration. It's riding every single syllable. 'I'm sick of it. The whole past year has been nothing but careening from the unknown to the uncertain, gripping on by our fingernails. Every time we've found one thing out, something else has reared up to throw us completely off balance, and I'm bloody sick of it. Now a poor lad who's had nowt but misery and suffering all of his days is being tormented yet again, and I...'

He breaks off and stares out the window, his eyes fixated on the silver car we're trailing along behind, though I don't think he really sees it except in a subconscious sense, keeping us a certain safe distance from it.

'I'm tired, Paul.' When he speaks again, there's a croak to his voice like it's close to breaking. 'This isn't what I want. After Jakob disappeared, I gave up on so much. The quiet of study and reflection eventually helped give me back peace. I don't want to live in interesting times, lad. All I want is to be quiet again. Is that really too much to ask?'

I think about it for a moment, mulling it over. It's a valid question, and it deserves a properly considered answer. 'Do you know what's the problem with living for such a damned long time, 'Zac?'

He shrugs nonchalantly. I think it's to say he could tell me a million problems with it, but he's waiting to hear me out on which one I'm concentrating on. 'Go on.'

'Sooner or later, you're going to find yourself living in interesting times again. It's the old Gandalf phenomenon.'

'I'm not sure I'm familiar with that particular branch of academic research, lad.' The wry tone in his voice does me good. It's so much more comforting than the edged despair that was there a second before.

'Look, Gandalf turns up in Middle Earth ages before, right? Like, I read the *Silmarillion* and all the back lore, but in effect, he's there for the first battle with Sauron. Then he has a period of considerable peace, where he gets to pootle around, befriending hobbits, setting off firework displays, meddling now and then in the affairs of humans or elves or popping off on adventures as and when the fancy takes him, right?'

Isaac nods. 'Seems about right. Been a while since I read any of the books.'

'But then there's the whole bit where one of the hobbits –I think it's Frodo– says about how he wishes that this shit hadn't gone down on his watch. And Gandalf says, "So do all who live to see such times," all wise and sagely. Except, what he means is, he's *seen* all of those times. He's seen each time the heroes, willing or conscripted by fate, have had to step up whether they wanted to or no. There might have been moments, hell, maybe millennia of peace in between, but sooner or later, it's all going to kick back off again, and it just has to be ridden out.'

'So what you're saying' –Isaac doesn't sound very impressed– 'is that this is just an unending cycle, and it's never going to change?'

'No!' I can understand how that's the point he'd draw out of it, but it wasn't the one I was trying to say. '*This* is the price. This is the price we pay to see it all. The price we pay for all those moments when we've time to indulge our passions, to invest in our projects. For all the times we get to see things through to fruition in a way that normal humans could only ever dream of. And more than that even. It's how we buy those times of peace for humanity as a whole to prosper. What's the point in living forever if you don't make any difference? We're the most hands-off shepherds you can imagine. We're not there steering the fold, making them follow along the paths we lay for them. No thank you. That way leads to god complexes, and next thing you know, you're building hundred foot tall ziggurats and baptising them in the blood of thousands.

'No, what we are are the ones who step out of the shadows when the wolves start circling. Before the howls can even send chills down the flock's spines, we're there, armed with our staff or slingshot, standing between them and the innocent they want to feast on. So that's the Gandalf phenomenon. We get to watch humanity prosper from the sidelines, get to enjoy the fruits of their labour, of their innovation and ingenuity. We get to watch all those changes and developments and growth and stunning mind-blowing moments of genius that don't require *talent* to create miracles and change the world. And because of that, we get to read the books they write, study the paintings they create. We get to chill in front of the TV, watching word-craft that Shakespeare would be proud of without moving from our homes, with fine quality food and even finer booze, safe and warm. While times are quiet, we get to smell the roses and savour their scent. And the price we pay is that when these moments arrive — these pivotal points where all stands balanced on a knife edge and might pivot into darkness, when it's taken from their hands because of the monsters we make sure they don't even know about? Well, that's when we have to step up and play our part. And sometimes,

sometimes it isn't all neatly done, wrapped up and put away in a neat little compartment, finished and finalised. Sometimes it isn't all over by Christmas, no matter how much we want it to be. And those are the times we go above and beyond. Those are the times when you taught me to go above and beyond, old Greybeard.'

Whew. That was quite a fucking speech. I'm pleased with it if I do say so myself, and I can see Isaac mulling it over, considering all the things I've said.

'But,' he says slowly, eventually, 'my beard's not grey.'

'That's your take away?' I can feel my voice mounting in exact correlation to my exasperation. 'That's what you draw out from that brilliant, stirring speech? From that revelatory moment where we gird our fucking loins ready for battle? Are you actually fucking serious?'

And just as I ask that, I see the twinkle in his eye. The one that's been missing. The one I'm inordinately pleased to see.

'Of course I'm not, lad. Stop being so bloody gullible.'

Oh, right. Totally fucking got me. The sneaky old bastard.

I'd love to come up with something to get him back with, but it'll have to wait. I make a note in my mental ledger that I owe Isaac a good winding-up and then put it away, ready to concentrate on the matter at hand.

We need to start coming up with a plan. Now. Because we're approaching the outskirts of Auch.

Chapter Thirty

Time to spring the trap. And hope we aren't walking into a
pair of crunching metal jaws. I did that once. Fucking
sucked.

I'm about to point out the signage telling us we're
approaching the city boundaries, but Isaac's picked it up.
There's a small breakdown lane on the right, and he swings
us into it, drawing to a stone-crunching stop. Fair play, the
car has a decent breaking system.

Isaac looks over at me calmly, but there's something else.
Something to the way his jaw's set, not quite clenched but
firm. Determined. 'Paul, my lad, you're not going to like
this suggestion.'

And just like that, I already don't. 'Okay, hit me.'

He grins. 'Don't tempt me.' Arsehole. That's two I owe
him. The smile fades away. 'There's something I can do
that'll help.'

'Okay, stop right there.' What he means is there's something he can do involving his *talent*. Except we both know the risks involved in that. 'I've brought you along because – well, frankly because I'd feel a bit of a bounder stealing your car, but you're here as an observer. No way are you and Nith about to start throwing down.'

'But that's just it!' Isaac's expression doesn't change. If anything, he looks even more certain. 'It won't be me. Just Nith. We reckon – and I'm not going to lie to you; we both acknowledge we could be wrong, but we reckon that if Nith pops off away for a moment, we'll be okay. The demon essence and the alp magic are battling each other to a stand-still without much input from us. So if it's only brief, it should be fine.'

'Or,' I point out, 'it might be all that the demon essence needs in order to overwhelm the effect of the hat and then you end up dead. Or worse.'

'What's life without risk, eh, lad? All just safety, hiding away, not doing our jobs as sneaky hidden shepherds, isn't that what you said?'

Oof. Low blow using my own rousing speech against me. He's right, of course. He usually bloody is. Which is precisely as annoying as it sounds.

'Look, lad,' he starts, his voice gentle but still utterly insistent, warmed steel but not flexible at all. 'If I'm Gandalf here, then this is my Balrog moment. Sooner or later, I'm going to fall. Darkness will take me if we don't move our behinds and find the little so-and-so who did this to me. Maybe it's better to plunge in and take it on rather than trying to run away.'

'But we already did the Balrog scene with Half-Marred Jack.' It's a reference back to his fantastic moment when we hunted the child-snatching Cagot bastard through the streets of Lyon, trying to catch him before he could deliver any more innocents to Queen Maeve of the Winter Court. When we managed to run him to ground through the traboules, the hidden passageways that criss-cross the old town, Isaac got to channel his inner Gandalf and break out the "You shall not pass" line, stopping him dead in his tracks shortly before I made him dead and stole his body. Still, it's a weak argument. *"We already used that pop cultural touchstone"* would mean we never spoke again.

'Well, sometimes these things come back around.' Which, of course, was my whole point before. Fucking hell, never get involved in a debate with an academic. It won't end well for you.

In the end, there's nothing I can really say except to acquiesce and let him crack on. 'All right, 'Zac, I trust you. Don't fuck it up, okay?'

'Yes, well, adding provisos like that on the end doesn't really scream out that you have implicit faith in me, just to be clear, lad.' He tips me a wink just to show he's not really worried or upset by it. Then he grins. 'Hey, Nith!' I've never heard him speak to Nith externally, and the grin is definitely fixed on me. I get the feeling this is more for my benefit. 'Fly, you fool!'

I'm about to give him top marks for working in an additional line, but I don't get the chance because my breath gets taken away spectacularly. Nithael explodes outwards and upwards from Isaac, roaring through the car's roof and expanding as he goes.

By the time he's disappeared, I'm already fumbling with the slick, modern door handle, trying to get the door open. As soon as I do, I practically fall onto the grass verdure. My eyes can't help but catch glimpses – controlled, minimised to save me from singing nonsensical hosannas at the sight but glimpses nonetheless – of the flight of an angel.

Nithael is grace incarnate. His wings expand outwards like neon signage picked out across the horizon, like lines of lightning flashing from impossible feather to impossible feather. Even without *looking*, I can see the heft of each unimaginably expansive wing that seems to stretch across the whole of the heavens, covering the sky, obscuring it behind crackling electric outlines. I know perfectly well, even if right now we're battling against demons, that there's nothing intrinsically better about going up the vibratory ladder than down. Still, watching Nith soar skywards, it's hard not to feel like there's something divine about his movements.

The Bene Elohim unfurls fully, hovering above us, gazing down onto Auch. Normally the cathedral in the centre stands dominant, hogging the high ground and carving visibility out of the clear blue sky. Not right now though. Nith pulls the eye upwards, far higher than any mortal building can manage.

Mind you, there's one slight concern with that. 'This isn't exactly fucking subtle, 'Zac,' I hiss. Tearing my eyes away from the spectacle is impossible. If that's true for me, though, it's probably true for every Talented being in a twenty-mile radius at least.

'You're right. Of course, lad.' Isaac's also looking upwards, but his expression is different. There's no awe in there – awe that, against my own nature and knowledge, I know is painted across my face. No, there's just pride, that simple kind of joy in seeing one of your own doing what they're best at. It's a "soccer mum on a Saturday morning" kind of expression, the one a friend wears as their mate tears it up at a Karaoke night when no one was expecting it. Nith's getting to cut loose, and Isaac's loving it.

'Okay, I was hoping for a bit more than that, 'Zac,' I say,

but then Nith breaks my concentration by stealing my breath away again. It's starting to become a bit of a habit, the sneaky angelic thief.

The angel folds his wings around himself, performing a tuck and roll in the air like a dive into an Olympic swimming pool, where the athlete seems to defy gravity itself for a moment. Then Nith plummets earthwards, straight towards us, so fast the electric neon that's streaking off his outline blurs, pulling backwards. It looks like nothing so much as a meteor entering atmosphere, burning with gravity's undeniable force, and it is both utterly astounding to see and mortally terrifying. It doesn't matter how much I know logically that Nithael doesn't occupy the same physical plane in the same way we do. Seeing him streaking downwards at unimaginable speed makes me want to cringe, to make one of those entirely human, entirely useless gestures like throwing my hands protectively over my head against a falling building. My instincts are screaming at me that impact is going to create a crater where I'm standing, a hole of demolition and rubble and bloody body parts scattered everywhere – parts that used to be attached to my body.

Of course that doesn't happen. There's no shockwave of impact, no drilling into the ground with explosive force. Nith hits Isaac dead on and disappears into him. Tiny roiling drops of electric fire roll down 'Zac's arms and crackle at his fingertips for a moment. Fucking hell. It's easy sometimes, with all the genteel nature and calm, quiet studiousness to forget just how mind-bogglingly powerful the duo in a single body in front of me actually are.

Isaac keeps his eyes closed for a moment, no doubt getting the lowdown from Nith, then opens them and looks at me, a little grin on his face that says he's happy his gamble's paid off.

'Fifteen demonic energy signals in Auch. One a possessed human; thirteen seem to be large apes.' Isaac's cheeky grin fades. 'And one large creature with a goat's head and the body of a bear. Rippling with dark magics.'

Isaac's already worked it out, of course, being several measures of intelligence beyond me, but I'm going to spell it out anyhow. 'Magical large apes? In those sort of numbers?'

There's only one real answer. 'Sounds like simiots.'

Isaac frowns, shakes his head slightly. 'But that doesn't make sense. They promised, on their *talent*, to stay in peace up in the mountains, not to bring war against humans.'

True. But there's an easy workaround for that. 'Except if they're possessed, it's not them using their *talent*. It's the demon using them both.'

I can see Isaac trying to work through that, looking for the holes in my logic. Sadly, he doesn't find any. "So thirteen simiots possibly. Not ideal but not undoable. But they're all packed with this special blasted demonic essence that renders Nith next to useless.'

A grim thought hits me suddenly. 'Your wrist, man. Let me see it.'

He rolls up his sleeve, and I'm beyond relieved to see there's still just a band of black around it. The poisonous infection hasn't started to spread back up his arm. It's still under control. Perhaps it's a tad thicker than it was but nothing significant.

'What about the hat, 'Zac?' I ask. 'You're not suddenly feeling the urge to transform into a stylish little bird or to jump on my chest and drink my blood?'

'Paul, my lad, there is rarely a day that goes by when I don't want to jump up and down on you. That's nothing to do with any alp magic though. No, no, just the sudden cravings to suck your blood.' He shoved two fingers up in front of his mouth and did the world's worst impression of a Transylvanian accent on the last line. Idiot.

But I'm relieved. That was a mad stunt to have pulled. Talking of…

'What about all the attention Nith just drew? They'll know we're coming now.'

'Paul.' Isaac's voice is gentle, kind but firm. 'This is a blooming trap, lad. It always has been. They've always known we're coming. Sure, they might know we're here now, but it's always only been a matter of time. That TV broadcast was a direct challenge, an invitation to roll up here, and we RSVP'd. At least now we know what we're up against and aren't just charging in blind.'

There's the world's gentlest little accusation in those last few words. A reminder, perhaps, that that is my normal MO and that I'm perhaps not in a position to cast aspersions when others get a touch gung-ho. Can't really argue with that.

'Okay, point taken.' What's done is done anyhow. No reason to dwell on it. 'Back to the matter at hand. One human possessed in there. Gil?'

'Seems likely.' Isaac purses his lips and furrows his brow. 'It's either that or whoever the demon is currently riding about in. Based on what we've seen so far though…'

'They're unlikely to meet us head on in direct conflict. Agreed. So Gil seems the most likely victim.' Damn it. I have precisely zero idea how to undo the possession. From what we saw on the news concerning the other passengers on the nightmare flight in Germany, it's not permanent. That was the demon letting them go though. I don't suspect he's about to do that with Gil. Not even if we say pretty please. Not even with a cherry on top, which is just ruthless.

And of course we've been skirting around the other

issue. 'Isaac,' I start quietly, carefully, that sort of tone of voice when you ask a question you're ninety-nine percent sure of the answer to, and it's definitely not the answer you want. 'How many creatures can you think of that have the body of a bear and the head of a goat?'

Please don't say only one. Please don't say only one.

'Only one I can think of, lad.'

Damn it, that was precisely the answer I didn't want. 'And that one would be the Warabouc?'

Please don't say yes. Please don't say yes.

'Aye, exactly.'

Shit. That's two for two answers I wanted different responses to.

Chapter Thirty-One

AUCH, 29 OCTOBER, PRESENT DAY

It's a bad situation. Guess we'll just have to make the m-
Auch-t of it.

There are times for subtlety.

Believe it or not, even I know that. There are times to go
full Solid Snake hiding under a cardboard box, picking your
way past the grunts to make it to the boss fight. There's a
place for doing the whole *Assassin's Creed* route, sneaking up
the sides of buildings with grace and elegance to find your
target. Or if you're me, turning around in circles, banging
into the wall, and leaping to your death rather than into the
conveniently placed haystack. Even outside of computer
games –I know, stop with the blasphemy; but there is a life
outside of computer games– there's a reason why ninjas and
assassins are so prevalent in our imaginations. Deadly
unseen tactical strikes are nothing to be sniffed at and
certainly not to be ignored as a potential plan of action.

This? This is not one of those times. We sent up our

own angelic equivalent of a position flare before we crossed into Auch. And they already knew we were coming. We know who's the big boss waiting for us, just like we know there's a shedload of cannon fodder to mow our way through to get to him. This isn't a sneaky, sneaky sort of situation. Gil might not like the comparison as it makes him a dead dog, but it's time to go full-on John Wick. At least until we get past the first checkpoint, so to speak.

So we just stroll straight into the town of Auch, the overhanging buildings covering architectural styles I've witnessed arrive hailed as the height of modernity and have remained to see become antiquated, outmoded. Everything that was once fresh sooner or later becomes tired and dated. Except me. I'm fresh as a daisy. And I'm ready for a date with a bunch of overgrown apes. Time to give them a day to remember.

The streets of the town are eerie, deserted. There's an echoing silence that makes me feel like somehow I've stumbled into a horror film, like hordes of undead have swept through on a forced recruitment drive. I know it's a result of the government. The demon definitely has its sticky claws in someone in the high-ups, playing with their mind, feeding them misinformation. I don't know how it would've pulled this off otherwise. If the public is just contained in their residences, I'd expect the streets to be swarming with police. Hell, even the army. Even then, I'd expect the odd window thrown open, people leaning out, watching the spectacle even if they'd been told their lives were at risk. There's always one or two who'd risk potential death just to have a goosey at what was going down.

There's not. It's a ghost town. All you need is a few shutter doors slamming in the wind and a tumbleweed rolling past, and you could be in the Wild West instead of the Normally Tame Southwest of France. It's unnerving, and it makes me wonder once more just how much power this demon actually has. Nithael is terrifying in how powerful he is, but he's also limited by his moral code. This demon doesn't have the same restrictions. I wonder how much chance I'd have against it if I didn't have Nith riding shotgun with Isaac. Thank the Good God for their apparent cowardice. Without it, we could be in even more of a pickle than we are, and I feel like we're practically swimming in vinegar, sugar, and preservatives as is.

As we step into the boundaries of the centre, the sloping banks of the Gers River visible down the boulevard, we make first contact. Around the corner, an echoing screech comes, reverberating and rebounding off the bricks and mortar, strong enough that I can see the pane in a shop's window shuddering under the sound. It's as though some-one's sawing through living metal that's screaming in harmony with the noise of the cutting. Except even less pleasant than that.

Then the first simiot steps around the corner. Think if you ran a howler monkey through Jeff Goldblum's machine from *The Fly* with a gorilla pumped up on steroids, and you'd start to have some idea what we're looking at. Then get it hooked on crack before smashing its pipe and insulting its mother. Also add some demon-marked eyeballs, and you have a picture of what we're up against.

I've met simiots before but not for a long time. Honestly, I didn't think there were any left. Crusading knights sweeping through the Pyrenees mistook them for demons – or more often for Moors because they were all both idiots and massive fucking racists. The simple crea-tures, living in the honeycomb caves of the mountains, eventually got pissed off with the whole thing and decided to go to war, attacking towns along the coast past Montpellier.

Eventually, a battalion of knights came riding over from nearby Montpellier, the local liege finally doing his duty, and barrelled into them, their lances raised. Isaac and I arrived, word having reached us of their march, just in time to watch them get decimated. A few hundred simiots had marched out to go to war with humanity, the poor mad fools. Ten died within seconds, even if they managed to bake one of the knights in his armour. A high price to pay for a single noble.

It took some work to save any of them. I swirled up a fog, screened the battlefield so as their numbers couldn't be further pruned by arrows and the imminent cavalry charge was thrown into disarray. Then Nithael swept the simiots to aside, hustling them into some nearby trees, where Isaac cast a *don't-look-here* over the whole woods. The knights stomped about the plain for a while, searching for their hidden foes, but eventually claimed divine intervention must have eradicated all the simiots. Which, in a way, was closer to the truth than they realised.

To the simiots' credit, they'd recognised with that first salvo killing off ten percent of their people, that they'd made a terrible mistake. So, we made a deal. They went back to the mountains, and swore on their *power* to leave humans be, and we'd keep them safe from the humans hunting them to get home. In the caves of the Pyrenees they'd be safe.

We got them home and heard no more from them, so assumed they'd accepted the way the world had changed, made peace with humanity's dominance. After all, they couldn't act magically against our species again. What threat were they?

More than I'd considered apparently. Really should have checked in on them after all. Made sure they were okay. Because the simiot in front of me? He's a long way from okay.

There's no sentience left in the giant ape. If the demon stains in its eyes weren't clue enough, the slathering foam around its jaws would give the game away.

Then the simiot explodes into flames.

Sadly for us, this is all part of its abilities. It's not spontaneously combusting, handy as that would be for us getting to Gil a whole damn sight quicker. No, when the simiots reach a state of frenzied rage, they ignite.

Do you know what's less fun to fight than a gigantic muscle-packed simian who could give a gorilla a spanking without breaking a sweat and tear sheet metal like a piece of paper? A gigantic muscle-packed simian with all the above characteristics plus fire magic.

'They've not gotten any better tempered over the centuries, have they, lad?' Isaac's words strive for humour, but I can hear the wistful regret in them. He feels precisely as shitty as I do over fighting these creatures after we thought we'd saved them.

I really wish Isaac wasn't here, that I could have left him back at the car, but I couldn't have. Nith can tell us where the various demon-marked creatures are now he's seen them, and our plan relies on them both. Thing is, I'm desperate that he doesn't use any *talent*, that he avoids putting any further strain on the stalemate the various magics raging through his frame have arrived at. Which means there's only one thing to do.

Make myself the clear and obvious target. 'Stay back, 'Zac, unless it really goes to shit.' Then I reach into my etheric storage and pull my sword out. Magical balefire crackles as green as a deep forest glade across the edge. They're going for *talented* ignition? Two can play this game.

I step forward, making sure the creature's eyes are on me rather than Isaac. I'm just about to make some sort of wisecrack about giving it a shave – completely wasted considering it's both possessed and unlikely to be fluent in modern English when I notice ripples in the rainbow-stained puddle in front of me. The ripples grow, getting larger and larger, the ground shaking harder as more arrive. I consider screaming, 'Don't move; they can't see us if we don't move,' but any humour in the situation rapidly evaporates when five more simiots, their lips curled back to reveal incisors made for tearing any and all flesh from bones quicker than you could say, 'Those were my good writing muscles, you blackguard.' Mind you, I don't know why they'd bother taking muscle. They're already more ripped than an eighties movie star. They scutter to a halt next to the original simiot. Then they take their cue from him and also burst into flames.

'Okay, six gigantic fiery monkeys. Still manageable.'

'Actually, technically, they're apes rather than monkeys, lad,' 'Zac pipes up from behind me.

I don't take my eyes off the threat, but my voice makes it clear that could I do so, I'd be staring at him in wide-eyed disbelief. 'Are you serious? Are you the fucking *Discworld* librarian? Is this really the moment to start getting into their genus?'

'Right, maybe not.' He sounds suitably abashed. So he should be. I really don't get what sort of simian they are. Either way, I'm more worried about us getting a bashing.

So half a dozen fire-controlling *apes* who'll tear me limb from limb without even breaking a sweat if they manage to get their hands on me. The odds are manageable. Difficult but manageable. I'm pretty handy with a sword if I do say so myself.

'Err, Paul, lad?' I can hear a nervousness in Isaac's voice, a tremulous note rarely there.

'What is it?' The simiots start to slouch forward, knuckling along the ground, their elongated arm muscles rippling with the movement. Fuck me, they're not playing about. Apparently, they spent the last few hundred years building a training gym under the Pyrenees and pushing some serious weight.

'Paul!' The panic level is distinctly higher.

'Slightly busy here, 'Zac.' The tone of his voice is infectious. Although that might just be from seeing the hairy, mind-controlled, flaming monkey men advancing on me, their enormous teeth glistening in the reflections of their friends' flames.

'*Paul!*' Fucking hell. Apparently, whatever it is that's stressing Isaac out, it's affecting his ability to use any words other than proper nouns.

Left with no choice, I risk a quick glance over my shoulder to see what's going on. When I see, I can understand.

The simiot fellas in front of us were just a distraction. Seven more of the giant apes have come sauntering up behind us, penning us in. Not only that, but they clearly sent the punier, less physically capable of their number to grab our attention. The seven advancing on us from behind look like if André the Giant had snorted testosterone and ran marathons until not an inch of fat was left on him.

Well, shit. Now it's fair to say the odds have swung away from our favour to the degree the Swing-o-meter arm just snapped off and started spinning round uncontrollably.

In other words?

We're fucked.

Chapter Thirty-Two

Everybody's in love with our simian drugs. Presumably anabolic steroids, looking at these simiots.

The apes continue to lope towards us down the deserted streets. I've no idea how the demon pulled off getting everyone to fuck off, but I seriously envy them all right now. I wish I could fuck off out of this situation too.

The only sound above the crack of tendons each time the apes move is the sizzling pop of water as they knuckle their way through the pools formed by the recent rains. Sadly, none of them melt away like the Wicked Witch of the West. There goes one potential option I was considering, hoping that the whole "water beats fire" elemental game might work in our favour. Based on the steam pouring up from the ground when they reach a puddle and the fact their flames don't even flicker on contact, magical fire trumps normal water every time. Damn it.

This isn't looking good. In fact, it's bad enough I need to

know all our options. 'What can Nith pull off here, 'Zac?' I'm beyond loath to ask them to use their power, but I'm even less inclined to be rendered into my component limbs like a kid's action figure during said child's experimental phase.

Isaac's backed up closer to me, so we're pressed against each other. I've swivelled us round so I'm facing the larger threat, both numerically and physically. I can hear him clicking his tongue on his teeth, a habit he has when he's calculating the odds.

'Little to nothing, lad.' Pretty much what I expected but still shit. 'He says he might be able to protect us, to keep the simiots out, but he can't do anything to stop them directly. The essence is still resisting all his attempts to overpower it, and combined with the stuff in our system...' He doesn't need to finish. The poison in his arm, even contained, is virulent. Not only that, but all the crap infecting the simiots is resonant energy. If they start throwing down against it, there's every chance the dark essence will overwhelm Nith and Isaac. Plus, even if the defensive magic works, it leaves us stuck here, trapped by an army of hench-monkeys. That allows the demon all the time in the world to come up with another attack, and I don't doubt whatever he concocted next would overwhelm us with ease.

So it's on me. Again. Sword work isn't going to be good enough. Good God, I wish Aicha was here. First, 'cos she'd make short work of slicing them all up. Compared to swordfighting a fae queen, thirteen simiots is child's play. But second, 'cos I don't doubt she'd have some genius plan, some clever trick up her sleeve or some sudden moment of incredible inspiration where she'd use the apes' magic against them. Something incredibly clever. Something I'm incapable of equalling. Honestly, the water thing was my big hope. Soak them, take off the fire magic part. Even the score at least slightly. Except it's no good. I need to power up the water, supercharge it somehow…

Ah. Ah ha! 'Back to back, 'Zac,' I shout, making sure he gets even closer to me than he already is. When I feel him press against me, I start to *push*.

Not at the simiots, not directly anyhow, although they can feel the power, the air whipping around them, sharp-toothed and bitter. It's enough to slow them, to make them hesitate, no doubt as they try to work out what's happening. What I'm *pushing* against is the water.

My talent whips out, stirring up the air currents, picking at every droplet of water, pushing it outwards from us. Every puddle, every tiniest little bit of condensed moisture clinging to the lampposts' metal. I'm forcing it away from us and towards the apes.

Of course most of it just evaporates, but that's okay too. The air's swirling constantly around the apes, cooling through movement, condensing it back to fall and pool at their feet. At the same time, I reach farther, past them, and start *pulling* more towards them from behind. Gallons of water come thundering down the quiet street, so as the noise seems reminiscent of Elrond's foam horses defending Rivendell. It hammers into the apes, stunning them. Finally the fires sputter a touch. They don't go out, but they aren't dispersing the water either. The creatures may be aflame, but it's a damp, dank burning now, like water-logged wood igniting against its will. The smell of damp fur, like wool left to rot in a forgotten storage locker, rises stronger, almost a stench, strong enough to make me wince.

'What's the plan, lad? Because if you're hoping to soak 'em into surrender, it's not working.' Isaac's voice pitches higher as he strains to be heard over the roar of the water and the wind.

'The plan, 'Zac? Simple. Normal water's not working. So let's supercharge it.' And I fling my sword upwards javelin-like as if I'm competing at the Olympics for a visiting team from medieval Europe.

My aim is still as true as it ever was, as true as it's been over the centuries from when I first learned the manoeuvre. Not an easy move to use, let alone to perfect. This is the second time I've been glad of it in recent months. The second time it's been tied to Gil too. The first was when we stood against the half-fae, half-dragon, all-wish-granting-death-incarnate Melusine. Then, the throw got her staff out of her hands and into Gil's. Gave him the chance to save us. A chance he took. Now it's going to give us the chance to save him back.

The blade approaches the top of its arc, but before it slows too much, before gravity overwhelms it and pulls it back earthwards, reminding it that swords can't fly...

It slices through the overhead tension cable.

The thick power-bearing cord whips free, springing back, no longer held taut. Then it, too, gets reminded of the pull of the ground, and even before the sword starts to turn and tumble, it falls. It lands, looping and coiling, the live wires exposed, sparking...

Connecting with the veritable moat of water I've built around us. A moat that all the simiots are standing in.

If I thought the smell of wet fur was bad before, it's nothing to the smell now. There are times in my long life... Times when plagues struck out at man and beast or when forest fires ravaged sections of the wild woods in such a way as the animals couldn't flee or when culls were required beyond what could be shared out and consumed or salted and laid down. When carcasses still thick of fur or bristles got consumed by the fire, each strand crackling and blackening as the flesh beneath blistered. That smell of animals roasting whole interweaves with that sodden hair smell, augmenting it, pushing it into sensory overload. It's the odour of an animal being soaked and burned at the same time, and my nose is yelling at me about how implausible and incomprehensible that is.

The judgement call I'm trying to make is beyond difficult, and it's one I'm going to err on the side of caution with. These creatures aren't acting of their own accord. Squid-ink eyeballs aren't one of their normal traits, believe you me. So I try to pour sufficient electricity through the simiots to overload their servos, to get their brains to shut down but without me burning out their entire circuit boards. It's a damn fine line to walk with any form of accuracy.

As much as it hurts me, I'll let them die if I have to rather than us, rather than Gil, and something in that makes me sick to my stomach. At the end of the day, they're innocent victims of the demon just as much as the possessed throng on the airplane were. And there's a little voice niggling away at the back of my conscious mind, pointing out I took a lot more damage from those humans, that I took a lot more risk in terms of potentially dying to keep them alive. That I'm more ready to kill these innocent simiots than I was a bunch of equally innocent humans. There's a bigotry there I don't like but I can't deny.

So I'm watching like a hawk, poised, ready. Desperately hoping. I watch as smoke plumes off their matted fur, completely disconnected from the flames that engulf them. And still I do nothing. I watch as the first one shudders and extinguishes, brown in place of the blue-orange-red flame that was just there.

And still I have to hold it. Still. Because some are still alight, and I can't take the risk however much it sickens me. I have to wait, watching them shudder, trailing wispy black tendrils towards the sky, my stomach turning over from the stench and from my actions. Then finally the last three flicker, and the flames die, and at last I can act.

I know it's probably too late, but I have to try. Reaching out with my *talent*, I wrangle the electric cable snake back up to its perch. There's no way I'm going to start re-wiring it, but the circuit breakers should pop soon if they haven't already. Double checking I'm wearing rubber soles, I start forward. Electricity isn't my area of expertise. I'm going to look like a damn fool if I manage to take them all out in such a stylish method, only to electrocute myself going to check on them. An extra-crispy fried fool at that too.

Nothing hits me. No remnants of electricity swirling through the waters like a ghost in the machine that's been transformed into a digital piranha, hunting the shallows of a rain pool puddle. Once I'm sure, I bend down and start checking the simiots.

If we're going to count the victories, they aren't all dead. If we're going to count the losses, some of them are, and my conscience is absolutely one hundred percent set on counting those losses, on numbering them and filing them away in little boxes it can flip open next time I'm alone in the dark of night, ready to show me pictures to prod my memory. Seven of them are still breathing, and it looks to be the seven who came up behind us, the bigger bastards. No real surprises there. Physical prowess still stands you in better stead of surviving being hit with that kind of live current, ignoring congenital heart defects and the like.

They're doubtless the ones I had to hold myself from pulling the plug on the electrocuting for. The ones it took the longest to put down.

The other six are gone. That crackling pig smell, one that haunts my dreams from bonfires and pyres I've had to stand witness to over the ages, is only a further reminder that they may not have been human, but they were people. The possession wasn't their fault. But damn, they paid the price.

The demon's gone. Now I can see their eyes, glassy and sightless but so damn close to our own.

Once the dead have been witnessed, I turn my attention back to the living. Of course, just because they're living doesn't mean they'll still be properly alive next time they come to. Between the possession that may or may not still be in place and the high voltage conducted by the liquid to every cell of their bodies, they may not be even shadows of the people they once were. It's highly doubtful I'll ever know the answer to that, but you can guarantee my guilty conscience will assume the worst however much I'm pathetically trying to count it as a victory. Sometimes, you just have to fake it till you make it. Or at least until you can take another step forward on your journey, even if you might avoid looking in any reflective surfaces for a while. Plenty of time for that weighted reflection later on.

There're questions to address right here and now that keep me focused, stop me from obsessing too much over the rights and wrongs of my actions. We can't leave the simiots like this. Taking on the Warabouc is already suicide. Trying to do it, then having an army of simiots suddenly turning up could be the difference between victory and defeat, where we don't just lose de feet but de legs, de arms, and eventually de heads too.

So we need some expert advice, and there's only one being I can ask. 'Are they still possessed?' I call over my shoulder from my crouched position. Nominally, it's addressed towards Isaac – or, at least, his body. But it's Nithael who holds the answer.

'No. Nith says the demon's essence has fled, lad.'

A part of my brain finds this interesting. It's that cold, clinical, analytical part that I try to ignore as much as possible, try not to acknowledge. The bit that can weigh up a choice between saving a child or their mother and come to a conclusion. It's that emotionless voice in my head that fills me with abject terror because it reminds me how easy it'd be for me to listen to it all the time. To make choices based only on cold logic, without any love or care or any other emotion. The world would have something to fear if I ever went that route. And it'd be so easy. That's what's terrifying for me. So very, very easy when you don't even really feel like a human anymore.

So that voice, even as I'm trying to marshal myself, to concentrate on the matter at hand and treat the simiots still living while another part of me is suffering with the guilt of killing innocents to protect myself, is asking questions. What made the essence leave? Was it the electricity overload that drove it out? Knocking them unconscious? Perhaps that broke the link? Or did the demon pull out, giving them up as a bad job? Could it feel the pain? If I hurt enough people who are possessed, will it damage the demon itself?

And that – that right there – is one of the reasons I prefer to just act rather than thinking things through. I'd rather be a clumsy, oafish Bear of Little Brain than the calculating one that my lizard brain would like me to be, blood so cold it'd turn my veins to ice.

Of course, these are all matters for another time. Probably the same time when the visions of the dead simiots come parading along, accompanied by the faces of all the other people whose deaths have been my fault. Right now, we need to get moving. Gil now, guilt later.

'Now they're not possessed anymore, can Nith do anything without it costing you both too dearly?' My mental touch isn't gentle. On top of what they've just gone through, if I start trying to keep them unconscious, I might turn them into drooling vegetables. Unconscious forever.

Isaac pauses, communes, then nods firmly. 'Aye, we can keep them under for the time being. We'll still need to come up with a better plan long term, but for now it'll work.'

Good enough for me. Long term planning can be left for future Paul to deal with. Yah, boo, sucks to be you. Except it sucks to be us right now.

'Get it done, please, you pair. Add a good, strong *don't look here* as well.' I shake my head, a quick little attempt to shove a touch of the weariness away. Raising my eyes away from the bodies lying around, living and dead, I look the body-sharing pair directly in theirs. It's impossible not to wonder if Nith is looking out as well, whether he needs to use such basic physical oculars, being stranded down here with us primitive primates. Whichever way it is, I can't help wondering what he sees when he *looks* at me. *Looking* at him for too long makes me weep blood. Does *looking* at me just make him want to weep?

Enough. Grim thoughts can fall by the wayside. It's not the time for them. Nope, it's time for something even harder than having to learn to live with our choices and actions. Asking for help. I drop a text to the Mother of the Sistren of Bordeaux – a woman who owes me a favour for saving her daughter – requesting she organise pickup and accommodation of the simiots until we're sure they can be returned home safely. I also ask her to investigate what's happened to the local inhabitants, to make sure they're safe. There's no one else I *can* ask, and she owes me a favour. More than one in my opinion. My phone beeps a couple of times, probably with enquiries in that elegant, enigmatic style of hers as to what precisely the fuck is going on. I ignore them. Worrying about updating the neighbours on the infernal shenanigans we've found ourselves drawn into can wait until we get out of Auch alive.

'C'mon,' I say, the weariness clear in my tone even as I try to toss a smile in Isaac's direction. 'Let's go fight the Warabouc.'

Chapter Thirty-Three

My diary's packed with cryptids trying to kill us. So when it comes to monsters waiting for their shot? Wara-book a slot.

We're not being any more sneaky, but we are being more cautious now. Nithael's assured us the two demonic signatures haven't moved, that they are still grouped together, one next to the other. But the Warabouc's not just sneaky. He's sneaky *and* magical. Which is a good combination for getting yourself caught out and eviscerated. So even I am ignoring my desperate desire to go charging in and instead am trying to keep hyper alert for whatever may come.

The streets are still silent, deserted. It's unnerving. Auch isn't Toulouse, of course, but it's still a decent-sized town. Even ignoring the tourist aspect —and it does well enough in terms of visitors each year— there're enough local inhabitants that it feels alive and bustling most of the time. Even if it's just some homeless punks sharing overly strong beer and dog chews on some government building steps or old folk laboriously dragging two-wheeled trollies behind them to complete the painful ascent of the sloping roads, the terrain mirroring, on a small-scale, the rolling grandeur of the mountains to the south. There're always people. Always.

Not now.

Shops stand lit invitingly, offering their wares – dummy-worn dresses and two-piece outfits, a la mode furniture, violet sweets, and tourist tat that's even less tempting than the confectionary. Only there are no vendors, no sales people ready to ignore you for as long as humanly possible until they have absolutely no choice but to engage and try to sell you something. There are no customers, no browsers. It's making me distinctly uneasy.

'You're sure there're only the two demonic essences still here, right?' The last thing we need is a large-scale repeat of the incident on the plane. I can see it now – the hordes of inhabitants pouring from their homes, filled with that same tar sludge ringing Isaac's wrist. All ready to tear into us.

'Absolutely positive.' That's something then. I hope anyhow. Fingers crossed it means my first thought was correct, and they've been evacuated somehow. Not that the new thought I've just had is correct. And the Warabouc has slaughtered the entire town.

Which is entirely possible. If they weren't ready for him, if no one was armed, if the gendarmes were caught unawares. Even if that wasn't the case, the chances of any mortals taking down the Warabouc? Infinitesimally small. Let's be honest, mine aren't a whole lot better.

We wend our way up the side of the hill that protrudes from the centre of the town. It's the bastion that the habitation has been built around. It's the easiest point to defend. So, of course, it's where we're trying to get to.

As we get closer to the top, the buildings become ever

more elegant or antiquated or both. Black wood beams run through the plasterwork of buildings that loom over the present from centuries past. The Napoleonic era white brickwork of the multi-storey houses, once single residences, now mainly divided up into apartments, looks brand new in comparison to these solitary moments of the past preserved as though in amber. Sometimes I feel the same way.

We slow, approaching the corner leading to the entrance to the Saint-Marie Cathedral. Even over the top of the imposing structures, the dual square turrets poke up, prominent, proud in their sky-climbing. The cathedral's the first thing you see when you come to Auch, and it's rare you lose sight of it anytime. The Church always did know how to dominate a skyline.

Round the corner is the beautiful little square leading up to the commanding entrance to the cathedral. It's surveyed by the magisterial gaze of the two towers, pillared by the archways underneath. You can see the twiddling finesses of the Gothic era still but only as highlights on the sturdy beauty of the brickwork that sits more solidly with that around it, confident in both presence and performance. The Renaissance arrived as the building was constructed, and you can see the influence in the design, so different from Toulouse's cathedral.

Of course, I'm not here to admire the architecture. I'd be more than happy to swap the upcoming battle with someone in exchange for going sightseeing, mind you. Sadly, I doubt anyone is going to be interested in making that particular swap.

Normally around the corner, there'd be pretty little terrace tables lined with tourists and over-priced beers. Not today. At least not according to my Demon Tracking Device, aka the angel Nithael.

'They're definitely outside?' Despite what legend would have us believe, I sincerely doubt the Warabouc is going to be bothered by the idea of holy ground. In the tale told in Meuse about him, he got led sedately into the local cathedral when a young girl made the sign of the cross, at which point he then burst into flames and returned down to the fiery depths where the Christian locals believed he'd come from. If that were the case, I doubt he'd have chosen to have a showdown with us just outside the doorstep of the one place in the whole of Auch he doesn't want to go anywhere near. Nope, just as the demon is going to be entirely unbothered by Christian structures or strictures, so the Warabouc is going to be similarly unimpressed, in my opinion.

Of course, something did happen to get the Warabouc to calm down. There was a period of time when he terrorised the area around Lorraine, in partnership with local darkly-inclined Talented. He gathered those with magic to him, and they did as he pleased. Mainly, "as he pleased" meant feeding on human flesh.

There's no way I'd have stood for that, of course. Certainly no way Aicha would have by the time she made her way to France. But something had happened. A geas perhaps, a working laid on him. Whatever it was, his coven disbanded, and the Warabouc became a solitary figure, holding the terrain of Meuse but restraining his darker appetites. At least as far as anyone could tell. No missing children, no wild slaughters that might draw the attention of the unTalented authorities. Nothing that merited our intervention.

He maintained the peace, and as a result, he got left alone.

Look, maybe that sounds shit to you. Perhaps you think

that we should have done something about him. That a creature that delights in eating people shouldn't be allowed to hold sway over a large swathe of a country. That's all well and good, but there are limits to what we can do for a number of reasons. First, getting a group of Talented to agree on anything and work together is like herding cats – but where the minute you turn your attention towards one of the moggies, another one is going to make your head explode with a fireball. We're too busy bickering, conniving, and backstabbing one another to act as an efficient police force against the rest of the Talented world. As long as they aren't bringing heat down on us, increasing the chances of the whole scam getting uncovered by the mortal authorities, then there's never going to be a group effort to shut them down. Shitty, but there it is. Meuse isn't noted as a terrible place to live. The statistics of people disappearing or dying aren't any higher than anywhere else. It's not Santa Cruz from *The Lost Boys*. He's kept himself to himself and kept the peace. That's been enough to protect him from any sort of concerted challenge by the rest of the Talented community.

The second reason is because *he's the Warabouc*. This is not a Talented you want to go head-to-head with. Not if you can help it. The collected Talented society as a whole might not have banded together to destroy him, but that doesn't mean he's never been challenged, never had anyone take affront to him and his actions and tried to take him down. It just means they've all failed miserably.

And now he's not just the Warabouc. He's the Warabouc under demonic influence. That is frankly fucking terrifying. If this arsehole from down under can forcibly recruit Talented as powerful as him, then I am honestly shit-ting my pants. Even if we survive this fight, which is far from sure, it means he can just take the time after to go grab up all the most badass monsters he can think of, then bring them raining down on our heads to wipe us out. It'll just be a matter of when, not if.

All of that's a problem for later though. Because we need to make sure there is a later first by surviving the upcoming fight.

I peek around the corner, jutting my head out just enough to try and spy the lay of the land. I might as well have just walked out, humming 'Eye Of The Tiger' while shadow-boxing because my subtlety is totally wasted.

The Warabouc is waiting for us.

In the middle of the flagstone square, there stands a creature I'd be lying if I said I ever wanted to meet. Have you ever seen the film *Donnie Darko*? Fabulous film about, well, I'm not entirely sure. I've a few ideas, but there's probably whole subsections of the internet set up to debating what the writer's artistic intention was. On the surface, though, it's about a teenager who starts getting visited by a terrifying gigantic metal-faced bunny, telling him the world's going to end. The bunny's called Frank.

The Warabouc looks like Frank if you tore off the rabbit face and slapped a ram's skull in its place. Then super-sized him. Both in terms of physical dimensions and scariness. He's at least eight feet tall, covered in a black shaggy down that might be wool, might be fur. It's too hard to see at this distance. He has a rippling physique that puts the simiots to shame, and the ram's skull is framed by more of the dark downy hair. It gleams like polished metal but moves like flesh, stretching and bending in a peculiar way that material resembling chrome-dipped bone shouldn't. The eyes are hollow empty sockets, but there's something in them right at the back. A burning in the depths. I don't want to stare at them too much. It's not just that they're unnerving – though they definitely are; it's that it feels like if I do, they might suck me in, swallow me down into the abyss contained within.

Behind him, a couple of the café tables are pulled together, the sunshade umbrellas torn out and carelessly tossed aside. Lain across them is Gil. His arms drape, limp, to the side, but there's no sign of any struggle. His blue bomber jacket doesn't look torn or dirty nor do the jeans he's wearing. I can't tell how he is otherwise. He's totally still, motionless. Unconscious? Dead? Hopefully the former but impossible to tell.

To find out, I'm going to have to go through a real-life monster, one who not only deserves the name but owns it, embraces it, considers it a badge of pride. The corpse-grimace, like a long left rotted ram discovered weeks late in a treacherous ravine, moves so unnaturally into a widening smile, I can't help the shiver that runs down my spine. 'Hello, dead man, so he says. Death awaits you here and now by his hand.'

That's new. So far, most of the possessed either haven't spoken, or they've been the voice of the demon. Despite him calling me 'dead man', he doesn't sound like the creature that hijacked the border guard's voice. I risk taking a *look* at him.

He glows like Peter Parker's little radioactive spider buddy when *looked* at. Sadly, I don't think he's about to give me a whole host of quirky superpowers. His *talent* shines out like a whole host of floodlights just got turned on straight into my eyes, a burgundy so deep and bright, it's as if I popped on infrared goggles and then stared straight at the anthropomorphic embodiment of fire.

What it isn't, though, is demonic. There's not the tar-swirl stains I expected to see painted through his being. In fact, there's not any evidence of possession at all. Studying him quickly because I doubt he's going to just let me stand here for long without responding to him or fighting him, my eyes catch on his wrist. A thin black line is wrapped around it, reminiscent of the demonic essence still present around 'Zac's. But when I stop *looking*, I see it's a twisted two-thong leather wristband bound there. What hide got tanned to make it…well, best not to think about it too much.

All of which can only mean one possible thing. 'He's not possessed,' I hiss out of the corner of my mouth to Isaac. 'He's working with the demon.'

Apparently the Warabouc has excellent hearing. Not an aspect I automatically associate with sheep, but maybe they do. Perhaps they're listening to everything, taking it all on board, plotting our downfall. 'He is not possessed, dead man. No, no. Why would he be? He's happy to have this new world, to be free. To come and fight the likes of you. That's his pleasure, all come true.'

'Fucking hell, what is it with magical creatures?' I don't have to force the disgust into my voice. 'Is it something about the way you're born or shaped by the magic? Or is it just an affectation, precisely as pretentious as it sounds?'

The flesh-metal of the skull bunches around the cheek areas, furrowing. 'What are you talking about, dead man?'

'Oh, what is he talking about? Which he is it this time, if I am also he because he, and this he being me and me being the Warabouc, is such a poncey little egotist that he has to refer to himself in the *third person*? You sound like a meth-head version of Gollum. Give it a break, will you?'

This is normally the point where I knock the bad guy sufficiently off kilter that they step off the poor fellow alto-gether and the maker of Scottish man-skirts can run away.

Possibly by making an obscure joke about the makers of kilts being called kilters while they were trying to threaten my very existence. Where the villain realises that their menacing dialogue has been undermined, and they search desperately for a way to regain their equilibrium.

Sadly, nobody informed the Warabouc of this. The required memo never reached him. Because instead of stuttering and stumbling or trying to justify himself or even just ignoring me and carrying on with his speech...

He roars loud enough that it would make a T-Rex piss their pants and head for the hills. Then he lowers his head, curled titanium-like horns looking like razor sharp corkscrews, specifically created for extracting my heart from my chest via my throat...

And then he charges. Straight at me.

Chapter Thirty-Four

If getting charged by giant deadly ram's horns was the plan,
then shofar, so good.

The one advantage about having pissed him off by mocking
his speech patterns is that he's concentrated on me. I really
don't want Isaac getting pulled into this battle as he's practically useless. Because the problem with fighting the
Warabouc is we can't use magic.

I mean, *we can*. But only if we want to die rapidly and
painfully. Why? Simple enough. Any magic thrown at the
Warabouc comes back on the caster, tripled.

There's a reason dark covens of hedge witches
worshipped the Warabouc and probably still do. Within
certain traditions of the Talented, the Rule of Three stands
prominent on their weavings. Any ill you intend or infuse
into your workings will come back on you but three times as
badly. My guess is that when those schools of magic started
up, they realised the only way to control those of a megalo-

maniac mind was to make dark magic carry a sufficiently high price to keep it from being thrown around like a pissed-up Jedi. It certainly connects into the idea of higher vibrations too; look at the Bene Elohim. They keep their *talent* strictly defensive, and I think it comes from similar ideas. Basically practicality and philosophy worked in together. An applaudable endeavour.

Then the Warabouc showed up, full of similar magic to that northern European tradition. Except, not only is he immune to the Rule of Three, but he twists it, wraps it around himself like some sort of magical armour, so that any power thrown at him regardless of intent gets hurled back and multiplied on his attacker. Basically, if I throw a fireball at his hiney, I'll end up with an even toastier backside, and he'll be unscathed.

So I come up with another plan. I pull my sword from my etheric storage, side-stepping as I do to put space between me and 'Zac, readying myself. As the Warabouc nears in his lowered charge, I roll aside, hurling myself into the manoeuvre and avoiding being gored by the merest of millimetres.

By the time I tuck my shoulder in and manage to turn the tumble into enough forward momentum to regain my feet, all without skewering my kidney on my drawn sword, and simultaneously turn my body to face the Warabouc who's carried on past me…the creature is already thundering back in my direction. My legs are still busy trying to get me upright again, to keep my balance, and I can't get myself moving quickly enough. It's close. I push off, trying to twist out of the space I can see the thundering gigantic ram skull head is about to occupy but just not fast enough. Searing pain whips across the back of my thigh. I drop to one knee. My free hand whips back and comes away soaking wet. He's torn a chunk of flesh out. The fact I'm able to take the knee, though, tells me he's not hamstrung me. Not yet, anyhow. Small mercies.

And, of course, being immune to magic, reflective of magic even, doesn't mean the Warabouc can't use magic. Oh no. Because that would be somewhat more fair. And the universe doesn't like being fair to me, except in the sense of a haunted house ride at a fair. Where all the ghosts and goblins are armed with baseball bats, complete with nails driven into them.

So by the time I've assessed that I can still stand and that even if my thigh's pissing blood, I've not been taken out of the fight on first contact, I look up to see the Warabouc's pulled together a ball of crackling red *talent*. It's elemental; that much is clear. Could be fire. Could be lightning. Either way, it's definitely pain. My shield slams into place just in time for the magic to splash across it. Heat blooms, radiating through the magical barrier; it's like putting your hand against a door with a raging inferno on the other side just begging you to open it so it can swallow you in the back draft. Fire it is then.

The Warabouc's not standing idly by, giving me a score out of ten for my magical defences either. Nope, my shitty version of spidey sense triggers in time for me to flatten to the hard ground and roll sideways. The first action stops me taking a ram's horn straight through my eye socket, and the second stops me getting trampled by The Undertaker's bigger, hairier, heavier brother. Damn it, that was too close – again.

Being on the defensive isn't really working out for me. I'm sore, bleeding, bruised from my avoidance tactics. He's only thrown one spell at me, and I've nearly ended up char-grilled and extra crispy. Time's not on my side. If we keep this up, sooner or later I'll not move quick enough, not weave a defence before he hurls his *talent* at me, and my goose will be cooked. Possibly literally.

So this time as I regain my feet, I do the last thing I think he'll expect me to do. I open my mouth, screaming my defiance. In my head I sound like William Wallace; in reality I probably sound like an enraged toddler crashing off a sugar rush as I charge straight at him, my sword out and to the side bushido-style.

It works to a degree. The unexpectedness of both my action and the horrible noise catches him off guard. It stops him from hitting me with whatever horribly dark magic he was drawing on, and he can't pivot to a physical counter quickly enough. Before he can ready himself, I'm on him, swinging my sword.

Luckily, the bastard's fast. He spins sideways, a Michael Jackson dance move, so that the sword just nicks across his bicep, slicing but not amputating. And I say luckily, because my left arm explodes into a cacophonous riot of nerves screaming about the amount of pain I'm in.

Looking down, I see a gouge exactly where I hit him, precisely as deep. It might only be a nick to him, but it's damnably deep for me, biting into my upper arm. My own *talent* diverts from the wound in my thigh, which has at least stopped bleeding, and into my upper arm, but the whole limb hangs numb for the moment. Apparently the Law of Three thing applies to physical attacks as well. Fuck me sideways with a wooden spoon. This is not good news.

The Warabouc obviously feels terribly sorry about how much pain I'm in with my arm because he decides to distract me from it...by clouting me with a clothesline as he completes his spin, clipping me in the back of the head as I go stumbling past. I swiftly forget about the cut, numb arm mainly because I forget most things, including where I am, who I'm fighting. Who I am. The world narrows down to a tiny square of light surrounded by blackness and a pain that echoes around that empty void, bouncing back off invisible walls and amplifying with each echo. There's a roar in my ears, and my legs start to buckle.

The Good God bless my instincts because there's nothing else left, but somehow they step up to the plate. The buckle turns into a half-barrel roll, pushing me sideways, keeping me out of the way of the huge swinging meaty cross between a paw and a hand that swooshes through the air occupied by my head only moments before. There's no question it would have decapitated me if it'd connected – unless the question is: Would it have also sent the severed head soaring over the top of the cathedral itself?'

My *talent* gives up entirely on my injured arm and goes flooding towards my brain. There may not be a lot of it, but apparently I need the little there is to be able to do things like walk, talk, fight, and not get shredded to pieces by a gigantic magic-proof Ram-Man. All useful things. Still pretty much blind, I throw up a protective barrier, hardening the air simultaneously. I get lucky again with that decision. Instead of catching his horns in my ribs and having them tear out of my body to festoon his cornets, he displaces the air with his lowering charge. I don't get eviscerated, but the force is enough to lift me off my feet and send me flying like a badly secured crash test dummy across the square, crunching into the wall of the building we came around the corner of. The air in my lungs gets driven out, completely emptied, and I'm wheeze-gasping, that desperate attempt to suck in air that seems doomed to fail. Either I'm completely winded, or my diaphragm's been crushed. Either way, breathing is next to impossible.

A glow like the first light of a spring sun floods my vision, and the pains wracking my body eases. I can get breath in again. Enough to swear.

'Fuck's sake, Isaac, no!' I don't want him taking the risk, wasting Nith's *talent*, potentially weakening their ability to fight off the two elements warring to reshape them.

His face swims into view, lines of worry etched into every aspect of it. 'You had a rib through each lung, lad. I didn't have a lot of choice.'

Oops. Yep, he definitely did me a favour there. And that – getting my magic shield up to get hurled across the square and impaling my lungs – was still the better option. It's fair to say I'm officially getting my arse kicked.

A booming staccato sound echoes across the square. It sounds like if you fired a machine gun in an echoey tunnel right next to your ear. High-pitched but full of promises of agonising pain. It takes a moment for me to realise it's a mixture between a human laugh and a chattering goat bleat, all wrapped up in one cacophonous package with the volume dialled up to maximum.

The fucking Warabouc is laughing at me.

'Not got so much to say about him and how he talks when there's no air in your lungs, eh, dead man?' The mockery is clear, but just to emphasise it, the Warabouc holds his sides, his hands where any decent creature would have love handles, but he just has hate muscles, and mirrors his laughter in his movements. It takes him close to a trip to the Uncanny Valley, making him look like an animatronic robot rather than a living being. He's deeply unsettling. Sadly, that doesn't make him any less likely to murder me in the next few minutes.

Nith's magic kept me alive, but there's a limit even to his miracles. He's not healed every bump and bruise. I didn't want him to, but it feels like every inch of skin from my back to my bicep is just one gigantic mass of blossoming purple soreness. At least I can move my left arm again. Small mercies.

With a wearied sigh, I push myself back to my feet with that arm. There's an unsteady sway, like a drunk sailor caught by the start of a swell, that suggests even between Nith's *talent* and my own, it's not been enough to fully repair all the head damage I've taken. That's deeply worrying because it speaks volumes to just how bad the impact was. Another strike like that, I might not be able to heal it. And that's the first clean hit he got in on me. It doesn't speak highly about my odds of success.

The Warabouc stops his school-play-level theatrical laughter and watches us, amusement written all over his creepy, weird face. Gods, I want to slap that expression off him. The chances of me managing it are slim. Doesn't mean I'm not going to give it a try.

I take a step forward, but a hand on my arm checks my progress. Looking back, I see Isaac's worry is as clear on his face as it is in my mind.

'It doesn't work!' he hisses at me, anxious, and then I remember. Oh, yeah. The whole plan. The whole plan doesn't work. I cut him, and it cuts me, so even non-magical physical attacks get reflected back. Getting my brain rattled like that drove it from my thoughts for a moment, but now it's back. Our entire plan is screwed.

And, of course, it's at that exact moment the Warabouc hollers his weird bleating roar.

Then launches himself directly at us.

Chapter Thirty-Five

I could write a bouc about Wara crock of shit this whole
fight is turning into.

Have you ever been in an emergency and suddenly
inspiration strikes? I don't know – the pipe under the sink
breaks, and water's pissing everywhere. Or all the electric
devices blow just before a work video meeting or the big
game, and the fuses have melted. And you're pulling your
hair out, no idea what to do, and then an idea strikes.
Maybe if you twist this hairband just so, it'll hold the pipe in
place. If you stick a bit of tinfoil where the fuse was, maybe
you can keep your job or catch the second half or whatever.
It's like lightning hitting your brain and electrifying you with
the possibility that this – *this* – might save the day and mean
you can do whatever you had planned, crisis averted. Slap
your hands together and dust them off, secure in the knowledge of a job well done.

And then it doesn't work.

Not only does it not work, it makes it worse. Now the water's pissing everywhere from three places, four, but you can't get to the bit of pipe 'cos it's jammed by the elastic. Or you pop the circuit breaker handle back on and promptly blow yourself across the room.

And now you're in an even worse situation and fresh out of ideas. Plus sporting some third-degree burns in the latter case.

That feeling you get in a situation like that? That utter hopelessness, that sense of futility and failure, that nothing you could ever come up with will be equal to this monstrous task facing you. How it feels in that situation? Take it, multiply it by a hundred. That's how I'm feeling right now.

And the task really is monstrous.

I shove Isaac aside and roll again. But moving 'Zac's cost me in terms of speed, in terms of agility, and one of those corkscrew horns goes straight through my calf. I'd be pinned, dangling like an overly proud major's chest medals, except for two things. His momentum and mine. The combination means it tears straight through, shredding the muscle, and I'm screaming, hollering in agony, pulled into a semi-twist by the impact, changing my angle so I come slamming down on the slabs with a crunch. Nith's magic might have fixed my ribs, but I get the feeling I might have just undone all the good he did. I definitely heard a *crack* or two on impact.

It isn't working. No matter what I do, no matter what I could do, it'll all just wash off him and straight onto me. And it doesn't seem *fair*.

I know what you're thinking. You're thinking that when bleeding out, unable to stand, with a villainous monster about to end your life and all your hopes of saving the man who saved you is a strange time to start complaining about *fairness*. All that tells me is you've never been deep inside a war zone, where people are catching blades or bullets left, right, and centre. You've never held a kid who's copped an injury that means he's done, finished. You've never seen that moment when the realisation lights up in his eyes and he knows that despite his youth, despite the promise of all the years that should lie ahead of him, all those dreams he's never seen through, his life has run its course. When he realises the one commodity he thought he had so much of – time – has run out, the hourglass shattered by some other stupid kid with a gun obeying their higher-ups, safely ensconced in some distant tent or bunker. When you hear Death's arriving wing flaps in that sort of situation, where you stood confident that you'd surpass it, make it onto the next stage, the next challenge, but instead you're lying waiting for the last breath to trickle from your lungs?

The weight of that lack of fairness weighs heavier than you can imagine.

Time's running out for me. I can hear my breaths hammering in my ears, like my heart's getting louder, operating harder as it pumps the blood out of my body through my wound. And that issue of it not being fair keeps running around my head. Because it isn't fair. And that's…

That's not right. That's not how it works.

I've touched on the whole "magical evolution" thing. I don't know if magic is alive. If *talent* itself chooses us or how it works for creatures that are innately Talented, whether they like it or not. But there are always rules. Whether it's the fae who can't lie or the alp turning up in the morning to pay back what he borrowed. Or poor old Lou Carcoilh, a deceased giant snail dragon who was stuck under a hill, away from the daylight until De Montfort took even that from him. Even the fucking Tarrasque, an apparently indestructible lion-turtle-dragon-wanker hybrid, can't break a promise, though he'll do everything he can to bend the rules because he's a massive arsehole.

There's a reason for that, whether deliberate by a sentient Talent or by the higher beings who regulate our existence like the one I had tea with in a shack outside of Life itself a couple times. It's simple. If not, either the Talented creatures would rule the world, or we'd have had the magical equivalent of Armageddon. Maybe we did once in some reality. Maybe that's why there're now *rules*.

And the Warabouc being immune to everything isn't playing by the rules. It's giving him the cheat codes to reality. It's the equivalent of the kid playing make-believe games who just keeps giving himself more and more special powers until there's nothing that can stop him, no kryptonite, no magic bullet to even the scores. And the Warabouc isn't Superman...

But he has to have a kryptonite.

So lying here, feeling the blood gathering, soaking higher and higher up my garments, so that now my T-shirt's sticking, pulling at my lower back, the legend of how the Warabouc got stopped comes to mind. The sign of the cross, the docility it causes. And I don't believe for a second that'll work. But a sudden thought as to how he might have been calmed down once many centuries ago pops into my head. It's a long shot. It's almost certainly the wrong answer. But I've nothing else, and the Good God loves a trier. So let's try once more, throw those dice one last time, and see what they come out with.

I push myself up onto my elbows, feeling the floor grabbing at my T-shirt, the damp stickiness not sure whether to cling tighter to it or to my skin. The Warabouc is stalking towards me, his gaze fixed on the blood, a savage gleam in his empty, cavernous fire-spark eyes.

And I make a sign. Not the sign of the cross. The sign of the T.

'Time out.' My words come out gasped, hoarse. Whether my lungs have been pierced again or not, I can't tell you, but they're certainly not working properly. 'Time out!'

Amazingly, the Warabouc does. Not because he has some weird allergy to a T shape –that would be too damn obscure for anyone to ever figure out– but because he's confused by his dying prey's desire to talk. And perhaps curious too. Enough so that he pauses and cocks his head, the sunlight catching on those deadly horns and blinding me for a moment.

Okay. So far, so good. Now I get to make my last attempt.

'Your...' My mind's blank, and I'm trying so hard to think over the pain. *C'mon, c'mon.* 'Your... horns look lovely.'

He blinks at me, this Billy Hulk Gruff, and stares silently. And I think I've guessed wrong, that I've messed up. That he'll tire of staring at me in a minute and start his slow stalk over to end my misery by making a pinata out of me.

Then he scuffs at the floor half-heartedly with his foot. 'You...don't look entirely stupid lying in a pool of your own blood.'

And it's shit, entirely forced, and unwilling. But it might just be the best compliment I've ever received in my life. Because it means my last desperate gamble was right.

I push all my *talent* in towards my wounded leg, trying to persuade the flesh to knit together. It'd be a fucker to bleed to death like a stuck pig now I've cracked the puzzle.

'Your face is wonderfully shiny and amazing in how it

articulates.' Amazingly fucking freaky, but he doesn't need that addendum.

The Warabouc grinds his exposed teeth so loudly, it sounds like repetitive revolver shouts echoing around the empty square. 'You survived longer than I would have expected.'

My wound's closed, although calling it healed would be a step too far. 'You fight phenomenally well.' That one doesn't require any effort. It's absolutely true. I've no idea how I've survived as long as I have.

The monstrous goat's head shakes back and forth, like he's trying to get rid of a drunken stupor. If he's trying to throw off the shackles of this constraining aspect of his *talent*, he fails. 'You're… annoyingly clever.' He winces, like the words hurt. 'Impressively clever, impressively clever!' He gabbles it out, and I have to wonder if they didn't actually sting him.

Now I have to make another gamble. They've paid off so far. Let's see if the second time continues the trend. 'I'd like to offer you a gift. My life. It's yours. You can kill me if you want to.'

The only sound for a second is the sharp intake of breath from Isaac from somewhere behind me. He's not near the Warabouc at least. Good.

A whine sounds up like a dog with a paw caught in a bear trap. It builds the same way a kettle does towards a boil. As I look at the creature, the miserable unhappiness on his face is clear. As I hoped, though, there's nothing he can do but carry on.

'No, no. He insists you keep it. It is your gift from him.'

I would pump my fist in celebration if I didn't suspect it'd re-open my wounds and possibly leave me bleeding out again. Instead, tentatively, I get to my feet. There's a gingerliness to my movements that relays exactly how much pain I'm in, but I make it. I'm back upright, even if the gigantic demon-goat-creature towers so high over me I feel like I'm still sitting down.

Time to make another dice roll, though my confidence is growing with each one. 'Then allow me to make you an offering of the life of the man next to me.'

The Warabouc backs up, making a *neuh, neuh* noise. It sounds like nothing more than a startled horse halfway to bolting. 'No, no, his life is his own. He gives it to him.'

The clauses make my head hurt – well, that, and the concussion I received, but I can work it out. Isaac's life is now safe too. Time to see if I can deliver the knockout blow.

Be ready, 'Zac. Please be ready. I have to hope this works. Otherwise, I guess we'll find out the answer to the Good God's enigma when she sent me back. Will I reincarnate once more when I die?

'I don't feel like I've honoured you enough, Warabouc.' I smile and pull a small knife from my storage. 'So I insist on giving my life for you.'

And then I cut my wrist.

It has to be real, genuine. I'm not faking it. If the magic works the way I think it does, anything less than a full, committed attempt to kill myself isn't going to work.

For a moment, the square goes deadly silent. I can't even hear a bird chirping, a sign squeaking. Not even the rustle of the wind through the twists and turns of alley runs. All I can see is the shock, the disbelief on Isaac's face as he looks at me, paling, and I'm urging him to work it out. *C'mon, Isaac, c'mon…*

And then the Warabouc wails.

It's a sound like that which a mother makes when the

news of her fallen son is brought to her door. The sound of loss so unbearable it breaks us, so though we might breathe on, we'll never live again. Not really.

But the Warabouc doesn't keen for a lost child. It certainly isn't for me, my life pumping out of a slice I daren't heal, not this time.

No, the Warabouc mourns for the only thing that matters to him. The Warabouc mourns himself.

Because the rules are there. And I found the loophole. Fair and square. Whatever is done to him comes back three-fold. That's what has made him so undefeatable. Each time someone attacked him with magic, they found the working striking them instead. Hitting him with my blade opened up cuts on me.

But giving him compliments meant he had to give them back to me. Everything done to him, for him, has to be repaid. So taking my own life as a present for him?

Now the Warabouc has no choice. He doesn't carry a knife, doesn't have a handy etheric storage to pull one out of. But he doesn't need to.

He lowers his mighty head slowly, unwillingly, like a great pressure is crushing down on him, bending him in two against his will. At the same time, his arm rises, closing in on the razor-sharp metallised bone horn on the opposite side. The noise he makes becomes chopped as he chuffs at the same time, his teeth chomping. His right foot stamps, scuffs, like he's trying to dig his way out through the floor, away from what he's about to do to himself. But there's no escape.

The Warabouc tears his wrist across his horn, slicing into the bone, tearing it open.

It's not a delicate affair like I did, genuine attempt though it was on my part. No, this rips all the flesh off, taking out a chunk the diameter of a football. I can see the bone underneath. It glistens, although I can't tell if it's also metallic like his face or just wet because a fraction of a second later, the hole fills with blood. Blood that pumps out under immense pressure, spraying across the courtyard. A torrent of dark life, erupting out of the form it has been caged in.

And I can almost relax. Almost. Because the Warabouc is done as long as Isaac does the right thing next. Panic is carried to my ears by the quickness of his breathing, by the sharpness of his movements – a rapid, uncertain jerkiness he never normally carries. He comes to check me over, not sure what to do. I want to tell him because I know. But I can't. There's a warmth settling in, a heat that's soothing away all those pains and fears, wanting to wrap me up in itself and rock me away to a sleep I'll never wake up from. And it's so damn tempting. It's taking everything I have to stay awake. I can't give him what he needs to know.

But Isaac gets it. Thank the Good God, Isaac gets it. Because even when he's panicking, watching the man he thinks of as a son disappear, he's still the cleverest bastard I ever met. And so he speaks loudly and clearly enough for the Warabouc to hear.

'This healing is a gift from me to you. A gift that costs me dearly.'

A gift given to me, at high cost. Meaning the Warabouc can't copy the effect, because it has nothing to do with him, nothing to do with what happened between us. I can be healed. He cannot.

I feel the touch of an angel. Then darkness takes me.

Chapter Thirty-Six

AUCH, 29 OCTOBER, PRESENT DAY

Apparently I'm not dead. That makes a pleasant change.

The light is softer when I come to, so as for a moment I think I've been unconscious for a long time, until the day's started to give way to an impatient night, and the light is diffused, pressed back by the advancing dusk. Then my eyes focus, and I realise I'm bathed in the luminous aura of a Bene Elohim.

Nithael holds me to him, cradling me, bathing me in this incredible light. I can feel it penetrating every inch of me, the glow radiant inside, fixing me and not just physically.

But then I see the light waver, and the memory of what this is costing him comes flooding back. With a cry, I leap to my feet, away from his aura. Away from the *talent* he's pumping into me. Healing me but at such a cost.

'Enough!' I don't know if I'm shouting at Isaac or Nithael or both, but the shock of it – of me coming to so suddenly and so violently – works. The light shuts off, and I'm left looking at the pale, drawn face of Isaac.

Except it's not just pale now. It's washed out, with a colour akin to that of motion sickness, carried across rough seas. It's just a tinge, but it's definitely there. A greenness around the gills, so to speak. Except it's every-where. And looking at his neck, I see red splotches, patches that could be skin that've been rubbed raw. Or could be the start of sores appearing, that might soon weep pus.

Just like an alp.

I nod at his wrist. 'Sleeve up.' If it sounds like an order, it's because it is. I'm close to gibbering in panic, so keeping my words to a minimum is a sensible decision. Isaac looks like he might argue for a moment, but then he shuts his mouth and lifts his sleeve.

The whole of his left forearm is stained black.

It's still contained. It's not that wild bubbling essence distorting the skin as though it might break through or reshape the flesh itself at any second. No, it's still a band. Just a band that now covers the whole of the bottom part of his arm, from wrist to elbow.

Saving me has cost him dearly. On both fronts he's fighting on.

And it doesn't matter how much I know the truth. That if he'd not done it, I'd be dead. Hell, probably they'd be dead or have used so much *talent* uselessly against the Warabouc as to be consumed by one of the forces warring for control of their body. Gil would be dead, and the demon would be celebrating right now, toasting its victory and putting whatever evil machinations it had in mind once we were out the way into operation. It doesn't matter that I know that's all factually correct.

I still feel guilty. The price he's paid to save me is enormous.

Isaac sees it, of course. Pity floods his face, and that only fans the self-doubt, the anger I feel at myself for not finding a different impossible solution to that unsolvable problem. Ridiculous, of course. That doesn't help.

And perhaps he realises that because he stops himself from saying whatever he was about to say. He knows I know it. Words aren't going to make any difference here. Healing him is the only thing that'll assuage my conscience on that front. So, instead, he gives me a nod – firm, solid, understanding. It says all the things he wants to without him having to — that he gets it, that it isn't needed, that he respects it, and he'll give me the space to sort it out as needs to be done.

Then he speaks. 'Let's go check on Gil.' Move the mission forward, switch the focus. Get away from this pointless, ridiculous guilt. He's right. There's nothing else that can be done.

As he moves, I can see the body of the Warabouc behind him, lying in a pool of its own ichor. The eyes might always have been empty in that oversized ram-skull, but the gleam is gone from the animate bone, and that infernal light at the recesses of the hollows has extinguished. The bastard thing's dead. There'll be a power struggle to come over in Meuse, but that's not my problem. Let the Lorranians deal with that. Right now, I need to go check on our friend.

By the time I've torn myself away from the corpse, Isaac's already by Gil's body. 'Paul, quickly!' The urgency in his voice makes me want to groan, but I bite it back. That's the selfishness talking, the voice that asks, "Haven't we done enough? Why should we have to deal with more problems?"

That voice can fuck right off and keep fucking off until it's fallen off the edge of the solar system. So I ignore it and heave myself over to Isaac's side. The aches and pains might be gone, but the bone-deep weariness isn't, regardless of Nithael's attempts. I just ignore it. It can fuck right off too.

What I see makes my heart sink down so low it's hiding out somewhere behind my lower intestine. Because Gil's lying on the café tables, but Gil...

Gil looks dead.

And I don't mean just-died-dead. With how often I've woken up in morgues or their equivalent over the centuries, I consider myself something of an expert in the freshness of cadavers, but it's not necessary in this case.

Gil looks several weeks – no, several months dead.

He still has flesh on his bones, so perhaps "months" is too long, but he looks like he's rotting. The skin is grey, sallow, a shade more than jaundice could ever change the tone. But that's not the thing that gives the effect. That'd be the worms.

His body is writhing without moving, and that's not a good sign. Looking closer, I see fat white grubs pop up from pores and wounds, then dive back into the... I catch myself from thinking 'dive back into the corpse'. Because he's not dead. He can't be.

Desperation starts building. Again. I've failed him again. I look over at Isaac. 'You said you could feel the demonic energy? Is it still here? Is he dead?'

Isaac frowns, almost a pout, and the concentration is clear in his expression. Then he's back. 'There's definite demonic energy in there. I... I think he's still alive.'

Fuck. That means those white worms, sausage-thick and

hand-length, are using his living body as their swimming pool. Disgust and nausea war, thickening the saliva in the back of my mouth, but I ignore it. I've mastered enough bodies. I'm not about to allow this one to start being physically sick whenever it chooses. Not when a friend needs our help. When a friend is fucking suffering.

One of the wiggling larvae pokes one end out of Gil's flesh, and I try to grab it with my *talent*, to heave it out of him. But the magic just slides off, unable to grasp the creature before it dives back into the safety of Gil's flesh. Fuck. Picking up my sword, I wait in ambush for another to appear, and jab at it, but again it's too damn quick, and if I'm honest, I'm too damn hesitant. Seems stupid to have gone to all this effort just to clumsily stab him at the last moment.

'What do we do?' There's a plaintive tone to my voice as I address Isaac. I know it, and I don't care. I just solved one ridiculously difficult enigma and saved us all. He's the genius. I'm the idiotic action hero. Let the smart thinker do some of that smart thinking. My head hurts and not just from the various concussions I've picked up.

'I don...' Isaac stops, his lips halfway to shaping the word know. Instead they purse, pensive, obviously considering something. For a moment, I think I see a waver of indecision, as might strike when one has to make a choice with no good options. But a second later that's gone, and there's only resolute certainty in its place.

'I have got an idea, actually.' He steps towards Gil, then turns back and looks at me with his hardest, most forceful glare. 'And, Paul, this is my choice. Stay out of it.'

Oh, fuck. That sounds absolutely spectacularly bad. But before I can do anything, before I can shout at him to stop and tell me what the Good God damn he thinks he's up to.

Before I can rush forward and restrain him and make him explain the plan step by step, so I can critique it and stop him from doing whatever utterly foolhardy course of action he's decided on…

He takes off the alp's hat and plonks it on Gil's head.

Chapter Thirty-Seven

AUCH, 29 OCTOBER, PRESENT DAY

Pity the little Gil-dren. But don't make Isaac pay the price for it.

I rush forward, horrified, intent on stopping him, but Isaac turns and steps into me, half-blocking my path, half-leaning on me for support.

'My choice, lad,' he says, but I can feel the weakness striking him. The essence is uncaged and starting its ineffable march on his body once more. Does he even know what he's asking of me, to stand by and let him do this, sacrificing himself for someone else?

And then his eyes meet mine, and his face is twisted with wry amusement. And I realise he knows exactly what he's asking of me.

Exactly the same thing I've asked of him time after time. To stand by and let me try to be the hero while he suffers in silence from the sideline. Guess this time it's my turn.

Damn it, it sucks, but it's fair enough. So I'm just going to put up with it. No other option.

There's a slight creaking groan, and Isaac looks back over his shoulder. He pulls away, dragging me towards the tables. 'Look!' he cries.

And I do. Fucking hell.

The worms are twisting, convulsing, popping out from the wounds, squeezing themselves out through impossibly tiny pores. Trying to get away. And I can see why. Green *talent* eats at them, chomping away at their rear ends, devouring them whole.

The alp's magic is overpowering the demonic essence.

But then I feel Isaac tug at my arm, and he points at Gil's head. It's not a one-sided fight.

The hat is glowing bright green, but there are oil-black cracks spreading through it, tearing away at the power it holds, shredding both magic and fabric. It's the battle that was going on inside Isaac but accelerated, intensified. Plus, with added flesh-worms.

The worms start glowing with the same intensity as the hat, but the hat's light starts to be subsumed into another almost anti-glow, like ultraviolet but in the bright sunshine. Both intensify, growing stronger and stronger until they hurt my eyes and my mind, digging into the very deepest parts of my being, and it feels like they might start consuming who I am to fuel their battle. I throw up my strongest barrier, and shut my eyes, wrapping myself in magic and darkness to protect myself from whatever is going on, too frightened for myself to stand witness to who wins this strange supernatural war.

Then a moment later, the sense of assault fades, along with the intensity of the glowing magic, and I risk cracking my eyes open to sneak a peek, to see who's won.

The answer in one sense is both and in another is neither. Gil's body no longer looks like a worm-ridden corpse. It looks like living flesh once more, the colour returning towards normality. Not only that but I can see his chest moving, rising and sinking. He's definitely breathing. I look over at Isaac, the question clear in my eyes, and he gives a firm shake. There's no demonic energy there anymore. Gil's free from possession.

But neither has he turned into an alp. Nor will he now, for where the alp's hat sat on his head is nothing but a small, tidy pile of ash, just underneath the back of his scalp. All that's left of the magical headwear.

I want to berate Isaac, to pour my utter frustration out on him for what's happened. For the price he's just paid, on his account and on my heart's. I can't though. Because as I watch, Gil opens his eyes, blinking confusion – no doubt at where he is and why the fuck we're here too, and I have to admit I'd have done the same thing in a heartbeat. Saving our friends, even at a heavy personal cost to ourselves?

Always worth it.

Because as the confusion starts to fade from his eyes, another emotion comes in at the sight of us. Relief. He may not know what's happened...

But he's glad we're here.

'Told you, Paul.' His voice is weak, reedy, and I can't bear thinking of what he's been through, but still there's that small smile. 'You and Isaac... always sort it out.'

By the Good God, I wish that was true. But I'll try and live up to that. *I promise you, Gil. I'll try.*

Epilogue

A new war then. But at least it started with an old – and
now very dead – Warabouc.

War. When all I want is to find my missing sister of the
heart, Aicha. Instead the threat has come even closer to
home. An assault on the man who is my father in all but
blood.

A first battle fought. And if the question is who won, the
answer appears to be – us. We won.

But we've paid a heavy price for it.

Sure, we got our friend back and saved an innocent who
should never have been involved and certainly who
shouldn't have borne such a burden just for knowing us.
We've destroyed the Warabouc, surely one of the demon's
strongest allies on this plane of existence – or at least I hope
to the Good God that's the case. Whatever the demon's
plans were, we've disrupted them, and we've more informa-

tion to give to Faust and Mephistopheles, information that might help us put an end to their plans once and for all.

But the timer is now ticking and fast. Because when Isaac rolls up his sleeve, the black band is no longer contained. I can see spikes of black starting to creep back up his arm. And there's a strange movement to the flesh. The darkness swirls in a way that makes me think of those fat white grubs tearing out of Gil. Worming upwards. Heading back for his head and his heart. Aiming to consume him all.

We've stopped this step of the plan, but we're still no closer to an answer. And still no closer to saving Isaac.

In fact, in many ways, it feels like we've moved nowhere or come full circle back to the beginning of this particular hellish jaunt – when I went hurtling into Isaac's kitchen and found out the truth about what had been going on since the battle of Bugarach. The struggle he'd been facing alone while I'd searched for Aicha.

That's not the whole truth though. Because I do know now. And so do our friends Faust and Mephistopheles. He's not alone. We know too that there's a manifested demon – here, on this plane and that if we get our hands on him, Mephy can undo this infection, drain the lower dimensional poison consuming 'Zac. And now, as long as neither he nor Nithael use any more magic, we've bought ourselves enough time to do exactly that.

So we need to get our hands on the demonic twatsicle. Get him to Meph. Then destroy him – or at the very least kick him the hell off our reality with his tail between his legs. Good riddance to bad rubbish. Don't ever fucking come back.

A new war. The Good God knows I don't want it.

But we've won, this time, and it gives me fresh hope. We've won, and we'll win again.

Looking at Isaac, I am absolutely determined to make that happen. No matter the odds. No matter the cost.

Movement catches my eye. Turning, I see Gil stirring on the café tables, pushing himself back up, his head swivelling around, getting his bearings. I correct myself mentally. That's not true.

Because the cost always matters. It matters, the price Gil paid for my refusal to help him. Matters that his brother died, that I couldn't save them both, that I chose Gil rather than Sebastien when I had to. For me, on a personal level, it matters that somehow, impossibly, he still believes in me, still knew I'd save him when the chips were down. I can't understand why. Can't imagine what holding onto that faith must have cost him.

He did, though. He paid that price, and if we hadn't paid our own, if Isaac hadn't used Nith's power to save me, letting the demon essence inch back closer towards his heart, I would never have survived today. Thanks to Isaac's sacrifice, I'm still here now. Plus we've saved Gil and bought ourselves some time.

We'll just have to make sure that that time is enough.

Save Isaac. Stop the demon. Find Aicha.

Three aims now tattooed on my soul.

And nothing – from this world or any other – is going to stop me from achieving each and every one of them.

Afterword

Well, there we are! The end of the first chapter in the next imPerfect Cathar story. And the stakes are higher – and more personal – than ever. What happens next?

If you're new to the series, then welcome! It's great having you join along on the adventures of Team Bonhomme. If you've been here since imPerfect Magic, it's fantastic to have you back with me once again for this next part of the saga. Believe you me, there's a whole heap of twists and turns to come before we get to the conclusion of the series.

As always, I like to let you know the parts that are true, or based on real legends in this part. The legend of Sir Ralph and the red mark is a real French legend, although the mark was supposed to have only passed down to the male heirs, ending once an all-female generation was born. The "Mummy of Old Lille" is also true. The body was found in bed in 2012 where it was believed to have laid, mummifying, for fifteen years. It took many more years before they finally solved the mystery of the strange death of Alberto Rodriguez, though obviously the authorities didn't believe it to have been the work of a magic cult. Little did they know...

The alp is a real German legend, including all the weird characteristics ascribed to him in this book – his shapeshifting, his magic hat, his strange caffeine addiction and his impeccable manners regarding repaying his debts. The legend of the simiots – and their attack against the towns towards Montpellier – is also a real legend, although the "magic mist" that saved them was my addition. According to legend they were wiped out.

The Warabouc is a myth from Northern France, and according to legend was destroyed by the little girl who led him onto hallowed ground, with him unable to resist. Considering his legendary connection to the supposed satanic witch cabals that he led, I thought the twisting of the Rule of Three might explain how she managed it, and give Paul a way to overcome his monstrous foe.

vinci-books.com/imPerfectblades

A legendary sword. A dying friend. A final test.

To save Isaac, we chase the myth of Charlemagne's blade—
Joyeuse. But the Pyrenees won't just test our strength. They'll test
who we are. And I'm not sure I'll pass.

Turn the page for a free preview…

imPerfect Blades: Chapter One

This town is an appropriate place to start. The sentence "Auch shit, what a mess we are in" fits perfectly.

Honestly, I miss the distraction of dying.

Allow me to clarify. Dying is no fun. Hurts like fuck nine times out of ten. And you can guarantee the tenth time is the most inopportune one because it means someone's poisoned you or murdered you so efficiently, you don't have time to feel any of the usual agony that really should accompany a body's final moments. Which normally means they got the drop on you. And that almost certainly means you wish they hadn't and doubtless will now have to pull on your new body like your big boy pants and go hunt them down. Recover whatever they've stolen or avenge whoever they've killed. A victim who doesn't have the advantage of popping back up in a new body like I do.

Like I *did*.

Thing is, I may still have it. The…god? Higher vibra-

318

tional being? Whatever the entity was I met a few times in that weird shack outside of life and who had the power to send me back to this plane of existence...they very deliberately chose not to tell me if I get a do-over if I kick the bucket this time or not.

So now I'm having to do something that does not come naturally to me in the slightest.

I'm having to be *careful*.

Although, by the number of dead bodies currently littered through the town of Auch, you might find that hard to believe.

The deaths have paid off though. Gil, our friend, the now non-magical kid who saved all our bacon in Lourdes by stabbing Melusine in the chest, is safe, and the demonic possession has been driven from his body.

Sadly, the deaths of the possessed standing between him and us weren't the only price to pay.

The Alp's hat. The headgear of a peculiar fae creature from Bavaria that we – well, that we just straight up robbed, if I'm being honest. Like the characters from the latest *Rockstar* console game, and I'm not feeling wonderful about that. Well, that hat burned up while fighting the demon essence coursing through Gil. It normally would have turned him into an alp as well, but with the two energies fighting for control, they cancelled each other out.

Problem is, that hat was also keeping demon energy from taking over Isaac, my mentor and father by all but blood.

And judging by the black mess crawling up Isaac's arm? The amount of time we have left before it swallows him whole is limited. Last time we had months. Months he wasted by hiding it from me, trying to find a solution on his own.

We don't have months till it reaches his head and his heart. We'll be lucky if we have days.

And that's why I miss the distraction of dying. It kept me on my toes. Bam, dead! Then popping back up in a new body. Where am I? What's going on? What physical shell am I dressed in this time? How long is it going to take for exercise combined with my magic to reshape this mass of previously dead fat and muscle and get it fighting fit again?

Questions. *Distractions*.

Instead of which, I have to be here, in the present, fully and totally. I can't take a quick breather by getting killed and worrying about simple things like making once-dead lungs remember how to suck in air.

Nope. Instead I'm stuck watching Isaac's life get eaten away before my eyes.

It's for the best. We don't have time to mess around. But I'd sure love something to distract me from all the pain and worry that's packing into my heart; it's going to burst if anything else gets added to it, good or bad. It just can't take any more than it's already weighted with.

Aicha, my sister soul, is missing in another dimension, and our mission to find her has completely stalled thanks to these fucking demons and their attacks on Isaac and the rest of us.

Why they seem so obsessed with Isaac, I've no idea. I can only assume it's the whole "he's sharing his body with an angel" thing. Everything we've learned so far has been a shock, to say the least. As far as either of us knew – as far as the angel 'Zac shares his body with chose to tell him – the angels' and demons' rivalry of the Abrahamic s was nonsense, an exaggeration. Now it's turning out to be far closer to the truth. A rivalry extending back over the millennia, a rift between a species divided. I only have to look at how those sort of divisions work in my own species to imagine what impact that could have. Plus, demons were supposed to be ineffective against angelic power, an irritating gnat's bite at worst.

The demon essence infecting Isaac, an oily goo creeping through his veins, consuming him slowly, working its way up his arm towards his heart, gives the lie to that one too.

Isaac rolls his sleeve down, tugging it tightly into place. His eyes flick to Gil, and he gives his head a sharp, tiny shake. The message is clear. *Leave it be. Don't worry him any more than he already is.*

Okay. He doesn't need to know about it for the moment. 'How are you feeling now, Gil? Any better?' He's regained his feet, but he's still looking more than a little thrown by the whole encounter. He's blinking, making occasional head movements, half-shakes like when you're trying to dislodge water from your ear after a plunge in a swimming pool. I'm not a hundred percent convinced he knows precisely where he is yet. I'm absolutely sure he doesn't remember what's going on.

'I think so, Paul, yeah.' His gaze drifts off towards the horizon. It's a spectacular view. Auch Cathedral holds a commanding position on top of the hill the town grew up around, but I think he has things other than the verdant scenery to worry about. Maybe he needs a distraction too. Understandable after the horror of being possessed.

Sadly, I don't have the luxury of time to allow him to process it all, to deal with what's happened and get his shit together. We've saved him. I'm extremely glad. Chalk a win up in the Team Bonhomme column on the blackboard. But my priority is sorting out Isaac.

'Can you remember anything? About what happened? Or…' I trail off.

I want to ask him if he can remember the demon's thoughts. That's what I'm really hoping for. Some kind of stroke of incredible fortune, where as a side effect of getting possessed, he got an unfiltered look into the demon's mind, seeing all the bastard's plans laid out. Ideally with carefully labelled diagrams and explicatory notes.

Of course, while that might happen in films, it doesn't tend to happen in real life. There'll be no equivalent of zooming in on some grainy group of pixels from a car park security camera and miraculously cleaning them up to give us a line for line treatise on the villain's evil plan.

Nope. They shared a connection, but no demon is stupid enough to allow unfiltered access. All we can hope for is that a little bit of *something* has leaked through.

'I remember the…whatever that is.' He gestures at the shaggy monstrosity lying in a pool of its own blood, its metal-like horns glinting in the sunlight.

'The Warabouc.' A nasty magical creature, supposedly unkillable. Turned out the trick was while we couldn't kill it, it could kill itself. There's always a get-out clause with magic.

'And…and I remember the worms…' His voice cracks, breaks as the words falter.

'Enough, Paul!' Isaac's by him in a moment, his arm around his shoulders. 'It's all right, lad. Just breathe. No need to go back there again.' He fixes me with a harsh glare. Bit unfair considering I'm doing it to save him, but I get the message. Stop haranguing the traumatised kid for answers he doesn't have.

Easier said than done, though, for one simple reason. I don't have anything else to go on. No other clue, no other lead. We've won a victory – got back Gil, killed the Warabouc, slew a load of poor possessed simiots, magical ape-like creatures who were forced to attack us. But none of that really helps us with the bigger game plan. With a lot of effort, we avoided killing all the simiots, but too many of them still died. We've no idea who this demon is, why they've come to our plane of existence, or what they want.

The startling vibration of my phone in my pocket breaks me from my frustrated reverie. It also makes me nearly leap out of my skin, but that's beside the point. Unless the point is "I'm so high-strung right now, you could pluck my nerves like a well-tuned harp". I look at the screen; it's the number of the Mother – witch-in-chief of the Sistren of Bordeaux coven and my new bestie since she made us go on a stupid fucking mission that got my magic eaten (thankfully, I got it back) and got us stabbed in the back by the Sistren's representative. Who happened to be my dead-for-centuries wife, come back to life as a fae. Because that's how my weird little headfuck of an existence works.

I hit call accept and get straight to the point. 'Did you manage to clean up the mess?' "The mess" in question is the simiots, living and dead, we left scattered in our wake as we battled our way to the cathedral. Somehow, the demon had got all the local inhabitants to clear out, setting us up for the showdown with the Warabouc. But we've no idea how long that's going to last nor what's going to happen now that particular plan didn't work out for him. The locals might come wandering back in, or governmental authorities might pour into the town. The latter would be spectacularly bad news considering the absolute fucking slaughterhouse we made of some of the streets, having filled them with barbecued flaming apes. And as they were already on fire by choice and magic prior to us frying them with a shitload of electricity, they're not something I particularly want the government to get their hands on.

'There has been a collection made. Living and dead, they're safely secured.' The Mother's voice is as serene and as unruffled as ever despite the whole "getting a call asking her to collect previously possessed fire apes". I guess her life has enough weird in it to stop that from fazing her too.

'Any idea what happened here to get rid of the locals?' I still don't know if they're even alive. The idea that the demon or the Warabouc might have slaughtered all the inhabitants of this medium-size town is crawling all over my brain like a drunken centipede.

'There was a government announcement. Possibly a gas leak or explosion risk. With that, there was a working, dark energy that, apparently, persuaded even the most contrary to follow the instructions.'

I don't even try to hide the sigh of relief. They're alive. That'll do for the moment. 'What are they saying now about it?'

A pause hangs between us for a moment, no less pregnant for the use of phones. 'They aren't. Nobody is mentioning it. There are no further announcements but also no questions. No demands for clarification.'

Good God damn it, that's a hell of a lot of influence the demon is wielding. Persuading authority figures to evacuate a town, getting all the inhabitants to follow along with such a massively disruptive order, then just cancelling it and not having anyone asking questions after? No inquisitive, pissed off locals demanding answers? No French civilians irritated by their government?

I look over at Isaac, who's listening in, grim-faced, to the conversation. 'This was all just a demonstration again, wasn't it?'

He nods, but it's the Mother who replies. 'There is… suggestion that this was the equivalent of a bicep flex. There are stories that need to be shared. Information needed for the coven to help both ourselves and you.'

Understandable. She wants to know exactly what the fuck is going on. Can't blame her. 'No question. I'll give you a ring on the way back to Toulouse, update you on everything. Right now, we need to get packed up and get the fuck out of Dodge before all the locals arrive and wonder why we've trashed their pretty little square.'

I'm about to hang up, but the Mother stops me. 'Wait, Good Man. There's one other thing.'

Of course there is. What are the odds it's good news? 'Go ahead.'

'The simiots. We found markings on them all, both alive and dead.'

Now I perk up. Fuck me. This sounds like that rarest of mythological beasts – a potential clue. The odds might have swung in our favour for once. 'Can you describe them for me?'

'There is a photo coming now, with a strong chance of recognition. There *will* be an explanatory call very shortly, Cathar.' The line goes dead.

Right. Don't forget to call her back unless you want a very *powerful*, very influential ally getting the hump. All jokes aside, our new alliance is massively beneficial, but I'm not stupid enough to believe we're really friends. Not pissing off the Mother is a very good policy indeed.

The phone buzzes in my hand, and I open up the image. Isaac and Gil crowd round, peering at the tiny screen. And I do know it. Though what I don't know is what the hell to make of it.

The symbol is a central diamond, with four compass

point lines coming off it. At the end of each is a letter. R at the north point, S at the east, L at the south, and K at the west.

'Karolus,' Isaac mutters. He's right, as per usual.

'Karolus?' Gil's brow furrows. I guess it's not a symbol he's seen. Of course, signum magnus have disappeared these days, and I suspect he's not had much chance to study ancient French history. Isaac and I are just showing our age.

'It's a signature.' I trace my fingers across the centre point, K to the R, then down to the L before ending at the S. 'The diamond in the middle is an A, an O and a U, where they used the letter V for that vowel before. It says Karolus. Latin for Charles.'

Gil doesn't look any more enlightened. 'Who?'

Isaac answers this one. 'The father of Europe himself. Charles The Great. Better known as Charlemagne.'

The legendary King of the Franks, creator of France, arguably, and holy Roman Emperor. Over twelve hundred years ago.

Which doesn't explain why his signature just turned up burned into the skin of a group of possessed, fire-elemental simians who came looking for a rumble with us.

My hoped-for clue raises a whole lot more questions than it answers. Probably because it answers precisely none.

imPerfect Blades: Chapter Two

Charles the Great's signature on the flesh of the simiots? I suppose it's more likely than Charles the Average's or Charles the Rubbish's though.

On the drive back, I call the Mother because I have precisely zero wishes to piss her off. She still owes me for saving her daughter; cleaning up the simiots doesn't scratch the surface. There's nothing she can do to help me in the search for my best friend, Aicha, but I'm hoping this might be more in her wheelhouse. Unfortunately, she has no idea regarding the meaning of Charlemagne's signature but promises to give us a call if inspiration strikes.

We discuss it en route, Isaac and I, batting back possibilities ranging from them being part of some secret cult created to protect his secrets, like something straight out of Dan Brown's shittiest book of plot ideas, to them being a bunch of history buffs who are also into scarification. A hipster's wet dream. It's only after about half an hour that

Isaac clocks something, his eyes flicking up to the tiny, little mirror in the sun-visor.

'Are you all right, lad?' I can hear the concern laced through his words. Of course. Gil. He's a quiet kid even at the best of times, but he's been through a heap of trauma, with him remembering enough details, I'm sure he wishes he didn't. I can't see his face, with him sitting behind me and my preference for not performing high-speed explosive crashes right out of *Grand Theft Auto V*, but based on Isaac's tone, he doesn't look well.

'I...' The hesitancy in his tone is clear, but it doesn't sound like trauma. It sounds like someone when they're trying to crack a particularly tricky puzzle, when the cross-word solution is just on the tip of their tongue.

'What is it, Gil?' I really want to have a look at him, see what's going on, try to read his features instead of just his voice, especially off a single word. My job is simple though. Drive us home. Get us behind the wards. Worry about the rest after.

'I...I think I remember something. To do with the symbol.'

I avoid swerving wildly off the road and screeching to a halt only because I can hear Aicha's voice in my head, mocking me for being a twat and fucking up the manoeuvre entirely. Me, I might come back from dying if I'm lucky; I might even be able to pull up enough magic to stop me from turning to toast if the car transforms into a fireball. Nithael, the angel inside Isaac, will keep him safe, but Gil? Gil has nothing, no magic to help save him. Outside of the fact that killing your friends isn't the best way to express said friendship, turning him into Barbecued Gil won't help me get the answer he's trying to give me either. Hard to talk when your tongue's been turned to charcoal.

So despite my instincts, I concentrate on driving, gripping the steering wheel's rubber so tight I'm pretty sure I've left grooves in it. I leave it to Isaac to do the delicate questioning, to tease out what we need to know.

'Remember? Are we talking about you, Gil, or...' By the Good God, between all the doubt and careful words, there's an awful lot of conversation trailing off. It's like everyone's just developed an allergy to complete sentences or something. My lack of involvement in said conversation may be making me a tad grumpy.

'Not me. Not...not me.' Apparently, the surety of that fact is enough to get us to a complete sentence. I can understand Gil feeling very definite about that. Poor kid.

'What can you remember?' Isaac's voice is as calm and as gentle as ever, a soothing monotone that promises no pressure. No harm, no foul if you can't remember; just give us whatever you can. Which is exactly why I'm leaving this to him. Me screaming in high-pitched frustration for *all of the fucking answers right now* probably wouldn't work as well.

'The symbol...I seemed to know it. Been wracking my brains ever since.' As always, Gil's words are sparse, deliberate. All carefully chosen. I don't doubt that for someone like him, who prizes self-control so highly, the previous time period must have been an utter nightmare. Not that "demon possession complete with skin-burrowing worms" is ever going to be anyone's idea of a fun Friday night, but I can imagine it must have hit him doubly hard.

'What did you get?' I really don't know how Isaac does it. Actually, thinking about it, he's had to pry information from my over-excited brain for eight hundred years. He's only had two real options dealing with me – to learn to reach a zen-like state of calm at all times or get struck down by a coronary.

'Just…some senses.' The frustration is clear in his tone. 'The demon…it wanted something. A task it had set for the simiots. A task they'd failed, which resulted in them getting the tattoo?'

The question, the doubt is evident as well. I'm not surprised. Demons are on a different vibrational energy plane to us; they live in a dimension that's incomprehensible to our spatially limited understanding of reality. The demon wasn't trying to communicate with Gil, just dominate him. I'm honestly amazed he got anything out of the connection at all.

Silence falls, and I know we're all ruminating on this fragment Gil pulled from the shit deal he found himself stuck in. Seems to be a specialty of his – getting one over on magical creatures well out of his league. Good on him.

'So what's the connection with Charlemagne then?' Isaac speaks up, breaking the silence. 'What could he be looking for?'

'I don't really know anything about him.' Gil's voice comes from the back.

Of course. He was raised in an abusive religious cult up in the north of France. They were more interested in praying the gay away – and failing that, resorting to extreme forms of torture to attempt the same – than giving him a good education in French history.

'Okay, big picture stuff.' I'm not about to go into all the ins and outs. 'Charlemagne was definitely a real person, although all sorts of legends and apocrypha have sprung up around him. Ruler of the Francs in the eighth century, he united a large swathe of western Europe for the first time since the Romans, earning him the name Father of Europe. Fought the Moors in Spain, I think the Saxons to the north too. Considered by many scholars as the origin of the

Arthurian legends – although I think Arthur and Merlin might have something to say about that – but definitely a source of tales of chivalric derring-do and legends of heroism and wonders. Lots of medieval poetry filled with them, not least his adventures with his equivalent of Excalibur, Joyeuse…'

'That's it!' Gil sits up so suddenly, he bangs his knees into the back of my chair, nearly sending us careening into the central railing. 'That's what he was after!'

'Joyeuse?' I can hear the doubt in Isaac's voice. 'Why would he send the simiots after Joyeuse?'

Gil's voice falters. 'Because he felt they were best equipped to seek it out?'

'Really?' Now suddenly none of this is making sense again. 'They're about the last people I'd have chosen. They'd never stand a chance.'

'Why not?' There's a plaintive tone to his words. Of course he doesn't know any of this.

'Because we know where Joyeuse is.' I avoid saying, 'Everybody does,' because Gil's a smart kid. Smart enough and easily hurt enough to read that as meaning, 'So why don't you?' even if that's not exactly what I mean. 'It's in the Louvre, under lock and key.

'And the simiots would have had even less success trying to penetrate through to the heart of Paris and stealing from the Lutin Prince than they did trying to block our path.'

Isaac's right. Which is why none of this makes sense.

'But…' Again the uncertainty in Gil's voice. Poor bastard. He's rummaging for snatches from a terrible, traumatic event, the little traces left inside his psyche. Precisely zero fun.

'But,' he starts again, 'they definitely weren't looking in

Paris. I can't say where, but it was *wild*. Natural. Not the city. Definitely not.'

Okay. Weird. Still, there's an easy way to solve this. I hammer the prerequisite numbers onto the car's touch screen without piling into the lorry that suddenly brakes in front of us, the carried load piled on its bed weaving back and forth. The familiar sound of a calling phone fills the car.

'Hello?' Precise but warm. Understandably cautious. Amazing how much can be carried in a single word.

'Al-Ruhban? It's Paul.' I wince, bracing myself for what's going to come next.

'Paul! Is *Lalla* there too?' There's evident delight in his voice. Delight I'm going to have to destroy.

'No. Aicha's missing. I'll call you back, explain it all properly later.' Easiest thing to do. We need to get moving, get this solved so I can get back to finding a way to rescue her. 'I'll get her back, but we've other problems standing in our way before we can. There's information I need. Can you get hold of Leandre?'

I could ring him myself, of course. I got his number from Al-Ruhban when we were playing at gathering our Infinity Crisis crossover team-up, thinking we'd bring all the combined powers of French Talented to bear on De Montfort before he could destroy the world. If you think I didn't lock those particular digits down safely in my Memory Palace, you're out of your mind, but I'd rather save ringing the Lutin Prince directly for real emergencies. Not least because my ability to savagely mock his mannerisms is limited, whereas his *talented* ability to savagely make my brains explode isn't. For a tidbit of information like this? Better to take a few seconds delay and go through Al-

Ruhban. I can always ring him myself afterwards if I don't get the details I need.

'Absolutely!' He's burning with concern and curiosity. I can tell that even without him saying anything else, but the Good God bless him, he sticks to what I've asked him. 'He's been most pleased with me since the whole Scarbo fiasco. Sees how trustworthy I am.'

'Can you give him a call, please? I just need to know something. Is Joyeuse still at the Louvre, and is it safe and guarded?'

'Peculiar.' He muses, obviously lost to the thought for a moment, but then he snaps back. 'Of course, anyhow, anything for you, *saabi.* I'll call him right now, then ring you back.'

He hangs up, and I risk a glance across at Isaac. 'The chances they've managed to get in there?'

'Almost infinitesimally small, lad, but those won't be the only agents the sod can put in play. First, make sure it's there…'

'Second, make sure it's well guarded.' Considering last time we contacted Leandre to tell him to guard something, it was stolen immediately afterwards, hopefully this time he'll be willing to listen properly.

If he has any sense, after our escapade, where Aicha and I evaded capture across the capital, he'll have rethought his security measures entirely. He might have been mistaken about us, having been fed phoney information painting us as the villains of the piece, but we still penetrated all the layers of security supposedly protecting his domain. I'd be amazed if he hasn't spent the past few months redesigning it, beefing it up, and patching up any flaws.

The car speakers start chirping at me, letting me know there's an incoming call.

'Hello?' Al-Ruhban. No surprises there.

'What did you find out?' I don't want to be rude, but I do want to know what the hell is going on, so my patience for small talk and social niceties is significantly diminished. Call it a tribute to my missing best friend.

'Well, the Joyeuse at the Louvre is still there, and Leandre is happy that it's safe and sound.'

And just like that, alarm bells start going off in my head so loudly, it's surprising I even hear myself speak. 'What do you mean, the Joyeuse at the Louvre? I thought there was only one Joyeuse?'

'Ah, well. Yes.' I want to yell at him to stop stalling, but he's obviously not looking forward to relaying whatever it is he has to tell us. 'According to the Prince, that's not the original sword. It's certainly the one that the nobles and names of France have owned for hundreds of years. The ceremonial symbol of power they've taken great delight in adding flourishes to, repairing and replacing bits as needed. But he said, as he owes you, he'll tell you the truth for free.'

Considering the fact that the Prince speaks like a throwback to the eighties trader mania, I bet he said something about 'being solution-orientated and circling back round to a synergistic collective market strategy when he touched base with us' or something equally brain-meltingly appalling. I appreciate Al-Ruhban translating it for us into understandable English.

That still leaves a burning question that needs answering. 'If that's not the real Joyeuse, then where is the original?'

'He has no idea. That's the problem.'

Of course he doesn't. Otherwise, there's no way he'd rest till it was under his auspices

'What does he know?' Worth asking, though I suspect the answer is "diddly squat".

'Only that it's been missing for a thousand years at least. Possibly since the time of Charlemagne himself.'

Otherwise known as diddly squat. Thanks a lot, Leandre.

Grab your copy…
vinci-books.com/imPerfectblades

About the Author

C.N. Rowan is the multi award-winning author of the imPerfect Cathar and the Broken Hotel for Magical Misfits series. His books have won the Pencraft Award for Literary Excellence, the Best Indie Book Award, the American Legacy Book Award and the Audiobook Reviewer Award.

It's been a strange, unbelievable journey to arrive at the point where these books are going to be released into the wild, like rare, near-extinct animals being returned to their natural habitat, already wondering where they're going to nick cigarettes from on the plains of Africa, the way they used to from the zookeeper's overalls. C.N. Rowan ("Call me C.N., Mr. Rowan was my father") came originally from Leicester, England. Somehow escaping its terrible, terrible clutches (only joking, he's a proud Midlander really), he has wound up living in the South-West of France for his sins. Only, not for his sins. Otherwise, he'd have ended up living somewhere really dreadful. Like Leicester. (Again – joking, he really does love Leicester. He knows Leicester can take a joke. Unlike some of those other cities. Looking at you, Slough.) With multiple weird strings to his bow, all of which are made of tooth-floss and liable to snap if you tried to use them to do anything as adventurous as shooting an arrow, he's done all sorts of odd things, from running a hiphop record label (including featuring himself as rapper) to hustling disability living aids on the mean streets of Syston.

He's particularly proud of the work he's done managing and recording several French hiphop acts, and is currently awaiting confirmation of wild rumours he might get a Gold Disc for a song he recorded and mixed.

Acknowledgments

My thanks go firstly to my beta readers – Becca and Becky – who've walked this whole journey so far with me; to Miranda my editor who I can promise has played a vital part in making this what it is; to my second line betas Brenda and Leigh for the work they've done pointing out my never-ending ability to make mistakes; to Mardie, Mel-Mel and Darin who stepped into the breach and did a fantastic job proofreading my audiobook; to my wife and kids, and all my family for bearing with me as I hammered away furiously on the keys incessantly; to my Semper Eadem sistren; to the FAKA authors for their endless support; to all my ARC readers who are always there with incredible feedback and the wonderful imPs, who encourage my constantly; to Jimmy and Rachel who help keep the imPs in line and me on my toes alongside Mel; to Perri for her amazing work translating the books (French language ones coming soon) and JL Henry for his support in beta reading those version, being a bilingual master. And of course to everyone else I've doubtless forgotten when I shouldn't have. You're all amazing. I am the Bear of Little Brain and even less memory, never doubt that.

And, of course, to you too. So, as always, thank you for accompanying me on these sojourns into my imagination. It's such an honour to be able to share them with you. Paul and co live rent-free in my head. Now I hope they get to share a little bit of your own mental freeholdings too. And I can't wait for you to find out what happens to the team in the next part of the adventure, 'imPerfect Blades'. Because, remember, for this part of their travails?

This really is only the beginning...

www.ingramcontent.com/pod-product-compliance
Lightning Source LLC
Chambersburg PA
CBHW011420010726
47494CB00011B/2430